T0301166

THE
OUTCAST
MAGE

ANNABEL CAMPBELL

THE
OUTCAST
MAGE

ANNABEL CAMPBELL

orbit-books.co.uk

ORBIT

First published in hardback in Great Britain in 2025 by Orbit

3 5 7 9 10 8 6 4 2

A CIP catalogue record for this book
is available from the British Library.

HB 978-0-356-52418-4
C format 978-0-356-52419-1

Typeset in Garamond by M Rules
Printed and bound in Great Britain by Clays Ltd

Papers used by Orbit are from well-managed forests
and other responsible sources.

MIX
Paper | Supporting
responsible forestry
FSC
www.fsc.org   FSC® C104740

Orbit
An imprint of
Little, Brown Book Group
Carmelite House
50 Victoria Embankment
London EC4Y 0DZ

The authorised representative
in the EEA is
Hachette Ireland
8 Castlecourt Centre
Dublin 15, D15 XTP3, Ireland
(email: info@hbgi.ie)

An Hachette UK Company
www.hachette.co.uk

orbit-books.co.uk

For Omar and Helen – without you none of this would exist

The Queendom of Dahran

BOOK I
THE GLASS CITY

1

NAILA

It felt wrong to be sneaking out in the bright light of afternoon.

Dusk would have been better; there would have been shadows for Naila to slip into, her dark robes and pitch-black hair blending into indigo twilight. As it was, she emerged into a bustling Amorian afternoon, robed strangers hurrying past her, shafts of purple light scattering through the glass dome high above their heads. She paused at the edge of the surging river of people, expecting someone to point out that she wasn't supposed to be here, but no one even glanced her way. They ignored her just as a real river would have, while she faltered at the edge of it, unsure of how or where to cross.

She slipped in at the periphery, her head bent, her bag clutched to her chest so she would look less like a student. She could feel her heartbeat through her tightly folded arms. It was ridiculous to be this nervous; pupils in the Southern Quarter ditched their lessons all the time. The difference being, of course, that Naila wasn't a normal student: she was a prospective mage, training at the magical Academy of Amoria.

Still, unless she was recognised, no one would suspect her truancy. Her robes were edged with a stitched-in ribbon of white, marking her as a mita – the lowest rank of mage – but she was old enough to simply be an untalented or unconnected graduate. No one else knew that the class she was missing, Introduction to Elemental Magic, was just another in a long list of classes she was failing year-on-year.

The crowds carried her away from the Academy, past the

pastel-painted shophouses which skirted the edge of the Market District, and the open fronts of teahouses with benches that spilled onto the wide avenues. Ahead of her were the narrower streets and crooked buildings of the Mita's District, paint peeling despite being sheltered within Amoria's glass. Naila's room was only a few streets away, in one of the old Academy dormitories that now stood mostly empty. She'd thought being close to home might calm her nerves, but it only made it worse. A low and menacing heartbeat pulsed beneath the normal murmur of the crowd.

She'd been hearing rumours of the march all day: the great Oriven was coming to speak to the people, descending from Amoria's lofty towers to the streets of the Central Dome. Mages were gathering from all over the city to hear him speak, and he could have found a crowd anywhere: the sparkling avenue of Artisan's Row or one of the wine bars in the Sunset District. But he had chosen to come to the Mita's District, to the poorest mage homes, to meet them on their own terms.

It didn't seem to matter that he was a lieno, the highest rank of mage, his robes edged in gold thread that cost more than most mages would earn in a month, or that he lived high above them in luxurious apartments framed in Amoria's violet glass. Never mind that he was a member of the Lieno Council, who ruled over all of them, and whose decisions made Amoria every inch of what it was today; the lower ranks of Amorian mages still clamoured for him, greeted him like one of their own.

Naila knew she should be going in the opposite direction. She was close enough now that the uneasy heartbeat was resolving itself into the shouts and chants of a restless crowd. The sound built like a roar in her ears. The streets near her home were almost unrecognisable, packed shoulder-to-shoulder, anticipation rolling off them in waves. Even if she wanted to leave, she was now caught by the current of people, dragged beneath its surface. Battered between shoulders and elbows, Naila clung to her bag, the buckles digging painfully into her arms.

But there was still that stubborn curiosity lodged in Naila's gut, the burning desire to see this Lieno Oriven for herself. Too many of her own classmates had whispered eagerly at the prospect, and Naila needed to understand why. Surrounding her were mages who not only looked down on people without magic, but who actively *hated* them, attending the rally of a man who had coaxed this hate from a flicker to a blaze. *Hollows* they called the magicless population of Amoria; empty inside.

In front of her, someone shot a spell into the air; a lurch of power, followed by a sharp crack which ricocheted off the inside of Naila's skull. Her heart seized and she stumbled backwards, her mouth filling with the hot, metallic taste of magic. Her foot glanced off someone else's and a man shoved hard into her back.

"Hey! Get off!"

Stumbling, Naila half turned to apologise and instead locked eyes with the mage behind her. His expression slipped from directionless anger to malignant interest, his gaze tracing over the raven sheen of her hair and the unusual black of her eyes. For an awful moment, Naila thought she'd been recognised.

She didn't wait to find out if it was true. She ducked further into the crowd, no longer caring if she was shoved sideways or took an elbow to the ribs. It was too late to fight her way back to the Academy, so she pressed onwards, using her long limbs and narrow frame to force her way to the edge of the crowd. She slipped under arms, pressed between shoulders, and dived for the briefest gap in the throng.

Breaking free into the alleyway felt like surfacing from underwater, a stumbling, breathless release. She pressed a hand against the cold wall of the neighbouring shophouse and bent forward, swallowing huge gulps of air into her lungs. Even here it felt like the crowd was pressing in on her from all sides, their magic and their intent thickening the air, making it heavy and harder to breathe.

She shouldered her bag, searching the smooth shophouse wall for likely handholds. There: a window ledge and the rusted bracket of the store's sign. It had been many years since she'd been a child scrambling over the rooftops of the Southern Quarter, but her body hadn't forgotten the way. There was one gut-lurching moment where her foot slipped against the smooth facing, her slipper hanging from the very tip of her toes. But she already had her arm over the lip of the shophouse's flat roof and she managed to wrench herself up in one final burst of effort.

She sagged onto her arms, her lungs heaving, but with the sweet taste of success on her tongue. She was so caught up in her accomplishment that for a second she didn't realise she wasn't alone.

Of course she wasn't. Mages had magic, and they had used that power to lift themselves up and out of the crowd. There were fewer people up here than in the street below, most of them with robes edged in gold or silver; levitation magic was no easy feat, and so those who had used it were from the upper classes of mage. But where lieno and trianne lined the other rooftops, there was only one mage on Naila's, a conspicuous circle of empty space around him. It was as if everyone else was keeping a wary distance, and in an icy moment of realisation Naila understood why.

This mage's robes were edged in the gold of a lieno, but alongside the gold stitching was a braided cord of vivid scarlet. A wizard.

There were only eight of them in all Amoria, mages with the power to level mountains and shape the world as they saw fit. A single wizard had more magic at their command than half the population of Amoria put together. They were the heads of Amoria's Academy, and even other mages eyed them with a mixture of awe and apprehension.

Worst of all, he'd know exactly who Naila was. There wasn't a mage in the Academy who hadn't heard of the *hollow mage*.

Naila found herself paralysed by fear. She was still crouching at the edge of the roof, her heart pumping ice water through her veins instead of blood. She couldn't even make herself look at him, her eyes instead fixed on the hem of his robes, her gaze level with his boots. The wizard himself made no move to acknowledge her, his thick coat perfectly still, his body angled towards the crowd. She could feel the enormity of his power, though, as if the whole world was bending down towards him.

Hardly daring to breathe, Naila dragged her gaze away, making herself stand and cross to the edge of the roof facing the street. She had to pass in front of him to do it, and she could feel his attention switch to her like a shadow falling across her back. She was trapped now, between the mob and this powerful stranger.

Below her, the crowd surged against a makeshift stage, individuals lost within a single, heaving entity.

And there he was, the origin of this commotion, like a stone thrown in water: Lieno Allyn Oriven.

He moved along the edge of the crowd, impossible to miss even among the clamouring throng of people. He bowed and waved, taking people's hands as he passed. The hem of his robes was so heavily embroidered with gold that he was dazzling to look at, the sun catching golden threads when he moved. The sinuous form of a dragon was stitched along one of his sleeves, the mythical ancestors of the mages, a badge of power. He looked like the perfect Amorian, composed and powerful, and Naila hated everything about him.

Oriven mounted the stage with one arm raised, his smile bright against the black of his beard. "My fellow mages!" he announced, his voice warm with a touch of amplifying magic. "I am so heartened to see so many of you with us, so pleased to be among our great people."

Another thundering cheer. Each of these mages possessed a thread of power, and they tugged at the magic around them, in the stone, in the air, in the glass walls of Amoria herself. To Naila, they felt like eddies on the surface of a lake – and no pull was greater than that from the wizard behind her.

But Naila found herself searching instead for the points of stillness in the crowd. She could just sense them, hanging back in doorways, pinched faces peering out of windows: the non-mages of Amoria. The hollows. It was their stillness and their fear that Naila could feel winding itself around her heart.

"Our momentum is growing. Soon the Lieno Council will be forced to listen to our – to *your* – demands!" Lieno Oriven opened his arms, embracing the crowd with his words. "Our fair city is in decline – we've all seen the signs. The Southern Quarter is so dangerous the Surveyors won't even patrol those streets any more, and the Mita's District is not far behind. We're overcrowded, our resources stretched: we must act!"

Oriven would never actually say that non-mages were to blame. He didn't have to. All he did was point to what was wrong with Amoria. It was true: the city was overstretched; the streets of the Central Dome were crumbling and crowded with people – but not with mages. As Amoria's magic-users dwindled, the number of non-mages only grew, and it was all too easy to infer the source of Amoria's apparent decline.

The rest of it seemed to happen on its own. Oriven had the mages in his feverish grip, his words creeping insidiously into their minds and falling back out of their mouths. They leaned into his speeches like starving flowers towards the sun, these people who didn't wear the gold of the lieno, but the bronze and white of the lowest ranks of mages. Their lives were as far from Oriven's as they could get while still having magic, and yet still they drank in his words.

Naila couldn't see the non-mages any more – the crowd had swallowed them up. Tension was building, thick and stifling. It was the same dragging sensation she'd felt in the crowd, as if all of them were being pulled down towards some inescapable conclusion – a long inhalation before the slow, inevitable unfolding of disaster.

The man who stumbled and fell was unremarkable. A non-mage, from the cut of his tunic and the absence of colour on the hem. He caught himself on his hands and knees, oblivious to the circle of attention growing around him – and of the mage who was sprawled at his side.

"He pushed her!"

Naila couldn't see who had spoken, but the words spread like fire through the crowd.

"The hollow attacked her!"

The mage drew back into the body of the crowd, but the man was still penned in. Naila saw his fear and confusion as he tried to push free, but he was met with a wall of bodies and shoved back into empty space. The first spell flew with a sharp crack, and threads of gold magic choked his arms and legs. He collapsed hard on the ground, mages closing in around him.

There were answering shouts of surprise and outrage. Non-mages tried to break through to reach the man, but their way was blocked by people wielding a power they could not hope to match. Naila looked with desperation at the stage – surely even Oriven didn't want *this*. He had to summon the Surveyors; *someone* had to.

But Oriven was already gone, the stage damningly empty.

No one was stopping them. *Naila* wasn't stopping them. Her heart was pounding, caught impossibly between helplessness and a burning desire to act. She was already edging forward, her toes over the seething crowd below. If she didn't do something, no one would. If she didn't act, she was no better than the other mages who were backing away.

Naila drew a sharp breath and—

A thin hand closed on her shoulder.

"Don't." It was the wizard who shared her rooftop, his voice hard and cold.

The buzz of magic was right against her now, a hot breath against her skin. The very air trembled with his anger.

"Why isn't anyone stopping them?" she whispered, her voice cracking. "I have to—"

"Go *now*." There was no spell or incantation, but the last word seemed to ring in Naila's mind like a word of power.

She was on her feet, stumbling towards the edge of the roof. Ahead of her was the path home, the path to safety, while behind her was the howl of the crowd and a city she didn't recognise any more. For a moment she hesitated, her heart aching to turn back, to do something to stop those awful cries. But what could she do in the face of such power?

Naila scrambled down the side of the shophouse and ran.

2

LARINNE

Larinne was unusually withdrawn when they left the council chamber. Her sister was doing what Larinne should be doing: greeting other senators, grasping the hand of an ally or offering a curt nod to her opponents. Dailem was born to this life: resplendent in butterfly-light robes, teal edged in gold, her dark hair curling over one shoulder. Despite being five years Larinne's senior, Dailem's tawny brown skin was flawless, her face rounder and softer than Larinne's. There was an ease and confidence to her, unruffled by the events of the council meeting, while Larinne could feel herself drawing inwards, becoming sharper and less approachable.

She had already seen a few weighted glances, could read the mood of her fellow senators like magic on the air; she needed to smile, reassure, pull others into her confidence, but she couldn't make herself do it. They shouldn't feel reassured, and there was certainly nothing to smile about.

The wide stairway was crowded with Amoria's political elite, lingering outside the council chamber like children after the school bell. There were too few of them, in truth. Every lieno in the city was invited to attend the Lieno Council, to understand the workings of their city, but around her Larinne could only see familiar faces. Like Larinne, they were the senators, the politicians and the heads of committia – the lieno responsible for running the city. The growing disinterest from the rest of Amoria only left more room for people like Allyn Oriven to thrive, unfettered and unobserved, his influence creeping through the Senate like a shadow growing in the dark.

There was a slight commotion by the arch of the chamber doors, and a small knot of people emerged: the representatives of the Shiura Assembly, the only non-mages invited to attend the Lieno Council meetings. They moved as a unit, a defensive formation if Larinne had ever seen one, their strides perfectly matched.

As the Consul of Commerce, Larinne worked closer with the Shiura Assembly than anyone else on the Senate. The members of the Shiura managed more of Amoria's exports than Larinne did; they were the ones with connections in the caravans and their representatives in Jasser. The non-mages of the isolated city wielded their own kind of power. She knew she ought to stop them, say something – but what would she say? *Oriven doesn't represent all of us, the council will protect you, we won't let him get his "Justice".* But how much of that was true?

She took half a step towards them, forcing a smile onto her thin lips, and tried to catch their attention.

"Honoured members of the Shiura," she started.

Only one of them heard her and looked up, his eyes narrowed in suspicion. He inclined his head exactly enough to be polite and then continued onwards, not even breaking his stride. Larinne was possessed by the certainty that she had failed a critical test.

"Your face is showing," Dailem said close to her ear, and Larinne bristled at the admonishment.

It was something their mother had always said to them: the council sees your position, not your face. Anything you gave of yourself was a weapon to be used against you.

With a deep breath, Larinne composed herself. "And you're not shaken by this at all?"

"Oriven preaching about the *hollow threat* isn't exactly new."

Larinne flinched at her sister's casual use of the word hollow. "Dailem!"

"What?" Dailem smiled coolly to a passing senator who had clearly wronged her in some way. "They're his words, not mine. Hollow is a meaningless term."

Anger flushed through Larinne's veins, but in the Tallace family tradition she kept it from her face. "You know it isn't. Haelius—"

"Haelius needs to watch himself now. That business with Oriven's rally . . ."

Larinne grimaced, an uneasy feeling twisting in the pit of her stomach. There wasn't a single person, mage or otherwise, who hadn't heard about the violence at the rally in the Mita's District. When Larinne found out that a wizard had stepped in, using magic to restrain the crowd and extract the unfortunate non-mage, Larinne had known immediately that it had to be Haelius. At first, she'd been relieved he'd been there to help, but the more she heard, the more it sounded like an innocent mage had been attacked and the wizard had only added to the violence.

Whatever happened, it was clear that Haelius was less popular than ever with Oriven and his allies.

"He's never made peace with the council," Dailem added, reading Larinne's hesitation. "Be careful with that one."

Larinne failed to suppress a scowl. "It's Oriven we should be careful of. He's using what happened as an excuse to push through this new 'army' of his. What if he succeeds?"

For the first time, there was the smallest wrinkle between her sister's eyebrows. "Even more reason to be careful."

"You think this motion will pass?"

The Justice, Oriven had called it, a special force of mages dedicated to the protection of Amoria. A magical army by another name. The Surveyors had always been the law enforcement; a constantly rotating group of lieno who anonymously patrolled the city. This would be different – a group of mages dedicated to combat and defence, and who answered expressly to Oriven. There had never been such a thing in Amoria, not even when they were still on the brink of war with Ellath.

"Dailem," Larinne urged at her sister's silence. "You can't think he'll get this?"

"Won't he?" Dailem asked quietly, and Larinne was surprised by the bitterness in her sister's voice. "I think this offers the Senate everything they want. They've been drawing lines in the sand for years; might as well get themselves an army to stand behind it."

"But the Assembly—"

"What are they going to do about it, except make their own army in response? This is the beginning of something, Larinne. If Oriven gets this, it will set us on a path we can't easily come back from. I've never seen an army without a war to fight."

Another council member bowed as they passed, and a warm smile spread across Dailem's face. "Ah, Lieno Gadrian, I was hoping to catch you – I hear we have an Ellathian visitor. A *priest*, no less."

Dailem was walking away, her hand on the lieno's arm, a brief glance at Larinne her only farewell. But her words lingered behind her, settling on Larinne's shoulders like a physical weight.

A war to fight. Surely such a thing was impossible. The Amorian mages and non-mages had lived peacefully alongside each other for hundreds of years. There'd always been some tension between them, rivalry even, but outright conflict? That would serve no one.

And if lines truly were drawn between the two halves of the city, on which side would Larinne stand? More to the point, on which side would *Haelius* stand?

Dailem's words continued to weigh on Larinne as she descended the Central Tower, making her way slowly back towards her own offices. The council chambers were situated at the top of the city's tallest tower, a true linchpin of Amoria. Up here, she was above even the glass dome of the lower city. It sloped away from the Central Tower like an enormous canopy, enveloping Amoria in a protective bubble of amethyst glass. Far below, she could just make out the wide streets and colourful shophouses of the Market District, and beyond that the glittering curve of the Aurelia, a circular canal which separated the city into two great concentric rings. The dome itself was so vast, Larinne could barely see the edge of it.

Amoria was the stuff of legends: a magnificent glass edifice, raised from desert sand and dust in a feat of magic that few now could even imagine, let alone understand. It towered above the Great Lake, delicate spires piercing the dome with bridges strung like ribbons between them. Here, Larinne could just make out the luminescent stone of the White Bridge, connecting Amoria to the mainland: a bright artery of life and trade. From this height, it looked like little more than a thread stretching out towards the distant shore, fragile enough that a sudden storm could sweep it all away.

These days, that felt all too true.

"Larinne!"

The call startled Larinne from her thoughts, but when she turned she found a familiar, old mage hurrying down towards her, one laborious step at a time.

When he reached her, Larinne bent to kiss him at the top of his forehead, the skin beneath her lips as thin as paper. "All right, slow down. You caught me."

"Good. Hmph, no, none of that." Reyan waved Larinne away as she offered him her arm. "I'm not *that* old."

Instead of answering, Larinne pressed her lips together and slowed her pace to walk alongside him.

"I sent a communication to your office today," he said with a thin note of reprimand; Lieno Reyan Favius was an old friend of her mother's, and he was the only mage in all Amoria who would still talk to her as if she was a child.

"Did you? Well, I'm afraid I haven't received it."

"That assistant of yours not doing her job, eh? I could find you a better one from among my people. A senator of your prominence ought to have no one less than a trianne working for her."

"My assistant is excellent and not *less than* anyone," Larinne snapped back; Larinne's assistant was a non-mage, a point on which he frequently voiced his disapproval. "She's worth ten of your witless new trianne. If you had any sense, you'd be trying to steal her for *your* office."

Reyan's eyes were pale grey and watery with age, but they'd lost none of their fire as he glared at her out of the corner of his eye. "Yes, yes, all right. I'm sure she's very good, if she's managed to earn *your* approval."

Somehow, Larinne knew this wasn't meant as a compliment.

"Still, didn't give you my message, did she? I suppose I'll have to get to the bottom of these missing documents on my own."

"What missing documents? And what does that have to do with me? Communications are *your* area, not mine."

"Clearly! If you'd got my *communication*, then you'd know." That imperious tone had entered his voice again, but he glanced over his shoulder, a touch of anxiety in his expression. "Best not to discuss it here. Get your 'excellent assistant' to put your poor Uncle Reyan into your busy schedule."

Larinne tolerated the rebuke with only a small twitch of her eyebrows.

"This business with Oriven . . ." she started.

"Yes, well, best to stay out of these things."

Larinne blinked, not expecting the suddenness with which he'd shut down the conversation. Eyeing him shuffling down the stairs beside her, Larinne couldn't quite tell whether his silence meant he was for or against Oriven's proposals, but then Reyan was as hard to read as her sister.

They walked the rest of the way in silence. When they reached the arched bridge that led across to Larinne's offices, Reyan stopped and looked up at her, deep wrinkles carving worry into the lines of his face.

"You need to meet with me, Lieno Tallace," he said gravely, startling Larinne with the use of her title. "This is important."

Larinne's mouth lifted in the edge of a smile. "I know, Uncle. It's always important."

"Hmph. You wouldn't think it, with the way you children ignore me. Give my regards to your sister. She's even worse than you – always rushing off somewhere."

"I've never seen you stand still for even half a minute."

"Yes, well, at my age you have to move twice as much to get half as far." He narrowed his eyes at her, unusually serious. "Stay out of trouble. Your mother asked me to keep an eye out for you both, and I intend to."

"When am I ever in trouble?"

Reyan dismissed her with a wave of his hand.

Larinne stood for a moment with her arms folded, watching him continue down the stairs, her fingers tapping an uneasy rhythm against the tops of her arms. When he'd vanished around the bend in the stairway, Larinne let out all of her breath at once. She straightened her shoulders, set the face of Lieno Tallace back into place and then turned to head back to work.

3

NAILA

The chimes of the noon bell reverberated through the Central Dome, announcing loudly that Naila was late.

It had taken hours, but when sleep finally came it had been of the kind that only left her more exhausted. She'd woken many times, the blanket twisted around her legs, her skin sheened with a cold sweat. Yet at some point, exhaustion must have dragged her under, because now half the day was gone.

She kicked herself free from the tangled mess of bedclothes. There was barely enough time to wash, so she splashed a little cleansing water on her face and pulled on her crumpled robes. They were made of a rough, homespun fabric, the coloured hem to show her rank nothing more than a dirty white ribbon. Too tight in places and too short in others, they barely reached halfway down her shins, but her pitiful Academy allowance wouldn't stretch to anything else.

She didn't even try to do anything with her hair: it hung limply round her face as usual, falling in a thick mess of tangled black strands. There was no time to care: Trianne Marnise had been looking for a reason to throw Naila out of her class for months – the last thing Naila wanted to do was give her one.

Naila's haste meant that she was ill-prepared for the wave of discomfort which struck her when she stepped out onto the street. Everything was entirely normal. Bright sunlight fell through the purple glass high above Naila's head, touching everything with a slight violet hue. Mages and non-mages hurried past her in purposeful strides, footsteps and rattling wagons filling the air with noise. It was as if nothing had happened, nothing had changed – and perhaps it hadn't. Yet Naila felt strangely sick at the normality of it, as if the scene in front of her sat over reality like a tracing that didn't quite match.

Maybe it isn't quite the same, Naila thought. There was still a tension in the air, a new way that people looked at each other: not a who are you, but a what are you, and are you the right type of person to be here? She saw the black robes of the Surveyors three times before she even turned a corner into Main Street, though their masked faces were anything but a comfort. Was this part of Oriven's great plan for the Mita's District?

She wished he hadn't been right about its decline. The district was named for the lowest rank of mage, but these days hardly any mages remained. It lay firmly in the shadow of the Academy tower, populated by old dormitories meant to house Amorian students.

In reality, the dormitories were homes now, housing non-mages rather than prospective students, many of the buildings sliding into varying states of disrepair. Something, no doubt, that Oriven would choose to blame on the encroaching non-mages, rather than the council's deliberate neglect. Naila lived in one of the only buildings that still functioned as a dormitory, and she was the last student living on her floor. Her classmates lived with their families in the glittering spires which pierced the Amorian skylines, in apartments meant for the higher ranks of mage; Naila wondered if they, too, were starting to feel empty.

The only tower Naila had ever entered was the Academy itself. It was not the biggest tower, nor the tallest, but it ran straight through the very heart of Amorian society. Every mage who showed the barest flicker of magical potential had to pass through its doors to learn control, and magic-users travelled far and wide to study from the great masters of magic, the wizards themselves. Most students, however, would never experience that lofty privilege: the wizards taught in the High Academy not the shabby classrooms below. The night before had been the closest Naila had ever come to a wizard, and it was probably the closest she'd ever come to one again.

As she approached the entrance to the Academy, Naila half broke into a run, her heavy bag bouncing hard against her back. Unlike most of the young mita, she couldn't use the pattern rooms: rooms woven with complex magic which allowed mages to travel between them in the blink of an eye. As a result, she was almost always late. She could already see the sour look on Trianne Marnise's face and hear the whispers of her classmates as she tumbled in at the back, an added edge to her daily humiliation.

The entrance hall was hushed in the way one would expect to find in a temple rather than a school. Naila's feet slapped loudly off the opaque glass floor, and she felt like she was drawing the heavy gaze of every disapproving mage in the room. Enormous, carved pillars of glass reached up to a cavernous ceiling, which seemed made to amplify every cough and dismayed intake of breath.

"Oomph." For a horrible lurching second, Naila didn't realise what had happened. Then her hands slapped hard against the floor and everything clattered down around her. Her bag, never properly secured, had spilled its entire contents onto the floor, all her worldly possessions scattering away from her in a mess of books, pens, coins and lint.

The mage she'd so dramatically collided with had also thrown up an armful of books, and they'd come to land around him in an undignified heap. He didn't quite seem to realise what had happened, blinking slowly at his scattered possessions. He got to his feet and brushed down his robes with short, brisk motions, tugging his wide sleeves straight at the wrist; sleeves which were edged in a braided cord of yellow gold and vivid scarlet. A wizard.

It was only once he straightened up, looming over her, that Naila *felt* him. His magic hummed in her ears, a bright heartbeat of power that threatened to overwhelm her if she looked at it too directly. Without even a syllable of an incantation, he extended a hand towards one of his books and it slid easily up through the air and into his outstretched hand, the casual gesture enough to manifest his will into magic.

There were perhaps three people in Amoria who could wield magic without speaking a word, and only one who could do it with so apparently little effort. Suddenly, Naila's hands felt like they were sticking to the cold glass floor, a sick feeling rising in her throat.

"W-Wizard Akana."

Recognition was beginning to dawn on him as well. He peered down at her as if she were a specimen at the bottom of a jar, his eyes sketching over her hair and then settling on the pitch-black of her eyes.

Wizard Akana's face was narrow featured and unkind, his drawn-down eyebrows etching deep groves in the centre of his forehead. A flat, angry scar marked his left cheek and jaw, disappearing beneath a high collar rumoured to hide worse scarring on his neck. The stories the students told suggested he'd burned himself with his own magic, experimenting with powers no one was supposed to understand.

His eyes studied her without mercy.

"You." He said the word almost like a question, but Naila had no idea how to answer it.

She pushed herself back from him, scrabbling to stand. Her legs and arms were trembling, and suddenly she was back on the roof of the shophouse, watching a man get attacked for merely falling next to a mage.

"Sorry, Wizard," she managed, her voice small and weak in her own ears. "I was running and—"

"You're late." He narrowed his eyes. "And now, so am I."

His thin mouth drew to one side as he looked down at the books scattered about his feet, but it only took one circular motion of his hand for them all to jump back up into his arms. Despite his lateness, he took a moment to glare down at her one last time and then – in the greatest display of power that Naila had ever seen – he vanished.

Naila had never seen a mage travel without a pattern room, and he'd done it without even a single word of a spell. His sudden departure sucked the air in towards where he'd been standing, fluttering the pages of her books and lifting the hair away from her face. For a moment, all she could do was stare in mute astonishment.

Then the first bell of the afternoon rang overhead, reminding Naila of exactly how late she was. She stumbled to her knees, scooping her belongings back into her bag without even looking at them. Then she heaved her bag over her shoulder and ran.

When she finally reached the classroom four floors up, Naila was flushed, sweating and out of breath, her hair sticking to the back of her neck. As she pushed open the heavy glass door, a familiar nausea welled up from the pit of her stomach. She took one long breath and braced herself for the wall of disapproving silence undoubtedly awaiting her.

What she found instead was an atmosphere of barely controlled chaos. It was clear there had recently been some kind of commotion: the whole class bubbled underneath with hurried whispers and exchanged glances. Trianne Marnise was gripping the lectern in front of her as if it represented her hold on the class, her brown fingers turning white at the knuckles. Her thin eyebrows were raised as she waited for the class to acknowledge their transgression, her lips curled inwards over her teeth.

Naila tried to use the agitation to slip in unnoticed but, of course, the only free desk was right in the centre of the room. Hugging her bag against her side, she half turned to slide between the desks, intently focused on not bumping into the other students. She kept her eyes down, having long ago learned it was always worse to meet their gaze.

The effect of Naila's presence was immediate: a heavy silence rolled in behind her. She'd been so focused on picking her way to her desk that she hadn't noticed the reason for the class's excitement, and now it caught the corner of her eye, a black shadow at the edge of her vision.

A Surveyor.

Naila froze, her hands tightening on the strap of her bag. The Surveyor stood in the corner, their body obscured in formless black robes, their face hidden behind a mask of concealing magic. For a moment, all Naila could hear was the rush of blood in her ears. What were they doing here? Who had they come for? Were they here because she'd knocked over Wizard Akana? Or maybe they were here because she had been at the protest the night before?

A million reasons flowed through her mind, each more ridiculous than the last. And yet, whatever the reason, Naila was possessed by a cold, awful certainty that they'd come here for her.

"Another interruption?" Trianne Marnise said with a thin veneer of patience. "Please, do keep standing there, *Mita* Naila. We're happy to wait." Trianne Marnise weighed the emphasis heavily on Naila's title, as if it were something that set her apart from the others. In reality, all the young mages in this class were mita, and would be until they sat their exams.

What set Naila apart was that she was sure to remain a mita forever.

"Sorry," Naila stammered for what felt like the hundredth time that day.

The focus of the trianne and her class was now firmly united on Naila. Whispers trailed her down the row of desks.

"He's here for you."

"Hollow."

"Hollow mage."

Someone stuck out a foot and Naila stumbled, hitting her hip hard against a desk, sending pens clattering to the floor. She wanted to glare down at the petty mage who had tripped her, but she couldn't make herself look away from the Surveyor. He had leaned forward, like a predator smelling weakness in its prey, and she felt the weight of his eyes behind the shifting blackness of his mask. Somehow, she managed to fumble her way to her desk, feeling the screech of her chair in her teeth.

"Good," said Trianne Marnise in a tone which implied exactly the opposite. "Let's begin."

Naila spent the rest of the lesson waiting for the axe to fall. She held herself very still, trying to keep her breath even, her pulse throbbing just below her neck. Her gaze kept sinking back towards the Surveyor and the inescapable gravity of his presence. The law enforcers of Amoria were not usually found in Academy classrooms. That one was here meant he'd been summoned.

Yet the only thing Naila could read from the dark form was boredom; once class resumed, the Surveyor leaned back against the wall, one black boot pressed against the glass, not even offering a pretence of interest.

Trianne Marnise's class was on the Theory of Magic, a lesson which was typically filled with long, ponderous lectures and very little practical work. It was, therefore, a class in which Naila excelled.

Like all mages, and better than most, Naila could sense and feel the energies which ran through all things, living and inert: the bright defining anima, untouchable and unalterable, and its strange sister-power, magic. Even now, she could feel the flickering threads of it swirling around her, magic being tugged this way and that by the competing presence of mages.

"Mita Naila, perhaps you would like to demonstrate."

Naila started, her gaze snapping back to the class.

Of course, this was what it had all been leading to. Trianne Marnise stood with her hand outstretched, a small marble of clear glass resting in her palm.

"Come now, Mita. This is a simple demonstration." She smiled with affected patience. "The infants in level one control could manage this."

There were a few sharp intakes of breath and more whispers. They knew, they all knew.

Naila stood anyway, her limbs heavy with dread. It wasn't enough that she looked like none of them, a physical imprint of how little she belonged here, but she was also at least three years older than any of her classmates. She felt it now more than ever, picking her way to the front, like an awkward bird that had outgrown its cage. She couldn't bring herself to look at the Surveyor, but she could feel the pressure of his gaze and hear the rustle of black fabric as he leaned forward. This was what he had come for.

"This is a magical item intended for the use of mages," the trianne explained, as if this were merely part of her lesson and not a carefully laid trap. "For a mage to use it, all they need do is touch it with a small amount of their power: set the magic within the item moving."

She reached out to drop the marble into Naila's hand, a shock of cold glass against Naila's skin. Its magic sang out in her mind immediately; it was made to train young mages and the magic was a swirling storm within it – easy to detect and easy to use, *if* one had the power.

"When the mita activates the glass," Marnise continued with her careful charade, "it will emit a bright white light. An item such as this is designed for the use of all mages, making the application of power needed very small. Mita Naila, please demonstrate."

Naila stared at the marble, her dread all caught up with the churning power within it. What the trianne asked was impossible, and Marnise knew that as well as Naila.

Never in all her seventeen years, never in any of her classes, never once in her whole life had Naila been able to do magic.

She tried anyway.

The classroom was oppressively quiet. Naila tried to focus her mind away from it, away from the sound of students clearing their throats and shuffling in their seats. Instead, she sank inwards, towards the well of power that was supposed to exist inside her. Frowning down at the tiny fragment of glass in her hand, she pushed all of her will towards it, reaching out to it, begging with it, pleading it to light. Everything she had here, her entire future in Amoria, all of it felt wrapped up in this tiny, insignificant marble. This time, it *had* to work.

The glass was utterly unmoved by her efforts. There was not the faintest flicker of power, let alone light. She felt empty – hollow – as if she were shouting inside an empty room. Next to her, Trianne Marnise blinked through her smile, the expression so fixed it could have been a mask.

"Mita Na—"

Naila was saved from whatever Trianne Marnise had been about to say by the loud, repeating chimes of the fourth bell.

As one, chairs scraped, pens clattered and bags were pulled out from beneath desks. Naila watched the students get up to leave, like standing on the edge of a flood and watching the boat pull away without her; somehow, she knew she wouldn't be leaving so easily.

As if on cue, Trianne Marnise hissed in her ear, "Stay where you are."

The Surveyor bore down on them, the black robes making him seem larger and more impressive than he really was. Trianne Marnise bowed her head in respect: Surveyors were called up to serve from within the higher ranks of mages, most often lieno, but Academy matters were usually solved from within, which meant that this was most likely one of the wizards. Naila half wondered if this was where Wizard Akana had been in such a hurry to get to – perhaps he'd find a way to punish her after all.

Holding herself straight, Naila stared up at the Surveyor, fixing her eyes on the deepening black shadow within his hood. The concealing magic was a disconcerting sight, and Naila's stomach did a strange flip as she tried to focus on where the mage's face should be. It only made her grit her teeth, more determined than ever that he wouldn't see her fear.

"Surveyor," Trianne Marnise began, "I'm sure you can see the reason you have been brought here. This is a school for mages, not for hollows." Naila flinched at such a casual use of the cruel word.

"Did the girl not test as a mage?" The man's voice sounded as if it was underwater, warped and distorted by magic, but Naila could hear a note of affected surprise.

"Perhaps she did, but there must have been some mistake. As you can see, she has shown no magical ability – as I said, less than I would expect from the children in the very lowest classes."

"Perhaps." The Surveyor stood very still, invisible eyes tracking over Naila's skin. "May I?" he asked, lifting one gloved black hand.

Naila's heart was beating so fast she felt sick. She stared at the hand, knowing exactly what it meant.

"I— yes ..."

The Surveyor placed two fingertips lightly on Naila's temple and she gasped; he'd sent the barest hint of his power towards her and it felt like someone had pulled on a rope attached behind her heart. Naila's power – her very sense of self – leapt to obey this mage's command, as if he could reach in and take her life into his hands.

"She is a mage," he said, as if it were the simplest matter in the world.

Trianne Marnise tried to maintain an expression of polite under-standing, but wrinkles appeared on the bridge of her nose. "They call her the hollow mage, Surveyor. She may appear to be a mage, but she has not passed a single one of the practical classes. I believe she sits in the infant control class. Though she may have been able to pass the exams to reach this class, she can move no further; she is already several years older than her peers and there is absolutely nothing I can hope to teach her."

Naila felt the heat of blood in her cheeks. It was true. It had been two years since she'd watched Ko'ani graduate from this class and move on without her, and she was the last student Naila had con-sidered a friend. Every year, the gulf deepened between her and her fellow students.

"Have you learned control?" the Surveyor asked.

And there was the crux of it. As if on cue, Naila felt the stir of the force inside her, a shift in the power that both elevated her to the life of a mage and condemned her. There was a simple reason all mages in Amoria had to attend the Academy. Naila had only ever heard rumours, but these stories were written into the very bones of the city. If a mage didn't learn to control their gift, it would grow wild, a seething storm caught within the fragile casing of a human body. In the end, it would crack them apart, tearing right through them and everything around them.

Naila's voice wavered when she answered him. "No."

The Surveyor addressed Marnise, his voice flat. "Then she cannot leave the Academy. Those are the rules."

"I believe this to be an exception!" The trianne's patience began to splinter at the edges. "This is a class for the talented young mages of Amoria. We are known here for our excellence. Why, this class even contains the daughter of Lieno Oriven himself."

"Does it, indeed?" Naila hadn't thought it would be possible to hear sarcasm through the strange warping magic of the Surveyor, but she did. She was possessed by a sudden, dizzying lightness: was he on her side?

"This is a disgrace. Lieno Oriven himself has—"

"What this is," said the Surveyor, "is a monumental waste of my time. I consider this business concluded. Good day to you, Trianne Marnise."

With that, the Surveyor turned and walked away, his footsteps clicking on the glass floor. Trianne Marnise watched him go with wide, unblinking eyes, her mouth pale at the edges.

"I see," she called after him. She lifted her chin and suddenly the calm expression of control was back, her dark eyes narrowing. "We've known for some time that this girl has support within the faculty. It is unfortunate that you were called to resolve this matter."

The Surveyor stopped abruptly in the doorway, the black robes swirling about his feet.

"It is a capital offence to allude to the identity of a Surveyor," he said without turning, and suddenly the air in the room grew heavier, charged with his power.

Even Trianne Marnise looked uneasy.

"I—" She swallowed. "I did nothing of the kind. This is not the end of this, Surveyor. I will be raising this matter again – with the Lieno Council, as well as the faculty."

For a moment the Surveyor just stood in the doorway, the magic of the room bending down towards him. And then he sighed, sagging a little within the black robes, his appearance suddenly smaller.

"Do as you will."

4

NAILA

Naila's legs were weak and trembling when she left the classroom. *Close*, was the feeling she had in her mind, *that was close*. But to what, Naila wasn't entirely sure. She hated her classes at the Academy, hated being forced to sit with children just so she could fail at everything, so what did it matter if they threw her out?

Except it was bigger than that; she felt it deep in the pit of her stomach where her power lurked like a living thing. Mages didn't live in Amoria without passing control; it was as simple as that. It was too dangerous. If Trianne Marnise forced her out, would she cease to be a mage? Every time they tested her, Naila felt that sickening lurch in her chest and watched the deepening frown on the face of the mage performing the assessment: they were always forced to admit she was one of them. So, what would they do with her if she couldn't ever pass control? Would they force her to leave Amoria?

There were times when she'd gazed out across the Great Lake with longing, to the town of Jasser which clung to the eastern shore, trying to imagine a life which wasn't defined by her inability to do magic. At night it was little more than a cluster of lights strung out against the immense blackness of the desert beyond. To go east into the Queendom of Dahran proper, one had to buy crossing with a caravan or else make the dangerous trek alone. Naila had no money with which to buy such a crossing, save the small allowance given to students of the Academy, and no skills, except a knowledge of a magic she couldn't control.

But none of those were the real reason she couldn't leave. Every time she resolved to turn her back on the Academy she'd feel the pull of magic beneath her skin, the stirring of the shadow that lived inside her. It would always be there, an ember that might one day grow to consume her.

For better or worse, Naila was stuck here.

Her feet carried her deeper and deeper into the Mita's District, putting the looming spire of the Academy to her back. She cut down the narrow side streets where the buildings leaned in together, the upper storeys crooked and overhanging. Following the streets south, Naila soon found herself at the edge of the district, where the city opened up and the reverberating roar of the Aurelia echoed ahead of her. Before her was the narrow bridge which led to the outer half of the city, and Naila realised that she had been coming here all along.

It was called the Southern Quarter, but really the Southern Half would have been more accurate. Across the canal from the Mita's District was the largest and busiest part of the Central Dome: sprawling streets of mismatched buildings which only grew more ramshackle and run-down the further out you travelled, as though Amoria was fraying at the edges. It was busier, louder and dirtier than the inner city, but it was every bit more alive. The bellowing of hawkers filled the evening markets and women in desert-stained clothing rumbled past driving carts laden with baskets and hessian sacks, the sharp smell of spices competing with the lingering stench of the animals.

The Southern Quarter was always a riot of noise and activity, seething with people from every cut and colour of cloth: mages, non-mages, traders from Jasser. Caravans made the desert crossing from all over Dahran to Amoria's twin city, and then associates of the Shiura Assembly would ferry goods across the bridge and into Amoria herself. The mage city depended on this lifeblood of commerce – grain, spices, silks, all traded for the intricate magical artefacts for which Amoria was renowned. Some of the less superstitious travellers would even enter the Southern Quarter themselves, easily identifiable from the way they gazed up at the vast dome overhead.

Even Naila could disappear in these busy streets, all association with the Academy forgotten. As she cut up another side street and heard the first familiar murmurs of conversation emanating from the inn up ahead, Naila thought she'd be hard pressed to find something in the Southern Quarter to surprise her. Anything was at home in the bright and bustling chaos.

It was as if the man sitting in front of the Dragon's Rest existed to prove her wrong. He was lounging against one of the magestone benches, one arm draped over the edge of the table, the other cradling a glass of wine in his lap. Everything about him was alien and peculiar. He was too fair to be an Amorian by far: he was the palest person Naila had ever seen, his skin paper-white and his hair almost yellow-blond. He was dressed so much like a mage but everything about the cut of his robes was just slightly wrong, and there was no coloured hem that Naila could see. The white and blue cloth was instead marked with a design Naila had never seen before: a single crescent moon embroidered in shining silver.

Naila didn't realise she'd been staring until she noticed him staring right back at her. The man next to him was also glowering at her, his dark face the opposite of his companion's in almost every conceivable way, except for the intensity of his gaze. Her cheeks flushing, Naila tore her eyes away and hurried towards the open doorway. She stepped through into the welcoming noise of the inn's common room, eager for the sight of a familiar and friendly face.

The Dragon's Rest was as much of a home as Naila had ever known and stepping into it was like falling backwards through time. Everything about it was familiar: the mage-crafted stone benches, always packed with a combination of animated groups of Amorian non-mages and travellers from Jasser hunched over their drinks. The enticing scent of Dillian's cooking wound through the room, mixed with the sharp aroma of wine and bodies pressed in together. The soft din of voices combined in an odd harmony of different conversations and languages, and when Naila stepped into that wall of noise she felt a sense of calm she knew nowhere else.

Only today was different. Almost as soon as she entered the common room, the conversations started to trail off, a poisonous thread of quiet twisting through the room. She saw the eyes of non-mages flicking up towards her, finding the white hem of her robes or lingering on the strange colour of her eyes. Naila felt like she wanted to cover herself, to hide the white strips of fabric with her hands.

Across the room, Brynda noticed the sudden stillness and looked up from behind the bar. Naila tried to smile at her, but the expression on Brynda's face was so different from what she expected that the smile froze on her mouth. Brynda recovered quickly, but the way she waved Naila into the kitchen was stiff and unfamiliar, and Naila couldn't shake the terrible, sinking feeling which followed her.

The kitchen was hot and humid from the stove, and the top of Dillian's head gleamed with a thin sheen of sweat. He was hunched over the table, chopping vegetables with the steady "clack, clack, clack" of his knife, his thick fingers stained yellow with turmeric. Glancing up, he grinned at the sight of Naila, but not before the briefest of frowns had flitted across his face.

Naila lifted a slice of carrot from the edge of Dillian's chopping board and popped it into her mouth, trying to act as if everything was normal. "Nice to see you too, Brynda."

"Gerroff." Dillian batted Naila's hand away, but her other hand slipped beneath his arm and stole a wedge of tomato. "Bloody thief."

Brynda was still staring at her, her eyes narrowed, lines forming at the edge of her mouth.

"What are you *doing* here?"

Naila froze, the tomato halfway to her mouth. "What do you mean? I came to see you. I could help out with the evening rush if you—"

"We don't need any help," Brynda snapped. "We have Ania to help us."

Naila felt a knot of jealousy tighten in her chest. It had been almost a decade since she had moved to the Mita's District as a prospective young mage-in-training, and Brynda and Dillian had taken in any number of children to help them since then. Somehow, though, it always felt a little like being replaced.

"Yeah, but that's never stopped me before . . ." Naila's voice trailed off as she glanced between them; Dillian was resolutely refusing to look at her, and even Brynda had turned her eyes down to the floor. "What?"

"Just not today, Naila," Dillian said eventually, turning to busy himself with the pot which had begun to rattle on the stove. "Have something to eat back here, and then you'd better be getting yourself back to the Mita's Quarter."

Naila felt cold with disappointment. "No, thanks. If you don't need me, I think I'll go."

"Don't be daft," Brynda caught Naila's arm as she turned to leave. "You're here now. Sit down and have something to eat before you go – you look half starved."

Naila shrugged out of her grip, her face hot. "No. Not unless you tell me what's going on? Why are you looking at me like that?" She hesitated: first the Surveyor in her classroom and now this. "Am I in trouble?"

"No, of course not! But you've seen how things are." Brynda's voice sounded thin and strange. "It isn't safe. There was another one of Oriven's marches last night and—"

"I know – it was in the Mita's District. I was there!"

"What?" There was a clatter as Dillian dropped the ladle and rounded on Naila. "What in the Goddess's name were you thinking of, going to one of those marches?"

Naila felt her exhaustion and anger sputter up like a flame in her throat. "What do you care? You clearly don't want me here."

"Oh, come on, Naila, don't be like that." Brynda gave Dillian a sharp look. "You know it isn't like that. Everyone is on edge just now. You shouldn't have come to the Southern Quarter . . ."

"Why, because I'm a mage?" Naila glanced between their severe expressions. "Is having a mage around bad for business? Has no one found *you* out yet, Brynda?"

"Naila!" Brynda flinched at Naila's anger, and her eyes flicked to the common room door. Her hands were tugging at her skirt, which bore no trace of the mita's white edging and hadn't for many years.

"There won't be any Surveyors around here," said Naila defensively, her guilt burning in her cheeks.

"Surveyors?" snorted Dillian. "What're you thinking? It's not Surveyors we're worried about."

Naila stared at him, still not understanding.

"She doesn't know," said Brynda, laying a hand on his arm. "Go on, I'll talk to her."

"Fine, fine," Dillian said amiably enough, though the tension didn't leave his shoulders.

"Sit," said Brynda, indicating the stone bench and smiling with only her mouth.

Taking her seat in silence, Naila watched Brynda gather her skirts and do the same, sliding onto the bench opposite her.

"Do you know what happened at the end of Oriven's procession?"

As if she could forget. Naila tried not to remember the sound as the man cracked his head against the road, or the hot scent of the crowd's magic. "Yes . . . a man, a non-mage, was attacked."

"Well, he's dead."

"*What?*"

"Not at the march." Brynda was gazing into her with an intensity which made Naila feel pinned against the bench. "Apparently some wizard put a stop to it—"

Behind Brynda, Dillian gave a snort of satisfaction, muttering, "Makes a bloody change."

"Well, it didn't help him any. Surveyors fished him out of the Aurelia this morning. Someone did for him – someone who didn't like that he escaped their judgement, no doubt."

Naila had the sensation that she was falling, like someone had wrenched the ground out from beneath her feet. *People are found in the canal all the time*, she told herself, but the thought was a feeble one; this was different, it was all different. She felt like she'd witnessed the man's death first-hand.

"People are angry, Naila," Brynda continued, relentless. "Angrier than I've ever seen them. It isn't safe here, not for a mage."

"What are you saying?"

Brynda looked down at her hands, folded on top of the table, one thumbnail picking at the other. "I'm saying that I don't think you should come to the Southern Quarter for a while. It's obvious you're a mage, but you don't have the power to defend yourself. People are angry: they're looking for a way to strike back, some chance of revenge. I just ... we just don't want anything to happen to you."

When Brynda looked up, her eyes were bright and shining. "It's nothing to do with us, with the inn, I promise. You mustn't think that." Brynda reached forward to place a hand on Naila's. "We took you in when you were just a babe – you'll always have a home here. You know we'd have kept you here with us, except ..."

Except Naila had tested as a mage, and it had ruined everything.

No one had expected it. When the shaking sickness had struck Amoria, it burned through the city's population so quickly, swallowing up entire families and leaving others weak and exhausted in its wake. Mages were by far the worst afflicted: once the terrible trembling took hold, anyone with the ability to wield magic died within a matter of hours. Not even their children had been spared. So when Brynda and Dillian had taken in a squalling infant found in the Southern Quarter, they'd had no reason to believe she'd grow up to show any kind of magical power. At nine years old, the Surveyors had come to test Naila and all the other children her age, moving through the Southern Quarter like shadows from another life. They'd found the dormant magic sleeping inside her, and from that moment nothing in Naila's life had felt like her own.

"It won't be for long." Brynda withdrew her hand when Naila didn't acknowledge it. "These things, they don't last—"

"Oh, like how I wouldn't have to stay at the Academy for long?" Naila snapped, seized by her own anger. "'You only need to learn control, Naila. It'll be at most a couple of years, Naila. You can come back and stay with us afterwards, Naila – no one will take any notice of you.' I've been there eight *years*."

Brynda took a slow breath. "We couldn't have known. What did you want us to do? Every child with magic has to learn control. We didn't have a choice."

"But I don't *have* magic, not any I can use. I never have! I'm just stuck there, year after year after year."

"Is that so terrible?" Naila could feel Brynda losing her temper, her words clipped and sharp. "The Academy feeds you, it houses you, and you've had more of an education than I ever had. We thought it'd be a better life for you . . ."

"Better?" Naila stared at her. "What about it is better? They want me just about as much as you do. The children hate me, the teachers think I'm worthless. They want me out. Today, when I went to class, there was a Surveyor waiting for me. He'd been sent to test me. Again. They're just looking for an excuse to get rid of me, and now you're telling me that I can't even come here, or see you, when you're supposed to be my . . ." Naila stopped short before saying the word "family", swallowing to wet her dry throat.

"They can't push you out." Brynda sounded hesitant, the unsaid words looming larger than the spoken ones. "You have to learn control. What would they even do with you?"

"I don't know."

"What did the Surveyor say?"

Brynda was watching her with round, worried eyes, and Naila felt her anger drain away. "It's fine, Bryn. He actually . . . he actually defended me."

Naila looked down at the table, picking at an old stain on the surface. *We've known for some time that this girl has support within the faculty* – that's what Marnise had said. At the time the words had been too impossible to comprehend, but the more Naila thought about it, the more it made sense. Why else had she been allowed to remain at the Academy for so long?

Haltingly, Naila recounted everything that had happened: everything, from the powerful wizard who'd stood behind her at the march, to the threats Trianne Marnise had made to the Surveyor. It felt good to tell someone, she realised, to lay all of it out in front of someone else's eyes. Brynda had always been a good listener, and she stayed silent while Naila unburdened herself, quietly taking in everything that had happened.

Brynda wet her lips. "I suppose it was only a matter of time until all of this reached our doorstep. I don't know what to say, Naila. We can't— you can't . . . I mean, you have to go back."

"I know, I know." Naila made herself smile, the expression stiff and wrong on her face. "I'll be fine. I'll get back to the Mita's District, keep my head down for a bit."

Brynda shook her head, not in denial, but because she clearly didn't know what else to say. Dillian placed a hand on Brynda's shoulder, and Naila envied their closeness, fervently wishing away the distance between them.

Brynda looked like she was about to say something, but there was a sudden swell of noise as Ania pushed open the door to the common room. "Yum'ma, there are—" Ania froze the moment she saw Naila. The girl was only a couple of years younger than Naila, but Ania had always seemed slightly afraid of her, dancing around some invisible obstacle between them. Now she just stared, her gaze lingering too long on the white fabric at her sleeves.

"Siditi," Ania switched to a formal address for Brynda, nodding her head in an awkward greeting. "The bar is very busy, and the priest has asked for more wine."

"I should go," said Naila, pushing herself away from table.

"Nonsense." Brynda was already on her feet. "You'll stay for your dinner. Dillian, I'll get this, you—" She flapped her hands in a gesture towards the stove. "Can't keep an Ellathian priest waiting."

"Wait, an Ellathian what?"

It was Dillian who answered Naila, not turning around as he clattered about the kitchen. "Yeah, you heard her. We have a holy guest. Didn't you see him when you came in? He's sitting right out the front there, bold as anything. Wonder what the mages will make of that, eh?"

The pale man she'd seen outside. Naila rocked back, stunned. Mages and non-mages came to Amoria from all over the continent of Omalia, from nearby Dahran, southern Cerisan and the Brevan Cities, but *never* from the Ellathian Empire; there was too much bad blood between them.

Before she knew it, Dillian was setting a steaming bowl down in front of her, a heavy hand settling on her shoulder.

"There you are," he said, as if the bowl of food would fix everything. "Eat up, now. I'd better go and see what I can do to get in the way. We'll be back through when things have quietened down."

Then there was another roar of noise as Dillian pushed through to the common room, before the door swung shut behind him, sealing the voices, and him, away.

Just like that, Naila was alone again.

She sat for a long time, not eating, stirring the soup and watching the steam coil lazily in the air. She could hear the clink and clatter from the bar, could pick out Ania's high voice, listening to the way she called out "Yum'ma" and "Yub'ba" so easily, when Naila had only ever called Brynda and Dillian by their names. Alone, Naila couldn't stop her mind from turning back in on itself. Even in a few short years, Ania was more at home here than Naila ever was.

With a sigh, Naila dropped the spoon onto the table and stood. She gave the common room door one last, lingering look. For a moment, she considered sticking her head through the door, waving Brynda or Dillian over to her, but in the end she decided against it. She had no idea what she'd say to them. Goodbye didn't really seem like it'd be enough.

Instead, she slipped quietly out of the back door.

5

LARINNE

Night had fallen by the time Larinne escaped her office, bathing the city in a soft violet glow. The lights of Amoria were reflected in the curving glass of the Central Dome, creating a mirror image of the city which hung high above her head. Amoria herself was far from quiet. Even as the last businesses closed their doors, mages and non-mages alike lingered in the streets, making their way slowly homeward or hovering in the yellow light of bars and teahouses. The murmur of voices echoed off the wide streets, a distant and otherworldly quality to them as if the hubbub of the day was filtered through a thick layer of Amoria's glass.

This was by far Larinne's favourite time of day.

She'd asked Haelius to meet her in the midaan, a square on the north side of the Academy. It was lined with young trees and bisected by a small channel of the Aurelia, a tributary of the canal which criss-crossed the inner city. One of the trees had stretched its branches out over the water, thin tendrils of leaves drooping down to trail on the canal's surface. Haelius stood underneath it, his arms folded across his chest, lost in thought – as usual.

He really had made an effort for seeing her, Larinne noted with a small smile. He was dressed in a traditional cut of Amorian robe: a floor-length coat of emerald-green, buttoned to his left shoulder. It was all edged in the red and gold which marked him as both a wizard and a lieno, but, in Haelius's way, it was only a thin, braided cord that skirted the edge of the coat: nothing like the glittering gold thread which wove through Oriven's robes or even the embroidery that patterned the edges of her own.

It suited him. Haelius was pale for an Amorian, his Ellathian heritage much more visible than Larinne's both in the shape of his eyes and the light brown of his skin. For once, the robes were pressed straight, and even his unruly brown hair was combed and pushed back behind his ears. Grudgingly, she allowed herself to be impressed.

"Look at you – you actually look halfway respectable."

He looked up with a narrow-eyed smile. "Only half?"

"No, really, I'm impressed. I almost didn't recognise you. What affected this transformation?"

"How unkind," he straightened up, though he wasn't tall enough to look down on her. "I suppose it is possible that Malek suggested I could make an effort from time to time."

"Thank the Goddess for Malek. How is he?"

Haelius raised one eyebrow. "I feel like *you* shouldn't have to ask *me* that."

Larinne answered with a grimace: Malek worked at the Academy alongside Haelius, but he also happened to be married to her sister. Haelius knew full well that she was terrible at making time to see either of them.

"I saw Dailem at the council," she said, letting her feet carry her down towards the edge of the canal.

"That definitely doesn't count."

"I know, I know." She sighed. She'd begun to relax – to feel her stiff shoulders sink away from her neck, slipping into the easiness of conversation with him – but the mention of the council reminded her of why she was really there.

"You think Oriven will get his *Justice*?" Haelius asked, misinterpreting her frown.

"So you've heard? I don't know. No. I mean, I don't— I didn't think so." Larinne wrapped her arms around herself. Amoria was never really cold, in the same way it was never really hot, but she felt a chill all the same. "Dailem thinks it will happen."

"Your sister has never been an optimist."

"She's right more often than you'll admit." Larinne frowned. "Listen, Haelius, I didn't ask you here to talk about this, and you know it."

He grew still beside her. "I don't suppose you wanted the pleasure of my company either."

He sighed and turned to sit on the stone bank of the canal, unbothered by the grit and dust which would dirty his coat; Larinne followed more carefully, spreading her own robes out beneath her.

"You've probably heard most of it already," he said wearily.

"I've heard a number of things, including that a wizard attacked a crowd of Oriven's supporters?"

"*What?* Where do these rumours even come from?" He pushed a hand through his hair, ruffling it up until he looked more like himself. "Tell me you didn't believe them."

"Of course not. Just – tell me what happened."

Haelius closed his eyes. He was tugging at his cuffs, like he always did when he was uncomfortable. "It was awful, Larinne. I've never seen them like this. I don't understand what happened. They turned on that man as if he was an animal. Less than an animal." He shook his head. "I thought they were going to kill him."

"And no one did anything to stop it?" A mixture of shame and anger burned in Larinne's chest; this was not the Amoria she knew, the one she had spent her whole life working to protect.

"No, no one. Oriven was gone before I even realised what was happening."

"So, you stopped them?"

Haelius nodded. "Just a couple of holding spells, nothing dramatic. I got the man out of there and little more. I certainly didn't attack anyone, Mother have mercy."

Larinne breathed out slowly, annoyed by the relief she felt; she'd known this was how it must have happened, but apparently part of her had still needed to hear it.

"Oriven should be thanking you for preventing a worse incident," she said quietly, remembering the way Oriven had spoken of *concerning interference* at the council meeting, lingering in front of Larinne.

"If that man ever thanks me for anything, I will strongly reconsider my actions."

They sat in silence for a time, surrounded by the peaceful murmur of the canal beside them. Almost without thinking, Larinne reached down and tugged the silk slippers from her feet, hitching up her long robes and slipping her feet into the clear water below. It carved a smooth, rippling path around her brown skin.

Like everything in Amoria, it was magic that drove water from the Great Lake and laced it through the streets of the city, so the canal still carried a prickling sensation of power along with the lingering warmth of the sun. Stretching out her toes, she felt the weariness of the day leach slowly out from her.

Haelius watched her with a quizzical expression and just a hint of judgement.

"What?" she said, trying not to picture how ridiculous she must look: a thirty-four-year-old senator dangling her feet in the water like a child.

"Nothing. Here—" She felt the touch of his magic again and then he was holding a small glass cup out towards her, steam curling off the amber liquid inside.

She laughed, despite everything. "Did you just teleport tchai here?"

"Yes, and it was extremely difficult." He wasn't lying – that Haelius could even use his magic to reach that far defied belief.

"So, this is how the most powerful mage in Amoria uses his magic?"

"What else is it good for?" He said it lightly, but she could see from his expression that he half meant it.

Holding the hot glass with the tips of her fingers, she took a small sip of the tea, sweet and spiced exactly as she liked it, but so hot that it burned the very tip of her tongue. "Hss, no, too hot."

"And yet," said Haelius, rolling his eyes. He didn't have to say anything else – they both knew that if it had been any cooler, she wouldn't have drunk it either.

"You'd think a wizard could manage to make a hot tea that doesn't burn."

"I'll put someone on it right away," he said, leaning back on his hands. "And while I'm at it, maybe light that doesn't actually illuminate anything."

Larinne pressed her lips together, trying not to smile. She curled her fingers around the warm glass and let herself enjoy a sense of normality. At least some things wouldn't change.

6

ENTONIN

Entonin took a slow sip of the wine, feeling the warmth and sweetness slide down the back of his throat. It was Dahrani wine, and good – better than he was expecting. It seemed that trade between the queendom and its magical neighbour was still alive and well, for now at least.

He shifted his back against the table, trying to make himself relax. He maintained a carefully benign smile, as if everything around him were just mildly interesting – as if he were not having a drink in the middle of *Amoria*, a city he'd only ever heard spoken of in breathless whispers, usually along the lines of "*how awful*" and "*can you even imagine it*".

The place had a horrible way of constantly reminding you what it was: it was hard not to dwell on the fact that the strangely smooth bench he was sitting on was almost certainly crafted using magic, as well as the floor, maybe even the glass he was holding, not to mention the monstrous great dome looming overhead. Out there in the crowds, there were people with *magic*, just walking around with the power to blast a hole through the side of a building. And they'd made their city out of *glass* – that was the truly ridiculous part.

In front of him, Amorians went about their business as if this were entirely normal. Carts juddered past, hawkers yelled, people drank, all of it bathed in that strange violet light. None of them looked up to the impossible glass sky above their head, none of them noticed as the sunlight began to fade and strange orbs of light blinked into existence above their heads.

In fact, none of them seemed to look up at all. Maybe that was how they coped with it.

These people were his kin, in a strange way. Amorian mages had once been Ellathians, fleeing the Empire to settle on the edge of Dahrani land. And yet it was *Entonin* who stood out here: he could feel their eyes on him, their sticky gaze lingering on his vestments, his pale hair. His robes had been washed and pressed by the inn after they arrived, so the white fabric was almost luminous in the evening light. It felt good to be wearing them again – the high collar, the stiff fabric: it felt like armour. Ardulath was with him, the weight of Ellath's greatest temple behind him. Let them look. He was here to be seen.

"You seem pleased with yourself," said his companion.

Entonin grinned. For a mercenary from some Dahrani backwater, Karameth was surprisingly perceptive. "It's good to be here, isn't it? Off the road. *Clean.*" He held up his glass. "And the wine is surprisingly good."

Karameth's gaze made Entonin's skin prickle with unease, the way it always did when the mercenary moved his full attention to him. He couldn't help it: Karameth was an intimidating sight. He was long and lean, moving in a way that felt like there was no wasted energy, and Entonin had seen enough to know that the long sabre he carried was not just for show. He looked exactly like the kind of person you shouldn't piss off, which was exactly why Entonin had hired him – and possibly also why Entonin took a perverse sort of delight in annoying him as much as possible.

Karameth seemed to be waiting for a better explanation.

"Not a fan of the wine?" asked Entonin, tipping his glass and smiling inanely.

When Karameth turned away, Entonin thought he could detect the smallest hint of exasperation on that usually expressionless face.

This was most likely the end of the conversation; Karameth wasn't exactly a talker. The mercenary was more like a human-shaped negative space than a companion, and that hadn't bothered Entonin in the least – the priest was quite capable of filling the silence for both of them. He wondered if that was the reason he still hadn't grown used to the mercenary: when Karameth decided to occupy a space, he suddenly grew a lot larger.

To Entonin's immense surprise, Karameth kept talking. "How long do you intend to stay here?"

"As long as Ardulath wills it," said Entonin, invoking the name of his god. It was another kind of answer which seemed to get under Karameth's skin.

"If he values your life, priest, let us hope he wills for us to be on the road again soon."

"Oh?"

"There is something very wrong here."

Entonin's surprise came out as a laugh. "Do you mean the fact that this is a city populated by magic-wielding heretics?" Entonin gestured above their heads. "Or that they've built a city in a bubble at the edge of a desert? Or was it the soup? I didn't think much of it either . . ."

Something twitched in Karameth's jaw.

"Oh, don't pull that face, Kara. You sound like some prophesying witch-mother."

"Good," Karameth turned his dark eyes back to him, and Entonin shifted uncomfortably before he could stop himself. "They have more wisdom than you do."

"Look, I'll admit that there is, besides the obvious, a certain *atmosphere*." Truthfully, Entonin had noticed it as soon as they had arrived: something guarded in the faces of the people who greeted them, an edge to the echoing shouts of the protest the night before. Not to mention the harrowed look in the landlady's eyes as she raised her head to listen. Entonin had felt this too many times not to sense the danger, yet this was exactly the kind of thing he was here for.

"My hands are tied," Entonin shrugged. "I have a job to do."

"And what is that job, exactly?"

Well, that's new.

They'd been on the road for months, and Karameth hadn't once shown any interest in what Entonin was doing here.

"Are you allowed to ask that?" Entonin took another long sip of his wine. "I thought it was against some 'mercenary code' or something. Aren't the Yenisseri's 'Grand Company' known for their discretion?"

Karameth almost looked uncomfortable. *Though perhaps I've just started imagining emotions for him*, Entonin considered. *The same way people imagine a dog's smiling.*

"I think you're mistaking me for one of your assassins, priest."

Entonin almost choked on his wine. "I really can't think of anyone who looks less like an assassin." He thought he saw the briefest flicker of a smile, though it was hard to tell through the shadow of Karameth's beard. Encouraged, he carried on, "Besides, what makes you think I know any assassins?"

"You're a spy for one of the ruling temples of the Ellathian Empire."

"The correct term is 'Seeker', thank you, and we're much more like ambassadors than spies. I am a humble seeker of truth; I offer guidance to those who look to the god of all knowledge, travellers who have lost their way . . ."

Karameth snorted. "You're about as humble as you are stupid."

Entonin blinked, unsure whether he had been complimented or insulted. He opened his mouth to answer, but Karameth interrupted him.

"Which is why I don't understand why we're not packed and ready to leave. You *know* there's trouble coming: you've felt it as much as I have. It may be tomorrow, or months from now, but this city is waiting for something. I don't think we should be here when that thing comes."

"But I have my *loyal* bodyguard to protect me."

"I'm one man—"

"That was entirely your decision."

"—and a hundred of the finest soldiers would not help you against magic." Karameth gestured towards Entonin, though at *what* exactly, Entonin wasn't sure. "None of *this* will protect you, not here. Whatever you've come to do, it doesn't matter. Go away and come back with protection, if you must – find some Dahrani mages to protect you."

Even the thought of travelling with mages made Entonin feel physically ill. Besides, there was something in the mercenary's tone, his casual disdain for Entonin's purpose, which had finally seeped beneath the priest's skin. Entonin had never been particularly good at mastering his temper: it had allowed himself to cut a path through the seething nest of politics and backstabbing back home, after all.

Whether it was because this awful city already had him on edge, or perhaps because it was the first time he'd had any kind of push-back from his uncommunicative companion, Entonin found himself retreating behind a wall of cold formality.

"Ardulath, praise be on his name, is the god of knowledge and wisdom. All knowledge. I am here to see and to learn. That means learning about what's happening here – *whatever* is happening here. So, no, I will not be leaving." He grinned, though it felt more like baring his teeth. "And if you want to be paid, neither will you."

He met Karameth's gaze without flinching, though he could feel the rapid thump of his heart. Sometimes Entonin's temper was like being drunk, like allowing someone else to take control of his tongue. What exactly did he plan to do if Karameth stood up and bid him farewell? The mercenary may not be able to fight against magic, but the very sight of him was a powerful deterrent.

The Dahrani mercenary *had* proved to be an invaluable guide through his country, and the last thing he wanted was to be alone in this gods forsaken place.

Entonin knocked back the rest of his wine. "Another?"

"No, thank you, Your Holiness."

"Are you sure? The wine really is very good." Though as Karameth got to his feet, Entonin could see that the mercenary's glass still sat on the table behind him, completely untouched.

He followed Karameth's gaze to the wide street before them. It had grown quieter even as they'd been talking, each shout seeming more distant. As he watched, the girl – the one who had stunned the common room into complete silence earlier in the evening – slipped out from the alley alongside the inn. She was an odd-looking creature, her hair almost the same blue-black as the deepening night, and the white on her robes was all the more noticeable in the low light.

A mage – perhaps the first he'd seen in this part of the city. She hesitated and glanced back over her shoulder before hurrying away, looking more like a frightened animal than a powerful magic-user. For some reason, this only added to Entonin's growing sense of disquiet.

"I don't know what trouble you're planning to cause here—" Karameth said without turning to look at him.

"What makes you think I want any trouble?"

"Ellath and Amoria are hardly friends. Your kind has a history of killing mages."

"That's really more the war god's domain; Ardulath doesn't kill people."

Not openly, anyway, his mind added. The god of knowledge preferred to get others to do His killing.

Karameth let out a low breath instead of answering, clearly deciding that whatever he'd meant to say wasn't worth the effort. Entonin was almost glad – through the haze of exhaustion and wine he was more likely to say something he shouldn't. Instead, Karameth turned to head back into the common room without so much as "by your leave", presumably to head back up to their room.

"Goodnight," Entonin raised his empty glass at Karameth's back.

There was no answer.

With a slight shrug, Entonin reached for Karameth's still full glass and tipped it into his own. Whatever the mercenary thought was "coming", he was sure he had time for another glass of wine.

7

LARINNE

The workshop was surprisingly dark after the dazzling sunlight of the dome, despite the glittering artefacts strung above Larinne's head. Delicately crafted bulbs and twists of glass swayed as she closed the door behind her, sending shadows dancing along the walls.

Haelius waited for her just inside, his hands tucked into his sleeves.

"You might be slightly overqualified for this, Wizard," she greeted him, unable to help her smile. "Though since nobody else has managed to tell me anything sensible about these artefacts, maybe we do need the Academy's help."

She was surprised when Haelius didn't match her smile; there was a bitter twist to the edge of his mouth. "Well, that's apparently a matter of opinion. Trianne Alenis didn't find me qualified *enough*."

"What?"

"She didn't want someone studying the artefacts who might have *mixed loyalties*." The air shuddered with Haelius's anger, the artefacts around him growing momentarily brighter and then fading again. "She asked that a *true* mage be the one to look at the artefacts."

Larinne stared at him, unable to comprehend what he'd just said.

It was absurd: mages and non-mages married all the time, and Haelius wasn't the first mage to come from a family with no magic at all. It was a fact of life; powerful mages struggled to have their own children – without children from outside mage families, they would have died out altogether long ago. Larinne was certain that if Haelius had been less powerful, or his father hadn't been a prominent non-mage of the Shiura Assembly, no one would have batted an eyelid.

Her own magic itched at her fingertips, anger giving it a path to the surface.

Of course, Haelius noticed even that tiny flutter of magic. "Why, Lieno Tallace, how unlike you."

She took a breath and forced herself to uncurl her fingers. "Well, I'm the one leading this investigation now, and I will use the experts I choose."

This finally coaxed a small smile from Haelius. "I serve at the pleasure of the Senate."

"Good. So, where are these 'sabotaged' artefacts?"

Haelius gestured further into the crowded workshop, and they began to pick their way towards the benches at the back.

"What do you think?" she asked, having to duck beneath another string of glass beads, each one glowing with their own soft light. Grudgingly, she was forced to admire the craftsmanship.

"I think Trianne Alenis made some lights that don't work."

"Oh, I'm so glad you're taking this seriously."

"Sorry," he gave her a sideways smile. "I will. Honestly, if there's anything to find, Malek will see it. He's far more familiar with artificing than I am."

That Alenis had requested Haelius's assistant inspect her work was a huge insult, but in truth Malek was well suited to the task. Dailem's partner was a talented artificer in his own right: Larinne had seen him turn what looked to her like a handful of sand and scrap metal into beautiful spun glass, and many of his own artefacts were sold at stores like this one. He was up the back of the workshop, bent over one of the lights. He looked like he hadn't heard them enter, but when Haelius spoke he snorted.

"*Better*, Haelius. I'm better at artificing than you are. It won't kill you to admit I'm better than you at something."

"Alas, it's true," Haelius replied. "Artificing, alchemy, speaking to people – the list is endless."

Malek looked up with a grin. He still had the magnifying eyepiece over his right eye and the strap made his thick, curling hair stick out from his head. He looked faintly mad.

"Beautiful Larinne!" He sprang to his feet with all the excess energy that defined him. "Goddess's grace, it's good to see you – it is always too long." He gave her a scratchy kiss on each of her cheeks, and then hugged her anyway.

For the longest time, Dailem had found no one, man or woman, who would live up to her exacting standards. When she had brought Malek to their parents' home – this cheerful Dahrani mage with twinkling eyes and a terrible sense of humour – a young Larinne had assumed he wouldn't last a month, and yet here he was nearly twenty years later. She was very glad to have been wrong.

"I know, I'm sorry. I'll make it up to you."

"Lies! No – don't look like that. Your sister is just as bad. And you don't need to pretend this is a social call. I know you're dying to find out what's wrong with these artefacts."

"Sorry," Larinne said again, following him back to the workbench. "There is a small disaster brewing out there and I need some kind of answer."

"Well, it's a strange one, no doubt." Malek lifted one of the lights up to his eyeline and turned it slowly between his thumb and forefinger. "It's of exceptional quality. It turns out that hateful woman is a talented artificer. One of the best I've seen."

Larinne leaned forward to get a better look at it. It was a beautifully simple design: a sphere of glass with a thin, twisting strip of metal in the centre of it, which extended to circle out around the globe. The metal was carefully inscribed with phonemes of magic which would make it glow and allow someone to turn it on with a simple touch to the outside ring.

It was meant for sale to people without magic, which involved the maker locking a part of their power into the artefact – a long and tedious process; an artificer could drain a good deal of their power and be without the use of magic for days. Still, it seemed odd that someone would spend so much time on something only to fail at the final step.

"Expensive," said Larinne.

"Very," agreed Malek.

"So, it's missing the magic to make it work?"

Malek tipped his head from side to side in a way that said he agreed but not entirely. "Yes, but there's more to it than that. I tried adding my own magic to it to see if I could make it work, but it just wouldn't take – as if the magic were draining right out of it."

"What? That doesn't make any sense."

"Indeed, no. And the metal feels … wrong, somehow. There's something I'm not seeing." He shook his head. "I'm afraid the good trianne's suggestion of sabotage is looking more and more likely."

"May I?" asked Haelius.

"Of course."

Haelius held one hand out flat and then crooked the tip of two of his fingers, almost as if he were beckoning the artefact to him: it flew from Malek's hand to his without Haelius uttering a word. Turning it slowly over in his fingers, Haelius shifted his gaze into that other sight, as if he were staring at a point far beyond the artefact itself.

He took a sudden, sharp breath, recoiling in surprise.

"What?" Larinne said before she could stop herself.

Haelius screwed his eyes shut before he looked at it again, a deep line forming in the centre of his forehead. "I don't understand. It's *gone*."

Larinne gritted her teeth against her impatience. "What is? What's gone?"

"The magic is entirely gone." He looked towards her, but his eyes were still vague and distant. He pinched the edge of the metal casing and snapped a piece off like it too was made of brittle glass. "And so is the anima."

"*What?*" Malek almost laughed in disbelief. "That can't be. It exists, Haelius, therefore it has anima."

Haelius shook his head. "Look again. You were looking at it like it was a complicated problem – look at it in the simplest possible way, the way you learned to see magic as a child."

They both huddled closer, and Larinne let her eyes become unfocused in the same way Haelius had. It was a different kind of sight, one which had as much to do with feeling as seeing. The magic was easy to sense, moving readily to a mage's call, but anima was always there behind it, vivid yet untouchable. It was a force which existed in everything, brightest in living things: it held the world together, defined what a thing was. Mages could use magic to manipulate the world around them – heat it, cool it, even break something down and combine it into something new – but they could not change anima.

For a moment, Larinne struggled to make out the artefact. The magic which clung to Haelius eddied around him like mist, obscuring the dark point in the palm of his hand. She had to focus her mind, push past the crowding magic and look only to that one point. Malek and Larinne saw it almost at the exact same moment, recoiling at the wrongness of it. It was less like an object and more like an absence, as if there were a gap where the artefact should be. Feeling suddenly dizzy, Larinne blinked and shook her head to bring herself back to normal sight.

While they still watched, Haelius tipped his hand and let the artefact fall onto the workbench. It didn't so much smash as crumble, parts of it disintegrating entirely into fine grey dust. Not even the metal remained.

"How?" was all Malek managed to say.

Haelius shook his head, looking more uncertain than Larinne had ever seen him. "I don't know. This defies just about everything I thought I understood about anima. I'd like to study some of the other—"

They were interrupted by a sharp cry from the street outside, followed by the sound of raised voices. Worse, Larinne could feel the faint prickle of magic lifting the hairs on the backs of her arms. She met Haelius's gaze for just a moment, before they both turned as one back towards the entrance.

Sunlight blinded Larinne as she stepped back out onto Artisan's Row, so that she had to lift an arm to shield her eyes from the violet glare. Yet even through the glare, it was impossible to mistake the dark figures that gathered around the shop's entrance.

Trianne Alenis had returned, and she'd brought Surveyors with her.

They had two non-mages with them, and Larinne recognised them as workers who collected goods from Artisan's Row for export out of the city.

She had to stifle a gasp when she realised that the magic she'd felt came from the restraints binding their wrists.

"—is a disgrace," one of them was shouting, struggling against the spell. "We're the ones who *sell* the artefacts! Why in the Goddess's name would we sabotage them?"

Alenis didn't even seem to register this commotion, her head bowed conspiratorially towards one of the Surveyors. Her eyes only flicked up when Haelius emerged from her workshop, and Larinne felt a sudden, powerful urge to put herself between Haelius and that gaze.

"What is the meaning of this?" Larinne barked at the nearest Surveyor, startling the small crowd to silence. "This investigation is under the purview of the Consul of Commerce, and I will be the one to make any decision on its outcome."

Even Alenis had the decency to dip her head in a small bow when she realised who was speaking.

"Lieno Tallace," Alenis said in a tone so deferential it didn't feel sincere. "I'm sorry I didn't wait for your judgement, but it felt prudent to get the Surveyors here as quickly as possible."

"And under what charge, exactly, are you holding these people?" Larinne turned her furious gaze to the Surveyors. "I haven't even determined what is wrong with these artefacts, much less whether a crime has been committed."

"It's sabotage!" Alenis said without hesitation. "Lieno, all of my items are made to code. You can see the quality of the workmanship yourself. These lights were working this morning when I sent them to sale; someone's clearly tampered with them."

"This is a serious accusation, Trianne Alenis. Why exactly would anyone want to sabotage your business?"

"Not me, *us*. They're trying to sabotage *our* businesses; everyone can see it. They want to discredit the magic of Amoria."

For a moment, Larinne was stunned. A chill crept down the length of her spine. She would have known exactly who the trianne meant as "them" even if she hadn't stared directly at the non-mages present, and Larinne very much did not want to be counted among "us".

It was all she could do to keep her voice even when she turned to address the Surveyors. "I think this has gone on quite long enough, don't you? Release these people at once."

"I'm afraid I can't let you do that."

Larinne had been so consumed with the scene in front of her that she hadn't noticed the figures approaching from her right. When she turned, everything seemed to stutter to a halt, the clammy fingers of dread tightening around her heart.

It was Malek who answered first. "Dailem?"

There were three mages dressed in a uniform Larinne had never seen before: long black robes which swallowed the person within them, covering them from ankle to stiff, high collar. But where the Surveyor robes were plain and unadorned, these robes were edged in thick gold embroidery, curling in from the edge of the robes like flames. Unlike the Surveyors, the mages' faces were uncovered, forcing Larinne to meet her sister's gaze.

They were the Justice. Oriven's Justice. And Dailem was wearing one of their uniforms.

How? was all Larinne wanted to say. It had only been days since they'd sat together in the council chamber, when they'd both heard Oriven's proposal with what she'd thought was equal horror. She wanted to grab the front of her sister's new uniform and demand that she remove it. But there were too many eyes on them, too many people looking to them both.

"Dailem?" Haelius, as ever, didn't care who was watching. "What is this? What are you doing?"

"Wizard," Dailem replied without an inch of familiarity. "I am here representing the Justice of Amoria, and we are taking control of this investigation."

"Justice?" Haelius looked sideways to Larinne, his expression uncomprehending. For an awful moment, Larinne wondered if he thought she already knew. "How? There is no 'Justice'."

But of course there was. Of course Oriven had secured every vote he

needed before he even brought his proposal to the Senate. The Justice
had been formed before Larinne even knew it was coming.

"The Justice's assistance is not required," said Larinne, her voice
sounding thin to her own ears. "My advisers and I have the situation
in hand."

"I'm afraid not." Dailem was all cold formality, but Larinne could
see the warning that was meant for her – *don't fight me on this*. "This is
not the only incident this morning. A number of merchants have had
their goods affected. It's become a matter of security. We'll be seizing
the artefacts and taking these people in for questioning."

"On what grounds?" Haelius shook his head. "The sabotage is
magical in nature. Just how do you propose any of these non-mages
did this?"

The word "sabotage" made Larinne grit her teeth; Trianne Alenis
looked positively triumphant.

"Artefacts across the city have been damaged." Dailem's voice was
tight as she carefully skirted the implication of any blame. She never
did have much patience for Haelius. "We must investigate all possibilities. I'd be grateful to hear what you've learned, Wizard. Lieno Tallace,
we will communicate with your committia at a later date."

"No." Haelius stepped forward, and Larinne could feel the dangerous shiver of magic on the air. "What is this, Dailem? Oriven is not
the Consul of Commerce. You can't take these artefacts; I can learn
more about them than any jumped-up—"

"Haelius, enough." Larinne grabbed Haelius's arm to stop him from
advancing on Dailem any further.

He looked back at her with such an expression of surprise and
disappointment that Larinne's heart sank in her chest. She held his
gaze and gave the smallest shake of her head. There was a moment –
she could feel the tingle of magic reacting to Haelius's anger and the
sharp, metallic taste of his power on her tongue. Then he seemed to
let it all go, his arm relaxing in her grip.

"As you wish," he said coldly.

Larinne squeezed his arm and smiled, but when she looked up, she
found Alenis watching them, her pale eyes fixed on Larinne's hand.

It made her feel too seen, an intrusion into Larinne's life rather than Lieno Tallace's. She dropped her hand immediately.

Instead, she turned to her sister. "My office is happy to assist the Justice in any way we can."

"Thank you, Lieno Tallace."

Everything Dailem was doing was performative: Haelius had missed all his cues, but Larinne wouldn't miss hers. In this moment, they weren't sisters – weren't even people; they were the offices they carried in their titles and the gold thread woven into their robes. And Larinne knew she would do almost anything to keep the peace.

She bowed. "You're welcome, Justice Tallace."

8

INTERLUDE

The air was unnaturally cold. The wind had a bite to it that felt closer to deep winter than late spring. Behind Ra'akea, the trees lifted and sighed, the sound stretching away from her like a wave pulling back out to sea. It was a mournful note, and she wondered if Mother Wind pitied the dead, even if they were humans.

The grass beneath her feet was stiff and frozen, but she left no footprints as she walked towards the settlement. It was little more than a single road and a cluster of low buildings, the sloping roofs gleaming silver-white and the paving stones slippery with ice. There was no building untouched by its icy breath, walls cracked with frost and long icicles hanging like teeth from the eaves.

The creature's wrath had swallowed an entire human village.

At the edge of the ruin, she passed the bodies of warriors, their faces frozen white with trails of silver creeping over their skin. At least, they looked like warriors. They wore a kind of armour, the red lacquer appearing milky under a layer of frost, but their weapons lay sheathed at their sides or unbroken on the ground: it didn't look like they had given much of a fight. Ra'akea supposed there wasn't much humans could have done.

As she stepped into the main street, the bodies began to look different. These people had no armour, no shields, no weapons. They hadn't even been running. They'd fallen in doorways, throwing open the shutters, their eyes turned up to get a glimpse of a shadow in the sky. They should have been running. She hesitated beside one small form, unable to fully pull her gaze away. She noticed the roundness of its face and the smallness of its fingers.

A child.

A human, came the immediate response, the voice clear in her mind as if the thought were her own. Tae had little interest in humans and even less concern for death.

It killed all of them, Ra'akea let the thought form in her mind. She did not hide her discomfort: she and Tae had been together since birth and their connection was absolute – her companion would sense her feelings whether Ra'akea wanted her to or not.

That is why we must kill it. There was no malice in Tae's thoughts, only an impatience to be done.

Ra'akea's mouth pressed into a grim line. It was true. She had not come here to mourn children.

Somehow none of this made hunting one of their own feel any better.

It is not *one of ours.* Tae's thoughts were full of revulsion. *The beast is wild.*

They both felt the other shudder: there was nothing more unnerving to their kind.

Ra'akea stalked through the small village, along a line of forlorn buildings these people had once called home. She hopped over a low fence, stepping over the bodies of dead chickens and one grey-muzzled goat which might well have been dead before the attack had come. She peered through half-open doors at tables set for supper, walked past a small shrine which held a single candle, tied with a blue and silver ribbon. And she searched – searched for something which might have caused this: some provocation, some crime these humans had committed.

It would have been easier if she'd found it. These were ordinary people. There was no threat here, nothing to explain the attack.

What did you expect? asked Tae, sensing her bitterness.

I don't know. An icy wind buffeted against her, pushing her thick hair back from her face and causing her cloak to flap against the backs of her ankles. *A reason. An answer.*

She had been to three different sites of attacks now and each of them was the same. There was nothing to see but death.

What have you found? she asked Tae, confident that her friend would have more success; if they couldn't understand why, they could at least put a stop to it.

The trail leads south. It has covered a great distance.

Can we catch it?

If you leave now.

Ra'akea nodded, even though Tae wouldn't see her. If they could catch up to it, if she could just *see* what had become of it, maybe she could get her answers.

And if not, then she knew what she had to do.

9

NAILA

Naila edged along one of the rows of stone benches, clutching her satchel to her chest. The lecture theatre was one of the largest rooms in the Academy, stretching almost the full width of the tower. Much like the lobby downstairs, it was a room too big for its purpose, all polished glass and carved stone. The light was muted: the outside walls were almost opaque, darkened to a deep indigo, and the soft glow from the lamps flickered over the glass like reflected water.

The small clusters of students made the room look emptier, if anything. Four of the advanced theory classes had been brought in together for this lecture, which meant there were students here who were close to sitting their ranked exams or graduating to the High Academy. Naila was probably still the oldest mita there, but many of these students were a similar age to her, born around the time of the shaking sickness or just after, at a time when so many mage children were lost.

Looking at the empty stretches of white stone, Naila couldn't help wondering if there was ever a time when this room had been filled with young mita, and, if so, if that time would ever come again.

She chose a seat almost in the centre of the room, far from the whispering knots of other students. Even this small number of people managed to fill the room with sound, their voices carrying up into the vaulted ceiling above them. It made her hunch smaller and pull up her shoulders, a sheet of black hair falling in front of her face.

"—that can't be true." Naila caught a snatch of the conversation from the group of nearest students. "An Ellathian priest would never come *here*."

"I swear it's true. He's staying at an inn in the Southern Quarter, some non-mage place—"

Naila flinched at the mention of the Dragon's Rest. Ever since Brynda's warning, Naila hadn't gone back there. She'd attended class, sat alone, returned to her empty dormitory, slept, and started all of it again. She hadn't spoken to anyone in days, and no one so much as looked at her. It left Naila feeling detached, withdrawn even from her own skin. She'd never felt as if her existence mattered so little to anyone.

Naila was startled out of her isolation by the sound of someone jumping down from the row behind her.

"Thanks for saving me a seat," said Ko'ani, grinning at her own joke.

"Ko." Naila's voice caught in her throat. Ko'ani was looming over her, her face haloed by a mane of twisting, brown curls. She was dressed in robes more Dahrani than Amorian, sleeveless and burnt orange, her forearms covered by a familiar tangle of bracelets. It had been months since Naila had seen her, and yet Ko was just as bright and easy as ever. Naila felt the bubble she'd been trapped in shudder and burst.

"What? Don't look at me like that." Ko punched her on the arm. "I might have escaped Marnise's class, but that doesn't mean you've escaped *me*."

She dropped onto the bench next to Naila and began rummaging through her bag, her bracelets jangling louder than anything else in the room. Like many of the other mita, Ko wore jewellery which matched the colour of the rank she expected to become when she graduated: gold, in Ko's case, because of her lieno mother. But unlike any other mage Naila had met, Ko also wore jewellery to match the lower rank of her father, with just as many silver bangles on her arms as gold.

"Where have you been hiding?" Ko continued her rummaging, her voice muffled by the pen she was holding in her mouth. "Even my mum's been asking after you. They're worried, you know, with how things are. Are you okay?"

Naila had been holding herself together so carefully, but the moment Ko'ani asked her if she was okay, she felt her eyes sting. She looked down. "Fine. No one's bothered with me yet." Naila cleared her throat and tried something like a smile. "Well, Trianne Marnise *did* try to get me thrown out of her class."

"Ugh, really? You should probably take that as a compliment. She hated me, too, even though I was clearly the most promising student she ever taught." Ko stuck out her chin in jest, though Naila could believe it was true. "I take it she didn't manage?"

"They let me come to this," Naila replied with a slight shrug.

"Yes, *lucky* us. Are you excited about a lecture from the great Wizard Akana?"

Even his name made a knot of anxiety twist in Naila's stomach.

"Well, that's a stronger reaction than I was expecting." Ko was staring at her with raised eyebrows. "Have you been to one of his lectures before?"

"No, Ko, I bumped *into* him – a few days ago, the day after Oriven's big march."

"You what?"

Naila slapped her hands together for emphasis. "Right into him. Bam. Knocked him over, sent his books flying everywhere."

Ko was laughing even before Naila stopped talking, so loudly that some of the clusters of students had turned round to glare at them. "Oh Goddess, Naila stop. He must have been *mortified*. That could only happen to you. Are you sure it was him?"

"Absolutely. Weird green eyes, that great scar on his face. He looked at me like I was one of his experiments."

Before Ko could answer, the wizard himself appeared on the dais as if they'd summoned him, his magic fluttering the pages of students' books and sending a whisper of gasps through the room.

"Show off," said Ko'ani, not even blinking at such a display of power.

Naila didn't answer, unable to take her eyes off the Wizard Akana.

As soon as he appeared, she felt his power like a beacon, as if he were a creature made more of magic than of flesh. The energies in the room were tugged towards him, and Naila had the sensation she was falling, sucked down towards the centre of the room.

If anything, Wizard Akana looked bored.

He approached the lectern like it was the last place he wanted to be and scanned the crowd with an air of disinterest, though Naila could feel him reaching out with his power, the magic twisting through them as if he were testing each and every one of them. When his eyes reached Naila, he paused, and Naila felt her breath hitch in her chest.

She was too exposed, too separate from her classmates, and he more than anyone could see what she was – or, more importantly, what she wasn't.

"Perhaps we should begin?" He leaned in towards the lectern, his voice awkwardly amplified by its magic. "I don't intend to keep any of us longer than I must. I am Wizard Akana, and I have been asked to speak to you today about the language of magic." He glanced sideways at Trianne Marnise, making it abundantly clear whose fault that was. "By now you should all be very familiar with the basic phonemes of magic. There are sixty-three common phonemes and more than two thousand uncommon ones – and probably more which we haven't yet discovered. The combinations are endless and allow us to manipulate magical energy in the form of spells."

He took a small step back and flicked his hand to one side. "*Mutacaeli visceler luxiveus figura. Teneminuas.*" Next to him the air shimmered like heat haze, and then the pictorial form of one of the phonemes of magic lit up, suspended in bright, white light. *Ignis*, Naila thought, though not one of the phonemes he'd used to cast his spell.

Wizard Akana stepped back to the lectern, appearing to ignore the phoneme, though it still glowed steadily behind him. A hushed murmur of surprise rippled across the room, students leaning forward in their seats.

Creating light was one of the simplest kind of spells, a case of altering the speed of existing energies until they produced a visible glow; Naila was probably the only mita in the room who couldn't do it. To produce a shape and hold in mid-air was far more complex, but to do it without maintaining a focus or constantly speaking the spell was remarkable. When Naila half closed her eyes to observe the movement of the magic itself, she saw that Wizard Akana was more impressive still: he wasted no energy holding the shape of *ignis* in one place – instead, the magic which passed through his spell would change and become light, but once it moved beyond the outline of the phoneme, it immediately went dark. Naila felt a grudging appreciation for his skill.

The wizard waved a hand carelessly and it disappeared.

"At this point in your education, I would expect each of you to know the sixty-three phonemes and at least two hundred of the more common combinations."

"Oh, come *on*," Ko murmured louder than Naila would have dared, adding her voice to the rumble of dismay.

"And you should also be aware that the phonemes themselves have no impact on magic itself, or the world around you." This time there was only silence and blank faces, Ko's included. "Some believe that the phonemes are left over from the ancient language of dragons, but I can assure you that this is nonsense. The phonemes we teach in Amoria are derived from ancient Ellathian, but spells can just as easily be cast in Dahrani, as I'm sure some of you already know. A more likely explanation is that the phonemes we speak are merely used to activate a part of our minds we use to control the magic in ourselves. This change in our *own* power allows us to influence the magic inherent in all things. I'm here to show you that the same thing can be achieved with gestures, entirely without words." He pointed two fingers and traced the shape of *ignis* in the air. In hardly the span of a breath, the phoneme was alight again.

Naila was relieved to see the other mita recoil with the same shock she felt. Wizard Akana was famous for his use of magic without incantations, but it was a different thing to see it in person – to witness the casual way he manipulated his power. The speed alone was unsettling.

"The idea that this is difficult or advanced is purely based on what you've been taught. In fact, some may even find this technique easier than more traditional methods."

Once again, Wizard Akana locked eyes with Naila. It was only for the briefest moment, but there was no denying that he'd stared right at her. Naila shifted back on the bench, her mouth dry.

"If you would start by considering the regions of the mind which we associate with magic, the limbic lobe and by extension . . ."

The lecture continued in much the same vein until the third bell. Apparently, it didn't matter all that much that Wizard Akana was a genius – it didn't mean he was able to teach.

The two hours for which he spoke were so rich in information that Naila thought she might have been able to learn more in that time than she had in three years of classes, had she been able to follow any of it. He spoke relentlessly, without so much as a pause for breath, and if you missed one word it felt like you'd missed everything. Ko hadn't even tried: she was slumped slightly forward in her seat, brown curls obscuring her face, but Naila could tell from her slow breathing that she was fast asleep.

"Well, I believe I have made good time," the wizard concluded, clearly satisfied with his work; he either hadn't noticed or hadn't cared about the extent to which he'd lost his class. "I will leave it there. I look forward to welcoming new attendees to the High Academy in the coming weeks." Though no expression graced Wizard Akana's severe features to suggest he looked forward to anything.

There was no invitation for questions, and as Wizard Akana stepped away from the lectern the auditorium slowly stirred back to life.

"Good nap?" asked Naila.

"No." Ko'ani screwed up her face and rubbed the back of her neck. "Did I miss anything?"

"No. I mean, maybe the whole of our education crammed into two hours? I don't know; I couldn't keep up with it."

"I've heard it all before," said Ko, as if a lecture by a wizard were something she experienced every day. "You'd think he could make it more interesting. He's a wizard, for Goddess's sake. Who can make *magic* boring?"

Naila was half listening to Ko, but her eyes kept drifting back down towards the dais. The wizard was still there, and Naila couldn't turn her back on him in the same way she wouldn't turn her back on a threat. He'd bowed stiffly to the mingling teachers, and Vetra Seith had fallen over himself to bow back. To Naila's surprise, however, Trianne Marnise hung back, barely nodding in response.

". . . my head. Do you think he even hears himself? I can't believe even *he'd* find that— Naila, are you ignoring me?"

"No, sorry." Naila tugged her attention back to Ko. "I don't think he's used to teaching us lowly mita."

"Or anyone else. I reckon I could keep up better than some of the idiots in the High Academy."

"If you weren't asleep."

"Exactly!"

Naila raised her eyebrows, smiling in a way she hadn't for days. "Well, we're unlikely to get taught by his like again."

"Ugh, speak for yourself." They'd followed the shuffling line of students back out onto the stairway, and Ko had to shield her eyes as they stepped out into the afternoon sun. "What now? Want to come down to market? My dad's going to be at Artisan's Row this evening – he'll definitely buy us dinner if I annoy him enough."

Naila's smile froze on her face. The invitation felt like a cool breeze on a stifling day, and she wanted desperately to lean into it, to go with Ko and feed the part of herself that had been starving since the Dragon's Rest.

Ko was watching her intently, somehow managing to get in the way of everyone trying to leave the lecture theatre. She was half brilliance, half disaster: as likely to get thrown out of a class as she was to be its best student. But she was almost certainly going to the High Academy, a young lieno with all the talent to become a senator or even a wizard. The last thing she needed was to be seen with someone like Naila.

"I— I can't." Naila looked down, avoiding Ko's penetrating gaze. "I haven't opened a book all week. I should study – at least try to find a way out of this mess."

"Oh." Ko was clearly surprised, but she smothered it with forced cheer. "I suppose I should probably do the same. Wizard Akana *would* be proud." Her lips twitched into half a smile. "Well, I'll head to the pattern room then. Just ... look after yourself, all right? Don't be a stranger. I know my mum's terrifying, but she knows the right people. We could help if—"

Ko hesitated, neither of them sure exactly what she could help with.

Naila forced a smile. "I'm fine. I only have to endure Trianne Marnise's classes until she throws me out."

"A fate worse than death," said Ko, and Naila wasn't sure whether she meant the classes themselves or getting thrown out of them. "Well, see you later. It's been really good to see you."

She turned to join the trailing end of the lingering mita, her bracelets jangling and her bag bouncing against her back. Naila watched her leave, hanging back by the lecture theatre door, unsure of where she meant to go herself. Ko's absence felt like a hollow had been gouged out of Naila's chest, all the more painful because Naila had done it to herself.

10

NAILA

In the end, Naila decided to settle herself on one of the bridges between the Academy and the Wizard's Tower, a residential tower meant for the staff of the Academy and its guests. It was where Ko'ani lived, thanks to her father, and although Naila had never crossed into the tower itself, her and Ko had spent enough evenings sprawled on the cool marble, watching the glow of the city below them. The bridges were always quiet – most mages used the pattern rooms to dart about the city – so that barely two or three mages would walk past them of an evening, and none of them would pay any attention to a couple of mita enjoying the view.

Maybe that was why she'd come here. The sun was halfway to the horizon, and it blazed a glittering path of fire across the Great Lake. Naila thought she could almost see the shadow of mountains on the northern shore, blurred and indistinct in the haze of heat and dust. She pressed her forehead against the glass and released a slow sigh, trying to breathe out the heaviness that had settled upon her. It wouldn't leave. It sat in her veins like poison, dragging her downward, as if someone were physically pushing her against the glass. When she closed her eyes, she could feel the hum of Amoria's magic in her jaw: that magic she would never touch.

It took all the energy she had even to reach for her bag and the books inside it. She hadn't opened her satchel since scrabbling on the floor of the Academy. What was the point? Nothing in these dusty old tomes would help her, just as nothing in the library books had ever helped her.

She tipped her bag, letting the books slide onto the floor, and then froze.

The first book to hit the floor wasn't one of her old library books – there was no cracked spine and peeling leather. The cover was pristine, dyed the rich, ruddy colour of wine, and the lettering on the front was tooled in gold: *Magical Devices and Their Use in Practical Magic*. Naila had never seen a book like it, let alone held one in her hands.

She gathered it into her lap, turning the pages slowly, reverently, only ever touching the edges with the very tips of her fingers. Each page was beautifully handwritten, accompanied by sketches and diagrams of different magical items: wands, gems, the enchanted glass that Amoria was so famous for. It was a careful and beautiful collection of knowledge, and likely worth more money than Naila would ever possess.

There was no doubt in her mind: this book belonged to Wizard Akana.

Her first instinct was to push the book off her lap, put some physical distance between her and the offending object. Maybe she could leave it here, walk away and pretend that this had never happened? *But he knows*, Naila thought, cold dread creeping through her. *That's why he kept looking at you. He knows you took it, and now he thinks you kept it.* She felt sick. She had stolen from the most powerful man in Amoria. How? How had this happened? She remembered gathering up her books. Surely she would have noticed picking up *this*?

She couldn't get herself to think. Instead, she could only imagine the disbelief if she tried to explain, the metallic taste of magic resonating with his anger.

She was coiled so tightly around her fear, she didn't notice the approaching footsteps until they were almost on top of her. Someone was laughing, and the sound of it kindled in Naila's frayed nerves. Before she could stop herself, she'd darted a look towards them, guilt written on her face.

They were mita – Naila's classmates – their arms heavy with gold or silver jewellery. Naila recognised two of them from Marnise's classes, Marcus at the front with more bracelets on his arms than thoughts in his head, and at the back, Celia Oriven herself, her robes the same brilliant scarlet as her father's.

"Who let *you* in here?" said Marcus, wrinkling his nose in disgust.

"It's bad enough you have to look at them all day," said a girl Naila didn't know. "Now they're invading your home, too."

Naila said nothing, her heart thumping so loudly she thought they must be able to hear it.

"Did you think you could just come and live here like a vagrant?" Marcus took a step forward, peering down at her and her scattered books.

"No, of course not," Naila snapped back before she could stop herself, fighting the urge to cover Wizard's Akana's book with her hand.

They laughed, and Naila knew that answering them had been a mistake.

"Well, don't just sit there on the floor then – do they not teach you manners in the Southern Quarter?" Marcus knew he'd found Naila's pride and he picked at it. "That might do for other hollows, but you're addressing the children of senators."

Naila stood slowly, hating herself for doing it. They were children – just stupid children picking a fight because they were bored. Except for one crucial difference: these children had magic.

She nodded her head in a stiff bow.

"That's better. See, you do know how to behave."

A second mita Naila didn't know had circled round behind her, and Naila began to feel more and more like she was their prey.

"Look," the boy said, his voice broken with laughter. "It still thinks it's a mage. It's trying to educate itself."

He kicked Wizard Akana's priceless book towards the others and Naila watched it slide across the floor, her crime out in the open for everyone to see.

"Don't be a beast, Tasian," said Celia, speaking for the first time, apparently far more concerned for the book than she had been for a fellow student.

There was a fraction of a hesitation as Celia bent to pick it up, a telling crease in her brow as she turned it over in her hands; Naila didn't breathe.

"What is this?" Celia looked towards Naila with narrowed eyes. "This can't be yours."

"It isn't." Naila made herself meet Celia's gaze, ready for the way the girl flinched at the black of her eyes. Naila suddenly felt too aware of herself: her frayed robes, the dirt-trodden white lining, the bare skin at her wrists. She folded her arms across her chest, as if that would hide who she was.

By contrast, Celia was the perfect mita: her silk robes were feather-light, long enough to skirt just above the ground, and wide sleeves trailed after every movement. A thick braid of brown hair coiled around her neck like a snake, and fine chains hung from her ears and criss-crossed her hands, the gold almost yellow against the brown of her skin. The book was at home in those hands. Oriven's daughter was everything Naila would never be.

"Then why do you have it?"

The tension took on a different kind of edge. Naila faltered. "I— it's because— I'm going to return it."

Marcus took a step towards her. "You stole it, then."

"No!"

"No, of course you didn't." Marcus took another step forward, forcing Naila to take a stumbling step back. "You just found it. Someone lent it to you. It appeared in your grubby little hands. Go back to whatever dank hole you crawled out of. Haven't you realised yet? No book will make any difference to you – you're still a Goddess-damned hollow."

Naila felt a fire light in her blood, tingling through her veins. "I'm a mage," she spat. "I have a right to be here."

"No, you're not." Marcus had forced her almost back against the glass. "You're a liar and a thief, and you'll never be more than that."

The anger burning in her skin felt almost like magic. For a moment, Naila let herself believe that Wizard Akana's words might apply to her, that she could push out her hands and power would rush with them. She clenched her hands at her sides, grasping for whatever power lived inside her – if there were *ever* a time she needed it to answer her, it was now.

"Reilin, go and get a teacher, or, better yet, a Justice. Let's see what they have to say about your horseshit story, hollow thie—"

"I'm not a thief!" Naila burst forward, slamming her hands into Marcus's chest.

There was no magic, but she hit Marcus harder than she meant to. He lost his balance, stumbling backwards.

His expression twisted into one of fury and disgust. "How *dare* you touch me."

Then there was magic: real magic from a *real* mage. Celia said the words so fast that Naila didn't hear them. The first she knew was a shudder in the air, the sensation of magic sliding away and then propelling back towards her.

The holding spell slammed against her chest, knocking the breath out of her lungs and paralysing every muscle in her body. She tried to breathe, but her chest was clamped in place and she could only make shallow gasps, gulping air like a fish out of water. Nothing would move. Every instinct in her was screaming to run, but she couldn't even blink.

"That's better," said Marcus.

Behind him, Celia stood as still and straight as if she were caught in her own spell, one hand outstretched, words of power spilling off her tongue.

Marcus stepped so close that Naila could feel his magic. He was no wizard, but power still coiled within him. He grabbed her face and tipped it up towards him, his fingers pinching into her cheeks. She wanted to scream. She wanted to run. But she couldn't even make a sound. They could do anything to her. Anything. She was a prisoner in her own skin.

"See?" said Marcus. "This is what magic is. There's nothing you can do about it." He leaned closer, his breath on her face. "Look at you. You're barely human, let alone a mage. Do you have any idea what they'll do to someone like you? You attacked the son of a senator. Stole from a respectable mage. They can't even expel you, because you haven't learned to control yourself. I hear they take people like you and lock them up in the cells beneath the city. You'll never see the light of day again."

There was the click of approaching footsteps on stone: Reilin had found her Justice already. This was it – they were coming for her and there was nothing she could do.

"*What is the meaning of this?*" Wizard Akana's voice was ice, and the air shivered with his anger.

Marcus let go of Naila's face and Celia fumbled her spell for just a moment. Naila's body staggered forward against the restraints that no longer held her, almost sinking to her knees. She didn't waste a second. Throwing herself forward, she barrelled past Marcus, every inch of her focused on getting away. She ran.

She knew she wouldn't make it. She knew that at any moment Wizard Akana's magic would seize her, or he would appear in her path. There was nowhere they wouldn't find her. Her chest heaved, her pounding footsteps reverberated in her skull and her feet slipped and skidded on the glass stairway. She didn't stop. She didn't think. She just ran.

It was only when she reached the bottom of the Academy tower that thoughts began to trickle through the haze of panic. Where was the wizard? Why hadn't he stopped her? She could feel her heart hammering in her chest, her head, her neck. Her lungs burned, and hot tears streamed down her face. But she couldn't stop – Wizard Akana could appear at any moment, materialising out of the very air. She had to keep going: force her weak, aching legs to move.

Naila pushed her way out into the street, her head down, trying to ignore the stares of passing mages. Where would she go? She couldn't go to the Rest; if she went to Brynda and Dillian, all this would come with her, and she couldn't bring Surveyors or Oriven's Justice to their door. She thought of Ko'ani and her promise to help her, but she couldn't bring herself to turn back to the Wizard's Tower. And what if Ko's mother didn't believe her? She was a member of the Senate – a friend of Surveyors and members of the Justice: she'd be forced to turn Naila in.

Naila was on her own.

Her only hope was to disappear. The Academy knew where she lived, but it would take a little time for Wizard Akana to find that information. If she could just get in and grab her belongings, the meagre amount of money she had hidden in her mattress, maybe she could hide in the Southern Quarter, or even cross the bridge to Jasser. There were a million places to hide, even in Amoria, and they'd have no way to find her. She would be forgotten. They couldn't hunt her forever.

Naila tried to ignore the prickle of magic beneath her skin, but she couldn't stop the images that crowded before her eyes: the terrible heat, the moment that her power would bubble up from within and burn right through her. Turning her back on the Academy meant turning her back on learning control. But she had no choice. Her power hadn't come to her in seventeen years – hadn't even stirred when Marcus had her in her grip. Surely that meant she didn't need to control it?

Naila skirted along the edge of the street. The Mita's District was too quiet, the air heavy and still. No one even glanced her way, but she felt their eyes all the same. She kept seeing Wizard Akana's cruel, scarred face, and feeling his long fingers closing on her shoulder.

Almost there, almost there, almost there. Her thoughts circled in her head, closing out the fear. He hadn't found her. She was only a few short yards from her home. She wanted to run, but she bit that thought down, taking step after measured step. *Only a little further.*

She was almost at the top of the dormitory stairs when she saw him. Her foot caught on the last step and her blood froze. He was already there. Wizard Akana was waiting for her, leaning against the wall next to her door, so casual about her fate. He was looking away down the landing, watching a different set of stairs, but it would only be seconds before he turned and saw her. She could still back away, but despair held her as tightly as the holding spell. How could she outrun this? Her whole body burned, her fingers trembling on the handrail. A sound like a whimper escaped her lips.

His green eyes snapped towards hers.

No was all her feeble mind could manage. She turned and half fell down the first step.

"Naila! Naila wait!"

The pleading note in his voice was so at odds with anything Naila expected that she stopped, her eyes dragged back to him.

He'd taken only one step towards her, his hands raised in a kind of surrender. "I'm sorry – I didn't mean to frighten you. I'm not going to hurt you."

It was too much. Without a battle to fight, without someone to run from, her body gave up: she sank against the step, tears of exhaustion hot on her cheeks. Closing her eyes, she grasped at the wall and the stone steps, trying to steady herself against them.

There were footsteps and the rustle of fabric as the wizard crouched beside her. A pause, and then the lightest touch on her back, a hand only just brushing the fabric of her robes. He stayed there without a word, letting her breathe. When she looked up, he snatched his hand away, his expression so uncertain that it looked wrong on his face.

"Are you hurt?" he asked. "Can I help you to your room?"

"No." Naila cleared her throat and tried again. "No. I can manage."

Her body screamed in protest, but she pulled herself to her feet. She forced herself to walk away from him without trembling, every step an exercise in willpower. It was only when she stood before the locked door to her room that she realised her bag – and her key – were still lying on the bridge to the Wizard's Tower.

"Let me." The wizard was standing a couple of feet back from her, maintaining a careful distance. He made one of his gestures, and Naila heard the *thunk* as the lock in her door slid back. Wizard Akana smiled, completely oblivious to how easily he'd eroded the security of Naila's home.

Her narrow room was cluttered and dark. Bedclothes were tangled into one corner, a small pile of ancient library books toppled over in another. The presence of this stranger in his rich green robes made everything seem grimmer, leaching the colour out of Naila's small life and into his.

She picked some clothes off the only chair and dropped them onto her bed, her movements mechanical and detached. They needed light, so she began to rummage through her desk, but before she even found her tinderbox, a soft, flickering glow filled her room. Naila felt the pinprick touch of magic on her skin, and when she turned there was a globe of white light suspended in the middle of her ceiling.

Wizard Akana still hovered in her doorway, as if he were a malevolent spirit who needed to be invited in. "I can light the candles if you'd prefer."

"No, it's fine. Please." Naila gestured to the chair and sat on the edge of her mattress, trying not to look too much like she was collapsing down onto it.

To his credit, Wizard Akana didn't appear to notice the mess. He stepped into the room slowly, as if he were afraid to disturb something, his fingers tugging at the red and gold braiding on his sleeve.

There was a long silence, Naila's ragged breath too loud in her ears. The panic had started to leach away, but in its place was a fog of exhaustion and confusion.

"Wizard Akana—" she started, her voice weak.

"Please, call me Haelius."

She stared at him, both of them knowing there was no way she would call him by name.

"I ..." she tried again, struggling to compose her thoughts. "I—with the book ... I can explain. I didn't mean—"

"You don't need to explain." A muscle in his cheek twitched, pulling at the scars. "All of this was my fault."

"What? I don't understand."

He looked down at his hands, lacing his fingers together. "The book is mine. I gave it to you."

"*You gave it to me?*" Naila swallowed. "No, but I found it in my bag. I had no idea. When we collided, I thought—"

"I switched them: your book with one of mine. When I bumped into you, I saw ... an opportunity. I thought this book might help you. I knew of your circumstances, and I wanted to help."

"*Help?*" The numbness of fear hardened into something sharper. "You *gave* it to me? I didn't know. I thought I'd stolen from you. *You.* A wizard. They called me a *hollow thief.*"

"I'm sorry. I thought—"

"No, you didn't think!" Anger spat from the back of her tongue. "You have no idea. They're waiting for a reason to expel me. I'm not allowed to be a non-mage, but to mages I'll always be a hollow. They're always watching me, waiting for me to screw up or make a mistake. They're just looking for a reason to throw me out of the Academy, and you just handed them one."

Whether it was discomfort or anger, Naila couldn't tell, but she felt the magic around them shift, and suddenly the wizard and his power felt far too close. The quiet man across from her, the man she was hurling words at like stones, was not only a mage but perhaps *the* most powerful mage, and she was shouting at him as if he couldn't destroy her with a gesture.

There was a long pause before he spoke again. "I'm sorry. You're right, I hadn't considered how it would look, or what you would think when you found it." He sighed, pushing a hand back through his hair, and for a moment he looked altogether human. "I've made a mess of things."

"But you can fix it?" Naila said tentatively. "You can just tell them you gave it to me."

His expression didn't fill her with hope. "It's not that simple. I mean, I can – I did – but that boy is claiming you assaulted him, and Oriven's daughter—" Naila noticed that his mouth twisted around that name, "—she used her power on you: a fellow student. She will need to justify why she did, so I'm afraid the Consul of Justice is likely to take a personal interest. Amorian children . . . Mage children . . ." The wizard grimaced.

Of all the things Amoria valued, it treasured its children the most. The children of mage families, that is. No one truly understood why, but the number of children being born to mages was decreasing year on year, especially in those who were most powerful; someone like Wizard Akana could never expect to have children of his own.

And Naila had just threatened those precious children.

"I'm going to be thrown out of the Academy, aren't I?" When he opened his mouth to speak, Naila hissed through her teeth and looked away. "No, it's not that simple. I haven't learned control."

"I came here directly." Wizard Akana stood, his robes spilling around his ankles. "There will be more I can do. I will try to make this right."

"And what will I do? I have nowhere to go. Do you know what it's like for mages in the Southern Quarter right now?"

"Just, stay here for now—"

"And wait for them to take me away?"

Naila saw his jaw flex again and he closed his eyes for more than a moment. "I hope very much it won't come to that. Here, let me return these at least." He lifted one hand and moved it as if he was drawing another phoneme in the air, as he had done in the class. The instant he moved, magic leapt to his command, eager to obey him.

Naila jumped when her bag and books thumped onto her desk. The pristine red book was conspicuously absent.

Wizard Akana stared at them for a moment longer, a small frown gathering in his forehead, then he made another gesture and something dropped into the palm of his hand.

"I think I can help you," he said, pinning her with an unnerving gaze. "Give me a day to settle things with the Academy, then use this to contact me." He held out his hand, and there was a small metal disc sitting in the dip of his palm. "It's an artefact. If you hold it in your hand and think of my name, then it will let us speak. It's made to be used by anyone." He carefully avoided saying non-mages, though she knew that was what he meant.

Naila stared at it but didn't take it. "And if I don't want your 'help'?"

His lips quirked into a thin smile, and he closed his fingers back over the artefact. "I suppose I deserve that. Then you don't have to use it and I won't contact you again." He set the disc on the edge of her desk. "I'll leave this here. I've felt your magic myself – I know that you have power. I think it's entirely possible that I could teach you how to use it."

11

NAILA

Waking up felt like reliving the previous day all over again. As Naila emerged from the void of sleep, the memory of the attack – of every disastrous moment that had led her to it – crashed over her. She curled tighter, screwing her eyes shut, trying not to see Marcus's face leaning into hers.

Even now, Oriven's Justice could be coming to find her.

She couldn't let herself think of it.

Instead, she rolled over and forced herself to her feet. The light left by Wizard Akana had long gone out, so she moved numbly to her desk, searching for her tinderbox in the gloom. It was almost impossible to believe that yesterday a wizard had sat here, his presence too large for her small life, but the artefact still sat neatly in the corner of her desk, making the truth of it undeniable.

She couldn't ignore the disc: the magic of it kept distracting her, like movement out of the corner of her eye. Once she lit the candles, she found herself staring at it, reaching out to touch it with the tips of her fingers.

She took it back to her bed, sinking down onto her mattress and shuffling herself into the back corner. Careful not to think of the wizard's name, she turned the disc over and over in her hands. It was a simple enough design: a circle cut from copper with a second green disc set on top of it. On the smaller disc, phonemes were scratched through the green to the bright copper underneath, etched in an untidy, spidery hand. She could recognise maybe *mentis* and the phoneme for speak, but the others were unfamiliar. Magic was locked into it, far too much for such a simple tool, and it throbbed beneath her fingers like an angry heartbeat.

She almost thought of Wizard Akana's power then, but, as soon as she did, she flung the disc away from her, afraid she might accidentally summon the man himself.

Never, she thought, twisting her fingers into her sheets. She would never ask for his help. Everything he had done had thrown her life into chaos. He was a wizard, one of the heads of the Academy; there was no chance he was acting with her interests at heart – there would be some cost, Naila just didn't know what it was yet.

And yet. She knew someone at the Academy had been protecting her – her years of education and her rooms in the Mita's District were proof enough of that – and that "someone" must have been him, mustn't it?

Naila couldn't shake the nagging suspicion that Wizard Akana *had* been going to her classroom the day she'd knocked him off her feet: it was in the Surveyor's weary sigh, so like Wizard Akana's reaction to Naila's anger, and the way Trianne Marnise had barely bowed to the wizard at his lecture. *He* was the Surveyor who had defended her, who had stood without hesitation between Naila and Marnise's hate, and he'd asked for nothing then, hadn't even told her who he was. Even now, he was giving her the chance to walk away.

That's the smart decision, isn't it? Naila rubbed her face with her hands and twitched at the sting of a bruise on her cheek. No matter what she did, Celia's father, Lieno Oriven himself, would come after her. Amoria would never be safe. Not while she remained the hollow mage.

Thump, thump, thump. There were three heavy knocks on her door, and Naila's heart seized in her chest. It was them. They'd come for her. She was out of time.

She pushed herself closer to the wall, small and still, as if that could hide her. She should have left. She should never have believed that the wizard could stop them.

The knock came again, insistent.

"Naila?" It was Ko'ani, her voice muffled behind the door. "Naila, are you there?"

It took a moment before Naila could speak, and in that time Ko'ani banged the door again.

"I'm here," Naila managed, the noise still rattling in her nerves. "Stop. Give me a second."

"Goddess, Naila, I thought something awful had happened. Open up already, it's only me!"

Naila forced herself to her feet, her legs wobbling. She stumbled over to the door and heaved it open.

Ko was waiting for her on the other side, and her eyes widened at the sight of Naila. Tentatively, she reached out and brushed Naila's bruised cheek with the tips of her fingers. "Oh, Nai. Those absolute bastards."

Naila tensed. It was clear that Ko'ani knew what had happened, but how? Did this mean that everyone knew? She tried to find the words to ask, but before she could speak Ko'ani had thrown her arms around her and pulled her into a hug.

"Why didn't you tell me?" Ko asked, speaking over her shoulder. "We would have helped. You don't have to face these things on your own."

It was a proper hug, Ko's arms tight around her, and Naila felt her eyes sting with relief. "I'm sorry. I didn't want to involve you in any of this."

"Mudammir piss on that," said Ko, invoking the name of the Dahrani destroyer and making Naila smile despite everything. "Well, too late, I'm involved. Can I come in?"

"Sure." Naila stepped back into her room, conscious again of the dark and the mess.

Ko'ani looked almost as out of place in Naila's room as the wizard had done, her fine yellow robes the colour of ripe silwheat. She was a less courteous guest than the wizard, glancing around with round eyes, her gaze taking in every untidy detail.

"You *live* here?"

Naila felt her cheeks burn with shame. "Yes. This is what the Academy gave me. It's not much but—"

"I'm sorry," said Ko, seeming to realise the discomfort she was causing. She pressed her lips together in a thin line, her expression serious for once. "I just— I'm sorry." She turned and plonked herself down onto the chair, an untidy mirror of Wizard Akana. "Listen, I have a suggestion."

Naila didn't sit.

"I think you should come and live with us." The words rushed out of Ko's mouth, as if she'd rehearsed them but nerves were still messing up the performance. "Just for a while. Wait, don't say anything. My dad's actually waiting downstairs and it was basically his idea. We can give you somewhere safe to stay to wait all this out. My mum's a senator on the Lieno Council. People are way less likely to come after you if you're associated with us."

"Ko, I ..." Naila was stunned. "I can't. I can't come and ..."

"You *can*. You have to. It isn't safe. Oriven's followers are ... well, you had a run-in with his *daughter*. No one else lives in this building – it isn't safe. Besides, Haelius said he's doing what he can with the Academy, but they might take this away from you."

"Wait, *Wizard Akana*?" Naila's blood ran cold.

Ko grimaced. "Yeah. He's, um, he's an old friend of my family. I know he looks like he's always angry, but he's all right really. If you get to know him," she mumbled the last part, sounding like a child who'd been caught in a lie.

Naila covered her eyes with one hand, her head reeling. It was too much. Wizard Akana was everywhere, somehow entangled in every part of her life.

"You don't have to decide now." Ko's voice was gentle, almost pleading. "Naila, you're as pale as an Ellathian. Please, just come with me now. We can have something to eat, you can get some proper rest and then you can decide for real tomorrow."

When Naila looked up, Ko's eyes were gleaming in the candlelight, her expression so hopeful that the thought of disappointing her felt unbearable.

"All right, maybe ... yes, thank you – if you're sure this is okay. I don't want to cause you any trouble."

Ko sprang to her feet, grinning. "You won't regret this. Let me help you pack."

Scooping up most of Naila's possessions and cramming them hap-hazardly into a bag, Ko seemed to have forgotten that Naila had only agreed to come for one night. Naila saw her eyes snag on the artefact lying on Naila's bed, but she didn't touch it and she didn't ask. Naila lifted the disc and held it at arm's length, as if it might erupt into flames at any moment, and slipped it carefully into her pocket. She wasn't ready to leave Wizard Akana's offer behind quite yet.

Ko's apartment was unlike anywhere Naila had been before. It was as wide as a classroom, but it was filled with the trappings of a home: there were comfy armchairs and shelves stuffed with books, and to one side was a beautiful glass table set for a meal. Ornate lamps hung from the walls and ceiling, though none of them needed to be lit as sunlight spilled through an outside wall of the tower. It stretched the full length of the room, a vista made of sky and violet glass, with the southern city and the Great Lake laid out beneath them. Even to someone who had lived in Amoria her entire life, it was a breathtaking sight: this view, this piece of the city, belonged just to Ko's family. It felt like they owned part of the sky.

Naila hung in the doorway, feeling more than ever that she had come somewhere she didn't belong. Ko shifted awkwardly next to her, unsure of what to say for once.

"Not bad, hmm?" Ko'ani's father, Malek, rescued them from the uncomfortable silence. "Amoria has its charms. Come in, come in – don't loiter on our doorstep."

Naila was about to take a step forward when a door to one side of the room clicked open and a member of Oriven's Justice stepped out.

Everything stopped. The dread yawned inside her like a chasm. They were *here*. She had brought them down on Ko's family.

Or they brought you to them.

The awful thought formed in her mind before she could stop it, casting everything in a different, ugly light. Was the wizard behind this? Had all this been an elaborate trap?

"Mum, what the hell?"

"What is this?" The Justice's eyes widened in a way so familiar that for a moment Naila thought she was looking at Ko.

Ko'ani herself looked more exasperated than horrified to find a member of the Justice in her home. "Do you have to wear that in here? Naila— I promise, it's not what you think."

"Naila?" The Justice raised her eyebrows and her gaze snapped to Malek. "What exactly is happening here?"

"Habibti, my love." Malek was unperturbed, striding across the room to place a kiss on the Justice's cheek. Naila thought she saw the slightest softening of her expression. "I didn't expect you home so early."

"Clearly."

Malek spoke to her so softly that Naila couldn't hear what was being said, but the Justice rolled her eyes in a way completely at odds with her uniform.

"And when were you going to tell me?" The Justice leaned away from Malek so that she could narrow her eyes at him, but something in the shape of her mouth belied the sharpness of her tone.

Malek smiled widely and shrugged. "It all happened so fast."

"Strange. I don't remember ignoring a communication from you."

"You are right, of course. I should have contacted you." Malek kissed her again, which was met with another narrowing of her eyes.

"Well, come in then, since I am so clearly outnumbered." The Justice turned her attention back to Naila, and Naila was struck by the full force of her gaze. "Perhaps these co-conspirators might consider making us some lunch."

As soon as the Justice disappeared back into the other room, Naila felt like a weight had been lifted from her shoulders. She took a deep breath, not sure if she had breathed once since she had appeared.

Ko made a disgusted sound. "I'm sorry, Mum's the worst."

"*Ko'ani*," her father snapped at her without turning around, already clattering through cupboards at the far end of the room.

"Well, she is." Ko dragged a chair back from the table and collapsed untidily into it. Unsure what else to do, Naila followed her example, sliding carefully into the seat opposite.

"Your mother is not 'the worst'." The way Malek mimicked Ko'ani's way of speaking made her sound ridiculous. "She cares about this family and the city, and she is doing what she thinks will best protect them both." Malek set a bowl of shining black olives in front of Naila, and Naila had to stop herself from grabbing a handful and shoving them all into her mouth at once. "She couldn't stop the Justice from being formed, so she is doing what she can to temper it from within. When all the fruit is rotten, you have to eat the best of it or starve."

"Baba, don't." Ko dropped her head back and groaned in a way that suggested she'd heard plenty of these expressions from her father before.

A smile lifted the corner of Naila's mouth. Seeing Ko with her family let her glimpse through all the layers of confidence and bravado Ko dressed herself in for the Academy. The person underneath wasn't any different, really, but she was relaxed and unguarded in a way Naila had never seen before. Ko and her father – and even her mother – seemed to fit together like parts of the same whole.

It was so different from Naila's own life that she felt the absence of this belonging like an ache.

12

NAILA

As the sun began to set and the pinpoints of light pricked on all over the city, Naila still couldn't believe any of this was real.

She had been given a mattress in Ko'ani's bedroom, the softest thing Naila had ever slept on, and Ko'ani's mother – Dailem – had insisted on giving her some of Ko's old robes, in a deep, almost midnight blue. Despite being a couple of years younger than her, Ko was slightly bigger than Naila in almost every way, so the robes were too long and too loose, but they were silk-soft, and the dark colour made the white hem shine like moonlight. It was all of it too much like a dream.

Ko was sitting on her bed, her legs curled underneath her and Wizard Akana's disc in her lap. "His handwriting is awful, isn't it? I'm surprised the enchantment worked."

"You're sure you're not going to contact him?"

Ko lifted both her hands and waved them to show she wasn't directly touching the disc. "I won't, I won't. I know how to keep myself from triggering an artefact."

Naila's shoulders sagged with relief.

"You really are frightened of him, aren't you?" Ko watched her with a frown.

"Terrified. I can't believe you're not."

"So, you're not going to contact him?"

Naila sighed and leaned back on her hands, avoiding the intensity of Ko'ani's gaze, which was too much like her mother's by far. Ko had explained how they knew about the attack, and of course it had been

Wizard Akana: he'd asked for Malek's help, knowing that Ko already had a connection with Naila, and they'd wasted no time in coming to get her. Naila should have been grateful – she owed the wizard so much already – but doubt still gnawed at her. He was a wizard, an embodiment of everything she had come to hate and fear about the Academy. She couldn't understand why he'd want to help her.

"Don't you want to try and learn magic, though?" Ko pressed.

That wish was locked deep, encased in so many years of failure; Ko's question cracked it open, digging into a part of Naila that she hadn't let herself acknowledge for so long.

"Yes, I mean ... of course I do." Naila was biting the inside of her lip, still not looking up at Ko'ani. "It's just that ..."

"I know. I'm sorry. I'm just excited. Just to think that you could— but, I know." Ko shuffled to the edge of her bed and held the disc out to Naila. "You're the one who has to decide. Whatever you decide, though, you can always stay with us."

Naila took the artefact, her smile warming her all the way through. "Thank you."

"Though I *promise* he's a better teacher in person than he is when he's lecturing."

"Wizard Akana a good teacher? Impossible."

The giddy relief had made Naila lower her guard: the instant she spoke the wizard's name, she felt the tingle of magic creep up the back of her skull and the disc grow hot beneath her fingers. She dropped it immediately, but it was already too late.

Hello, Naila. The words formed in her mind as if she'd thought them herself, but the voice was unmistakably the wizard's.

Naila couldn't help looking back over her shoulder, her heart thumping, her mouth suddenly dry. "Shit, no. I mean ... hello?"

"It's a communication spell," said Ko, practically falling off the edge of the bed in her eagerness. "You only need to *think* your answer to him. Be careful – he'll be able to sense a little of what you're feeling."

"What?" Naila panicked. She tried to smother her fear of the wizard, but in doing so she knew it was all she was thinking about.

The barest tinge of regret formed through the spell.

Wizard Akana? It was the only coherent thought she could manage.

The same.

The sensation of being connected to another person was deeply strange. Naila could feel his emotions almost as if they were hers, and yet she remained somehow removed from them. He was holding back a great deal, but she could still sense something, like shadows moving along the bottom of a closed door. She thought she could feel an edge of apprehension creeping from beneath it, the same hesitation she had seen in her dormitory. Abruptly, she could picture him sitting in her room, tugging at the edge of his sleeves.

Wizard Akana could clearly see it, too, and he didn't manage to conceal his surprise.

A bad habit, he admitted, but there was a warmth to the words. *Can we talk?*

I— um . . . The panic was rising in her throat again, but Ko'ani's steady gaze met hers, her eyes gleaming with excitement. *Don't you want to try and learn magic?* Ko's words circled her thoughts, pulling her down towards the obvious answer, the only answer. Learning magic could free her, let her move on with her life. She had to try.

Can you teach me? she asked.

There was a long pause before the wizard gave his answer. *I don't know. I think so. The only way we'll know is if we try.*

Naila swallowed and nodded, forgetting he couldn't see her. She tried to smother some of her hope, even though she knew there'd be no locking it away again. *I'd like to try.*

Good. Where are you?

What? Now? Naila glanced up at Ko, forgetting that she hadn't been able to hear the conversation.

If it's convenient, he answered, and Naila thought she could detect the barest hint of sarcasm in his tone.

Ko raised her eyebrows in a silent question.

"He wants to meet," said Naila. "Right now."

"Ha, of course." Ko grinned. "He's like that. If a thought occurs to him, he just does it. Are you going to?"

Naila felt paralysed. She looked down, biting on one side of her lip.

There was the thud of bare feet on the floor and the tell-tale jangle of bracelets, and then Ko was crouching in front of her. "I promise it's safe. I'll come with you if you want."

Naila took a deep breath and smiled at the friend who had already given her so much. "Thank you."

Wizard Akana knew she'd made her decision before she put the thought into words.

Where are you? he asked again.

I'm with Ko'ani— I mean, the Tallaces.

The wizard's gladness warmed her like stepping into a patch of sunlight. *In the Wizard's Tower? I'm only a few floors above. I can meet you outside.*

In just the same way as he had vanished out of her room, Wizard Akana disappeared from Naila's mind. His sudden absence felt like forgetting the end of a thought, and it left Naila reeling.

"Is he coming?" asked Ko.

Naila nodded. "Right now, I think."

"Well, come on then." Ko sprang to her feet, her yellow robes crumpled down one side from sitting on the bed. "You know what he's like. He'll just appear outside – 'poof!'."

Striding across her room, Ko threw open the door without even pausing for shoes, though Naila pulled on her battered slippers and jogged to catch up with her. In the next room, Malek and Dailem were sitting together on the sofa, leaning in over a glass board on the table, set with the brightly coloured pieces of the game rudimenta. They barely glanced up as Ko stormed past them, clearly well used to their daughter's ways, though Malek gave Naila a small wink.

They emerged onto the landing outside Ko's home, a circular corridor around a central stair. The lamps cast rectangles of yellow light across the floor, but they did little to dispel the gloom, the corridor curving away into shadow. There was no sign of the wizard.

"Huh," said Ko. "Weird. I was sure he'd already be here."

Naila turned away from Ko and squinted into the dark, just in time to see Wizard Akana emerging from the shadows. He was striding towards them, an intimidating sight with his long robes billowing out behind him. Naila still had to fight the urge to run.

"He's there," she whispered to Ko, who was still looking in the wrong direction.

Ko spun on the balls of her feet. As soon as she turned, Wizard Akana's face lit up with a smile in a way Naila hadn't seen before.

"Ammi!" Ko exclaimed, using the Dahrani word for uncle. She ran the last few steps to meet him and threw her arms around him. The wizard made a sound like she had knocked the air out of him, but he was still smiling. He kissed her on the top of the head in the way reserved for family, though Ko was tall enough that he had to stretch to do it.

Naila stared.

"Wore yourself out again?" Ko asked, untangling herself from the embrace.

His mouth pulled to one side in a half-smile. "Something like that. You look well rested, as well you should, given how much sleep you're getting in class."

Ko had the good grace to look embarrassed. "Ah, you saw." She wrinkled her nose. "I knew most of it already."

"Really? Excellent. I'll expect your application for wizard tomorrow morning, then."

And then Ko punched him on the arm, as if it were nothing, as if he were not the most powerful magic-user in all of Amoria – as if he were just a member of her family, or even a friend.

Wizard Akana saw Naila watching over Ko's shoulder. He patted Ko'ani's arm and then stepped carefully around her, dipping into a formal bow. "Naila. I'm glad to be meeting you under much better circumstances."

"Wizard." Naila returned the bow.

"Haelius, please," he tried again, though his tone suggested he knew it was pointless. "Can we talk? There are some things I need to explain to you. You could come to my study; I live only a few floors up from here."

Naila looked at Ko again: she was nodding encouragement as if the wizard couldn't see her.

"I— will we be long?" Naila's mouth was dry, a cold sheen of sweat on the palms of her hands.

"No, I won't keep you." He stepped to one side and gestured along the landing.

Naila followed, her heart fluttering like a butterfly, her legs like lead weights; she wasn't sure if it was excitement or fear that had her in its grip.

She hesitated as she passed Ko'ani, and Ko squeezed her arm and whispered, "Do you want me to come with you?"

"I'm okay." Naila smiled, so grateful for her friend. "I'll tell you everything when I get back."

As soon as they stepped out of the landing and onto the twisting stairway, the wizard heaved out a breath which sounded a lot like a sigh of relief. "I'm glad you came," he said.

Naila had no idea what to say to that, so she nodded, even though he was ahead of her and wouldn't see. The silence felt like a physical presence between them, as if it would swallow anything she tried to say.

When at last they reached the floor on which the wizard lived, Wizard Akana was flushed and out of breath. He slowed to walk alongside Naila, glancing towards her with an unreadable expression.

"I still frighten you." It was a statement more than a question.

Hunching her shoulders, she looked away, still unable to force any words from her mouth. He didn't press her, but she thought she heard another small sigh.

Wizard Akana didn't need a key or even to touch his door to open it – he flicked his hand in front of him and the door clicked obediently open. His rooms were almost a mirror image of the Tallaces' below, if slightly smaller, and Naila could see immediately why the mess of Naila's dormitory hadn't fazed him in the slightest: there was not a single surface in his home that wasn't covered in clutter. Most of it was books, heaped up on creaking tables, or piled into crooked stacks which lined a winding and precarious path across his floor. It was a stunning wealth of knowledge. No wonder he'd thought so little of swapping that beautiful book with one of hers.

"Come in," he said, picking his way through the mess as if he didn't see it. "We'll go through to my study."

To Naila's surprise, he lit none of the lamps and made no move to create a light as he'd done in Naila's rooms. The sun had set fully now so that the glow from the rest of Amoria was the only thing illuminating the wizard's rooms, casting everything in blue-grey shadow and the deep indigo of night. Twice Naila almost kicked over a shadowy mountain of books.

"In here." He beckoned impatiently for her to follow him.

He sat behind the large desk at the centre of his study and gestured for Naila to sit opposite. He still didn't cast any kind of light. Rummaging through one of his drawers, he produced two candles, which he dumped unceremoniously on his desk, as well as an old, battered tinderbox. He began to strike the flint so clumsily that Naila half wondered if he'd ever done it before.

As usual, it was her pride that finally summoned her voice. "You don't have to avoid casting magic around me," she snapped. "I'm not frightened of magic."

"What?" He looked up with an expression of genuine surprise. "Oh, this? You think I'm not using magic because of you?" He laughed but very gently. "No, it's not because of you. I'll show you."

He set the tinderbox down and held out one hand, bunching his fingers into a fist and then splaying them wide. A fire kindled in the palm of his hand and immediately roared upwards, easily two feet of yellow-gold flame. There was an unsteady flicker to the magic: where before his use of magic seemed so effortless, Wizard Akana was rigid with exertion, staring intently into his spell. He set his jaw, his eyes narrowed to slits, and Naila saw his fingers tremble when he snapped his hand shut to smother it, plunging them back into darkness.

"I tried to make a flame large enough to light a candle," he said, as if that were an explanation.

"What?" Naila stared, uncomprehending. Magical exhaustion was what mages called the overuse of magical power: it would leave a mage depleted and cold, unable to use their magic and at risk of burning through their own strength. She knew of nothing that could cause a mage's power to rage out of their control like that, save for in the children's classes where young mages had yet to learn control. *Oh.*

The wizard saw the realisation on her face. "My power is ... well, to do a small thing, I need to exert a great deal of control. When I'm tired, that control becomes harder, and if I'm exhausted then it's better if I don't use magic at all."

"You can't use magic when you're *tired*?" Naila couldn't stop her eyes shifting to the burns on Wizard Akana's face, wondering if losing control had caused those scars. She could see where they twisted beneath the high collar of his robes, and who could guess the extent of the burns concealed beneath..

He touched his left hand to his jaw, it too wrinkled with scars.

"Something like that," he said quietly, all too aware of her scrutiny.

Naila looked down at his desk, feeling the heat of shame burning in her cheeks. She knew what it was like to feel the needling gaze of people who never looked at *you*, their eyes only snagging on the parts of you that were different. She loathed that she had just done it to someone else.

Snatching the tinderbox out from under his fingers, she struck the flint and file with practised ease, her eyes focused firmly on the glow of the kindling flames and not on the wizard's expression.

"Thank you," he said, watching her light the candles. "It is possible to become too used to magic."

"I wouldn't know."

"You'd be surprised." At that, Naila looked up, ready to protest, but she stopped when she found an amused smile on the wizard's face. "So much of Amoria's existence depends on magic; some of what we use we're barely even aware of."

"That isn't what I meant."

"I know."

Naila had to bite her lip to stop herself from snapping back at him. Something about his calm manner infuriated her, and part of her knew it was because she wanted to hate him. She had to remember that he was perhaps her only chance of learning magic, and that *he* had been the one protecting her at the Academy all this time.

"Why did you bring me here tonight?" she asked instead. "If you're so tired you can't use magic, couldn't this have waited?"

"No," he said simply. "We needed to talk as soon as possible. Besides, I thought perhaps it might ... help, if I was unable to use magic. I know I make you uncomfortable."

Naila opened her mouth and closed it again, shaking her head in disbelief. "You thought being unable to control your magic would make me *less* frightened of you?"

"Well, when you put it like that, it does sound ridiculous."

"You showed me you couldn't control it with *fire*."

At that, the wizard laughed, the sound of it so contagious that Naila almost smiled.

"No one has made me feel quite this stupid, quite so many times in a long while." Wizard Akana pursed his lips in feigned annoyance. "Well, except perhaps Ko'ani's aunt."

Naila didn't trust herself to answer. Instead, she looked down at her hands, folded in her lap, with her bare wrists and ice-white hem. "It isn't just your magic."

"I understand that. Better than you think. I sensed some of your feelings, through the communication spell. Your ..." he struggled to find the word. "Your hope. I remember what that felt like. I need to tell you, learning to use magic won't solve everything. There will always be people who won't let you forget what you were."

His words felt like he'd taken that raw, exposed part of her and sunk his nails into it. "You don't know *what* I am," she snapped. "Don't pretend you understand. You're a wizard. You've never had to live in Amoria without magic."

He sat back a little at her anger, his fingers toying with the red and gold banding on his sleeve. "You're right. I've never lived without magic." But lines had formed at the corner of his mouth, where his scars met his lips, and Naila could sense the words he wasn't saying.

She scrubbed at her eyes with her hands, feeling the warmth in her cheeks again. She wanted to say she was sorry, to acknowledge everything he'd done for her, but she couldn't force the words past her lips.

"Why?" she asked instead. "Why are you doing this? Why help me?"

Wizard Akana didn't answer immediately, his eyes down, one thin finger tapping the edge of his desk.

"I was there," he said eventually. "When they first assessed you for magic and it ... it was like nothing I'd ever felt before. Even then, I knew I had to understand it."

"You wanted to *study* me?"

"What? No! I mean ..." There was that doubt again, that uncertainty that seemed so wrong on the face of the most powerful man in Amoria. "I wanted to help. And, well, there's more. I hope you'll agree to learn magic from me, but the truth is that you don't have much of a choice."

Naila's head snapped up. "What?"

"The situation is complicated. Because of his daughter's involvement, Allyn— Lieno Oriven can't simply let this go; for Celia to be innocent, you need to have been attacking a mage. The punishment for that would be suspension or expulsion from the Academy, but since you haven't learned control, that's impossible."

Naila's hands tightened in her lap, her nails digging into her skin. "What are you saying?"

"I had to step in. I said I would take responsibility for you, that I would teach you. If I can teach you to use magic, teach you control, then they will continue with your expulsion from the Academy and you can return to a normal life in Amoria, though you will no longer attend the Academy. I assumed that would be no great loss to you."

"And if you can't?" The words were out of Naila's mouth before she could stop them.

The wizard hesitated, but the expression on his face was far from concerned. "There would be consequences – for both of us, I imagine. But I can assure you that I don't intend to fail."

Naila's emotions had been pulled in so many directions it left her heart feeling bruised and strung out. It wasn't too late to run. She could still turn her back on all of this, disappear into the Southern Quarter or leave Amoria altogether. If even the great Wizard Akana didn't understand her power, perhaps it *was* different. Perhaps she could live a normal life.

But somehow the belief that she might finally learn magic still simmered in her after all this time. This didn't mean she had to stay. It wouldn't tie her to him forever. All she had to do was learn control, learn enough that she could do the rest on her own.

"Okay," she said. "Okay, yes. I want to learn. When can we start?"

His smile completely changed the shape of his face, and Naila found herself struggling to remember the way he'd glowered down at her in the Academy. "Not tonight. As you've seen, I'm worse than useless this evening. We could start tomorrow? If you use the disc when you would normally attend the Academy, I can bring you here or to my office in the Academy tower."

"I'll do that."

"Good." The wizard got to his feet and Naila stumbled to do the same. "Then let me take you back. Thank you; I'm so glad you're letting me put this right."

Naila could see that was true.

"Thank you, Haelius," she said, trying out his name as if it were a foreign word.

Haelius's smile widened. "You're very welcome. Come, let's get you back – Ko'ani will want to hear everything."

BOOK II
THE WIZARD

13

INTERLUDE

They had travelled quickly, the lands of Omalia sliding away
beneath them in a blur of green hills and sprawling human settlements. They'd had no issue tracking their quarry: they needed only
to follow the line of death and destruction which cracked across the
continent like lightning. The trail led them always to the south.
Neither of them had ever seen anything like it, and Ra'akea doubted
there was a living rider among the Miatha who had. Each one was
like the first Ellathian village: small human settlements drowned
in the beast's wake, their last moments written in silver frost and
blistering cold.

Ra'akea should have ended this by now.

For weeks it had stayed ahead of them, moving with some un-
knowable purpose. There had not been many hunts in her lifetime,
but every beast she had tracked had been the same. They were lost,
mournful creatures, their minds shattered by what they had become.
They would cling to some lonely memory – a lake, a cliff face – some
place that held a sliver of their former lives, and no matter how much
they hungered, they would always return there.

This one was different.

Further south, she came across the first burned town. She saw the
smudge of black smoke long before she reached it, a blossoming bruise
against the pale sky. Where the ice had preserved, the fire had obliterated. Buildings had been melted to black slag, and even the earth
beneath her feet was brittle and broken. At least here she didn't have

to look into the faces of the dead – there wasn't enough left of them for that.

There are two of them. It was an impossible thought, but an irrefutable one.

There are two lost ones, Tae agreed. *Miatha and Tiatha.* Water and Fire.

Ra'akea stood in an icy silence, her long cloak fluttering against the back of her ankles, her eyes stinging from the smoke. These creatures were an aberration, the sad shame of her people. Each of the tribes had spawned them, air and water, fire and earth, but had there ever been two of them at any one time? Ever, in all the long years of her people?

No, answered Tae, her voice clearer in her mind than her own thoughts. *There are more of them than ever before.*

Then she felt something as unfamiliar to her as this blackened town: Tae's fear. In all the long decades of their life, bound together heart and mind, she didn't know if Tae had ever been afraid. But this – this was the most awful fate for any of their kind, and they had no clue as to why it was happening; no clue how to stop it.

Which do we follow? Ra'akea asked, more to herself than to Tae. It was a choice she'd never had to make.

There was little chance of hiding this now. There had been too many towns, the path of the beast too bloody. Humans were resilient creatures; they would come scurrying out of disasters like cockroaches, and Ra'akea had not been close enough behind to silence them. It was too much to hope that the Sha'arin had remained hidden. If there were two to hunt, then she could not pursue both. The Mothers would have to understand – it would not be her failing.

But which one?

You do not have to choose, said Tae. *They are going the same way.*

Ra'akea stiffened, the drumbeat of her own heart growing louder in her ears. *How can that be?*

I do not know. She felt Tae shift, felt the change in her focus. Ra'akea could smell the air almost as she did, feel the cool breeze as she turned her face into the wind. *I feel . . . something. A pull. A call. I think it is what leads them.*

Ra'akea took a deep breath, felt her heart slow. *Then that is what we must follow.*

14

LARINNE

By the time Larinne reached her office in the Western Spire, she was exhausted. Her meeting with the Assembly had been a disaster from start to finish. Before she'd even taken her seat at the Majlis, she'd been on the back foot. The Shiura Assembly had harried her without pause, demanding explanations and dismissing any of her requests out of hand. They'd even threatened to block the sale of artefacts to any visiting caravans, a move which would be disastrous for all of Amoria, not just the mages. More of the sabotaged items had been discovered, and Larinne knew the Justice had been hounding the non-mage council for answers. But, even so, this felt like more.

The Shiura members had treated Larinne like a combatant, interrogating her as if she'd been hiding information; it felt like they'd been waiting for her to reveal a hand she didn't even know she had.

Someone is playing games, she thought, gritting her teeth. *And I will not be one of their pieces.*

Larinne balanced her bundle of papers under one arm and shouldered her door open with the other, still half buried in thought as she backed into her office.

"Ah, good, you're here" came a voice from behind her, almost making her drop the papers in surprise.

When she turned she found Reyan sitting behind her desk in her chair as if it were *his* office, his wrinkled hands folded on her desk.

"Lieno Favius?" she sputtered in surprise, all too aware of the open door and the interested eyes rising from their work. Briskly, she shut the door behind her and rounded on Reyan with fire in her veins. "Get out of my chair."

"My dear, you wouldn't make your poor Uncle Reyan get up, would you? My old bones—"

"*Get out of my chair.*"

Reyan made a big show of standing up, groaning and clutching at his back, though she could see the wicked glint in his eyes. She watched him with her arms folded and her lips pressed together, utterly unmoved.

"Youth makes you heartless," Reyan muttered, lowering himself into the chair opposite without being asked. "One day it will be you hoping to rest your weary bones in a comfortable chair."

"And when it is, I will have the good manners not to invade other people's offices." She reclaimed her seat. "How long have you been hiding in here?"

"Only as long as it took to get your attention."

Larinne could see that several of her papers were out of place, as if someone had been rifling through them. She felt her stomach tighten with anger. "You have exactly ten seconds to explain to me why you're here, or I'm going to throw you out of my office, old bones be damned."

Reyan sat back and crossed one leg over the other, clearly unconcerned. He tapped his gnarled fingers on his knee as if to count out the seconds. "I expected to hear from you after the council meeting."

"What?" And then she remembered: that strange conversation on the stairs, something about missing documents. She pressed the heel of her hand against her forehead, screwing her eyes shut. "Does this have to be now? I'm very busy and this morning has—"

"So, you *had* forgotten me," Reyan observed. "Well, this is not so easily forgotten." He produced a piece of paper from a pocket somewhere within the folds of his robes and set it neatly on the table, pushing it across to her with two fingers.

Larinne didn't pick it up. "What is this? Can't you just tell me what's going on? Reyan, don't play games with me. I'm tired and—"

"You need to see this," he said, fixing his gaze on her in a way

Larinne had learned to be wary of. "Go on. I'm sure you'll spot it more quickly than these old eyes did."

"Fine, but if I find nothing to do with me or my work, I'm having you removed from my office."

Reyan's eyebrows arched, but he tipped his head to one side in acknowledgement.

Pressing her lips together, Larinne unfolded the paper, half determined to see nothing before she even started reading.

It was a list of missing documents, written in a cramped and trembling hand.

Reyan's office dealt in communication: the spell which allowed mages to communicate via thought wasn't especially taxing, but it required a strong connection to the person you were trying to contact, and it could leave your thoughts and emotions exposed. As a result, most mages avoided it where possible. Instead, documents and messages were teleported across Amoria by a complex web of magic, something between the pattern rooms and Haelius's teleportation spells. The mages responsible for that magic reported to Reyan.

"I don't see—" she started, but then her eyes caught the words repeated over and over again through the list: Lieno Allyn Oriven, Consul of Justice, Committia Justice, Oriven.

"They don't turn up anywhere else either," said Reyan, carefully watching her. "Naturally, I began to pay special attention to the communications from the Committia Justice. I even worked some of the spells myself. I'm not infallible, of course ..." He spread his hands and smiled in a way which suggested he absolutely thought he was infallible. "But I am certain that at least some of these were redirected between my spell and their intended destination."

Larinne swallowed. "Really? That doesn't seem likely. Someone would have to detect your spell and interfere with the magic *remotely*. The speed with which they'd have to ..."

"I can think of only one person capable of that kind of magic, can't you?" Reyan didn't take his eyes from Larinne's face.

Haelius, Larinne thought before she could stop herself. She leaned forward, her elbows on her desk, and massaged her temples with the tips of her fingers, a headache coming in behind them.

"He wouldn't be so stupid." Even as she said it, she could see the tense faces at the Shiura Assembly, their impatience as they waited for her to share something she didn't know. A heavy dread sank through her: Haelius had done more than just steal the documents; he'd given them to the Assembly.

"There's more," Reyan continued, merciless. "After the missing communications, there was a flurry of successful messages between the Consul of Justice and his committia. I try not to read the letters that come through my office—" Reyan's eyes were bright with the obvious lie "—but the urgency of these communications following the failure of my office was, of course, a concern.

"It appears something important was stolen, an artefact of great value to the Consul of Justice himself. It vanished out of the city archives without any sign of break-in or interference, just ahead of Oriven's people getting to it. As if someone had received advance notice of the Consul of Justice's interest, perhaps."

"Haelius isn't a thief," Larinne said weakly.

Reyan just looked at the list of stolen communications between them as if that were evidence enough. "This isn't exactly the first time he's been at odds with Oriven."

"At odds? Yes. But this— this is something else. Do you know what was stolen?"

"No."

Larinne clasped her hands on her desk. "And how do you know that this item was ever *in* the archives? That it hasn't been missing for years?"

A pause. "I don't. But Oriven certainly believes that it was."

"Then this could all be a misunderstanding." Larinne straightened in her chair, willing her heart to slow. "The archives are chaos – you know that. None of this is proof of anything."

"Proof? No." Reyan's voice was cool and unreadable. "But a suspicion is more than enough, especially in these times. You've seen the mood of the council, this new Justice." He said the word as if it left a bad taste in his mouth. "Don't pretend to me you don't share this suspicion. I know you too well for that."

Truthfully, Larinne didn't know what she believed. Everything Reyan had said was true – there was no love lost between Wizard Akana and the Consul of Justice, and if anyone could have intercepted those messages, it would have been Haelius. But would he really steal from Oriven? And, worse, would he do it without telling her?

"Why have you come to me about it?"

Reyan's weathered skin crumpled into a frown. "Larinne, really, do you have to ask? A courtesy to you. I know you care about him. I can't sit on this much longer; if it continues, it will implicate *me* and my people." He uncrossed his legs and sat forward, forcing her to look at him. "I suppose there's a part of you thinking 'this must have been justified'. Ah – don't make that face at me. I don't know where this Oriven business is going, but if you want my advice you'll stay out of it."

"Will I?" Larinne asked drily.

The corner of Reyan's mouth twitched. "Hmph. Goddess save you, you're too much like your mother by half. You think I'm old and losing touch, but I tell you I've seen enough men like Oriven come and go in their time. They all play for power they can't have; I see no reason why this one will be any different." Reyan hauled himself slowly to his feet, groaning as he straightened his back. "Never fear, I'm done trying to impart wisdom to you for one day: I know a hopeless task when I see it."

Larinne followed him to the door.

"Oriven has his army," she said. "This is different."

"That he does," Reyan agreed. "All the more reason you and your pet wizard should stay out of this."

Her cheeks burned, but before she could answer Reyan reached up and placed a hand on her shoulder.

"I was very fond of your mother," he said, the frown deepening, carving thick lines across his forehead. "And I remain very fond of you. You need to look out for yourself, Larinne: think about how you present yourself to the council. That wizard—" Larinne scowled.

"No, listen to me. He's unpredictable. Only yesterday, he threatened to resign his title if he can't teach some hollow girl magic."

"*What?*"

"The point is, that title offers him more protection than he knows. Wizards may just run the Academy, but the title means something to Amorians. Oriven will hesitate before bringing one of them down. I'm quite certain nothing will keep him from going after Haelius Akana, nothing and nobody. This is not the first time that wizard has acted in a way unbecoming of his rank, and he doesn't have many allies left. Your association with him is ..."

"Unbecoming of my rank?" Larinne did not try to hide her revulsion at such a ridiculous turn of phrase.

It washed off Reyan like water off glass. "Dangerous." He squeezed her shoulder, his expression filled with a wistful affection. "Well, I can see you want rid of me. I'll take no more of your time, Lieno Tallace."

15

LARINNE

The rest of Larinne's day passed in a blur of meetings, paperwork and a throbbing headache.

Larinne felt like she was being pushed from six different directions, all her stress compounding in on top of itself until she hardly had room to breathe. At its heart was her anger at Haelius, pressed hard and sharp like a stone lodged in her gut. Worse, she knew she was failing to keep it in check.

By the time the fifth bell rang, Larinne was ready to cast the communication spell to tell Haelius she wasn't coming. The quiet of her empty apartment beckoned her. All she wanted to do was retreat into solitude, kick off her shoes and sink into her armchair, but she knew she wouldn't do it. To make it all worse, she'd been looking forward to seeing him; the last time Larinne had spoken to anyone outside work it had been an argument with her sister about joining the Justice. She'd been longing to see her friend, to have a conversation without the shadow of Oriven looming over it.

Little chance of that now. She rubbed a hand over her face. She needed to talk to him before this anger burned right through her.

She didn't cast the communication spell. Instead, she lingered at her desk until the last of the evening sun was slanting through the glass walls. She plucked her cape from the back of her chair and looped it around it her shoulders, blue silk cascading down her back, all of it edged in glittering gold. In a way it felt like donning armour, though in all Amoria Haelius was the one person she really had no protection against.

The pattern room took her straight to the Solis, or Sunset District. She could hear her destination before she saw it, voices filtering through the still evening air, the burble of a fountain amplified strangely by the empty streets. The popina itself was quieter than usual, only a scattering of mages seated around tables or lounging beneath small trees lit by artefacts high in their branches. The wine bars of the Solis were primarily frequented by mita and vetra, so – like everywhere else in the inner city – they'd begun to feel empty. Most nights, however, there were a good number of non-mages adding to the clamour of voices and the festive atmosphere. Tonight, Larinne couldn't see a single person in Solis who wasn't wearing the coloured hem of a mage.

Haelius was already waiting for her at a table by the fountain, his hands tucked into his sleeves and his head bowed as if that could keep him from people's notice. He looked up almost as soon as she entered the courtyard, sensing her magic before he saw her. It was somehow worse that he smiled at her as if nothing was wrong. He had no idea she knew about the letters, and even less idea of the consequences.

She tried to smile back at him, but she knew she hadn't managed it. The response was slight, but she saw it, the blink of surprise, the way he sat slightly straighter. When she pulled out the chair across from him, he watched her sit without saying anything.

"Larinne?" he tried eventually.

Stupidly, stubbornly, Larinne didn't answer. It felt like all her anger lay right behind her tongue and she wasn't sure what would come out of her mouth when she opened it.

But when he stood to leave, Larinne was instantly filled with regret. She turned to tell him to wait, but he had only gone to the bar. She watched him pick his way across the popina, mages hurrying to pull their chairs out of his path, their eyes following the red and gold hem of his robes or drawn to the scars on his face.

He ordered a beer for her and tchai for himself, and when he turned back she didn't look away quickly enough.

"You're angry with me," he said quietly, setting the beer down in front of her and retaking his seat.

"You noticed."

"Give me some credit." He smiled one of his helpless smiles, half apologetic and half hopeful, but it only stoked Larinne's anger. "I'm sorry. I know I haven't been in touch much lately. It's . . . things have been busy."

So I heard, Larinne thought. She didn't answer him, taking a long swallow of cold beer.

"But that isn't why you're angry." He was watching her, his eyes bottle-glass green.

"Is it true?" she asked. "Did you threaten to resign from the Academy?"

He sat back a little in surprise. "Is that what this is about?"

"Partly."

"Do you know why I did it? I didn't just 'threaten to resign'."

"The girl. Naila. Again. Reyan said—"

"Oh, good, do tell me what Reyan Favius had to say." He looked away from her and huffed out a bitter laugh. "He always has such wisdom about the *proper* way for a wizard to behave."

Reyan's words, "unbecoming of his rank", crept unbidden to her mind. "He is *trying* to look out for you. The title of wizard protects you, when you're—" she shook her hands in exasperation. "When you're behaving like this."

"Like what, exactly?"

"Like *this*. The Academy is your life, Haelius! What are you going to do?"

"I didn't resign."

Larinne looked at him in disbelief. "No. You just said you would if you couldn't teach a non-mage magic."

"She isn't a non-mage," he snapped. She could feel a flutter of his anger, a faint tremor to the air. "And I *didn't* resign; I said I'd stake my position at the Academy on teaching her magic. You know what Oriven is like – I had to give him something, a reason to give me a chance."

"Because he wants to see you fail!"

"I won't fail."

"When no one else has managed to teach her in all her years at the Academy? Of course you won't."

It was the arrogance that got to her the most: the absolute belief that none of this would catch up to him. He'd thought the same thing when he'd stolen from Oriven; his magic was infallible, no one could possibly know it was him. He only ever looked at the problem that was right in front of him – never followed the thread of his actions down to their consequences.

Yet it was Larinne who would have to untangle the knot at the end of it. It always was. She was the one who had to work with the Shiura Assembly every day, struggling to keep the peace between the two councils, and more than once Larinne had called in a favour at the Academy to keep Haelius out of the trouble he'd made for himself. From the first time he'd tested this girl for magic, he'd felt compelled to step between her and the other wizards, despite her being no relation to him whatsoever. And Larinne was quite certain the only reason Oriven hadn't insisted on the girl's immediate expulsion had been because Haelius had risked his own position to protect her.

But none of that mattered to Haelius because he saw far too much of this Naila in himself. Born to a family of non-mages, he'd always been caught between two worlds. When the enormity of his power became clear, it only served to isolate him further – alienating his peers and frightening his father. There had been no chance of an ordinary life for Haelius Akana. So when a girl had appeared in the Southern Quarter with a mysterious power, Haelius had been drawn to her as inescapably as magic was drawn to him.

Still, someone had to protect him from himself.

Shouting at him hadn't been the right way to reach him, though. His face was closed off to her now. He had the same insufferable, superior expression he always got when he felt threatened. With his eyes narrowed and his chin raised, he looked so much like his father that it threw Larinne right back to the Majlis that afternoon, where the members of the Shiura had eyed her with such obvious contempt.

All the tension and humiliation of her day crashed back over her in a cold wave.

"Reyan came to warn me," she said, reaching under the folds of her cape and taking the list of missing communications from her pocket. She placed it on the table and pushed it towards him.

Haelius snatched it out from under her hand.

"What is this?" His eyes scanned dismissively over the page and then slowed, snagging on the meaning of the words. "Where did you get this?"

"Reyan gave it to me. It was you, wasn't it? You've been stealing communications from the Committia Justice."

He lowered the paper and met her gaze, his eyes rounder, eyebrows drawn together. "Did you find them? Do you know what they're about?"

"Does it matter?"

"Yes!" He raised his voice without meaning to, swallowed, and softened it again. "Of course it does. Larinne, they're about moving non-mages out of the Inner Circle. Out of the Central Dome, even."

Larinne stared at him. "You can't be serious."

"I am. Some of these came to me first. Oriven wanted my expertise to assess the outer towers for their safety; I told him they were unsafe, *unstable*, but he was insistent, suggested I divert my attention to their repair." He raised his hands. "Magic over the cracks, somehow, I don't know. I knew something must be happening, so I did some digging." He dropped the damning list back into the centre of the table. "This is what I found."

Larinne sat very still, her eyes not quite seeing, the murmured voices of the popina suddenly much louder in her ears. The night felt breathless, as if the air around them had ceased to move.

"This is— this could tear Amoria apart."

Haelius didn't answer.

"And you've just given this to the Shiura Assembly?"

Haelius opened his mouth, looked as if he was about to deny it, then pressed his lips together and nodded.

"Have you any idea what you've done?"

"What do you mean 'what I've done'? I had to tell them. They had to know what Oriven was planning!"

Larinne lowered her voice to a hiss. "You think turning the Lieno Council and the Shiura Assembly against each other helps anyone?"

"Oriven is already doing that."

"Yes, Oriven, but until now we might have found a way to deal with him on our own. This implicates the whole Lieno Council, Haelius! The Shiura Assembly won't differentiate between Oriven and the rest of us. I was at the Majlis this morning and I was treated like an *enemy*. Months of negotiations were shut down; they threatened to block all trade from the artificers. I couldn't understand why they were so hostile, what they thought I'd done." She jabbed a finger onto the piece of paper. "Now I know."

She saw his throat move as he swallowed. "What was I supposed to do? Ignore it? Ensure a quiet life for the council?"

Larinne clenched her hands into fists and gave a strangled laugh of disbelief. She was so tired of people assuming the worst of her – that Haelius would do the same was too much. "No. You should have told *me*. We could have looked into this together. We could have petitioned the Senate – solved this *before* it reached the Assembly."

"I didn't want to involve you." Haelius's voice was barely audible above the sounds of laughter and the clinking of glasses.

"No? It just involved my work, my city, my family, oh, and you, of course. What concern is it of mine?"

Silence.

Larinne felt numb with anger, like every other feeling had been swallowed by it. She knew this had turned out wrong, that everything she'd meant to say had come out laced with poison. She hadn't even begun to process what Oriven was planning, and yet all she could think about was how much danger Haelius had put himself in, how little she'd be able to do if Oriven found him out.

Haelius was looking away from her and into the deepening shadows of the courtyard, his jaw stiff, his fingers worrying at the scars on his cheek.

She wanted to stop, but she couldn't leave the rest unsaid.

"And the artefact?" she asked quietly.

She was hoping for a frown of confusion. Instead, Haelius flinched. "So you *did* steal it."

There was a swell in Haelius's magic large enough to make the mages at the nearest table mutter and twist in their seats. "I, as a wizard of the Academy, withdrew an artefact from the city archives to study it."

"One that the Consul of Justice just *happened* to be interested in?" For a moment, Larinne looked away, her mouth working round her anger. "So, what is it? What's worth bringing the anger of the most powerful man in Amoria down on your head?"

Haelius's shoulders sagged, the sharp vibration of his magic softening to a familiar hum. "I don't know. But it's important. Oriven was obsessed with finding it, sent half of his committia to search the archives. I think it has something to do with the damaged artefacts. If I could just get my hands on one of—"

"Put it back."

"No." There was a stubborn twist to his lips, one that Larinne had seen too many times to count. "Not until I understand what it is."

"And when they find out it was you who took it?"

"No one knows. It couldn't possibly be traced back to me."

"Reyan knew. He knew it was you."

Haelius raised his eyebrows. "He couldn't have."

And there it was again, that arrogance.

"Of course he knew! Who else could intercept those messages? Or would have reason to interfere with Oriven's interests? I knew it was you before he finished telling me."

"But what proof—"

"Do you think Oriven needs proof? He *is* the Justice. He has an army. A suspicion would be enough."

That at least gave Haelius pause. "And is the good Lieno Favius going to turn me in?"

"No, of course not."

Haelius's eyebrows twitched upwards. "Why not? He doesn't owe me anything."

"Because he knows you're associated with *me*." She regretted her choice of words immediately, the coldness of them. *Because you're my dearest friend*, she thought, *because I care about you*. But her anger wouldn't let her say it.

"I can't imagine that pleases him." Haelius looked at her strangely, studying her expression. "And does that 'association' worry *you*?"

She was so tired. The people who'd noticed Haelius's magic were still watching them, their eyes lingering on her, on Haelius. A senator and the famous Wizard Akana. She hesitated just a moment too long before she answered him.

Haelius reacted immediately. "Oh" was all he said, sitting back in his chair.

"Haelius—"

"No, I think I understand."

It was the very last thing. All her anger had grown out of fear for *his* safety. Now she was faced with the potential of city-wide disaster, and he was *still* all she could think about. That he would question their friendship was a blow she didn't have the strength to take.

She pushed out her chair and stood, barely able to make herself look at him. "Goodnight, Haelius."

He didn't answer her.

16

NAILA

Haelius turned out to be a more traditional teacher than Naila had expected.

That first morning in his study there were no magical tests or secrets of his craft. He thumped a heavy tome onto his desk in front of her, rattling the multitude of ink bottles and artefacts crammed onto its surface. *Magical Devices and Their Use in Practical Magic* – the book that had started all this.

Naila stared at it like an old foe.

"Did you read it?" he asked.

"What, all of it?"

Haelius raised his eyebrows, as if it hadn't occurred to him that a person might not read an entire book in two days.

"I had some other things on my mind." Naila shifted in her chair, her pride prickling her cheeks with heat.

"Well, that would be a good place to start." He turned away from her and towards the shelves which covered the walls from floor to ceiling, each one of them sagging beneath the weight of his books. "Though maybe …" he added, softly enough that she knew he was no longer talking to her. "Some of the fundamentals …"

It was impossible not to watch him. He stood with one arm raised, a flick of a long finger enough to coax a book from its shelf and draw it to his waiting hand. More than once he studied a cover and sighed, murmuring "No, of course not" to himself. Then he'd set the book seemingly in mid-air and dismiss it with a twist of his wrist, sending it back to the shelf and, though he never looked, always to the exact same position it had occupied before. Every movement he made was casual but exact, as natural to him as breathing, but Naila could feel the immense tide of power that flowed in behind him.

She couldn't help the part of her that still recoiled with fear.

He heaved another four tomes onto his desk alongside *Magical Devices*, the books leaving smears of grey dust on his arms and chest. That, at least, served to ease some of Naila's nerves.

He eyed *Magical Devices* with one eyebrow raised. "Traditionally, one opens a book to begin reading it."

"You're a bit distracting," Naila snapped back.

As soon as she realised what she'd said and who she'd said it to, her face flushed and her stomach twisted itself into a knot.

To her relief, it was a smile that drew his thin mouth to one side. "Forgive me. I'll just retrieve my own work then and let you study – if you don't object." He sank into his chair and waved his hand, summoning another book. "What about the rest of your education? How many of the phonetic combinations do you know?"

It was the same way she'd felt when Trianne Marnise had called on her in class, and her tongue felt like it had died in her mouth.

Haelius waited for an interminable length of time before he answered her silence. "Well, no matter; if you know the basic phonemes the rest will follow. You do know ..." At the expression on her face she saw him make a mental readjustment. "How many of the basic phonemes *do* you know?"

"I— I don't know."

He exhaled slowly. "So not all of them."

Naila looked down, mortified, her hands curling into fists in her lap. She'd barely begun her first lesson and already she was failing at it.

But Haelius's frustration didn't seem to be directed at her. "Sorry, sometimes I forget what level of knowledge students come to me with." He was slamming open the drawers of his desk. "Though, really, I have no idea what the Academy is teaching these days. I think I need to have words with Vetra Seith." He twisted round in his chair to look at the shelves directly behind him. "*Where is it?* Ah – there we are."

He beckoned over another book, though this one was different from the others. It was grey and dog-eared, the leather cover cracked and peeling at the edges. When he handed it to her, she opened it slowly, the binding so loose that she thought it might fall apart in her hands. On the first page, she found the title, *Phonetic Magic*, along with a name scribbled on the inside cover in the same untidy handwriting she'd seen around the edge of the artefact in her pocket: *Haelius Akana*. She looked up and thought she saw a slight flush to the wizard's cheeks.

He cleared his throat. "It was my copy when I started at the Academy. I imagine that book's a fair bit older than you are. If you want, I can find a less decrepit copy next time I'm—"

"No, this one suits me fine." She smiled and placed a protective hand on the front cover, feeling strangely privileged that he'd let her use it.

"Good. Then I suggest you start there. Learn the first sixty-three phonemes, and then really you ought to know two hundred or so of the common combinations."

Naila knew the panic was showing on her face, but if anything Haelius only looked amused. "I'm sure I've seen Ko'ani make that exact same face at me."

"I just don't understand," she said, looking down at the book. "You don't even use the phonemes?"

He'd already returned to his own reading, but he raised a single eyebrow without looking up at her.

"Don't I?" was all he said.

In the weeks that followed, their lessons continued in much the same fashion. Naila was summoned to Haelius's study, where she would be directed to a new stack of enormous tomes. Haelius was buried in his own work, either reading or scratching out notes in his illegible handwriting. He spent long hours staring at a small shard of obsidian that he turned between his fingers, and Naila could feel his magic reaching out, probing it, scratching at her attention. But whatever the wizard was doing, he would look up almost hourly and begin quizzing her on the phonemes, picking them at random or asking her to recite them in order. He was an exacting teacher, not allowing even the smallest of mistakes to go uncorrected, and sometimes those corrections were decidedly at odds with what Naila had been taught: when she wrote out the phoneme for *push*, one of the first she'd ever learned, Haelius simply reached out and turned the paper upside down.

"This way," he said, and then returned to his reading.

"But Vetra Seith always . . ."

He peered at her over the top of his book, his eyebrows almost disappearing into his hair. Naila found herself glancing down at the red and gold stitching on his sleeves and swallowed the rest of her sentence.

"I didn't think so," he said, looking altogether too pleased with himself.

He might have been arrogant, but he was never cruel. If Naila didn't know the answer, he would gently lead her to it, and the humiliation which had dominated her education at the Academy never featured in her lessons with him. Gradually, Naila learned not to fear the moment when she didn't know the answer.

The work was *hard*, though. Naila threw herself into her lessons, desperate to grasp at every thread of knowledge Haelius would offer her. She would stagger back to Ko'ani's under the weight of Haelius's books, and she continued to mutter phonemes to herself throughout dinner.

In the weeks that followed, Naila and the wizard began to feel out how they fitted into each other's lives. Naila became more used to Haelius's exactness, and the way the currents in the air could change with his mood. And she began to notice other things, too: the dark smudges under his eyes, or the way she would often find him hunched in the same place she'd left him, as if he had barely moved from his desk. On the days when they studied long into the night, Naila wasn't convinced she saw him eat once, even as her own stomach began to grumble in anticipation of Malek's cooking.

So on the third week of their lessons Naila brought a cloth-wrapped package and set it right in the centre of Haelius's desk where he'd be forced to look at it.

He eyed the package with all the suspicion of a child being forced to take medicine.

"What is this?"

"It's food, Haelius," Naila said drily. "You eat it."

Haelius's expression darkened, and Naila felt her heart skip a beat. In the recent weeks, she'd spent more time with him than anyone else, yet she still didn't always know where she stood with him. Sometimes he felt like an old friend, sometimes a teacher, and sometimes the most powerful living mage, capable of bringing the whole city down on their heads. Too often Naila forgot that last one.

"I can see how much you're working," Naila amended hastily. "You never seem to stop, and I've never seen you eat. I just wanted to bring you something – to say thank you, and ..."

Haelius looked at her in a way she associated more with "Wizard Akana" than Haelius, his lips drawn thin at the edges and his chin raised so he could look down at her. Once, she had thought it was a look of anger or disgust; now, she was beginning to realise it was an expression of discomfort.

"I don't need Dailem Tallace looking after me."

"You *know* it wasn't Dailem. Malek gave it to me because I asked for it. He's worried about you." *And so am I*, she added silently.

Haelius rolled his eyes and looked away, and Naila thought she could see a slight flush to his cheeks. "Malek is always making a fuss."

"Is there any wonder? We can all see how much you're pushing yourself." Naila looked down, feeling the question she'd been trying not to ask forcing its way to her tongue. "Is it because of me?"

"What?"

Naila swallowed, her mouth suddenly dry. "What happens to you? If they throw you out of the Academy?"

"Naila." Haelius's expression softened to a tired smile. "They won't throw me out of the Academy."

"But it's been weeks, and I haven't managed to do anything." She'd been keeping these fears locked away, but now that she'd let one of them crack through, the others hurried out behind it. "I'm trying to learn the phonemes – and I try to … I think about every lesson in magic I've ever had, and I …"

"I think perhaps I'm not the one who's been pushing herself too hard." Haelius finally closed his book and set it to one side. "We haven't even begun to use what you're learning. This is a start: a framework, that's all. Building on that will take time. You're expecting too much of yourself."

"Do you even have time? What if the Academy demand to see our – my – progress?"

"Do *I* have time?" He tipped his head to one side, narrowing his eyes, studying her. "Are you not more worried about what will happen to you?"

"I …" Naila swallowed and sat back in her chair.

"Maybe it's time we started some new lessons." Haelius was still watching her, and she had the sensation he was looking straight through her, down into her darkest thoughts. "I've been thinking it's time we put some of this into practice."

"Really?"

"Mm, but never fear, we still have time to test your phonemes while I eat." He undid the red cloth with a wave of one hand and pushed a piece of paper across to her with the other. "Write out the phonemes for mind, pull and repel, please, and then tell me the correct pronunciation of each of them."

From that day on, the nature of Naila's lessons changed. She still studied Haelius's books during the day, the two of them working alongside each other in near silence, but in the evenings the wizard turned his full attention onto her. He would instruct her to stand in the centre of his study and then he would fix her with that unsettling gaze, the one that looked beyond normal sight and down to the beating heart of her magic. He would lead her through thought exercises, hardly seeming to blink, or order her to stand a certain way, correcting even the position of her fingers. Sometimes he would pull artefacts from his shelves, or summon the ones hanging from his ceiling, pressing glass, or metal, or stone into her hands. But where they grew warm and bright almost as soon as Haelius looked at them, they remained dead and cold in her fingers, their magic absolutely disconnected from her own.

It felt hopeless.

During those evenings it was almost as if the man Haelius Akana disappeared and was replaced by the force of his will alone. He spoke only to instruct her, focused and relentless. Sometimes, Naila could wait half an hour or more while he tore through his shelves, looking for one particular artefact. At other times he would place two fingers against the side of her head and reach for her power with his own, magic hooking into her like claws. It was one of the most disconcerting feelings Naila had ever experienced; it left her buzzing and disoriented, as if someone had passed a hot current through her bones.

Nothing worked.

As the weeks raced away into months, Naila could feel Haelius's apprehension grow. He never voiced his frustrations, but sometimes she found him pacing at the long outside wall of his apartment, the air heavy and thrumming with his magic. On seeing her, his face would always crack into a smile and the oppressive atmosphere would break apart, like the passing of a sudden storm. Yet every time Haelius used his power, Naila felt the tension return, a discordant note to his magic.

No matter what Haelius said, Naila was sure the council was leaning on him for an answer – a solution to the *hollow mage*. There was only so long Oriven would wait to dole out his punishment to the person who had threatened his daughter, and somehow Naila didn't think that Oriven had handed Haelius an open-ended agreement.

The truth was, they were running out of time.

17

ENTONIN

The Southern Quarter was fully awake by the time Entonin and Karameth made their way out into the busy streets. Amoria lived and breathed like almost every other city Entonin had been to, but you could never escape the strangeness of it. Even now, after months living in the Southern Quarter, Entonin couldn't be easy. Nearby, someone was hammering on stone: "clack, clack, clack", an implacable heartbeat. The sound echoed, up and up, seemingly never-ending, trapped beneath the glass.

Like they all were.

Maybe it was the Ellathian he could hear being spoken all around him – or Amorian, or whatever they wanted to call the coarse dialect of Ellathian these people spoke – but this place still *felt* like Ellath in its bones. Five hundred years this city had stood on Dahrani land, and although the people had changed beyond recognition, their city had stayed the same. They still clung to so many Ellathian ways: the architecture, the language, even the mage Senate all tied them back to the Empire they'd supposedly left behind. Amorians themselves were now a people apart, neither Ellathian nor Dahrani, nor really anything in between.

And yet what Entonin found strangest of all was the complete void where the gods should be. Oh, they invoked the name of a "goddess" casually enough, though whether it was the old Ellathian goddess of magic or Dahran's goddess of all creation, Entonin wasn't sure. He wasn't sure the *Amorians* knew any more. Even the temples felt somewhere in between, tucked away in forgotten corners, dark and smelling of stale air. The first time Entonin had visited one, he'd felt a deep and unsettling chill at the base of his spine.

Perhaps it was natural they'd turned away from the gods, considering what the gods had done to them. The fall of Sisephia, the former Ellathian goddess of magic, had led to the execution – the *annihilation* – of Ellathian mages, the temples hunting any who carried "Sisephia's curse". When the Ellathian mages fled and built their own refuge in Amoria, they had founded it across desert, mountain and water, as far from the eyes of the gods as they could feasibly get. Who could blame them? Entonin had often passed the scorched ruins of Sisephia's temple, the blackened rubble a dark warning stamped onto the heart of Artainus. He'd never expected to set foot in the city of her children.

And what was Ellath without her temples? What was the Holy Empire without the gods? These were questions Entonin had never asked, and he certainly didn't want to know the answer.

Yet here he was, on the way to meet with one of Amoria's ruling councils. Not the council he'd *wanted* to meet, certainly, but it had taken months of bowing, scraping and weaselling his way into people's offices to get this much.

This would have to do.

It was the hour of Trebaranus, and back home the war priests would be marching through the capital, beating their chests and bellowing to anyone who would listen: *"Break those who will not bow. The hour of Trebaranus is upon us."* He could almost imagine himself standing back in line with the other Seekers, trying to look solemn and serious, instead of grinning at the smirk on Remaia's face.

What would she say if she saw you here? Entonin wondered. *Mages are worse than war priests, surely.*

He hadn't thought of *her* in a long time.

Ah, here we are, thought Entonin, as they crossed from the Southern Quarter into the Adventus. *The Shiura Assembly do know they're second best. And they clearly don't care for it.*

"Impressive?" said Entonin, his tone half a question.

"Odd," answered Karameth with his usual brevity.

He wasn't wrong. The Majlis loomed over the whole district, a strange monument to the power of those without magic. It looked like a Dahrani temple with no roof, raised up on wide steps which surrounded it on all sides. The elevated courtyard, if that was the word for it, was lined with ornate pillars of white stone: pillars which held up nothing at all. After all, what use had the Amorians for a roof, living as they did beneath a glass sky?

"Compensating, perhaps?"

"Mmm," agreed Karameth. "Who could say why?"

Entonin grinned despite himself. Karameth might not speak much, but when he did he possessed a delightfully dry sense of humour. He would deliver it with the exact same stoic expression he always wore, but for the slightest curl to the edge of his mouth. Entonin had started to look forward to the moments he could wring that small smile from his companion's lips.

As they approached the Majlis, Entonin was careful to turn his own smile inwards, so that he wore the appropriately respectful expression for the men and women waiting for him at the bottom of the stone steps.

"Lord Seeker." One of the members of the Shiura addressed him, an older man with piercing green eyes and an expression like he'd just swallowed something sour. "Welcome to the Majlis, I am Mustashaar Wylian Akana. These are Mustashaar Mokkadir, Drusa and Bitar."

It was difficult to pin down exactly what each member of the Shiura Council was responsible for, as they didn't have fixed duties like the mage senate; the title mustashaar literally just meant counsellor. But Entonin knew their names well enough. Mustashaar Akana, he was sure, was related to one of the heads of the Academy. An interesting dynamic; Entonin didn't particularly want to imagine what those family dinners were like.

Unlike the mages, none of them bowed to greet him, again more in keeping with Dahrani traditions than Ellathian. Entonin had a feeling that these differences were carefully cultivated: though the mages of

Amoria were originally Ellathian settlers, now Entonin doubted that the mages and non-mages were any more or less Ellathian than the other. Yet here they were, the mages with their Ellathian rituals and the Shiura Assembly with their Dahrani ones.

"Honoured Mustashaar." Entonin gave a small bow, as was tradition back home, even if it pained him to bow to people who had offered him no such courtesy. "It is my pleasure to be here."

Karameth said nothing, and Entonin could see the Shiura members eyeing him dubiously as they began to mount the steps. He'd turned out surprisingly well: the mercenary was dressed in a sleeveless black and red coat, typical of the Dahrani, and his hair was tied into a thick knot at the nape of his neck. He looked decidedly military. Entonin pretended not to notice the questioning glances of the Amorians – let them think what they wanted.

The silence was a palpable presence, hanging like an unanswered question between them. Entonin had expected the script for this meeting to have been carefully rehearsed, but everyone seemed to be waiting for somebody else to speak. *How interesting.*

"The Majlis is quite beautiful," Entonin said, enjoying the thought of prolonging their uncertainty. "Is it as old as the rest of the city?"

"No, Seeker," Mustashaar Akana replied. "It has been complete a little over two hundred years. Its construction took decades."

Entonin knew better than to ask if it were made from magic. Around each of the pillars, the sinuous form of a dragon had been carved into the smooth stone, every feather etched in eye-aching detail. A particularly odd choice, given the strong association between the mythological creatures and magic. Or perhaps it was exactly the right choice, a defiant symbol of the Shiura Assembly's own power. Regardless, it was clear the whole thing was hewn from blocks of solid marble, not an inch of Amorian glass or magestone in sight. The stubborn impracticality of it was oddly comforting: this was the kind of showmanship he was used to.

"It's a Dahrani word, isn't it? Majlis?" Entonin asked mildly.

"Yes. A meeting place. Many of the non-mages in Amoria came originally from Dahran. Though the mages follow the ways of their

Ellathian ancestors, we try to honour both our Dahrani and Ellathian heritages."

Entonin smiled, struggling not to raise an eyebrow at even the acknowledgement of Ellathian heritage.

"Please, this way, Seeker," said Mustashaar Bitar, speaking for the first time. She gestured them towards what looked like a wide rectangle cut down into the stone, Shiura perched around the edges.

There were several of these lowered seating areas scattered across the Majlis, men and women clustered together on the stepped-down benches or standing behind them. People seemed to drift between them as was required, a wave and a shout being enough to extract someone from one cluster and pull them into another. It was less a series of individual meetings and more an interconnected web, with no part of the Shiura Assembly being completely independent of the others. This, too, felt far more Dahrani than Ellathian.

Entonin sat as he was directed, pulling his white and blue robes straight beneath him. Karameth stood at his back. *Good. He knows what he's here for.*

"We have to admit that we are surprised by your visit, Seeker." This was Mustashaar Mokkadir, his voice soft but no less direct. "It has been a long time since an Ellathian has come within our city's walls, let alone a member of your distinguished order."

"I am honoured to represent the Temple of Ardulath, praise be upon His name, god of knowledge and wisdom, greatest of the Ruling Six." It was an unnecessary introduction, but tradition was tradition. "Let me begin by setting your minds at ease, honoured members of the Shiura, I am here with a hope of putting our troubled past behind us." Entonin spread his hands, as if he could erase five hundred years of hostility just like that. It wasn't non-mage blood his people had spilled, after all.

"We are glad to hear that, of course," said Mustashaar Akana, though he didn't exactly sound it. "We would like to extend our own assurances, that we too seek to look to the future and not the past."

As if on cue, a child arrived at Entonin's elbow, offering him a glass of mint tea from an ornate metal tray. Entonin took it, glad of the distraction and hoping his surprise hadn't registered on his face. He had, of course, hoped the Shiura Assembly would receive him politely enough, but he had hardly expected to be welcomed with open arms.

"That is most gratifying to hear, Mustashaar Akana." Entonin watched them carefully over the rim of his glass, wanting to dig into the cracks in their expressions and uncover whatever it was they wanted of him. "The Ellathian Empire has always had strong ties with our neighbours—" *just not always peaceful ones* "—and you'll find we make a beneficial trading partner."

"Amoria is but a small diversion from the Spice Road," added Mustashaar Bitar.

You only have to cross a desert, thought Entonin, but he tipped his head towards her in acknowledgement.

"Would it be beneficial to involve the Lieno Council in this discussion?" he asked, his heart tripping into a gallop even as he opened his mouth. "Any trade deal would involve the work of mages, would it not?"

Ah, yes, they don't like that. He took another sip, his expression carefully benign, pretending not to notice the exchanged glances. A number of Shiura members looked like they were hiding behind their cups, as if they were Dahrani courtiers hiding behind their silk fans.

"Most of Amoria's exports are handled by the Shiura Assembly directly." Mustashaar Akana's voice was tight. "Our resources extend far beyond the magical 'artefacts' you've heard of."

"You may not find the Lieno Council so eager to meet with you," Mustashaar Mokkadir added, so quietly that Entonin had to lean forward to hear him. "They are ... particular about who can address the council. Especially in these times. Perhaps in the future, it may be possible to establish contact with the Lieno Council, but for now it would be wiser if you dealt through us."

Entonin frowned. It sounded a lot like they were forbidding him from speaking to the mages.

"Let's be direct, shall we?" Mustashaar Drusa spoke for the first time, cutting through the quiet murmurs of the Majlis. The others glanced towards her with unease, but also with a kind of deference,

Entonin thought. They sat a little back, giving the impression that she was at the centre of their circle, without her having to move at all. "I'm sure you're aware of Amoria's troubles. You're not blind, Lord Seeker – Entonin, is it?"

Entonin gave a single nod, having to bite his lip to keep from smiling. Oh, he liked this one.

"There is some," she waved her hand in a circular gesture, "ongoing business between this assembly and the Lieno Council. You must understand, we live among people with immense power – we aren't looking for conflict, but we *are* looking for allies. We would like certain assurances from the Ellathian Empire. I'm sure you understand my meaning."

The only thing Entonin was sure of, was that "direct" had exactly the same meaning in Amoria as it did in Ellath: not direct at all. He couldn't help his eyes drifting up to the rest of the Majlis, to the people who crossed so close to them or the other seating areas which were surely within earshot. It was all so *open*, and this conversation felt like it belonged behind solid walls.

Entonin swallowed, took a deep breath, let his heart slow down. "I think that Ellath doesn't want to reignite old conflicts." *Or start new ones.*

"We're not talking about old conflicts; we're talking about new allies." She didn't say "keep up" but it was there in the arch of her eyebrow.

"Well, if we're being direct, Mustashaar Drusa, what does Ellath stand to gain from these ... assurances?"

"That is something for discussion, though I was under the impression that our goals here might align."

Align. That is, with the goals of Ellath – the empire that had killed mages for hundreds of years. It was not often that someone cut to the point quicker than Entonin, and it was an uncomfortable sensation. He kept his face carefully blank as he considered her. His entire life, he had been raised to believe that magic was evil: Sisephia was a treacherous creature who disrupted the natural order, cheated death and conspired against the other gods. Drusa's offer was an innately pleasing one, and it spoke to the part of him that had lived within sight of the ruins of Sisephia's Temple, had been raised on the sermons of his elders and had seen rebel mages hanged from the city gates for their crimes. Any priest would be tempted by this offer.

Instead of answering her, Entonin set down his cup and sat a little taller. "Be sure you don't mistake me for a priest of Trebaranus. Their speciality is war, not ours."

"I mistake nothing" was all she said, holding his gaze almost without blinking.

"Good. Then you'll know, too, that I'm a Seeker, not a Ruler. I will happily hear your 'discussions', but this is a matter for my temple. Only they can offer the *assurances* you're looking for."

"Certainly, Lord Seeker. It's a start."

18

NAILA

Naila lay on Ko'ani's floor, one of Haelius's books open in front of her, her chin propped up in her hands. She was sure she'd read the same sentence more than seven times by now, the words shifting and blurring in front of her. Screwing her eyes shut, she tried to blink the words back into focus. One long blink. Then another.

"Did I just hear you snore?"

Naila startled awake, her face barely an inch from the page.

"I did, didn't I?" Ko was grinning down at her. She was up on her bed, another of Haelius's books resting against her knees, the tips of her hair tinged with violet in the low evening light. "You can give yourself a break, you know?"

Naila groaned, letting her head drop all the way forward. "I can't," she mumbled into the floor. "I just know the Academy are starting to get restless. I can't do this. And if I can't do it, then . . ." Neither of them tried to finish that sentence.

Naila still didn't know what would happen to her if she couldn't learn control or stay at the Academy. No one seemed to. But there were far too many stories in Amoria about unstable mages who had vanished in the night, stories which featured the faceless Surveyors and underground prisons with blackened walls. Naila couldn't shake what Marcus had said: *you'll never see the light of day again.* She shuddered despite the warmth of Ko's bedroom.

"Is the answer likely to be in that book?" Ko asked, the bangles on her ankles clinking as she shifted to peer down at Naila. "What is it anyway?"

"*Metaphysical Magic*," Naila replied, lifting the front cover so Ko could see.

"What does that even mean?"

"I don't know, and I've read almost a fifth of the book."

"Mudammir piss on that," said Ko, invoking her favourite curse. "No wonder you're dying down there. Come here and try this one – it's way better."

Naila heaved herself to her feet, shaking off the discomfort of sitting on the floor. She left *Metaphysical Magic* where it lay and climbed up next to Ko'ani, shuffling along the mattress until they were shoulder to shoulder. Ko had studied with Naila since her first lesson with Haelius, testing her on phonemes and helping her understand some of the more complex concepts. In turn, Naila passed on everything she could from Haelius's lessons, watching Ko tip her head to one side as she listened, absorbing every word. Leaning in over the book with her friend, Naila realised that – even with the threat of the Academy looming over her – these had been some of the happiest months of her life.

"Which one is it?" Naila asked, as Ko slid the book to rest between them.

"*Silent Casting: the fundamentals of magic without incantation*," Ko intoned gravely.

"One of Haelius's?"

"It has to be. Yeah – look there: that's his handwriting on the diagram."

Silent Casting turned out to be vastly easier to understand than *Metaphysical Magic*. Naila and Ko'ani flicked through it together, Ko choosing what she considered to be the most pompous phrases and reading them out in a mockery of Haelius's voice, usually while she waited for Naila to catch up with her. The book was on Haelius's favourite subject: magic cast with movement and gestures, not words. Out of the corner of her eye, Naila could see Ko making shapes with one of her hands against the mattress, copying the positions in the diagrams.

"You want to try it?" Naila asked.

"What? No." Ko immediately balled her hand into a fist. "Well, I mean, of course I do. I just know that you can't, and I didn't want ... you know."

"Don't be stupid. Try it! What's all this for if you can't actually use it?"

"All right then." Ko shuffled off the bed in a jangle of bracelets and then stood stiffly in the centre of her room.

"Just don't do anything that might wreck the place," Naila joked, though there was a part of her that was completely serious. "What do you want to try?"

"Light, maybe? That's always the safest place to start."

Naila flicked back through the book until she found the right diagram, and then pointed the book at Ko'ani. When she looked up, she found Ko standing ready to cast, one hand raised in front of her, a look of fierce determination on her face.

All her awkwardness had been shrugged away. Naila could see the same exactness to her stance that she saw in Haelius, the way her whole body might serve as a conduit for magic. If Amoria was a city of people who could use magic, Haelius and Ko were true spellcasters. Naila couldn't help the knot of jealousy that tightened in her gut.

Ko arranged herself exactly to match the diagram, half closed her eyes and stared hard at the air just above the palm of her hand. With a small twitch of her fingers, a light sputtered into existence above her hand. It was feeble and diffuse, drifting apart almost as soon as it had formed, but it was light: Ko'ani had cast without speaking a word.

"You did it!" Naila leapt off the bed, all her jealousy forgotten, and threw her arms around her talented friend.

Ko was laughing, breathless, her expression triumphant. "Did you see that? It was so small and pathetic, and now I'm exhausted."

"But you *cast* without speaking. How many people can do that? You'll be a wizard in no time."

"Wizard Tallace." Ko considered it, tasting the words. "I like that."

Naila. The voice whispered at the back of her head almost as if it was her own thought, and the smile froze on her face. Haelius's presence in her mind grew slowly, almost as if he hesitated before opening the door. *I know it's late, but do you want to come for lessons this evening?*

It was phrased as a request, but they both knew she'd never say no; she didn't have the luxury of choosing not to try.

Before she answered, Naila tried to swallow the guilt that suddenly swept through her. She shouldn't have been messing around with Ko. How could she even laugh when so much depended on her?

When Naila failed to keep her thoughts from the wizard, Haelius would almost always let through the smallest shadow of his feelings in return. This time, it was regret she felt sink through her.

I'm sorry. You don't have to come. Perhaps you should rest?

No. No I want to. Where are you?

My study. Do you want me to bring you here?

No. Naila grimaced, trying not to remember the sickening lurch of Haelius's transporting magic. *I'll walk.*

She thought she felt the barest hint of amusement from Haelius, before the wizard's presence dropped from her mind.

"You're going?" Ko said out loud. She'd understood what was happening the moment Naila's smile disappeared, and she'd perched on the edge of her bed, waiting for Naila to come back to her.

"Yeah, I'm heading upstairs."

Ko flopped back onto her bed with a dramatic sigh. "We were just starting to have fun."

"Well, there's nothing stopping *your* fun." Naila picked up *Silent Magic* and dropped it onto Ko's stomach, making her splutter. "Keep it. I have enough books to drag upstairs anyway."

Ko scowled up at Naila. "What's the point if you're not here to cheer every time I do something amazing?"

"Then you'd better work on something truly impressive for me when I get back."

Naila found Haelius standing at the outside wall of his study, his hands folded behind his back, peering down at the ghostly form of Amoria beyond the glass. That was never a good sign with him. Naila's arms were aching beneath the pile of books she'd lugged up the stairs, part of her regretting her refusal to be transported by Haelius's spell. She dropped them onto his desk with a *thump*, sending one of his pens rolling off the edge of the table. He caught it with magic without even looking. Instead, he eyed the pile of books with one eyebrow raised.

"Where's my book?" he asked, by way of greeting.

"Good evening, Haelius," said Naila, used to how abrupt he could be. "Here." She took the parcel of leftovers from where it had been balanced on the stack of books and handed it to him.

He received it with the air of someone doing her a great favour, and he still had his eyebrows raised in the way that told her he was waiting for an answer.

"Ko has it."

"Does she indeed?"

Naila dropped into her usual chair and gestured to the chaos all around them. "I don't even know how you notice when a book is missing."

"I assure you, every book is in its proper place. What is the young Mita Tallace doing with my book, exactly?"

"Casting." Naila smiled warmly, her chest swelling with pride. "She managed to create a light without saying a word. It dissolved pretty quickly, but it was definitely there."

"Did she, now? Casting a spell and maintaining it are two different skills – it will follow, in time." He rubbed his forehead with one hand. "I really should make more time to teach her."

Naila could see how pleased he was: he sat a little straighter, his green eyes alight with the thought of teaching Ko'ani. She couldn't help it; all her pride at her friend collapsed, swallowed into a hole that had been growing steadily in her chest. There, her own failings weighed much heavier than Ko'ani's success.

The smile slipped off her face.

"Ah, but *we* haven't made much progress, have we?" Of course, Haelius had noticed. His eyes softened, and the apology she could see in his expression was almost unbearable to look at. "This is my failing, Naila; not yours."

Naila gritted her teeth with frustration. "No, it's not. How can it be? You're doing everything you can. I just can't use magic." To Naila's horror, her voice wavered. "I'm a hollow. I always have been. No amount of teaching, or books, or learning phonemes can change that."

If Haelius was shocked by her use of the word "hollow", the only sign he gave was a slight widening of his eyes.

The magic in the room lurched suddenly, wrenched down as if something was stealing the very air itself. The intensity made Naila gasp. She felt like she had stumbled forward, someone dragging her towards the floor, but nothing in Haelius's study had moved at all.

"Feel that?" Haelius asked innocently, releasing his grip on the magic.

"Very funny," snapped Naila, rubbing at her chest as if he'd really reached forward and grabbed her. "That felt *horrible*."

"Strange, seeing as how a non-mage would feel nothing at all."

Naila scowled at him.

"Naila, you're incredibly sensitive to magic." He sat forward, his gaze pinning her to the back of her chair. "You can see and feel magic. You can even see anima, which not every mage can. You're not a 'hollow', whatever else you may be."

"But what if I'm not a mage?"

"Then we'll have to deal with that when we come to it."

"But the Academy—"

"We'll deal with them, too, if we have to."

Naila didn't have the least notion of what "deal with them" meant, and she wasn't convinced Haelius did either. Instead of arguing, she let out a long sigh, trying not to imagine Haelius's robes stripped of their red braiding.

"Well, do you want to learn magic or not?" asked Haelius, though the bright note in his voice still didn't quite ring true. He stood and beckoned her to the centre of his study. "Come. Let's begin."

It was an intense lesson. If anything, Haelius seemed more driven than ever before. He guided her hands and arms into precise positions, making her hold them until her fingers twitched and her muscles ached.

"Focus," he said for what felt like the hundredth time. "Don't just see the magic, *feel* it. Feel the connection between the power in yourself and the energy all around you."

"I *am*." Naila could hear the whine in her own voice.

She did feel it, as vividly as her own skin: the anima, steady, still, holding everything in its place; and the magic, which seemed to spill through all existence. It was sliding down towards Haelius, the very shape of it changing, like he was a weight pulling at the centre of a web.

The wizard had his fingers against the side of her forehead, so close that Naila could feel the prickle of his power across her skin. His frustration was a tremor, a change in the taste of the air.

"It's right there," he hissed the words through his teeth. "I can *feel* it."

Naila braced herself for what she knew was coming next. It was the moment in their lessons she hated most, when Haelius would use his magic to reach for hers. She gasped, feeling him turn that immense power towards her, sinking his magic into her like a knife through butter. It was the rope behind her heart again, held firmly in his grip, dragging on something that should belong only to her. If the holding spell had left her trapped within her body, this felt like the opposite, like someone was trying to prise her out of it.

Haelius pulled harder than he ever had before, relentless, as if he were trying to physically remove whatever blocked her power.

Naila couldn't help it: a moan of discomfort escaped her lips.

In an instant, the grip on her was gone, the magic collapsing into stillness. The look of concentration vanished from Haelius's face, replaced instead with one of worry.

"Did I hurt you?"

"No." Naila lifted her hand to her eyes, her body trembling like a plucked string. "No. I . . ." She gritted her teeth. "We should go again."

"Are you sure? I don't think . . ."

Naila had already shifted her sight back to magic, frustration burning through her. She looked past Haelius, to the immense world of magic behind him: a rich tapestry she would never touch.

And then she felt it.

There was something on Haelius's desk, its magic standing out against everything else, a point of light bright even in blinding sunlight.

It was the piece of obsidian, the one Haelius had been studying, but now it pulled on her the same way Haelius's magic had, only softer, more enticing, like being led by the hand towards it.

"That stone," she asked. "What is it?"

"What?"

"The obsidian you've been staring at for weeks?" Her voice felt separate, as if it didn't belong to her.

"Oh." Haelius sounded confused but unconcerned. Oblivious. Could he not feel the vastness of its power? "I don't actually know. It's an artefact from the archives, but I can't seem to get it to work."

Naila was at the edge of his desk now, though she didn't remember moving. She could see it twice, both as the physical object and as a bright bead of magic which called to her more strongly than anything ever had. It was no bigger than the tip of her thumb, polished and smooth on one side, cracked and jagged on the other. It wasn't truly obsidian, she realised – it was a deep black, but not in a way Naila felt like she'd ever seen before: it seemed to drink in the light, a dark pool into which she could fall.

"How did it break?" she asked.

"Break? I don't know what you're talking about. Naila, are you all right?"

Naila almost didn't hear him. She reached out and picked up the artefact.

And then everything changed.

The stone erupted into life, magic and light rippling across its surface. It was no longer dark but alive with colour. First it was the shimmering iridescence of a raven's wing, then there was a thread of sapphire through it, dark as deep water. Light skittered across its surface, and Naila was dully aware of that light building all around her. She could feel it – she could feel it all; something had filled that emptiness inside her, and now it unspooled, connecting her to everything by a million tiny threads. She could follow those threads to the ends of the world, reach out, and reach out, and feel endless magic and anima all woven together.

She could reach all of it.

"Naila!" Haelius's voice was little more than a distant vibration. "Naila, stop!"

The artefact in her hand had grown hot, so hot it was almost burning. Yet that didn't matter. Even through the blinding light, a darkness was creeping in at the edge of her vision, closing over her like a fist. She tried to shrug it off, to lean further into the light, but the blackness only rushed in faster.

"Naila!"

The darkness swallowed her.

She woke slowly, feeling the softness of a bed beneath her, her head throbbing as if something had tried to split it open from the inside. Her eyes ached, too, but she forced them open, trying to blink away the heaviness in her skull. A sense of unfamiliarity was creeping over her skin, and she realised she was on a bed she'd never seen before, in a room that was completely unknown to her. The panic shocked her fully awake.

Haelius was seated on a chair nearby, his fingers steepled in front of his face. As soon as she stirred, he looked up with wide, anxious eyes.

"Naila! Thank the Goddess."

She sat up, pressing the heel of her hands against her eyes. "What happened? Where am I?"

"Easy," said Haelius, perching on the bed next to her. "May I?"

She had no idea what he was asking her, but she nodded at him anyway, instantly regretting any movement of her head.

He touched the back of his hand against her forehead, and for a moment Naila thought he meant to do magic of some kind, but he only sighed in relief and dropped his hand back into his lap. "You're not cold. The worst of it has passed." He looked hard at her, and she could feel his gaze tracking over her face. "It was a kind of magical exhaustion. The artefact pulled on too much of your strength; magic is tied closely to the energies which keep us warm and alive. It won't have done any permanent harm, but it took a lot out of you."

"The stone!" All of it came back to Naila in a heady wave. The obsidian, the light, the *magic*. "I . . . was it magic? Did I do magic?"

"Wait, slow down. Give yourself a moment of rest, please." Haelius tried to look stern, but there was a frenetic edge to his words that told Naila he was almost as excited as she was. He ignored her mutinous expression and reached over for a glass of water set next to the bed. "Drink. Then we can talk about what happened."

Naila obeyed, and quickly found that she was desperately thirsty.

Haelius watched her with a satisfied smile. "See? I might know something about this." He took the glass and refilled it, handing it back to her. "You should eat as well – I think I have something in my study."

"No, wait." Naila grabbed the edge of his sleeve as he tried to stand. "Tell me what happened first. You can't say I suffered from magical exhaustion and then not tell me what happened."

He frowned down at her. "All right." He pushed a hand through his hair and sat back on the edge of the bed. "The truth is, I don't really know what happened. You touched that artefact on my desk – that one I've been studying for months. I still don't know what it is.

"I took it from the archives. It . . . there were mages interested in it, in what it could do, but I've never got it to work. It looks like an artefact. *Feels* like it should have magic. But when I tried to use it, it did nothing." His voice trailed off as he clearly realised the same thing as Naila: it was just like her.

"What happened when I touched it?" Naila asked, breathlessly.

Haelius shook his head, his gaze distant, as if he was trying to see what had happened in his mind's eye. "I don't know. You connected with it. You connected with each other. It was drawing on your strength just as you were drawing on its. It was too much; I don't know what would have happened if I hadn't knocked the stone from your hand."

"So does this mean . . .?"

Haelius's eyes shifted back into focus and he frowned. "I don't know what it means, but there will be time for this later. First, let me get you something to eat."

"But where's the stone?"

The wizard arched one eyebrow. "Far away from you. You've had quite enough excitement for one evening."

"What?" Naila stared at him in disbelief. "You can't mean that. This is the closest we've come to . . ."

"I *do* mean it. We'll be just as close tomorrow morning." He smiled, some of his own excitement creeping onto his face. "Trust me, I want to understand this just as much as you do, but for now you must rest. I know better than anyone how dangerous it can be to push yourself too far." He held his left hand out towards her, the one wrinkled and darkened with scars, and tipped his head so that she could more easily see the scars that covered his lower face and jaw. "You must promise me not to try any magic this evening, or to try anything until you're back here with me. The magic I felt was powerful – you need someone to protect you from it while you learn."

It was the first time he'd ever alluded to the cause of his burns, his green eyes flat and unreadable. There was no self-pity in his expression, but there was something hard buried there, and it left no room for argument. Naila had no idea what to say, so she only swallowed and nodded.

"Okay, I promise."

19

INTERLUDE

They'd followed a great river west, life clinging to its edges, a stark line of green against a barren landscape. Tae could still hear the call, stronger now, pulling her south and west. As they followed it, they witnessed more of the Sha'arin's destruction, leaving them in no doubt that they too followed this strange call. Yet they always arrived a heartbeat too late to find the beasts. There were places the river had burst its banks, violent floods sweeping away entire towns, and others where great swathes of land had been blackened to nothing but char.

And then suddenly there was nothing at all, all sign of the Sha'arin gone, all sense of their path evaporated. Tae and Ra'akea circled a wide area, skirting human settlements and vast rolling dunes that seemed to stretch out to infinity. They couldn't find anything: no smoke on the horizon, no sense of water being pulled out of balance, no humans trampled in their path. The lost ones had vanished.

In a place too far from the sea, Ra'akea had lost her way.

There hadn't been much choice: ask for help, or turn back and admit their failure. Ra'akea left Tae at the river, keeping her as far away from the town and its humans as she could. Within water was the subtlety of illusion. It wasn't true magic, but it was enough that Ra'akea could hide her appearance. Still, she lifted her hood, pulling the rough fabric close around her face; anyone who looked too closely would know there was something off about her, something that wasn't quite human.

The establishment she chose was dark and filled with people. The air was damp and warm, as if it had been breathed in and out too many times, but at least here there was water. Ra'akea held her hood close around her face and picked her way between the low tables and strewn cushions, careful to let nothing touch her.

I can still feel the call, Tae spoke into her mind. *We must be close. Ask the human what is west of here.*

She slid up onto a seat by the bar, as some of the other humans had done, and warily eyed the man behind it. He scrutinised her in return.

"Welcome, sister," he said. "Welcome. Please, make yourself at home." He gestured to her hood, as if he wanted her to lower it. "What can I get for you?"

"I am hoping I can ask you a question," she said carefully. "I am a new person in this place. I do not know what lies to west of here."

"West?" The man's eyes widened. "This is Tuabet, most western wilaya of Dahran. What's west of here is desert, sister, and nothing else. Just sand and oasis towns, until you reach the magi city and their Great Lake."

"Magi?"

"The magic-users, spellcasters. Magi. Mages. Out west is Amoria, their glass city."

"Ah-mor-ee-a." Ra'akea sounded out the word carefully. She had heard of this place – an unnatural edifice raised by humans using the most dangerous of their gifts.

"Most who come here are seeking the magi," the man said. "Looking for their knowledge or their wares. Nothing west of Amoria but desert, and nothing west of that but death. Strange that you come here and don't know of it."

She could feel the weight of his suspicion closing in on her along with the thick, stale air in this place. Tae's anger was like the thrashing of a tail, but Ra'akea only smiled her thanks.

And then she choked.

The feeling was like nothing she'd ever experienced. It shone in her mind and Tae's, blazing like someone had cracked open Tokar itself, right down to the molten fire at the heart of world. Ra'akea stumbled forward, gripping onto the bar, but instead of falling she felt like something was rushing up towards her: an ancient thing, sleeping and locked away. It was free, its power calling out like a beacon, its song discordant and broken, scraping at her mind.

The Sha'arin had heard it – she knew it deep within her bones.

And now she knew where to go. It was the first real clue: the first sign that something more was at work here. Yet no matter what it meant, even if it had nothing to do with the fate of the lost ones, she knew she had to find what had just been unleashed. She had to find it, and she had to stop it.

She was going to Amoria.

20

LARINNE

Stepping into the glasshouse was like pushing through into a wall of heavy, humid air. The cloying stink hit her at once, filling her nose and mouth with its sweetness. It was the scent of rotting earth and decaying leaves, and Larinne didn't know if the roiling nausea she felt was because of the smell or because of the panic which had begun to take root in her stomach.

It was so much worse than she'd imagined. She took a small step forward and then stopped, her wide eyes unable to take in what she was seeing. They were dead. All the plants were dead. All of them.

Larinne stepped towards the first row of silwheat, hardly registering her own movement. These weren't just sickly, not drooping or spotted with brown: the leaves were withered and black, brittle and desiccated as if they had been dead for days. When Larinne tugged on one of the bladed leaves, it came away easily, already crumbling to dust between her fingers. How could this be?

The panic grew up from the pit of her stomach, wrapping itself around her heart like tightening vines. Sil was the currency of Dahran and Amoria, and silwheat was so named for its immense value. The golden heads of the wheat made the flour and breads which Amoria so depended on, while its strong leaves could be pulped to make paper. It was a precious lifeline for the mage city, tempering Amoria's reliance on trade with Jasser. With the loss of income from so many sabotaged artefacts, the city was already teetering on the edge of a knife; if even a fifth of the silwheat was lost, people would go hungry.

This was a catastrophe, and there was nothing Larinne could do to fix it.

"All of it?" she whispered, raising her eyes to the incomprehensible blackness stretching away from her.

"All," said the assistant, startling Larinne back to herself. She'd forgotten he was there.

To his credit, the young trianne had remained still and silent, letting her take the time she needed. He seemed to have recovered some of his composure in the journey down from Larinne's office, as if in finding Larinne he had handed the burden of his fears to her. Now, he raised his arm and gestured towards a cluster of people further into the glasshouse, their distant forms faded in the misty air. "Please, come with me."

In front of someone else, it felt easier for Larinne to reassemble herself. She donned the role of Senator Tallace as if she was stepping into a different skin. It was a part she knew well, and it didn't leave any room for her fear. *Find out what you can, fix what you can*, she told herself. *Then deal with the next thing.*

The group was a mixture of mages and Shiura Assembly members, though Larinne could see a line being drawn between them. They were speaking in low, urgent voices, hushed as if they were in a place of worship and not this field of death. On the non-mage side, Larinne could see Mustashaar Drusa and Akana. Mustashaar Akana watched her approach with the same green eyes as his son, his lips pressed tightly together.

It was a relief to find Dailem already there, standing alongside a wizard from the Academy – though it was the first time Larinne had ever felt comforted by the sight of a Justice.

Mages dipped their heads in greeting, while non-mages eyed Larinne like she was reinforcements for the other side.

"Lieno Tallace. Thank you for coming on such short notice." The man who spoke was Lieno Fintas, the mage who'd sent his assistant to find her. He seemed to be keeping his calm better than his young colleague, but behind his eyes was the same haunted look growing in all of them.

"When did this happen?" she asked, wasting no time on pointless pleasantries.

"In the night, we believe." There was the slightest hesitation. "It was discovered at the seventh bell, on the arrival of the earliest workers."

"Where are the workers who discovered it?"

"My people have them," said Dailem. Her sister's calm, steady voice was a balm to Larinne's soul, soothing the part of her still shivering at the back of her mind. Dailem looked like a Justice: tall, stern, every inch of her in control. Larinne could see the cracks that no one else would, the quick movement of her eyes, the tension in her straight back. They were both of them playing their roles, just as they'd been taught. "They're being questioned, and the knowledge of this is contained for now, but ..." Her dark eyes flicked back to the entrance and the gathering crowds.

"And when will the Shiura Assembly have a chance to question these workers?" Mustashaar Drusa's voice snapped like a whip, no hushed whispers for her. Larinne set her teeth; of all the Shiura Assembly, Drusa had the least time for mages. "Some of those workers were non-mages. Or are we to assume they have already 'disappeared' into Oriven's system?"

Larinne saw the dangerous flash in Dailem's eyes, and so she spoke before her sister had a chance to. "Mustashaar Drusa, I am certain that the Shiura Assembly will have the opportunity to speak to the workers shortly. Right now, our only aim is to discover what happened here, and then forge a path out of this. For that, I am most grateful for your help and support."

There was a slight twitch to the corner of Dailem's mouth which told Larinne her sister didn't approve of Larinne's platitudes. Nothing new in that.

"Tell me what we know," Larinne pressed on, gripping tightly to the fragile threads of control.

Everyone looked towards the wizard, so Larinne turned, too. Wizard Marinet was as different from Haelius as it was possible to be. The hem of her robes was heavy with elegant red and gold embroidery, the fabric pressed and immaculate. Her thick grey hair was piled on the back of her head in a bun, and she held herself with an air of utter certainty, as if the world held no more mysteries for her. She was the only one who seemed free from the cloud of dread, her head lifted above it; clearly Marinet had no notion of how much Amoria relied on this silwheat.

"Is it magic?" Larinne asked simply. "Did someone *do* this?"

"If it's magic, it's no magic I've ever encountered." Larinne had no doubt from the wizard's tone that Marinet did not believe in magic she hadn't encountered.

"So it's natural then?" Larinne turned back to Lieno Fintas. "Some kind of blight?"

He hesitated, unwilling to contradict her – or perhaps more importantly the wizard. "We, ah, don't think so. It's struck too quickly, too completely. It's like nothing we've ever seen."

"Poison, then?"

"Maybe," said Fintas, his expression bleak. "We just don't know."

"Could we detect poison with magic?" Larinne pressed on, relentless; she wouldn't let any of this, any of them, stop her from moving forward.

At this, the wizard bristled slightly, as if such a request were preposterous. "I have analysed some of the plants, but unless the poison is magical in nature, it will be near impossible to detect. Perhaps at the time of administration, or perhaps if there were any clue as to the source."

A simple "no" would have sufficed. Larinne took a slow breath in through her nose. She closed her eyes, her index finger tapping against her upper arm. *What next?* There had to be something. She couldn't help wishing that they'd called on Haelius instead of this intractable wizard, to have his mind working on this as well as hers. Despite the way they'd left things, she missed his steadfast presence at her side.

She thought of the way he could extend his power, reaching out over vast distances with his awareness. Surely he would see something they couldn't. "So we need to find the source. Wizard Marinet?"

"I could bring a team from the Academy, of course, though it would take several days and be little more effective than searching by more conventional methods. Might I suggest that my abilities are put to better use elsewhere?"

"Could Wizard Akana do it?" To Larinne's surprise, it was Dailem who said it, sparing no thought for Wizard Marinet's pride.

Ah, there it is. For the first time, Larinne felt the wizard's power, shivering with Marinet's temper. It was so like Haelius's: an immense creature sleeping somewhere beneath the surface, only visible to them through the ripples of its movement.

"I'm sure he would believe he could, Justice Tallace." The wizard's voice was tight with anger. "Though that wizard's opinion of himself . . ."

"We need him," Dailem interrupted. "He is our foremost expert in magic. We should use everything we have."

Larinne nodded, steeling herself against the flutter of nerves she felt at seeing him again.

To Lieno Fintas, she said, "Assemble a team as Wizard Marinet suggests and search the glasshouses. I want the state of every plant – *every* plant – reported back to me. Justice Tallace, I want the crowd outside dispersed. I'll contact Wizard Akana."

Dailem made a signal with her hand, and two Justice immediately stalked away, their black robes whipping out behind them. With that, it was like the tension that had been holding their small group together dispersed. Larinne sighed with relief, filled with a sudden lightness; it felt like she'd been using her strength to hold them together, weaving a careful spell to keep them from each other's throats.

She tried to find a quiet place to contact Haelius, but in reality it was the quietness she couldn't escape. Everywhere she turned, the blackness stretched away from her. If she considered it too long, if she thought about what it really meant, she felt herself tipping forward, as if she would plunge right into that darkness.

A hand touched lightly against her arm. "Are you all right?" said Dailem, an unusual gentleness to her voice.

Larinne closed her hand on her sister's, the warmth pulling her back from the edge. "No. You?"

"You did well." Dailem sidestepped that question as she usually did. "They were about ready to start a brawl before you turned up, and I have to admit that I was ready to throw the first punch."

Despite everything, Dailem managed to wring a small smile from Larinne's lips. "I'm glad I didn't find you with your hands around Mustashaar Akana's throat."

"Well, there'll be time for that yet. Oriven is coming. He'll be here soon." Dailem's brown eyes locked on Larinne's, and Larinne knew what she was about to say. "Haelius needs to keep his calm."

Larinne blew out her cheeks and nodded, wondering when she'd become the wizard's handler. "He will. I'm surprised you want him here."

"We need him. This is ..." Dailem's gaze lifted to the sea of dead plants stretching away from them and, for the first time, the mask of calm slipped. There was a glassy quality to Dailem's stare, a weary downturn to her eyes and mouth. That, more than anything, stirred the panic that lay coiled around Larinne's heart. "You know what this means. We need to find a cause that doesn't implicate either side, or this will only get worse."

She meant the mages and non-mages, but the use of the word "side" sat like a weight in Larinne's chest.

"If anyone can find the answer, it's him. I'd better do this."

"Coniumentis loquesemo," Larinne began, while at the same time thinking, *Haelius. Haelius, I need you.*

Larinne? His response was immediate. She felt a sense of his power rushing to meet hers, almost as familiar to her as her own, and he gently exerted control over the spell between them, maintaining it so she wouldn't have to.

She held the image of the dead plants in her mind. *The silwheat is dead.*

There was a pause while he processed the grim image, and then Larinne felt the smallest flutter of his fear. His control was normally better than that. *Where are you?*

Again, Larinne showed him rather than explaining in words, and she felt his immediate comprehension. *I'm coming.*

Haelius dropped the connection and Larinne rocked back into her own mind. "He's on his way," she said aloud.

The wait was agonising, though it could barely have been a minute before Haelius arrived. He materialised ten feet from them, Malek at his side. Malek almost stumbled, his whole body faltering at the sight of the silwheat. His hands dropped to his sides, and he turned slowly on the spot, his brown skin paling.

Haelius came straight to Larinne.

"Are you all right?" he asked, his eyes tracking over Larinne's face.

Larinne tried to swallow down the relief she felt at seeing him. "*I* am. But this . . ."

Only now did Haelius turn to look, deep lines forming in the centre of his forehead. Larinne could see the same hopelessness roll over him as it had over all of them.

"How many are like this?" he asked.

"All," Dailem answered. "All the glasshouses. The silwheat is all dead."

"How can this be?" Malek's voice was weak and devoid of its usual warmth. He went to Dailem's side, gripping her hands in his own, and for a moment Larinne envied their closeness, the comfort of physical touch.

At least we're together, she thought.

"What can I do?" asked Haelius. "Tell me what you need."

"This lieno thinks you might have some *unique insight* into why this happened." Wizard Marinet's sharp voice came from behind them.

"Wizard Marinet." Larinne saw the twist to Haelius's mouth, before he turned and dipped into a bow lower than was necessary – his small way of trying to keep the peace. "Any sign of what caused this?"

"No. Poison most likely, though it's beyond detection now. However, I'm told *you* can do the impossible."

Larinne felt the barest twitch of Haelius's temper, before he drew a long breath and mastered himself. "I'm afraid not, but perhaps between us we can find some sign as to where this came from." He moved to the nearest row of withered plants, his eyes catching on Larinne's as he turned. "You want me to look?"

"Please." Larinne nodded.

Haelius closed his eyes, but he had barely stretched out his hand before he snatched it back, a hiss of shock escaping his lips.

"What? What is it?"

"There's no magic."

"As I said," sniffed Wizard Marinet.

"No. I mean *no* magic."

"They're dead, Wizard Akana, what did you expect?" She spoke as if she addressed some upstart young pupil, not a fellow wizard.

"Even in death, some magic remains," Haelius snapped back, his temper finally getting the better of him. "And how would you explain the lack of any anima?"

"What? That's impossible."

"Then it seems I *have* done the impossible. Come and see for yourself. You were so busy looking for *something* that you failed to see what was missing. Stop looking for an answer – just *look* at them. Really look."

It was an echo of the words he'd said to Malek when they'd first discovered the sabotaged artefacts. *The artefacts,* Larinne thought, shivering as the realisation rang through her like the toll of a bell. *It's the same. Goddess, how did I not realise?*

They all moved to the plants as one, all of them shifting into that other sight, reaching, concentrating, trying to see the invisible. They all saw it at the same time, shock rippling through them. The magic of the silwheat was even more horrifying to witness than the dead plants themselves. Around them, the air, the ground, all of it still shimmered with power, magic spilling down towards them, drawn always towards the wizards. At the silwheat, the pattern abruptly stopped, coiling away as if the plants actively repelled it. They were a grey void – a blankness printed onto the surface of reality. That emptiness was an impossibility, and it surrounded them like the yawning mouth of a pit.

Larinne felt a steadying hand on her arm, Haelius stepping in close to her.

"Look away from it," he said, his voice barely above a whisper.

She closed her eyes and tried to shake the image away, letting herself lean into his hand. When she opened her eyes, he was watching her, the obvious question written on his face – *what now?* Larinne had no idea.

"It's magical, then." Dailem spoke first. "Deliberate?"

"It must be, though how …" Haelius shook his head. "I don't know."

Dailem's expression hardened, her eyes searching out the Shiura members who still drifted among the ruined plants, looking for their own answers. "This can't get out. Especially not to the Shiura Assembly."

"What—?"

"This can't get out." Her gaze snapped back and her eyes pinned Haelius as if she'd reached out and grabbed him. "Tell them nothing. The Assembly can't know that magic was involved until we've found out what caused it."

Haelius's expression darkened. "This disaster will affect all of Amoria—"

"And it will split Amoria in half if the Shiura Assembly are made to think that mages are responsible. This is a matter of security. A matter for the Justice." Dailem had hesitated before she said those last words, but she drew herself taller now, staring each one of them down in turn.

A cold dread settled around Larinne's heart.

She could feel the tension radiating from Haelius, the metallic taste of his magic on her tongue. Every part of him had stiffened, pulled so tight he was almost trembling. Larinne knew what it meant, knew how quickly Haelius's anger would lead him into fights he couldn't win. And at the other side of the glasshouse, Larinne could see the unmistakable approach of someone who could only make it worse.

Oriven.

Larinne closed her fingers around Haelius's arm and squeezed, trying to drag him out of the path of his anger. When he turned, he looked at her like a stranger, like someone else was staring out from behind his eyes. Larinne didn't flinch, willing him to understand everything she couldn't say out loud. *Don't give him a reason to suspect you*, she begged. The power it would have taken to destroy the silwheat was vast – beyond the reach of almost every mage in Amoria. Almost.

"Please" was all she said out loud.

His expression didn't change but she felt him soften beneath her fingers. "I know."

Oriven strode towards them, the light fabric of his robes billowing out around him. He wore the same uniform as his army, though his was more gold than black; even his gloves were soft black leather edged in a fine filigree of gold. She saw Haelius's gaze lingering on Oriven's gloved hands. His fingers twitched, and Larinne knew he was fighting the urge to reach up and touch the scars on his face.

"Justice Tallace," Oriven greeted Dailem first, a practised order to his every action. "Wizard Marinet, thank you for your expertise. Senator Tallace, Larinne." Larinne moved to bow, but to her great surprise Oriven took her hands and kissed her on both cheeks in a display of familiarity he hadn't expressed in many years. The gesture snatched away the last of Larinne's calm.

"Justice Oriven," she managed, hearing the surprise in her own voice.

"Allyn, please. What do we have in this mess if not each other?" Though "each other" clearly meant the lieno and wizards present – there was no such acknowledgement for lowly Malek, and certainly no move to approach the Shiura members.

With a sense of dreadful inevitability, Larinne watched Oriven turn to Haelius. "Wizard Akana, I didn't expect to see you here."

Haelius bent in a rigid bow. "I'm here at the council's behest."

"Good. Good. It is important that the council and the Academy work together on this. Tell me what you've found."

Haelius recited what they'd seen with a cold detachment, describing the magical void like a lesson from the Academy, not like the stomach-churning sight it had been.

Oriven didn't turn towards the plants to confirm this strange information with his own eyes. In fact, he had barely glanced towards the silwheat since he'd arrived. He made all the right expressions: he nodded attentively, his brow furrowed, his expression grave, but there was something off about him – as if he twitched for Haelius to finish speaking.

"Only magic could have caused this," Haelius finished, placing each of those words carefully, his eyes flicking towards Dailem.

"Perhaps." Oriven clasped his hands. "Or perhaps not. You say this is like nothing you've ever seen. Do you know of a magic that could cause this? Wizard Marinet?"

"No," she answered immediately. "I know of no magic that could do this. And the reach needed to cover such a vast area – I think it beyond even a wizard's skill." Though as she said it, her eyes slid towards Haelius for just a moment.

"Just because we don't know about it," said Haelius, "doesn't mean it doesn't exist."

"No, of course," agreed Oriven. "But consider that there may also be poisons of which we know nothing, which could have effects we perceive as magic. We have the greatest mages of Omalia, perhaps the whole world. What is more likely: that we lack the expertise in magics or poisons?"

At this, all Haelius's patience crumbled and he scowled. "Come on, Allyn, you don't really believe that."

"I don't know what to believe." Oriven's eyes tracked over Haelius, the slightest twist to his mouth; he'd always hated when Haelius acted like he knew more than he did. "What mage would do this? What could they hope to gain? No mage benefits from this."

"No *Amorian* benefits from this."

"No? A destabilisation of an already weakened Amoria? A disruption to the status quo?" Oriven's expression was carefully naive. "Who might benefit from such a thing?"

Who controls much of our trade? Larinne found herself thinking; her heart started to thump an unsteady rhythm in her chest.

Haelius remained still, his eyes dangerously bright.

"Well, whatever the answer, we must find it." Oriven stepped back and, just like that, the tension cracked apart. "We thank you for your expertise, Wizard Marinet, Wizard Akana. The Justice will handle it from here."

Larinne started in surprise. "But— wait—"

"Of course, Larinne, we will need your help as well." Suddenly it felt like the use of her name wasn't familiarity at all, but just a different type of control; she felt lessened by it, diminished next to the mighty Justice Oriven. "Whatever the cause of this, we need someone to guide us out of it. I feel your office is best suited to gain control of the situation."

"And any magical analysis of the plants?" Haelius asked, his voice cold.

"Done, thanks to you. Any further investigation can be carried out by the Justice. We may not be wizards of the Academy, but we're still mages. I'm sure we can manage."

"But perhaps a more experienced perspective . . ."

"Thank you, Wizard. We will of course contact the Academy if we require assistance, though I understand that you have more pressing matters to attend to." Oriven tugged at the edge of his gloves, and Haelius's eyes followed the movement. "We've both witnessed the consequences of you overextending yourself."

Larinne held her breath, dreading Haelius's answer, but he only bent into a low bow, a cold void where his magic should be. "Of course. Please, contact me if you need anything." He was addressing Oriven, but as he straightened his eyes locked with Larinne's, and she knew the words were meant for her. "Senators. Justice. Wizard Marinet."

He strode away, Malek hurrying to bow and follow behind him. Larinne saw Haelius extend two fingers and twitch them towards the silwheat, three plants tipping forward as if they'd been cut. They vanished along with the wizard.

21

HAELIUS

Haelius grimaced and rubbed his dry eyes. Looking up to the dark expanse of his window, he realised that he'd been staring at the silwheat for hours, his vision slipping in and out of the sight for so long that it took him a moment to centre himself back in the physical world. In front of him, three of the dead plants lay across his desk, their leaves already disintegrating; the world would not tolerate the impossibility of their existence, magic and anima rushing to fill the void they'd created. His chance to study them was passing, crumbling away between his fingers.

And he'd learned nothing.

He heard the shudder in his breath, frustration and fear rising in his throat like bile. His gift seemed to sense it, too, and the magic in the room bent down towards him, even the fire of the lamps leaning out from their brackets, blackening the glass with their flames. Who would understand this if he couldn't? *This is what you're for*, he told himself. *This is what you do.* If he couldn't find an answer, Oriven would, and it would be whatever damn answer he wanted it to be. Haelius sighed and stood, the lamps shuddering back into place.

At the outside wall, he cast a light in the palm of his hand, letting the golden glow spill across his fingers, bleeding away a little of his magic. It lit his image in the glass, blocking out the soft light of Amoria with his own dishevelled reflection. His hair stood half on end from where he'd pushed his hands through it, and even in the dim reflection he could see the dark mark of the scars on his face. They had itched ever since he'd seen Oriven, and when he reached up to touch them, he could feel that he'd rubbed his skin raw. The shame still burned even after all these years.

It was all of it too much. The artefacts and now the silwheat – Haelius had spent hours pulling down old Amorian texts in the library, and he'd found nothing to suggest even influencing anima was possible, let alone *draining* it. He had no clue, no understanding of what had happened. It felt like being adrift in the dark, nothing to anchor him, no idea which way was up. And in the dark lurked harder questions: who? *Why?* He couldn't stop thinking about Oriven's calmness, the way he'd refused even to consider that magic had caused the silwheat's death.

Who might benefit from a disruption of the status quo, Oriven had asked him.

Who, indeed?

He'd reached for the communication spell before he was even fully aware of what he was doing.

Larinne?

Haelius? I'm here. She didn't manage to keep her weariness from him, the exhaustion pressing down on him through their connection.

With a pang of guilt, Haelius realised he had no idea what time it was. *I'm sorry – did I disturb you?*

No. No, I'm up. There was a pause, and Haelius knew she'd be glancing around her immaculate apartment, looking for mess. *Do you want to come here?*

If you don't mind?

Come. I'll make tchai.

Larinne's rooms filled in around him, the shape of her home emerging from the patterns of magic he had used to bring himself there. He was immediately struck by the familiar scent, the smell of her – of spiced tchai and the dried jasmine flowers she bought from visiting merchants. Even after the events of the day, Haelius felt a sense of calm wash through him. It had been too long.

"It's the middle of the night," Larinne said by way of greeting, the side of her mouth curving up in that wry smile he loved.

"Sorry. I had no idea."

"I didn't think so. Come and sit down. You look the way I feel."

Instead, Haelius lingered by the dining table, watching her prepare the tchai. She handled everything so precisely, touching the glasses only with the very tips of her arched fingers. Her hair was down from its usual bun, so that the dark brown waves fell across her shoulders – she kept pushing it out of her face with an irritated sigh.

"You look lost," she said, turning back to him. She had two glasses of steaming tchai on a metal tray, the gold patterns on the glass worn away by frequent use.

"I feel it," he agreed. "How did we get to this?"

He looked down at the table, the weight of the day crashing back over him. On the table was the only mess in the whole apartment – a rudimenta board, abandoned in the final turns of a game. The shining beads of glass for earth were clearly winning, their dragon pieces already in play, despite the innate advantage of the opposing player who had chosen fire. Water and air remained in the defensive formation which showed that this had been a game of only two players.

"Dailem has been here," he said, his anger rekindling as he thought of Larinne's sister and her new allegiances.

"Mmm," mused Larinne, coming to stand by his side, setting the tray on the table. "Weeks ago now. I keep thinking she'll come back to finish our game, but, well ... I was losing anyway." She sighed. "Haelius, you mustn't be angry with her. Her goal is the same as ours – the safety of Amoria."

"Which part though?" he asked and knew he hadn't kept the bitterness from his voice.

"That isn't fair. Conflict between mages and non-mages helps no one. If it got out that a mage destroyed the silwheat, it could turn the non-mages against us."

Us, thought Haelius, and wondered which "us" he really belonged to. Unconsciously, he flexed the fingers of his left hand, trying to lose the pins and needles that so often weakened his scarred arm. It was a constant and damning reminder of what happened when he tried to answer that question.

"What's the alternative if a mage didn't destroy the silwheat?" he asked, instead. "That a non-mage did? How is that outcome better? Oriven has already stirred up plenty of hatred to the non-mages – and they don't have *magic* to defend themselves."

"I'm not saying we blame anyone—"

"But someone will be blamed. Someone *did* this."

"And we'll find out who." There was a hard edge to her voice now. "Dailem was just trying to give us time; she couldn't have known Oriven would do this."

Haelius stiffened. "Do what?"

"Goddess, you don't know, do you?"

"Know what?" Haelius felt like the ground had vanished from beneath his feet, and Larinne was the only one who could throw out a hand and keep him from falling.

"Oriven declared a state of emergency." She took a breath and blew it out slowly, as if she was trying to prepare herself as much as Haelius. "He convened an emergency meeting of the Senate today, and the Senate voted him in as 'High Consul'. He took control of the Senate, the council. All of it."

Haelius rocked on his feet, his fingers closing on the edge of the table. His scars felt tight on his chest, as if his skin was constricting, making it harder to breathe. "He can't do that. The Senate would have to give up their own powers."

"They're frightened." Larinne was no longer looking at him but wrestling with her own demons, her brown eyes burning gold in the lamplight. "They threw away their own power, and with it any chance they'd need to take responsibility for this mess. Cowards, all of them."

Haelius didn't know what to say. He thought of the Shiura Assembly, his father, what must be happening in the Majlis right now. His head reeled. There was no way they'd stand for this.

You have to stop this. There must be something you can do. All this power. He could flatten half of the buildings in the Central Dome or crack open the earth with a wave of his hand. Surely there was something he could do.

He felt Larinne's hand on his arm, gently tugging his hand away from his face; he hadn't even realised he'd been worrying at his scars again. "Stop that."

"Sorry, I— I need to go. I need to speak to my father, or . . ."

"Haelius, it's the middle of the night." Larinne's voice was gentle but firm. "There's nothing we can do right now." She took his hand and pressed the warm glass of tchai into it, closing her fingers over his. Haelius watched as if all of this were happening to someone else, someone far, far away from him. "Come and sit down. Get some rest. It's been too long since you were last here."

Neither of them had mentioned the subject of their previous fight, or the long weeks they'd gone without seeing each other. Haelius didn't know how to – how to apologise, or explain, or tell her how much he'd longed to see her.

He didn't have to.

"Come on, sit," Larinne said again, moving to her own armchair and gesturing to the one that was his. "It will be waiting for us in the morning. Just . . . let's just sit for a bit."

Haelius nodded and managed a weak smile, so grateful for her, for the safety of these rooms – the way Larinne could close the doors and shut out the rest of the world. But the weight of responsibility didn't leave their shoulders as they sat, both of them hunched forward, a heaviness to their every breath.

He couldn't keep himself from saying it. "What if Oriven did this?"

"You can't believe that," she said, but the hesitation, the way her eyebrows knotted inwards, told Haelius that she'd had the same thought.

"He has always needed to be at the top, always. When he couldn't do it with magic, he just found another way. Now he has everything he ever wanted."

"This will hurt all of us, mages as well as non-mages." Larinne looked away, rubbing her temples with the tips of her fingers. "Do you really think he's capable of this? I know how he was with you, but that doesn't mean . . ."

Haelius's fingers tightened on the arms of his chair. "It was never just me, Larinne. You just didn't see the worst of it. Non-mages are nothing to him, even the lower ranks of mages. They're irrelevant. He only concerns himself with how he can use us; components in a spell. Even the powerful only matter to him long enough for him to find his way to the top."

Larinne didn't answer, but Haelius knew she was listening, turning over every word. He waited.

"I just don't understand how this happened," she said eventually, sinking back into her chair. "Even if he is capable, *how* did he do it? Could anyone do this with magic? Could you?"

Haelius felt all his useless frustration come rushing back through him, compounding his failure. "No. But it *is* magic. There's no poison on Tokar that would do this." *There's nothing I know of that could do this*, he added silently.

"Be careful, Haelius. The more you insist this is magic, the more dangerous it becomes for you. If you accuse him, he'll only turn it back onto you. He's never forgiven you for being better than him, not when you're—"

"*Hollow-born*," Haelius finished, feeling his mouth twist, tugging on his scars.

"Someone who disproves everything he stands for." Larinne gave him a reproachful look, but she placed a hand lightly on his. Warmth spread down Haelius's arm like the prickle of magic. "What matters right now is finding out what happened. Maybe once we understand that, we can figure out who's behind this and, more importantly, stop them from doing it again. For now, we just need to hold Amoria together long enough to do it."

Haelius didn't answer, taking a long sip of the now cooling tchai and staring at the ghostly outline of Amoria's towers through the glass. He didn't know which of those tasks was more impossible: holding Amoria together or understanding the magic that was tearing her apart.

22

NAILA

The death of the silwheat brought an abrupt halt to Naila's lessons. Haelius had vanished into his work, his search for answers consuming every hour of his days – and probably nights as well.

Naila could hardly blame him. If Amoria had been unstable before, now it teetered on a knife edge.

"You need to stay here, inside our apartment," Dailem had said, her expression belonging as much to the intimidating Justice as to Ko'ani's mother. "People are frightened, tempers are high. Out of sight is out of mind."

"I can't leave?" Naila's mind had immediately conjured an image of the Dragon's Rest, its warm yellow light, the smell of Dillian's cooking. She'd hadn't been back once since that awful day when Brynda had turned her away. She'd told herself that she'd been staying away for their sakes, making their lives easier by keeping out of their way, but she knew she was still nursing a bruise from Brynda's words. She could have gone to the back door into the kitchen so many times, told them that she still thought of them, that she still hoped to come back when it was safe.

Now they were impossibly far away. "I have friends ... in the Southern Quarter. They're like family to me."

Dailem's expression had been sympathetic but uncompromising. "I'm sorry, Naila. Of all the places, the Southern Quarter is somewhere you absolutely must not go."

The days which followed were long, strange and lonely. She was left to study Haelius's books alone, with Ko out at her lessons at the Academy, Malek and Dailem working days which seemed to start earlier and finish later.

Without Haelius, studying magic was an impossible task. His books felt like a vast and impenetrable landscape; she could turn in any direction, start down any path, and only travel further from the knowledge she needed. She hadn't realised how much she'd relied on his guidance, how much she needed him there to mark her progress or pull her back onto a safer path. Without him, she was lost, unable to tell if she moved any distance at all.

It had been such a frustrating place for their lessons to end. After touching the obsidian artefact for the first time, Naila had returned to Haelius's study with the sense of her power living inside her. She knew what it *felt* like now, how it could move. She had expected to reach for the stone again and feel her magic stretch and respond, a new muscle she now knew how to control.

Instead, nothing.

She and Haelius had stood for hour after hour, the stone cold and dark in the palm of her hand, her power like a wall she could only push up against. It was all just the same as before, but worse – because now she *knew* the power was there, knew how it felt to have magic rushing to her fingertips.

Sitting up at Malek's table with books spread out across the glass, Naila felt the silence close in. She leaned on her elbows, her head resting in her hands, trying not to feel the despair welling up inside her. She just had to keep reading, keep her mind focused on something she could actually do. *Just one more sentence*, she told herself. And then, *just one more*. Over and over again. None of the words seemed to stick in her mind.

Naila?

She jumped and then grinned, unable to hide the dizzying rush of relief at the sound of Haelius's voice. *Haelius!*

As usual, his response to her excitement was slight bemusement, along with a small tinge of regret. *I'm sorry, I've been neglecting you. Things have been . . .*

I know.

Do you want to come to my study? He sent her the sense of his office in the Academy rather than his home, the shelves slightly less crowded, an untidy workbench to one side of the room.

In response, it was Dailem's warning about leaving the apartment which filled Naila's mind. She still found it so hard to guard her mind against the communication spell's connection, to draw a line between her feelings and his. She knew he'd be feeling every inch of her anxiety.

Ah was all Haelius said. Naila felt his dismay and wondered if he had meant to let that through, or if his own control was also less than perfect. *I can transport you here, if you'd prefer?*

Naila hesitated. She still hated the feeling of his travelling magic, the moment you were entirely unanchored from either place. Still, it was the safest way. *Okay. Do it.*

She stumbled a little as she arrived in Haelius's study, her stomach feeling like she'd left half of it behind. The wizard had stood to cast his spell, and now one hand was half extended, as if he was readying his magic to catch her if she fell.

"I'm all right," she managed, brushing his concern away with an irritated wave.

"You get used to it." He smiled and Naila scowled back at him. The scowl didn't stick, though; she was too glad to see him.

"I'm sorry I missed our lessons." He stood a little awkwardly, as if not entirely sure what to do with himself. "Believe me, I hadn't forgotten how important this is."

Naila made a sound that was somewhere between a laugh and a sigh of exasperation. "I know. You've had other things on your mind."

She found her gaze inescapably drawn to Haelius's workbench; there was a large bell jar on one side, part of a withered plant suspended beneath. Magic hummed around the glass, thick and unnaturally still. Inside the jar, the plant seemed to be disintegrating, fragments of its leaves trailing up and away from it as if it were dissolving into the very air.

"The silwheat," she said, and took half a step towards it, her gaze sliding effortlessly into the sight.

It only took her a second to see the true nature of the damage. It was impossible not to: there was an awful grey void where the anima and magic should be, the natural fabric of the world ending at the leaves of the plant. It looked like a tear in reality, a crack opening into the dreadful emptiness beyond. Naila's stomach turned, and she found herself taking a step back.

"It's ..."

"Gone," finished Haelius. He gave her an appraising look. "You know, a wizard of the Academy didn't see that immediately. Not me," he added, when Naila opened her mouth to ask. "Still, you're more sensitive to the arcane energies than you know."

"How did this happen?"

Haelius shrugged, his expression tired. "Your guess is as good as mine."

There was an unusual bitterness in his voice, making Naila turn back to him with a frown, seeing him properly for the first time. In the week since she'd last seen him he'd grown thinner than ever, and there were dark smudges under his eyes. He smiled at her worried expression.

"Come on, sit down," he gestured to the chair in front of his desk. "There's much we need to discuss, and none of it is about that cursed plant."

They both sat, Naila eyeing Haelius's desk with a frown. There were some unusual items set among all the notes and tools of spellcraft: a jug of water, cups of tchai, and even a small dish of nuts and dried chickpeas. Naila stared at them as if they were the strangest things she'd ever seen in the wizard's study.

"Returning the favour," he said, gesturing to the food with one hand. "Though ... well, I guess it's a small start."

Naila looked back to him with narrowed eyes. Something in Haelius's behaviour had triggered a small tick of worry at the back of her mind.

"There's no need to look so suspicious." He reached for one of the cups of tchai and blew across the top of it, as if he couldn't just have cooled it to the exact temperature he wanted. "I just think we should talk for a bit, before we start your lessons again. That's all."

"What's wrong?"

"Can't we just have some tchai for a . . ."

"*Haelius.*"

He sighed, defeated, closing his eyes for a moment before he spoke. "All right. All right. The truth is . . . well. The truth is, I'm not sure what to do next. Oriven is losing his patience, and we're running out of time."

Naila knew it, had known it for days, but to hear him say it was like having him reach into her chest and crush all her fears down into hard certainty. "But . . . with the stone? Shouldn't we be trying to make it work again, with the time that we have . . .?"

He made a gesture with one hand and the stone dropped onto his desk with a small *clunk*. "The obsidian artefact. You know, it doesn't respond to me at all." His smile was rueful. "I kept trying. For hours after you first touched it. There was a part of me that wouldn't accept that I couldn't make it work. There aren't many things of a magical nature that I can't influence in some way."

The unsaid words rang louder than anything else: if the great Wizard Akana couldn't touch its magic, why could she? Naila had a dreadful feeling she knew why.

"I'm not a mage, am I?" she said, her voice so quiet that it hitched on the words.

"I don't know."

She pressed her fingers against the edge of Haelius's desk, feeling like it was the only thing tethering her to reality. *You knew this*, she told herself. *You knew you weren't a mage. You always knew.* But she'd spent the last months letting herself believe that she might be.

"Is that why you want to stop trying?" She held her eyes shut, not trusting herself to look at the expression on Haelius's face. "With the stone? In case I'm something else? In case it's . . ." *bad*, her mind finished for her.

"No, no, of course not." When she finally made herself look, she found him watching her with a sad smile. "I'm not going to stop teaching you. I don't know if I could – I'm almost as desperate to understand this as you are. Mages and magic are just one small face of an enormous power. Here, in Amoria, it's easy to think this is all there is, because it's all we know – but there's so much out there that we *don't know*." There was a brightness to Haelius's eyes as he said this which made him look more like his usual self. "I might be a wizard, but I'm still a mage. All my knowledge is here, wrapped up in Amoria. I might not be showing you what you need to know. And the question remains, how am I going to placate the Academy?"

"You promised to give them a mage." Naila reached out to the obsidian, feeling it pull at her, drawing her always towards it. It was easier to listen to its call than it was to let herself hear Haelius's words; if the meaning of what he was saying caught up with her, all of this – her lessons, her life with Ko'ani's family – all of it would come breaking apart.

"I did."

Naila tightened her grip, feeling the shard's uneven edges digging into the palm of her hand. "We were so close." She could feel it, feel the part of her that had come alive that night. It was *right there*, her skin a thin border between her magic and the stone.

Naila's cup of tchai tipped over as if someone had pushed it, the brown liquid seeping out across the table, staining the edge of Haelius's papers and dripping onto the floor.

They both stared at it, neither one reaching to right the glass.

"Why did you do that?" Naila asked.

Haelius looked up at her with a frown and a small shake of his head. "It wasn't me." As realisation dawned on him, excitement lit in his face. "Naila, look!"

Naila didn't have to look – she could feel the warmth growing against the palm of her hand, the light of the stone spilling out between her fingers.

"Do it again." Haelius pushed his tchai towards her.

"But your desk . . ."

"Never mind the damn desk." He was on his feet already, and he used magic to sweep the top of the table clear, papers scattering out across the room. "Again."

Naila could feel it now: not magic exactly, but the water itself. She could feel the cup of tchai, its heat, even the steam as it coiled away. The water in the jug was a solid presence, cold and still, a mass which she could almost just reach and touch if she …

The jug tipped over with a *thunk*, water glugging out across the scratched glass. Naila had to stand and scramble away to avoid getting soaked, knocking her chair over as she did. Haelius laughed.

"You never do anything by halves," he exclaimed, delighted, standing over his soaking desk. He used his own power to stop the jug before it dropped onto the floor.

"I …" Naila stared at what she had done, her head reeling. She could still feel it, feel every drop of water, sense a single drip gather and plummet from the edge of the desk. It was overwhelming. "I did this?"

"You did." Haelius was at her side, though she hadn't heard him move. "Can you move the water on its own?"

Naila shook her head. "How? I don't know how."

"You do. Think, Naila, all those phonemes you learned. Push, pull, slow, harden. They're really just *ideas*. Concepts for what we can do. We use the words to help us control magic, but what matters is your will. Use the phonemes, their meaning, to shape that."

Naila drew a slow breath, in and out, closing her eyes so that she could better sense the shape of the water. She kept one hand closed tightly around the obsidian artefact, but the other she extended towards the desk, standing as she had seen Haelius do so often when he was casting. She felt faintly ridiculous, like she was a child pretending to be a wizard, but she made herself focus, emptying her mind of doubts and filling it only with the sense of the water.

Gather, she thought, remembering the shape of the phoneme in her mind. *Pull.*

The water shivered and Naila opened her eyes. Ripples were forming on the shallow pool, rolling towards her as if a breeze was blowing in from the other side of the room. The water began to creep across the desk, droplets beading up on the glass and merging together. When it reached the edge of the surface, it didn't run off the edge or spill onto the floor; instead, a long tendril of water snaked out into the very air, reaching out towards Naila's hand.

Naila gasped in surprise and her concentration broke, the water pattering to the floor, splashing both her and Haelius in the process. Haelius laughed again.

"You did it!" He gripped her arm in his excitement. "This is it – this is your power. I've never seen anything like it."

Naila blinked slowly, a little unsteady on her feet. She loosened her hold on the stone and felt the sense of the water recede from her awareness, centring her back in her own body.

"Is this magic?" she asked. "Do I have an affinity for water?"

Haelius let go of her arm, but he stayed close, half guiding her back towards her chair. "Not exactly. Here, sit, let me show you."

Naila saw the moment his sight changed, switching from seeing her to seeing magic. He turned his palms face up, fingers curled inwards, and began to move his arms in a wide, circling gesture, as if he were weaving the air together with his hands. As with Naila, the water on the floor and the table began to gather up into shining beads, drawn up out of the rug and even out from the hem of Haelius's robes. They rolled together like marbles, gathering into a shivering pool.

"Naila." Even through his magic, Haelius fixed his gaze on her. "Focus. *Look* at what I'm doing."

Understanding, Naila unfocused her eyes and switched her awareness back to the sight. Now she could see the complex patterns of magic the wizard was weaving together: he'd drawn on the magic in the water, in the air around it, combining it with his own power to wrap around and guide the water. The magic had slowed and hardened, used almost like a cup to hold the quivering mass together. Haelius's arms were always moving, and when he went to lift the water from the floor he kept circling one arm while he lifted the other, a faint line of concentration appearing in his forehead. He deposited the water back in the jug and then released his hold on the magic with a sigh; it was obvious that this was many times harder than what Naila had done.

"Do you see the difference?" he asked. "I used magic like a tool to move the water. You just . . . moved it."

Naila bit the edge of her lip. "But what does that mean?"

"Hang on." Haelius glanced around him, and then summoned

paper and pen to his hands, unconcerned that his possessions were still scattered across the floor. He sat opposite Naila and slapped the paper on his desk, drawing a large square in the middle of it, and then drawing an "x" from corner to corner, dividing the square into four triangles. In the top triangle, he drew the symbol for fire, then the one for earth, then water, then air, until there was a symbol in each quadrant. Then he labelled the corners where the "x" and the square intersected: between fire and air, he wrote "hot", between fire and earth "dry", between earth and water "cold" and between water and air "moist".

"The rudimenta, right?" he said. "The fundamental elements which make up all things, in one combination or another."

"The elements of dragons," Naila blurted out before she could stop herself.

"If you will." Haelius twitched an eyebrow. "There are some who believe that is where the rudimenta came from – that the power of mages is descended from ancient dragons, even though there's no real evidence they even existed."

He said it with such obvious disdain, but even the mention of the great elementals had sent a tingle of excitement up the back of Naila's neck, her ears filled with the sound of beating wings.

"And anima is the prime energy," Haelius continued, oblivious to the strange excitement bubbling beneath Naila's skin. At the centre of the x, he drew the symbol for anima. "Or the prime element, if you will. It makes up everything, defines everything."

Naila nodded. All of this was from the earliest lessons in magical theory, things she'd learned as a child.

Haelius drew a large circle around the square. "And this is magic. It's none of these things and all of them – a force that is both separate from and inseparable from anima." He saw Naila's confused expression and shook his head. "It doesn't matter. The point is, a mage can use magic, can alter it or move it to affect these." He jabbed his finger at the square. "But we cannot change the rudimenta, not really. I can affect property, but not substance. What you did was affect this directly." He pointed at the symbol for water.

Naila shook her head. "I don't understand. How is that different from an affinity for water?"

"Because you didn't use magic at all, Naila," Haelius looked up at her, and she felt herself pinned by his gaze. "You didn't reach for magic, did you? Affinity is just ... magic that is drawn to one element over another. My affinity is somewhere around here." Naila wasn't surprised when he pointed at the section for fire, his finger close to the line separating it from air. "I can make fire, but not without magic, and not without air or energy to ignite it. If I give it no fuel, it will burn through my magic instead. Do you understand? What you did was more like ..." and then he hesitated, staring down at the diagram he'd drawn, his face strangely blank. His eyes flicked towards the dead silwheat.

"What?"

"No ... I ... nothing, it doesn't matter. I was getting carried away."

Before Naila could press him, there was a sharp rap at the door. Haelius sat back and frowned. Interruptions were not unusual at his Academy office – there was always someone coming to ask Wizard Akana for help or advice – but there was no denying the urgency in that knock.

"Who is it?" called Haelius, eyeing Naila and clearly thinking the same thing she was – were they out of time?

"It's me," Malek's muffled voice came from behind the opaque glass.

Haelius's shoulders instantly dropped. "Come in."

But his smile vanished the moment he saw Malek's face.

"What is it?" asked Haelius, immediately alert. "What's happened?"

Malek's eyes flicked between Naila and Haelius, clearly unsure if he should speak in front of Naila.

Haelius stood. "She's not a child, Malek. If this affects her, too, she should know. Are you all right? Tell me what's happened."

"It's the silwheat," Malek answered, then swallowed to wet his throat. "The food shortages. Larinne hasn't managed to secure what we needed from Dahran – something has happened to the nearby towns."

Naila saw Haelius falter at the mention of Ko'ani's aunt. "Is she all right?" he asked, his voice strangely thin.

"She's fine. But Oriven fears the coming shortages, and so he's seized control of everything, all the food, the remaining glasshouses. The non-mages have been cut off, left with nothing. The Southern Quarter is rioting."

23

NAILA

Naila almost didn't hear what was said next. She watched the scene unfold as a series of unconnected images – watched Haelius take a step back and drop into his chair, watched Malek push a hand through his beard, watched her own fingers grow white as they tightened around the obsidian shard.

"How bad is it?" Haelius asked, his voice faint behind the ringing in her ears.

"I don't know. Dailem says the Justice are moving to secure the bridges. There's smoke visible from here. We could have conflict before the night is out."

Haelius closed his eyes and rubbed his hands over his face. "What do we do?"

"Nothing, my friend, there's nothing we can do. You know you can't go down there."

Naila was already stumbling to her feet, her hand shoving the stone into the pocket of her robes. Her legs felt numb, her movements disjointed, but she made herself turn and step towards the door as if she knew what she was going to do.

"Naila?" Haelius appeared in her path, blocking the way to the door. "Stop – where are you going?"

"Brynda and Dillian. They're family to me. I have to make sure they're okay."

Haelius stared at her as if she was deranged. "Oh, so you're just going to walk into the most dangerous part of Amoria, right now, in the middle of a riot?"

If anything, Haelius's reaction hardened her resolve. She met his blazing green eyes without flinching. "I have to. They could be in danger."

"Listen to me. These riots are happening because of actions by *mages*. Do you really think it will help if you turn up? You *look* like a mage."

"That's exactly why I have to go! Brynda *is* a mage."

That surprised Haelius enough that he faltered, and Naila used that moment to shoulder past him and head for the door. Malek stumbled to stop her, but before he could reach her Haelius had vanished and appeared in front of her again.

"Stop this, now," he hissed. "What can you possibly do to help? You're just putting yourself in needless—"

"Places are on fire. Maybe I can help put things out . . ." her voice trailed off as she thought of her new power, the obsidian shard heavy in her pocket. Maybe she could move the waters of the Aurelia? Redirect it to the buildings that were on fire?

Haelius seemed to realise what she was thinking. "Don't. Don't even *think* it. Your power is new, untried and untested. You have no idea what you can do or what strain it might put on you. No. I forbid it."

Naila lifted her chin, her face only an inch from Haelius's. "You *forbid* it?"

There was just a brief flicker to his gaze, before he narrowed his eyes and set his jaw. "Yes."

"You don't understand. Everyone you care about is a mage – they're all safe, here on this side of the city. I can't just hide up here in these lofty towers and forget about the people I care about. You have no idea what that's like!"

Out of the corner of her eye, Naila saw Malek grimace.

And then she felt it – Haelius's anger. The air in the room became charged, the hairs on Naila's neck standing on end. Haelius himself almost seemed larger, the magic a living extension of his skin.

"Don't I?" he asked, and Naila felt her breath catch in her lungs. "Then I suppose Mustashaar Akana is no relation of mine."

The realisation sank through her like a stone. "Oh" was all she managed to say.

"Oh," Haelius replied, his voice cold.

So much about Haelius finally clicked into place: he'd understood more about Naila's life than she'd ever realised. She'd never even asked him, she'd just assumed he'd always been a lieno, always on the path to becoming a wizard. There was still so much she didn't know.

Right now, though, it didn't matter. Naila took a deep breath and clenched her hands into fists.

"I have to go," she said, emptying her voice of anger. "I have to. If you want to stop me, then do it."

"You think I couldn't?" The unfamiliar ice in his voice made Naila shiver. "You think I couldn't hold you here?"

She knew he could. The memory of Celia Oriven's spell made her heart stutter and her mouth go dry. She took another breath and met Haelius's gaze. "Do it, then."

He stared back at her for three long heartbeats. Then he looked away, sighing with exasperation. Magic melted away from him, and Haelius diminished back into his usual self.

"Thank you," she said. She reached into her pocket and touched the metal disc he'd given her, knowing he would sense that connection. "I still have the artefact you gave me. I'll let you know as soon as I reach the Dragon's Rest."

"Let me know? Naila, don't be ridiculous. You're not going to walk into the Southern Quarter, and certainly not on your own." He shook his head. "In and out. As soon as we ascertain your friends are safe, we leave. No magic. No one can know we were there."

"Haelius, no . . ." There was a dawning look of horror on Malek's face. "Both of you, stop. Think about this for a minute. If the non-mages see a *wizard* in the Southern Quarter, do you know what they'll do? And if the mages think you're in any way associated with these riots . . . Haelius, there's no way this won't end in disaster."

"They won't know we're there. I promise."

It was the most complicated spell Naila had ever seen; she lost track of the movements of Haelius's arms, each careful positioning of his hands. He altered the pattern of the magic as if he stitched with a real needle and thread, working the intricate magic around Naila first and then himself. Naila felt the spell settle over her like a second skin.

When he was done, Wizard Akana was gone. In his place, Haelius stood wearing the short tunic and loose trousers common to non-mages in Amoria. His familiar high collar, the red and gold of his rank had all vanished. Even his scars were gone, the skin of his jaw smooth and even brown. Naila couldn't help staring. It felt wrong to her, like it wasn't really his face looking back at her.

Even more disconcerting, when Naila looked down, she found herself wearing similar clothing to Haelius, only she could still feel the shape and weight of the robes she'd borrowed from Ko'ani. When she reached to touch the fabric of the tunic, her fingers passed right through it, making Naila's head spin.

"Just an illusion," Haelius said. "Don't come too close to anyone and try not to look at it; I know it feels odd. The spell will last as long as I have magic to give it."

Malek touched Haelius's shoulder, unperturbed by his friend's transformation. "Please, Haelius, don't do this."

"We won't be gone long." Haelius gripped Malek's arm. "This gives me a chance to see what's happening down there – see if there's anything I can do to help."

"There *isn't* anything you can do. Don't reveal yourself. Just get in and out, as fast as you can."

"I will. I promise." Haelius let go and turned to Naila. "All right. I'll get us as close to the Dragon's Rest as I can, but I don't know that part of the city well, so I'm limited to where I can take us. Stay close to me. *No* magic, under any circumstance. And you must do everything I say. Understand?"

Naila nodded, her heart thumping against her ribs.

"Good."

*

They appeared next to one of the larger tributaries of the Aurelia, pressed in close to a building which would hide their arrival. The noise was immediate: the whole city trembled with a thunder of voices, punctuated by the high sound of breaking glass. The roar echoed down the streets, coming and going like the crashing of waves. Amoria had finally cracked open, splintering under the force of Oriven's grip. There were so many years of anger living in that sound.

Naila took a moment to lean against the cold stone of the building. While she recovered from Haelius's magic, he checked for anyone who might have witnessed their arrival. When he was sure no one had seen them, he paused, watching the thick smoke billowing towards the dome, curling against the glass until it was caught up in the city's circulation and drawn away.

When he turned back to Naila, Haelius's expression was grim.

"It's worse than I thought." He had to stand close and raise his voice for her to hear him. "I don't know how much more Amoria's magic can take – I've never seen it tested like this." He closed his eyes and gave his head a small shake, as if he was trying to keep away his own thoughts. "This is as close as I could get. The bulk of the crowds are concentrated near the bridges and the Adventus." For the first time, Naila could see Haelius's own fear hovering just behind his eyes, in the rigid set of his shoulders. "It's quieter here, but there are buildings on fire to the south. I don't know the Southern Quarter well enough to tell you what they are."

The Rest, Naila's heart cried out, but she bit down hard on that thought.

"Do you know where we are?"

"Yes. We're not far."

"Good." Haelius leaned in closer to her. "Listen. I know it might seem like I could easily protect us or get us away from here, but if I'm surprised, or too many people get in close to me, there's not much I can do. The transport spell takes my full concentration, especially if I'm moving someone else. This is dangerous, Naila. You must stay close to me and do exactly what I tell you."

For a moment, her resolve wavered.

It was too easy to think of Haelius as invincible, his magic untouchable. To be faced with his vulnerability was a new and different kind of fear. Naila nodded, pressing her lips together to keep them from trembling.

"Okay, good," said Haelius. "Lead the way."

He was right: the shouts they could hear were distant, the streets near them all but deserted. Even that was an alarming sight. Naila couldn't remember a time when she'd ever seen these roads without the bustling crowds. Empty windows peered into the streets like eyes. Every now and then, Naila would look up to find a frightened face pressed up against the glass. She kept to the shadowy edges of the main road and hurried down smaller side streets whenever their journey allowed it, keeping them out of Amoria's sight.

Behind her, Haelius was grim and silent, never letting himself get more than a step away from her. When she looked back, she found him with his attention halfway into the sight, using his magic to sense if anyone came near.

They crossed a bridge over a thin finger of the Aurelia, and the hollow sound of their footsteps were unfamiliar in Naila's ears. Ahead of them, the buildings opened up in a way she hadn't expected, the Amorian skyline falling away and exposing the curved glass of the dome above their heads. Everything about the empty district had felt so unfamiliar that Naila had ignored the sense of wrongness growing at the back of her mind. It had shadowed her steps ever since they'd turned off the main street, and now she was sure of it. She'd gone the wrong way.

The market square was only one street over from the Dragon's Rest, but it was exactly what Naila had been trying to avoid. Here the path of the riots was all too apparent. Carts and stands were smashed to rubble and kindling, one blackened stall still smouldering in the corner.

Worst of all, there were people. A group of five of them were still in the square, carving a path of pointless destruction. They were dressed in the way of non-mages, their clothes grey from the dust and lingering smoke. They hadn't noticed Naila or Haelius, but it was only a matter of time. One of the men stepped back and raised a hand towards a glass shopfront, shouting words that Naila couldn't quite hear over the din.

The flash of magic that followed, however, was unmistakable.

They were mages.

"What are you *doing*?" Haelius's voice carried across to them even over the distant roar of the crowds. The air grew tight with magic, all thought of secrecy evaporating with his anger. "What *is* this?"

They spun round to face him, each of them grasping at their own magic, ready to fight whoever challenged them, but they were tiny ripples before the mounting wave of Haelius's fury. She saw them glance between each other, saw the widening of their eyes. They were starting to realise whose power this was.

Haelius stepped around Naila. "Stay behind me."

"Haelius—"

"I know. I'm sorry."

Haelius's hands were held out from his side, magic crackling at his fingertips. Naila's heart was beating so hard she thought she might be sick.

Then something changed. Haelius felt it before any of them. The sense of his power shifted, and Naila saw him falter and look up.

The *crack* was so loud it rang through Naila's skull, yet what followed was worse: a sickening creaking, a grinding that hummed in her teeth, so loud it seemed like the world was coming down around them. The dome of Amoria was so far above their heads, so vast that it felt endless, but Naila could see a change in it, something shifting that should have been solid; something moving that should have been still. Before she understood what she was seeing, a sliver of blue sky appeared above their heads.

And then the glass fell.

Everything slowed. Naila could only stare as an enormous piece of the dome broke free, death reflected in every inch of its glass. The whole sky was plummeting towards them, and there was nowhere for them to run. Nowhere that would be far enough. Naila couldn't even breathe. They were going to die.

Haelius took three steps forward, each step gathering power. On the second step, his illusion broke, his robes spilling down around him. On the third, he lunged forward and thrust his arms upwards, sending forth a power so great that Naila felt her breath go with it. Every single thread of magic pulled down towards him, twisting around him like he was the eye of a mighty storm. He stretched his arms towards the glass, trembling with exertion, pushing back with all of his strength.

For a terrible moment, the glass kept tumbling towards them.

And then it stopped.

It froze, still high above Haelius's head, held by the force of his will alone. Naila could see the strain in every line of his body. Another surge of magic rolled in towards him, as if he'd taken a giant breath, and he let it out as a strangled cry between his teeth. Then the glass began to move back upwards, slowly, slowly, towards the hole in the sky.

If Naila had thought the illusion magic was complex, the magic Haelius used to repair the dome was beyond anything she could have imagined. His whole body became a conduit for power. He turned one foot, and Naila could see the magic around it lock into a complex array, phonemes carved in the pattern of magic itself. He moved his arms, and she could feel him reaching out, gathering the magic to him for the next part of his spell. And his reach was so far. Naila couldn't sense the end of it, sure that every mage in Amoria must be able to feel his pull on their magic.

She'd learned to fear Wizard Akana when she could feel the tremor of his anger, but she should have learned to fear the cold, the way the air grew icy and still as he stole every last bit of energy from it. If she thought she'd understood how powerful he was, she'd been wrong. *This* was why they called him the strongest mage of a generation.

As with all things, that strength took its toll; to draw on so much power had taken too much of his own. When at last the final sliver of blue sky was locked away, Haelius dropped his arms as if he couldn't hold them up any longer. He swayed and took an unsteady step to the side, his shoulders sagging. Naila wasn't the only one to see it.

Wizard Akana was defenceless. The mages were watching him;

the man who'd stood against them, a man they could never hope to fight, had suddenly lost all his strength. This was the only chance they'd have.

The first spell flew towards Haelius in a crack of white light. Somehow, he threw out one arm and cast the spell aside, pushing it away as if he were swatting away a fly. But his body followed the motion, and he lurched sideways as if he were going to fall. Before he could recover, the next mage hurled a fragment of broken stone, their magic propelling it through the air faster than Naila could move. Faster than Haelius could react. It slammed into his head with a sickening *thump*, and Haelius crumpled to the ground.

"Haelius!" Naila screamed. "No!"

They were turning their attention to her now, still readying their magic. They eyed the unthreatening white of her hem, their mouths sliding into smiles at their triumph over a wizard. A wizard who had just saved *all* of their lives. Naila felt the anger burn through her hotter than anything she'd felt before. She put herself in front of Haelius's prone body. They would not touch him again.

Plunging her hand into her pocket, she tightened her fist around the obsidian shard.

Water blazed into her awareness, the tributary of the Aurelia like a fork of white-hot lightning behind her. This was nothing like the jug on Haelius's desk – the river was a living thing, a channel of raw power. She had no idea if she'd be able to control it, but there was no time to doubt.

Naila sank her concentration into the water, her mind plunging into its turbulent depths. It pulled at her, the gurgling of running water filling her ears, slipping through her fingers. She seized onto it with everything she had.

Naila threw her arms upwards and a towering wall of water rose behind her.

The phonemes, a memory of Haelius's voice came unbidden to her mind. *Push, pull, slow, harden. They're really just* ideas. *Concepts for what we can do.*

Cold, she thought, clenching her teeth together. *Hard. Fast.*

She punched one arm forward, and a dozen shards of gleaming ice shot out from the wall behind her, hurtling towards the approaching mages. They were too fast for them to block, and at least one struck home, sinking deep into a mage's arm. His shriek of pain was almost enough to break Naila's concentration, but she thought of Haelius behind her and held tight to her control.

She'd startled them at least, scattered their concentration enough to interrupt their magic. They were starting to back away from her, to falter in the face of magic they didn't understand. *Again*, she thought, and another rain of arrows shot out from behind her, ice smashing up against walls and skittering across the ground.

The mages ran.

For a moment Naila stayed frozen, her arms raised, hardly able to believe what she'd done. Then she sagged with relief and felt the wall of ice collapse behind her. She went straight to Haelius's side. By some miracle, he was conscious, trying to push himself up onto his arms. Blood was dripping down one side of his face, splatting thickly against the ground.

"Haelius, Haelius we have to go." Naila looped her arms under his, trying to find a way she could pull him to his feet. She could feel his body trembling beneath her hands. "Come on, they'll be back any second. We have to go."

He looked up, but his eyes were glazed. "Where ..." he started, and then stopped, gritting his teeth against the trembling. "How far is the inn?"

"Just one street over. Not far. Come on, you need to get up."

"Get to the Rest." He grimaced with effort, his eyes fixing on her clearly for just a moment. He grabbed onto her arm with one hand.

"No!" Naila knew exactly what he meant to do. "Haelius don't—"

They appeared on the street outside the inn, just a few buildings down from it. The transport spell had taken the very last of Haelius's strength and he collapsed against the ground, cold and still. Panic seized Naila's chest. When she touched him, she gasped: his skin was like ice beneath her fingers.

"Haelius, Haelius, please wake up." Even the shivering had stopped.

She rolled him onto his back and his head tipped limply to one side. Blood had started to clot in his hair, thick and dark. He lay so still that Naila could hardly see him breathing. "Come on, please."

The Dragon's Rest was so close to them, solid and safe as always. Out in front of it, a crowd of people had gathered, all of them looking up towards where the dome had cracked, their faces painted white with shock.

"Help!" Naila shouted as loud as she could, her eyes searching for Dillian and Brynda in the crowd. "Please help us!"

It was the Ellathian priest who saw them first, his strangely pale eyes visible from halfway down the street.

Naila didn't care who came, as long as someone did. "Help! Please!"

Her heart plummeted when the Ellathian turned away from them, but he was only seeking out his Dahrani companion. He grabbed the other man by his arm, his mouth moving with hurried words Naila couldn't hear. Then the two of them were running down the street towards her and Naila felt herself sway with relief.

The Ellathian hesitated when he saw the red and gold on Haelius's robes, but to his credit, only for a moment. "What happened here?" he asked in accented Amorian, crouching by Haelius's side. He immediately pressed one of his immaculate white sleeves hard against the wound on Haelius's forehead and reached for the wizard's wrist with the other hand. "Gods almighty, he's cold. What in Ardulath's name happened to him? How long has he been like this?"

"Just a few minutes." The words tumbled out of Naila's mouth. "It's magical exhaustion. We were attacked. We . . ."

"We need to get him inside. Karameth, give me your scarf."

The Dahrani man pulled the red scarf from his shoulders without question and passed it down to the priest, who swapped it with his sleeve and continued to press it against Haelius's forehead. "Can you lift him?"

In response, the man crouched and lifted Haelius with ease, positioning him carefully and following every muttered instruction from the priest.

"All right, good. What about you?" Naila felt firm fingers close on her chin, tipping her face towards him. "Any injuries? Can you stand?" He didn't even try to hide the way he stared at Naila's strange eyes, his pale gaze peering into her dark one. Naila twisted herself out of his grip.

"I'm fine." She stood, ignoring the wave of dizziness that swept through her. "Please, I need to find Brynda."

"The landlady? She's just inside. Let's go."

Stepping into the Dragon's Rest was too much. So much of it was the same, the buttery yellow light, the sweet smell of wine and spices. And yet painted on top of that was a hushed and sombre atmosphere, people huddled into corners, their eyes down. They were seeking refuge today, not company. Naila could see visible signs of injury on some of them, cloth ripped into strips for bandages, a sharp smell of spirits on the air.

Brynda was the first one to spot her. "Naila? Goddess, Naila what in all the— why are you here, you stupid girl?" She was in front of Naila in an instant, her hands cupping Naila's cheeks, feeling across her shoulders and then wrapping her into a hug. Naila felt the dam she'd built inside herself start to crack, hot tears filling her eyes.

"Brynda, I'm sorry, I had to come." The first tears gathered and spilled over her cheek. "I had to see you were okay."

"We're fine, we're fine, shhh." Brynda was smoothing her back, but Naila felt her stiffen when the priest and the Dahrani came in behind her. "Your Holiness? What are you bringing into my ..." Her voice trailed off completely when she saw Haelius. "Goddess save me."

"Please, Bryn, you have to help him." Naila stepped back but kept hold of Brynda's hands, reluctant to let go of that familiar warmth. "He's used too much of his magic and ... and he's so cold. I don't know if he's going to be okay."

"Naila, a wizard?" Brynda's gaze slid back from Haelius to Naila, her eyes round. "What are you doing with ... Do you know what's happening here in the Southern Quarter? What was he even doing here?"

"He came with me." Naila could feel her voice rising. "He followed me because he didn't want me to come here alone. Did you see the dome? It was *him* who stopped it. He saved just about every person in the Southern Quarter. Please Bryn, I need a ..." Naila stopped herself from saying the word mage, but Brynda glanced anxiously around the common room anyway. "You know what he needs."

"That was him?" Naila heard the priest suck in his breath behind her. "Gods, that's some kind of power."

Brynda was biting hard enough on her lip to draw blood. "Just ... come on, come upstairs."

Together, they barely all fitted into the small guest room. The Dahrani Karameth laid Haelius down on the bed and then stepped back out to the landing, carefully keeping himself out of everyone's path. The priest stayed by Haelius's head, his hand still pressing firmly down on the scarf. Despite the red fabric, Naila could see the blood soaking steadily through it. *This is my fault*, she thought, unable to look away from where the blood stuck to Haelius's face and hair, the damp pallor of his skin. She perched on the edge of the bed, her hands curling into the blanket, desperate for his eyes to open, her heart aching to tell him how sorry she was.

"How bad is it?" she asked, her voice barely above a whisper.

"This bit isn't as bad as it looks," said the priest, not unkindly. "Head wounds almost always look worse than they are. I'm more worried about this cold. Kara, can you get my bag from downstairs? And get the innkeep to bring us something warm. More blankets."

Karameth nodded and headed to the stairs without a word.

"I'll go and help." Brynda tried to follow him.

"No, Bryn, wait." Naila locked eyes with her. "It's magical exhaustion; you know that's not all he needs. Please, can you help him?"

Brynda's eyes flitted to the priest and then back to Naila, deep lines forming at the corners of her mouth.

"It can't wait or I wouldn't ask," Naila pleaded. "You're the only mage I know of in the whole Southern Quarter right now." The priest flinched but blessedly said nothing. "I can't do it. Please, a little of your magic could bring him back from the worst of it. I ... this is my fault. Please."

Brynda was still chewing her lip, but her fingers loosened on her apron. "I don't know if I can, Naila. He's a wizard. I barely have enough power to light the stove." She stepped towards the bed and closed her fingers around Haelius's wrist. "Goddess but he's cold. This is the worst I've ever seen it."

Naila tried to swallow past the tightness in her throat.

"*Visdo tribuo.*" Brynda murmured the words, closing both of her hands around Haelius's scarred wrist. Naila felt the gentle whisper of her power, felt the small channel of magic slip through Brynda and into Haelius. Leaning forward, Naila kept her gaze fixed on his face, desperate for his eyes to open.

Haelius drew a sudden, deeper breath, looking for just a moment as if he might wake, but then the trembling began again. He didn't open his eyes.

"Good," said the priest, reaching out to touch Haelius's cheek with the back of his hand. "The shivering is good. It might shake off some of this cold."

"Entonin." Karameth was looming in the doorway, holding a skin of water out towards him, and a moment after Dillian pushed past him with a bowl of steaming water.

"Hello, trouble." Dillian managed a quick smile at Naila, before he set to helping the priest make Haelius as warm as they could. They tucked the skins in against his side, and heaped blankets over his robes, covering him up to his chin.

Once the priest had his bag, he made quick work of Haelius's injury. He had the deft hands of a healer, and he cleaned the blood away and dressed the wound with a practised efficiency. Naila watched her friend's face slowly emerge from behind the caked blood and the clotted hair. He looked just a little more like himself, though his skin was still a sickly, ashen grey.

Brynda watched, too, her hand wrapped tightly around Naila's. "I did what I could," she said, almost as if it were an apology. "I just don't have any more to give."

Naila gripped Brynda's hand back in answer.

"Well, that's about all I can do for him." The priest stood and stretched, his hands on his lower back as he bent to assess his work. "The wound itself isn't so bad, but he's had a nasty knock. Someone should stay with him."

"I will," Naila said immediately.

"And the cold ... I don't know." The priest waved his hands in a gesture Naila assumed meant magic. "I don't understand any of this. If it's anything like normal hypothermia, I think he's through the worst of it. Keep him wrapped up and warm, and hopefully it should pass."

Naila nodded, unable to quite find the words to thank him.

"Thank you," Brynda did it for her. "Dill, will you see our guests get everything they need?"

"Of course. Anything you need is on us, Your Holiness."

On his way out, Dillian ruffled Naila's hair and gave her the full warmth of his smile. In answer, Naila felt her mouth twist down, tears pricking at her eyes.

"Don't cry, little thief, and definitely not over a wizard."

"He's the good one," Naila said, hoping Dillian would remember their conversation all those weeks ago – about the wizard who had saved the man at the march, the Surveyor who'd defended her, the one who had been protecting her all that time. All of them had been Haelius.

"Ah. Well, I'm glad you found him. He'll be all right, you'll see. Don't think these wizards are so easy to do away with."

Naila just nodded, her lips pressed tight, not trusting herself to speak.

She couldn't keep it in. When it was just Naila and Brynda, Naila felt herself cave in under the full force of her tears.

"It's my fault." The sobs heaved out of her. "I made him come. He told me not to. I had no idea ... I just wanted to see you." Naila found herself leaning into Brynda, letting herself bend towards that comfort in a way she never had before. If Brynda was surprised, she didn't show it; she just tightened her arms around Naila and let her cry.

Naila didn't know when she'd fallen asleep, but she woke to a sharp rap on the door. The last of the light had gone, the world diminished to blue shapes and grey shadows, Haelius just an outline beneath the blankets.

Naila sat up and pressed her hands to her eyes, before she called out, "Who is it?"

"It's me." Naila could immediately hear the anxiety in Brynda's voice. "Someone is here – they're asking for Wizard Akana."

Naila hardly had time to feel the knot of panic, before the door was shoved open and whoever it was stepped right around Brynda and into the room.

"*Igni*," came an impatient female voice, and the lamp by the bed flared up with yellow light.

The woman who glared down at Naila was tall and thin, all sharp angles and narrow, hawkish features. Naila could see a little of Ko'ani and more of Dailem in her face, in the prominent cheekbones and high forehead, all the more severe because this mage wore her hair tied back in a tight bun. Naila had no doubt as to who this was.

"Lar . . . Lieno Tallace," Naila scrambled to her feet, too hopeful that Larinne could help to feel the fear she ought to in front of a senator. "Please, he's used too much magic, hours ago, and he's still cold. He needs your help."

Larinne had already shifted her gaze to Haelius. Without a word to Naila, she perched on the very edge of bed and reached beneath the blankets for Haelius's hand, drawing it out and into her lap. "*Visdo tribuo*," she whispered.

The spell barely resembled what Brynda had done. The magic rushed from Larinne's hands into Haelius, as bright to Naila's eyes as the lamplight. Haelius stopped shivering almost instantly, colour flushing through his skin as if Larinne had breathed life itself back into him. In a way, Naila supposed, she had. His breath evened out, his body relaxed back against the pillows.

"Haelius, you fool," said Larinne, still holding onto his hand. She huffed out an irritated sigh, but the expression on her face had softened with such tenderness that Naila finally understood why Haelius startled every time someone said Larinne's name.

"He's just sleeping now." Larinne turned her sharp gaze back to Naila, and all the softness in her face had vanished. "Sit. I need you to tell me everything that happened."

24

LARINNE

Larinne listened to the girl's account of what happened with the thud of her heart in her ears. Every detail of Naila's story was another clarifying drop of dread. Larinne had seen the dome crack, had heard the gut-wrenching sound of the glass breaking free, but it was another thing to hear what it had been like to stand beneath it, to know with certainty that it would have crushed half the Southern Quarter. The only comfort was the warm weight of Haelius's hand in her lap, and Larinne tightened her grip on it, brushing her thumb over the back of his fingers. *He's safe*, she told herself. *You got here in time.*

Throughout her account, the girl's eyes shifted about the room, never quite looking directly at Larinne. Her gaze fixed on Haelius more than once, and every time it did her expression wavered at the edges. It was clear how much she cared for him.

Larinne had been determined to dislike her. It would have been easy to – she'd caused enough trouble for her friend. Her unteachable magic had put Haelius in the most precarious position Larinne had ever seen him, and yet she knew exactly how little of it would have been this girl's choice; there'd been no chance of a quiet life in Amoria for her. Even her appearance singled her out: those eyes so dark Larinne couldn't see her pupil against the black of them, and the oily sheen of her hair, somehow so different from the darkest brown of an Amorian, or even a Dahrani.

It took a great deal of effort and reassurance to send her away. The girl's skin looked thin and washed out, and she was swaying slightly where she stood; more than anything, she needed food and rest. In the end it was the stern expression of Lieno Tallace that sent her away, Larinne frightening her into looking after herself.

Alone, Larinne had nothing to keep her own grief away. Her hands tightened around Haelius's and she tried not to think of how close she'd come to losing him. It was the worst magical exhaustion she'd ever seen. Magic always took its greatest toll on those with the greatest gift – it was life and warmth, as well as power; if he let it, the vast flood of Haelius's magic could drag every inch of him with it.

His hair was stuck to his forehead, still damp from where someone had cleaned his face. Larinne brushed it back with the tip of her fingers, careful not to touch the bandage or the dark, swollen skin around it. He looked so frail and small beneath the heaped blankets, as if it would take only the smallest tug to drag him away from her. There was nothing she could do to stop the memories which swelled in her like a rising tide. The years melted away and she was back at his side the last time she had seen him like this, when the burns on his skin had been angry and new.

Before the accident they had been— what, exactly? Something. Too young, for one thing; near enough to children. She'd been the only one who could make the sullen boy from the Adventus smile, who could get that proud mask to slip long enough for his mouth to draw to one side, a slight dimple in his left cheek, his eyes the colour of leaves in sunlight. But Oriven had hounded him even then. He'd plagued Haelius's days in the Academy, daring a hollow boy to prove he belonged there. Eventually, Haelius had decided to prove not only that he belonged there, but that he had more power than their entire class combined.

After the fire, she hadn't been able to see him for weeks; at first because he'd been kept unconscious through the worst of the pain, and later because he refused to see anyone, including her. When at last she'd forced her way back into his life, she'd sat exactly like this – perched on the edge of his bed. Only when she'd reached for his hand, he'd snatched it away from her, turning his head so that she couldn't see the burned side of his face.

"Haelius?" He'd given her no answer. "Haelius, come on. Look at me. You don't know how hard it was to see you."

"You shouldn't have come."

Larinne had tried to smile through her surprise. "Well, when has that ever—"

"No, I'm serious." He'd turned back then, revealing the full extent of the burns on the left side of his face. There was gauze over his cheek and jaw, but Larinne could see that the wound was still seeping through the fabric, the skin underneath wet and raw.

Haelius's eyes were flat, almost grey, and Larinne flinched away from the anger she saw in them.

"See?" he hissed. "Look at what I did. I'm dangerous, Larinne. Allyn was right. You should stay away from me."

"It was an accident—"

"It was me. This is what I am." The air in the room had changed: charged, humming with power. Haelius's eyes widened with a desperate, almost wild look. "Do you feel that? Even now. Even now, when all I want is to swallow this power and keep it from ever rising to the surface, it keeps coming. I'm lucky not to be locked up with the mages who can't learn control. You should go. Get away from me. Go."

And she'd gone, when she should have stayed.

Now, Larinne kept hold of his hand in a way she couldn't do for him before.

Part of her ached to let him sleep, knew that he needed every minute of it, but she couldn't wait any longer; no amount of rest would save them if there was still a chance the dome would come down on their heads.

She pressed a hand against his shoulder and shook him gently. "Haelius, wake up."

When he didn't stir, Larinne felt a sudden beat of fear and gripped his shoulder more tightly. "Come on, Haelius, wake up."

His eyelashes fluttered and he groaned.

"I'm sorry," she said, though she felt a giddy relief to see him move. "I need you to wake up."

"Larinne?" He blinked blearily up at her, his fingers tightening on hers. "Where am I? What happened?"

"The dome." She made herself press her own feelings down, cloaking herself in a cold practicality. "It broke. A part of it nearly crushed the Southern Quarter. You stopped it, repaired it, and nearly ended yourself in the process."

"The dome!" Haelius sat up too quickly and all the blood drained from his face, leaving his skin the colour of old parchment.

Larinne caught his chest against her hand, steadying him. "Slowly. You've taken a bad knock to your head. It's okay – you stopped it, you repaired the glass."

Haelius closed his eyes and nodded once, and then immediately grimaced at the pain.

"I'm sorry to do this," Larinne pressed on, "but I need you to tell me if we're in danger of it falling again. Do we need to evacuate the Southern Quarter – or the dome, even?"

For too long, Haelius didn't reply. He sat with his eyes closed, and Larinne knew he was centring himself, remembering, considering his answer before he spoke.

"I think we're safe," he said at last. "Or as safe as we can be. There are protections in Amoria's glass, magic which no one now would know how to cast, let alone break. There was something wrong with the part that fell, an erosion." He winced as if the effort of remembering hurt him. "When I repaired it, I reconnected it to that magic. If anyone can break that, then it's not just the central dome we need to worry about."

All Larinne's breath left her at once, her shoulders sagging beneath the weight of her relief.

"Naila!" Haelius's eyes snapped open and he leaned forward again as if he meant to push past her and stumble out of bed.

"She's safe." Larinne increased the weight of her hand on his chest. "She's downstairs. She stayed with you until I got here – it took some effort to force her to leave your side."

His breath shuddered out of him and he curled forward, his forehead resting against her shoulder. "Thank you."

"I'm sorry I woke you; I had to know." Now that she had nothing else to hide behind, she felt the full force of her fears for him return at once, an ache right beneath her sternum. "You should rest. Here, let me help you."

"No." His fingers twined tighter around hers. "No, I'm okay."

"You're *not* okay. What were you thinking? This was ... I can't even imagine what you thought you were doing. This was a monumentally stupid plan."

"It wasn't actually my idea."

"*Haelius.*"

"I know. I can hear myself."

She could feel the silent shaking of his laughter through her shoulder, and she wondered if he could hear the thundering of her heart. It was as if this – everything – had removed the last fraction of distance between them. A distance that never should have been. Did it really take almost losing him to get here?

"No, listen, I'm serious," she pressed him.

Haelius lifted his head from her shoulder, and Larinne immediately missed the weight of it. The warmth. Instead, she met his gaze. They were so close she could see the flecks of brown in his eyes, the slight lines in his forehead.

"Haelius, I almost lost you." Larinne's heart was in her voice now, she could hear it – knew he would hear it too. "I can't— I ..."

His eyes softened, tracing over her face like fingers brushing across the strings of an oud. His breath deepened, and Larinne felt aware of every inch of movement, as if the air between them changed with each breath.

Then he wrenched his gaze away.

There it was again, the wall that he always pushed between them. This time, at least, he didn't pull his hand away.

For a while they sat in silence, Haelius with his eyes closed, Larinne unfocused, gazing down at their linked hands.

She started when he cleared his throat.

"I don't ..." He swallowed. "I don't remember how I got here. I remember the dome breaking, the magic to repair it, but then ... There were mages in the square – Oriven's people acting like rioters."

"Naila said. They waited until you repaired the dome, and then they went for you." The anger simmered in her blood, burning the rest of her feelings away. "They waited until you were weak and then attacked."

Haelius was touching the bandage with his other hand, feeling out the edges of his injury. "I don't remember. Did I get us away?"

"No. Naila did."

"What? How?" His gaze snapped back to hers.

"She defended you. Used her power to scare them, I think. Haelius, I didn't know you'd managed to teach—"

"No," he interrupted her, his eyes growing wide. "No, no, no, no."

Larinne didn't think it was possible for Haelius to go paler, but he did.

"What is it?" she asked. "You're both here, you're both all right. Naila's okay."

"No, you don't understand." Haelius's expression was desperate. "No one can know. No one can know what Naila's power is. Least of all Oriven."

Larinne just shook her head, waiting for him to explain.

"It's the obsidian shard – the artefact I took from Oriven. That was the key to Naila's power. If he realises … If they saw what she can do— Goddess, Larinne, it might already be too late."

25

ENTONIN

Entonin was early to breakfast. Most of the tables around the common room lay empty, and the staff of the Rest were still busying themselves with the morning cleaning. It wasn't yet the hour of Ardulath, or the eighth bell, or whatever these mages called the first hour of the god of knowledge.

Of course, it wasn't just the early hour which meant the common room was deserted. Even the street was near enough empty, which was another warning he really should have heeded sooner; any traveller with even a lick of sense had fled Amoria long ago, and even the ones without any sense had gone after the dome cracked. It was long past the time for Entonin to do the same, and he wondered what it said about him that he hadn't yet put the glass city far behind him. Failing the temple of Ardulath was no easy thing to live with, but it had to be better than the possibility of not living at all.

The clack of a bowl being set in front of him was the first Entonin knew of the landlady's arrival, and he utterly failed to hide his jolt of surprise.

"Lovely Mistress Brynda," he greeted her, the cheer in his voice sounding false even to his own ears. "Good morning."

"Breakfast, Your Holiness," she answered simply, as if the events of the previous night had been nothing but a strange dream.

"Entonin, surely," he tried with a sly smile. "Surely we've been through enough together that I might be counted among one of your regulars."

He found himself studying her, looking for some difference, something that would have given her away if he'd seen it before, but she looked the way she always did: almost Ellathian, with a heart-shaped face and olive skin, the curl of her hair already escaping her tight plait. Entonin had liked her, until he realised what she was. It was hard to take the image of this handsome, likeable woman and overlay it with the word *mage*.

She studied him back, her eyes lingering on his robes; it was her who'd washed away the blood of the wizard they'd saved together. Even unconscious, there'd been no mistaking what *he* was.

"All right, Sidi Entonin," she relented, using the respectful Dahrani address, her tone still guarded. Entonin wasn't even sure it was a step in the right direction.

"Any sign of my sullen companion yet this morning?" he asked, changing the subject.

"Not yet." That finally wrung a small smile from the edge of her mouth. If all else failed, it seemed making fun of Karameth was a universal language.

Entonin smiled back, despite the sudden pattering of his heart. Karameth's bed had been empty when Entonin woke, the mattress creased and dimpled with the mercenary's outline. They'd argued most of the night, Karameth insisting with increasing vehemence that they needed to get out of the city. Entonin hadn't considered that he might actually leave without him.

At that moment, the door of the inn slammed open, yanking on Entonin's already frayed nerves. His irritation was quickly replaced with a horrible, yawning dread when four Surveyors entered the room. They were dressed head to toe in black – though with the formless robes and awful masks, Entonin couldn't be sure they had either. They stepped in line with each other, creating a black wall between him and the exit. Looking beneath their hoods, the concealing magic made it feel like peering down into a bottomless pit, only it pulled you towards it as if you'd already lost your footing. For a moment, his mind believed it would happen, his body tipping forward at the edge of a terrible fall.

The landlady pressed herself right back against the table, her fingers gripping the edge of the stone until they were white.

"Surveyors," she said, her voice frightened and small. She bowed with only her head. "How can we help you?"

As if their distorted voices were not terrifying enough, the words they said were worse. "Stand aside. We're here for the priest."

"What, me?" He'd meant it to sound casual and bemused, but his voice came out as if they already had their hands around his neck.

Everything in him wanted to run. The room resolved into startling clarity: the small gap to the left of the Surveyors, the exit he knew lay out the back, the hard shape of the dagger concealed beneath his robes. But what use was any of it? None of that could help him in the face of magic.

Ardulath protect me.

"Priest of Ellath, please come with us. If you resist, we will restrain you."

Entonin felt a flicker of anger, and he grabbed onto it with both hands. "Come with you? For what? Don't you need to tell me that?" Silence. "Do you know who I am? I'm Entonin tyr Ardulath. A Seeker of the high temple of Ardulath. That's a priest, of the Holy Ellathian Empire – you see the robes, right? Have you any idea what that mea—"

"Will you resist, Entonin tyr Ardulath?" was the only answer he received, the modulated voice sounding like someone was speaking to him from underwater.

"*I* won't, but you'd better believe that if anything happens to me, my temple will. The Seekers are protected by a sacred contract", but even as Entonin said it, he knew that contract existed with Dahran, and Brevin, and just about every nation except Amoria, because when had the priests of Ellath last had dealings with the mage city?

Two of them stepped forward and yanked him to his feet, their fingers pressing into his arms so hard that he could feel his skin bruising. It was strangely disorientating to acknowledge there were people under those uniforms, someone solid and real with a beating heart just like his own.

"The Dahrani?" said another of their watery voices.

"He left this morning," the landlady answered quickly, "with his bags. Paid us his coin. He's already gone."

That bastard, thought Entonin, stumbling ahead of his captors, a hand pushed into his lower back and thin bands of gold magic snaking around his wrists. Somehow, that final betrayal sank deeper than everything else. He hadn't really believed that the mercenary would just leave him to his fate.

The cell they pushed him into was entirely sandstone: it was probably the least glass Entonin had seen in the whole of Amoria. A single torch in a metal bracket was the only light, flickering with a not-quite-natural life of its own, the colour of the flame just a shade away from what it should be. The bars, too, were *almost* what you'd expect in any prison. They were thick metal, iron or something similar, but if you looked close enough you could just make out a sketching of strange symbols carved into them, some of them embossed in copper or silver. Entonin didn't have to be a mage to see the magic in every line of this room.

A Surveyor followed him into the cell, standing so close that Entonin could feel him like a pressure at his back. The air was stagnant and too still, depleted by every breath. *We're underground*, thought Entonin, and somehow that knowledge made everything worse.

The Surveyor clicked a heavy metal collar around his neck, which pinched Entonin's skin and made his eyes water.

"This will prevent the use of any magic," said the Surveyor.

"Along with the fact I don't have any," Entonin snapped back. He lifted his chin, trying to stretch his neck, but the movement only made him more aware of the restriction. "I'm a priest, gods damn it. Don't you remember what Ellath does to mages?"

The Surveyor didn't dignify this with a response. He stepped out of the cell, finally freeing Entonin from his suffocating presence, and carefully enunciated a single word that Entonin didn't understand. In response, the door of the cell clanged shut and the gold bands on his wrists evaporated into insubstantial light. It all felt a little too final.

He knew it would make no difference, but once he was alone he stepped up to the door of his cell and shook it hard enough that his body rattled instead.

"Let me out, you fucking godless heathen bastards!" He threw all his anger up against the immovable gate. "The Sallow Lady take all of you! No, I hope you rot under the sky and the Sallow Lady never comes to claim your souls." He slammed his shoulder one more time against the bars, and then let himself slide slowly down to the floor. "Gods *damn* you."

Entonin had no idea how long he'd been sitting on the floor of his cell, but it was long enough that his shoulders had begun to hunch and his back ached. Every time he tried to stretch, he felt the collar against his skin, as if it tightened on his neck with every movement.

Apart from the protests of his body, there was nothing else to mark the passing of time – no natural light, no sound of the city's bells. It could be the middle of the night and he'd know nothing about it. *What a dark heart lies under all that glittering glass*, he thought bitterly.

Aloud, he recited one of the acclamations of the hours, keeping his own time. "Lead them from the dark," he whispered to the empty room, as if it might drive back some of the shadows. "The hour of Ardulath is upon us."

The sound of the outer door creaking open made him jump before he could master himself. Like the Surveyors, the woman who entered was dressed all in black, except for the thick gold embroidery that marked her as the highest rank of mage. She, however, wore no mask or shrouding aura of concealing magic.

"Oh, thank the gods, a person with a face," remarked Entonin, staying seated on the floor.

And what a face. She had a wide, sloping forehead and sharply pronounced cheekbones, making her face severe but unmistakably striking. She was the quintessential Amorian, her light brown skin a shade darker than the wizard's or even the landlady's had been, but still pale enough to suggest a lifetime behind glass. Her hair fell over one shoulder in waves of chestnut and russet brown, though there was nothing untidy about it; everything about her appearance was as rigid and regimented as her uniform. Under somewhat different circumstances, Entonin might even have found her attractive.

"Entonin tyr Ardulath," she said, pronouncing each word carefully and precisely. "You carry the name of a god."

"So do most of us who join His family. And you are?" he asked, still not getting up. "You find me at a disadvantage."

She smiled, but the expression didn't reach her dark eyes. "I am Justice Dailem Tallace."

"I'd say 'pleasure to meet you' but I think we both know that's horseshit."

"You're a long way from home, priest." She came to stand outside his cell, considering him, her arms folded across her chest. "What brings you to Amoria?"

"I wasn't aware there needed to be a reason to enter Amoria."

"Perhaps for an Ellathian priest, there does."

Entonin felt suddenly exhausted. "Look, can we just skip to the part where you accuse me of whatever it is you want to accuse me of?"

"No one's accused you of anything – yet. I just want to ask you some questions."

"Well, good, because believe it or not, I'm not your enemy."

"Let's start simply, shall we?" She raised one black eyebrow, her expression revealing nothing. "You're staying in the Dragon's Rest in the Southern Quarter, correct?"

As if they didn't know his every move from the day he'd stepped into Amoria. "Correct. Nice place. Food was good back when Amoria had such things, though a bit too much fish for my taste. Is this some kind of test?"

She gave no reaction. "And how long have you been staying there?"

"Gods, Ardulath only knows. Three months?"

"That's a long time to stay in an unfamiliar city." The way she said unfamiliar made it sound like she really meant to say another word entirely. Unfriendly, maybe, or outright hostile. "What have you been doing for all that time?"

"Drinking, mostly. Do you want a day-by-day account, or hour-by-hour?"

Her dark eyes seemed to glint in the torchlight, but Entonin couldn't tell if he'd managed to rile her.

"Why don't I start by telling you what I know?" she said evenly. "For the first time in hundreds of years, an Ellathian priest – from the very order who murdered mages and drove them into exile – appears in our city unannounced. Around the same time, there are several attacks on Amoria, each of them using a type of magic this city has never seen before. These attacks strain existing relations between our councils, and this priest uses the opportunity to meet repeatedly with the Shiura Assembly. I am reliably informed the Assembly sought a deal in which Ellath would support them exclusively, particularly in the case of any conflict against mages. Any of this sound familiar to you?"

Entonin swallowed, feeling his throat graze against the strangling hold of the collar. Laid out like that, it didn't exactly sound good. "Well, for a start, it wasn't *my* order who drove the mages out of the Empire. The priests of Trebaranus did that." *We just told them to do it.*

The unnatural torch flickered in its bracket and cast leaping shadows across her face, lending false movement to her expression. She waited.

Entonin wetted his lips. If she waited long enough, his temper was likely to do her work for her. Instead, he drew a slow breath, calming his mind as if before prayer. "It's not what you think. Did you know that I've been trying to meet with the Lieno Council since the day I arrived?"

Silence. But Entonin was sure he saw the slight widening of her eyes. She hadn't known.

"Do you know what I am?"

"A Seeker," she answered instantly. "A spy."

Entonin had to bite down on everything he wanted to say to that. "An envoy. A representative of my people. An ambassador. We seek knowledge, yes, but we also seek allies."

"And manipulate foreign courts, sabotage any who would oppose you and pave the way for your empire. Yes, I know what you are, priest."

"I came to make *peace* with the Lieno Council. Amoria was, is, a growing influence in Omalia. Ellath could no longer afford to ignore that. I came to test the water, to see whether the councils would be open to receiving a more *official* envoy from my people. I guess we know the answer to that now."

It was most of the truth, though the reason he was there had less to do with Amoria's influence and considerably more to do with the sabre-rattling of the Temple of Trebaranus.

"You can't expect me to believe that." She almost *laughed* at him. "A priest seeking to ally with mages? Are we just supposed to forget our bloody history? The thousands of mages that you've killed? And I suppose your secret meetings with the Shiura Assembly were all in aid of peace as well."

"What about them was secret?" Getting through to her was like shaking the metal gate of his cell. "You wouldn't speak to me! I met with the council that *would*. We talked of trade, of a future relationship. I agreed to *nothing* about standing against mages."

"And you expect me to believe that?"

"If you think that a priest of Ardulath would willingly lead Ellath towards war, you know *nothing* about my people. I would be handing the priests of Trebaranus a bloody crown. While Ellath is at peace, it's the priests of *Ardulath* who rule."

This, at least, gave her a moment of pause.

"And yet," she said. "You were in the Southern Quarter during the riots and breaking of the glass—"

"Where else would I be? I was saving the life of one of your damn wizards!"

"—and there's the matter of this magic, unlike anything ever seen in Amoria, or in the nations who send their mages here to study."

"Magic?" Entonin sat back, unable to comprehend how someone could know so little about his people. "Are you honestly suggesting an Ellathian *priest* knows anything about magic?"

"Your priests have their miracles."

Entonin's mouth opened but no words found their way out. He felt strangely sick, as if someone had told him that left meant right. "Miracles are *not* magic."

He was saved from her answer, as the outer door creaked loudly open again. There was a scraping, scuffing kind of sound, along with grunts of exertion as if something – or someone – was being dragged across the floor. Then four Surveyors stepped into the prison, wrestling a large man between them. They threw Karameth forward, so that he stumbled and fell at Dailem's feet.

Entonin felt a powerful shudder spread through him, from the base of his spine up to the top of his skull. He had never been so simultaneously relieved and devastated to see a person.

"Oh good, you got captured, too," Entonin said, making a vain attempt at sarcasm – his voice was shaking too much for it to work.

Karameth instantly turned his face towards Entonin, the torchlight catching in his round, startled eyes. Entonin thought he could see the exact reflection of his own feelings looking back at him.

Karameth turned away too soon, angling his fury back towards their captor.

"Let us go," he barked in Dahrani. "We've done *nothing*. Mudammir take you and your family, and their fam—"

"I'd prefer it if you left my family out of this," said the Justice in perfect Dahrani, only a slight Amorian lilt to her words. "And who are you, exactly, to be travelling with an Ellathian priest? His pet?"

Karameth drew back like a snake and then launched himself forward, even though his arms and legs were tied with ten times as many restraints as Entonin's had been. The woman didn't even flinch. She said one of those strange, incomprehensible words and Karameth froze, even the individual strands of his hair fixed in place. He teetered for a moment and then toppled forward, unable to lift his arms to protect his face.

"Enough of this." The Justice jerked her head towards the cell adjacent to Entonin's, and the Surveyors hauled Karameth to his feet just long enough to throw him into it. Entonin couldn't help but notice that they didn't try to fit a collar around *his* neck. "Leave them. I don't have time for this nonsense. Perhaps, given some time, you can think of a more convincing story, Entonin tyr Ardulath."

The outer door squealed shut, the sound hanging in the still air like a final judgement. Entonin and Karameth were alone.

Entonin stayed on the floor, his fingers threaded together in his lap, trying to keep his head above the different emotions that threatened to overwhelm him. In the adjacent cell, the object of a number of those feelings groaned and pushed himself to his feet.

Karameth didn't even hesitate before he stalked across to the gate of his cell and threw his shoulder against it.

"I already tried that," said Entonin, though he had to admit there'd been considerably less weight behind his own efforts. "You know, if this is a rescue, it isn't going very well."

Karameth turned on him, and Entonin was suddenly very glad there was a wall of metal bars between them. "I *told* you to leave."

"And then you decided not to wait for me." As usual, it was anger that most easily found its way to Entonin's mouth. "Did you make it to the bridge? Or were you still in the Southern Quarter when they caught up to you?"

"What?"

"The landlady said you left early this morning."

"To see if there were still ways out of the city." Entonin didn't think he'd ever heard the mercenary so angry. "To get supplies. To be ready to drag you out of the city if I had to."

"Oh." The landlady had lied to the Surveyors. Of course she had – she'd tried to protect them in her own small way. "Well, turns out you should have left."

The sound Karameth made was too strangled to be a laugh. For a moment, he remained by the gate, one hand on the bars, his head hunched forwards, brown hair falling in front of his face. Then he let go, put his back against the bars between his and Entonin's cell and let himself slide down to the floor.

There was something like solidarity in the way he'd sat as close as he could, and Entonin found himself wanting to close the remaining distance. He pushed himself across the floor to sit beside Karameth, their backs against the bars. Despite their separation, there were only a couple of inches between them. Entonin couldn't deny the relief he felt at being back at the mercenary's side; the black despair that had been gathering in his gut felt just a little lighter, the situation just a little less bleak.

It shouldn't. If anything, they were worse off than ever – no one remained to rescue either of them. Yet it still felt better than the thought of the mercenary abandoning Entonin to his fate.

"I hope you're secretly someone important and your people are on their way even now to rescue us," said Entonin, only half joking.

There was a hesitation, a moment too long before Karameth answered, and then, "No. No one is coming for me."

"That's too bad."

"What about you?" Karameth turned his head, so Entonin could see the profile of his face through the bars, the long nose, the neat black beard which lined his jaw. "You keep telling everyone how important you are."

Well, that cut to the very heart of it. Entonin grimaced. "Not important enough. Don't tell *them* that, though."

"I thought an Ellathian priest could walk from one side of Omalia to the other without fear of attack, so great would Ellath's wrath be if any harm came to them."

"No one really believes that, do they? Besides, even if they avenge me, we'd already be dead."

Karameth didn't answer. Entonin was close enough that he could hear his breathing: a little too quick, a little too shallow. The mercenary was frightened.

"You should have left," Entonin repeated. "I don't pay you enough for this."

This time it was more like a laugh, but the sound was too small against the quiet of the prison.

"True. But it's too late for that. Looks like we're stuck with each other."

26

NAILA

On her return from the Dragon's Rest, Naila had braced herself for Dailem's anger, but none of it unfolded quite like she expected. They returned before dawn, Ko'ani's aunt deciding that the darkest hours were the safest time for them to limp out of the Southern Quarter and back to the inner city. When at last they reached the Wizard's Tower, Dailem wrenched open the apartment door before they'd even had a chance to knock. For a moment, her expression wavered, almost as if she'd lost control of an illusion. Then she grabbed Naila and pulled her into a tight hug.

"You idiot child," Dailem said, though there was no real anger in her voice. "What in the Goddess's name were you thinking?" She leaned away to get a better look at Naila's face, still gripping her upper arms with vice-like strength. "That wizard. When I get my hands on him, I'll—"

"He claims it wasn't his idea," Larinne said coolly from behind Naila.

Dailem stepped back, composing herself in that single movement. "Well, we've never heard that before. Where is he? He might come to defend himself."

"Resting." Out of the corner of her eye, Naila could see the disapproving arch of Larinne's eyebrows. "I sent him ahead to his rooms. You know he's the reason the Southern Quarter isn't crushed to dust right now—"

Naila didn't hear the rest of their budding argument, because at that moment Ko pushed open her bedroom door, lured from her bed by the sound of raised voices. The moment she saw Naila, she broke into a run, her bare feet slapping off the glass floor. Again, Naila felt her breath knocked out of her lungs, Ko slamming into her, arms looping around her neck.

"You're okay!" Ko's voice was muffled by Naila's shoulder, the curls of her hair tickling against Naila's cheek. "When the dome broke ... Dad said you and Haelius were ... Goddess damn you, Naila, I thought ..."

Naila tightened her arms around Ko. "I'm okay. Haelius is okay. Your aunt saved him."

In a movement so like her mother's, Ko gripped Naila's arms and peered intently into her face. All Ko's worry had melted away into curiosity, her dark eyes burning bright with questions. "Did you see it? Were you there when it broke?"

Naila swallowed, trying not to hear that awful screeching, or feel the dreadful weight of her death plummeting towards her. "I did see it. I saw him fix it, Ko. You should have seen him – *felt* him. I've never seen someone reach for so much magic. I could have sworn you'd sense it from here."

The edge of Ko'ani's lip twitched, and Naila knew there was just a hint of jealousy in that expression. "You should have told me you were going. I'd have come with you, I could have—"

"That's enough of that." Malek's voice had an unusual edge to it, as he too emerged from his bedroom. "Haelius and Naila are lucky to have made it back in one piece."

Ko broke away from Naila, keeping her eyes on the floor, her lips pressed together; she knew what that tone in her father's voice meant.

Naila swallowed.

"I'm glad you're all right," said Malek, placing a heavy hand on Naila's shoulder, and with it Naila could feel all the weight of his disappointment.

"I'm sorry," she managed to croak. "I put him in danger, I know."

Malek sighed. "It's not just *him* I'm worried about. You put each other in danger." He squeezed Naila's shoulder and let go, stepping past her and leaving her to sink beneath her guilt.

"Habibti," he said, addressing Dailem, "I didn't know you were back."

"Only just." Dailem let Malek kiss her on the cheek. "Larinne told me they were coming. I need to get back out there. Everything is just ... Even before the dome, we—" She froze mid-sentence, her eyes gaining a glazed, faraway look, and Naila felt the prickle of magic from a communication spell.

"What is it?" Larinne asked even before the magic faded. "What's happened?"

It was an alarming thing to see Dailem lost for words. She closed her eyes, and Naila saw her shoulders lift and fall before she spoke. "I have to go. They want me to bring him in."

"Who? No. Wait. No, Dailem." Larinne's face twisted with such raw emotion she was almost unrecognisable. "No, they can't. He just saved the Southern Quarter. That can't be right."

Haelius, Naila realised. *They mean Haelius.* She felt as if the floor had dropped away from her feet, her lungs paralysed in shock.

"It's just to ask some questions. He was in there during the riots, during everything – you have to see how that looks. I need to go to—"

"This is too far, Dailem." Larinne grabbed onto Dailem's arm. "You can't do this. I won't let you. He's done nothing wrong!"

Dailem wrenched her arm free and drew herself to her full height, the stiff uniform of the Justice making her seem like she was carved from obsidian. "He's done a thousand things, and you know it. Don't be a fool. It has to be me because I can *protect* him. It will be questions – just questions. I promise that will be all. Now let me go, before someone else gets to him first." Dailem hesitated for just a moment, reaching out to touch Larinne lightly on the arm. "Trust me."

When Larinne looked up, there were a thousand unspoken words in her stare. She nodded once, and then Dailem swept out into the shadowy corridor, heading out to arrest their friend.

The following days were an agony of waiting.

The breaking of the dome changed Amoria. The glass was a constant: it didn't fade, or change, or *break*. It just was. The moment it had cracked, so too had a central pillar of the city's faith. For so long, Amoria's sense of safety and security had been slowly eroding away, layers and layers of it scraped back, until all that was left was the cold glass at its heart. And now even that was breaking. Naila felt like she was trapped in that heart, confined to Ko'ani's apartment high up in the spires, able only to sit and wait while the city fell apart around her.

From Haelius, they heard nothing.

Naila stayed in Ko'ani's apartment, turning the disc Haelius had given her over and over in her hands. It didn't matter how many times she thought his name and felt the pull of the spell under her fingertips, she would hear nothing in return, not even the flicker of a connection. It felt like something was blocking her out, and Naila didn't know if that meant Haelius couldn't or wouldn't answer her.

There was nothing left to occupy her but worry. She couldn't even practise her magic; before they'd left the Rest, Haelius had taken the obsidian artefact from her, his long fingers closing around it, his eyes flat and unreadable. "Promise me you won't try to use your power again until you're with me," he'd insisted. "Promise me, Naila."

She *had* promised, even though losing the stone only made her more helpless, made the glass walls of her prison close in tighter around her.

It was unbearable.

This time, at least, she wasn't alone. Where Dailem was almost never home, and Ko'ani was forced back to her classes, Malek seemed to spend most of his time in the apartment, and Naila couldn't help wondering if he'd been left to watch her. He made for an amicable enough jailer, bringing her cups of tchai or sweet mint tea.

Most often, though, Naila would look up to find Malek simply standing at the outer wall of the tower, still and silent. He was doing just what she was, she realised: waiting for word from Haelius.

"Why don't you leave?" Naila blurted out one morning, unable to stand the brooding silence or the slump of Malek's shoulders.

Malek turned and blinked at her, as if he hadn't fully understood her question. His brow furrowed, and for a moment Naila worried that she'd angered him, asked a question she had no right to ask.

"And where would you have us go, young Naila?" he asked amicably, crossing back to the dining table and pulling out a chair opposite her.

Naila wetted her lips. "I'm sorry, I know Amoria is your home now, but—"

"—but Amoria has its complications?" Malek raised an eyebrow. "Don't worry, I won't be offended by questions. Wisdom is found in questions as much as in answers."

"You're Dahrani. You must have family outside Amoria? Somewhere you could go, at least until the worst of this blows over?"

The look on Malek's face was strange, his eyes looking towards a point that Naila couldn't see.

"We could, I suppose. Though I can't imagine Dailem would be best pleased by the idea. How much do you know about Dahrani mages, Naila?"

Naila shook her head as she tried to remember any of the little she'd learned of the Queendom from Ko'ani, or from visitors to the Dragon's Rest. "Dahran has mages just like we have – they're not persecuted like they were in Ellath."

"We're called magi, and we're quite rare." Malek's smile seemed completely detached from any feeling. "Only in Amoria do you see mages in anything like this number. We're not hunted down like Ellathian mages, of course, but we're not entirely welcome either. People tend not to like people who are different from them."

That sounded all too familiar; Naila tried not to let the bitterness show on her face.

"I guess I don't need to tell you that. People are people." He reached for one of his sleeves and pushed it back, the brown and silver fabric bunching around his elbow.

Naila knew she was staring but she couldn't stop herself. On Malek's brown skin, under the black hair of his arms, a flowing script was inked up the full length of his arm. He turned his hand over, so that Naila could see where the writing twisted underneath, the black ink stark against the paler skin of his wrist. It was the flowing, joined-up writing of the Dahrani script, so that even where it was clearer, Naila still couldn't read a word of it.

Malek noticed her small frown as her gaze tracked across the looping words. "They're phonemes, just written in Dahrani and not the characters you're used to. It can be used to help in casting, but mostly it shows other people, 'look out, this man's magi'."

Naila's eyes flicked back to Malek's face, to his utterly humourless smile.

"Most magi are called to serve in Dahran's army," he continued, holding Naila's gaze. "Magic is one small advantage we have against Ellath, and not one the Queendom is willing to lose. Most children of magi end up in the army before they're fully grown."

There was something awful about trying to imagine Malek as a soldier. Everything about him was soft and scholarly. In so many ways, he was the opposite of his wife: even the silver thread which marked him as a trianne seemed too ostentatious for the simple brown robes he favoured. Malek belonged at his workbench, making beautiful things with his hands, or pulling them apart to better understand them.

Naila blinked, and before she knew it she was seeing Ko instead of Malek, her friend's arms spiralled with black ink, all her wildness locked in behind the rigid lines of a uniform. Somehow, she knew this was what Malek saw every time he thought of leaving.

"So you see, Amoria is our home in a way nowhere else could be," he said gently, his expression softening when he saw that Naila understood. He tugged his sleeve back down to cover his arm. "And it's a home mages will fight for fiercely if they think it is threatened. Whatever Oriven is, whatever he does, he thinks he's protecting his home – the only home for his family."

The gathering silence was interrupted by the click and creak of the front door opening, followed by the jangle of bracelets which marked Ko'ani's return.

"I'm back," she called in a sing-song voice, followed by the usual sounds of Ko dropping her bag and everything else she carried right at the door. Naila thought she heard a faint sound of disapproval from a second person.

Ko darted round the corner and into the main room, a bright smile lighting her face, as if recent events hadn't quite managed to lay their hands on her.

"Look who I found wandering the corridors like a ghost," she said cheerfully, gesturing behind her.

It was Haelius who followed her into the main room. It had been a few days since the dome broke, but he still looked pale and tired, an angry purple bruise standing in sharp contrast to the pallor of his skin. Even from across the room, Naila could see that something was wrong: his eyes were too bright, and one of his hands was already picking at the edge of his sleeve.

She was on her feet before she really realised what she was doing, crossing the room in three steps that were half a run. "Haelius!" She threw her arms around him, grabbing him as if he might disappear at any moment.

He stiffened in surprise, and then Naila felt him relax, a hand patting lightly against her back. "Hey, I'm all right."

She stepped back to look at him, her heart dropping at the dark, swollen mark on his forehead. *I caused that*, she thought.

Haelius raised his eyebrows at her scrutiny, but for a moment a smile chased the shadows from his face. "I'm all right," he said again. "You?"

Naila nodded.

"You look like you need a stiff drink, my friend," Malek said, even as he began to fix the tea that was the only thing Haelius would drink.

"Just tchai," Haelius answered automatically.

The feverish look had returned to his eyes. He was standing too still, his stiff posture seeming only to imply more turmoil underneath. The sense of his power was strangely absent and that only added to his appearance of unnatural stillness.

"What's happened?" she asked, knowing beyond a doubt that something had brought him there.

"I ..." Haelius looked more unsure than Naila had ever seen him. "There's been more conflict, at Merbridge."

"I heard," Malek said heavily. "It was almost inevitable. Oriven is using the entrances to the inner city like choke points; the bridge is where they're most vulnerable."

"It was with the Justice. Is Dailem—?"

"She wasn't there, thank the Goddess."

Naila heard Ko'ani let out a held breath.

Haelius nodded mutely, and somehow Naila could tell this wasn't what had brought him here.

"Will all of you sit down," Malek called from behind the clink and clatter of glasses. "It's like being surrounded by a bunch of—" and then he said a number of Dahrani words that Naila didn't know.

Ko caught Naila's gaze and gave a conspiratorial roll of her eyes. "It's better not to ask," she said, dropping into one of the chairs at the dining table.

"Better," said Malek, setting the tea in front of each of them. "You shouldn't have stayed away so long, Haelius. We've been worried about you."

"I'm fine," Haelius answered too quickly.

"Have you found anything more about the dome?"

"No. I'm still certain it isn't something that can be easily repeated, but I'm struggling to sense it." Haelius closed his eyes and lifted his chin, as if he meant to reach for the magic in the glass at that very moment. Instead, he flinched.

"Don't push it," Malek chided gently.

"It still isn't back?" Naila had to clear her throat to make her voice sound. "Your magic hasn't come back?"

Haelius opened his eyes and smiled in a way that only touched the corners of his mouth. "These things take time."

"Magic begets magic," Malek explained. "It's self-perpetuating. Our friend here left himself with less than enough to fill a thimble and now he needs to fill a whole ocean. It will speed up – give him another couple of days and he'll have more magic than he knows what to do with. *If* he's smart enough to rest and leave it alone."

Haelius rolled his eyes, and the familiar expression warmed Naila in a way she hadn't realised she needed.

"So." Malek took a sip of his tchai and winced at the heat. "Are you going to tell us why you're really here?"

Haelius's eyes were fixed on the table, twisting his small glass back and forth with the tip of his thumb and middle finger. He took a long moment before he answered, and, when he did, he looked at Naila. "Actually, do you mind if I speak to Malek alone for a moment?"

Naila sat back in surprise. "But . . ."

"It'll only be for a moment."

"But we have every right to know what's going on," said Ko'ani, and there was an edge to her voice that was more than a little reminiscent of Dailem.

Haelius raised his eyebrows and opened his mouth, but Naila didn't give him a chance to speak. "You said we're not children. You said that we have a right to know what's happening."

"I know what I said."

This rebuff made warm blood rush to her cheeks. It felt like she'd been trusted once, like she'd been invited to the table and then her reaction to the riots had seen her shut out again.

"But—"

Under the table, Ko squeezed Naila's fingers so tightly it made her wince. When she turned to her friend, Naila found an unusual look of calm on her face.

"Come on," she said quietly.

"But—" Naila tried again.

In response, Ko widened her eyes meaningfully, and almost crushed Naila's hand in hers. "Come *on*."

Naila left the table without looking Haelius or Malek in the eye, anger burning like a hot coal in her throat. As soon as Ko closed the door of her bedroom, Naila rounded on her, a protest half formed on her lips.

"Shhhh," said Ko, holding a finger out in front of Naila's face.

"Ko, what are you—"

"I said shh," Ko hissed again, dropping into a crouch next to her bedroom door and gesturing that Naila should do the same.

Naila did as she was told, but her anger hovered on her tongue.

With only her finger, Ko reached out and traced the phoneme for "sound" on the door, and Naila could see the magic in the opaque glass shift, sliding into the shape of the symbol. Then Ko pressed her hand to each of the four corners of the phoneme, whispering a spell as she did so. The magic flared bright on Naila's awareness for just a moment, before settling in the pattern Ko willed, as if she'd had turned the door itself into an artefact.

The silence from the other room was so long that for a moment Naila thought Ko'ani's spell hadn't worked.

"Haelius?" Malek said eventually, and when he spoke it sounded as if he was standing right next them, his voice coming from the glass itself.

Naila smiled in amazement, and Ko raised her eyebrows, as if to say, "*and you doubted my brilliance?*"

"Talk to me," Malek tried again.

There was a rustle of fabric as someone stood, and that too felt like it happened a breath away from them.

"They took you in for questioning?"

"Yes." There was sharp, bitter edge to Haelius's voice he had never shown Naila.

"You know Dailem went because she was trying to protect you, because—"

"I know. It's ... Actually, it isn't fine. None of this is."

From Malek there wasn't a sound. He was waiting again, giving his friend the room to speak. Next to Naila, Ko'ani swallowed.

"They searched my study." Haelius's voice was breathy with the savage shadow of a laugh. "They took nearly everything. Books, tools, a letter I was writing. Nothing that meant anything to anyone else. Oh, and what was left of the silwheat, so I guess we'll never find out what happened to that."

"I'm sorry."

Haelius made a sound of disgust. "It doesn't matter."

There was another silence. The spell made Haelius's deep, unsteady breath sound like it was right at her ear.

"People died today. At the bridge."

"I know."

"If I was there, I could have stopped it."

"Stopped it how, my friend? Who would you have stopped? What would have happened if you did, and how long would it have lasted?"

"Malek, I have all this power—"

"Not at the moment. I was never much of a dueller, but I would bet even I could best you right now. I know you don't like to admit it, but even *you* have limits."

There was another small breath of laughter, softer this time.

"Even if I were recovered, I . . . I don't know what I'm supposed to do. I have something – an ability with magic that surely I'm supposed to use? What use am I, if—"

"What if magic isn't the solution?" There was the sound of someone standing and the softer scuff of Malek's footsteps. "Force isn't the answer to this, and you know it. Maybe you can't fix this, because it's not up to one person to fix it."

"I can't fix anything. It turns out I can't even protect Naila."

Naila's heart, already bruised with guilt, lurched painfully in her chest.

"What's happened?" For the first time, the calmness was gone from Malek's voice.

Next to her, Ko'ani shuffled a little closer, and Naila felt a warm hand close over hers.

"We've run out of time. Someone saw her use her powers during the riots. Oriven's people were there, causing damage, pretending to be rioters. She confronted them, and they ran straight back to their master. Oriven has commanded the Academy to end this: to bring her before the other wizards and decide what should happen to her. We have days, if that."

A pause and then, "All right. She has a power now – you said so yourself. She can go before them and . . ." Malek's voice trailed off, and Naila could almost see the shake of Haelius's head.

"It isn't magic. Malek, she manipulates *anima*. It bends to her will just like magic bends to mine. Anima. You know what that means, don't you?"

"Goddess," Malek breathed. "The silwheat."

"Yes, and the artefacts, and maybe even the dome. It will give him everything he wants. An answer to all of it, and a known 'hollow' to pin it on. Everything tied squarely away."

"Could we do something to make them believe it's magic? Use your magic to conceal hers, or, I don't know ..."

"No. If it were before the council or Oriven's people, maybe, but the other wizards? We wouldn't fool them for a second."

Ko'ani gripped Naila's hand so hard it hurt, but she was grateful for the sensation, something solid anchoring her in place. She tightened her grip back, feeling the tremble of Ko'ani's arm.

"Have you spoken to Larinne yet?" Malek asked, a strange note of hope in his voice. "Perhaps she could persuade them to bring it to the Senate instead, or Dailem could—"

"Wait, did you feel that?" Haelius's voice was followed by rustle of fabric and the quick click of his footsteps across the floor.

Before either of them had a chance to react, the door to Ko'ani's room banged open, both Naila and Ko'ani stumbling back against the floor. Haelius loomed over them.

"What is this?" His eyes flicked to the back of the door, his gaze slipping into the sight. "I see. Very clever." Haelius turned on Ko'ani, his green eyes blazing. "I asked to speak to your father *alone*. I can't believe I didn't feel this. If I'd been at my full strength, I would have sensed this the moment you cast it."

To Naila's surprise, Ko shuffled backwards, her face suddenly pale, and Naila realised she'd never seen Haelius angry like this before. But Naila had.

"And what?" Naila felt her blood grow hot, all her fear and guilt twisting itself together into one blazing thread of anger. It was so much easier to be angry than afraid. "You'd have blocked us from hearing you talk about *me*?" She scrambled to her feet, drawing herself taller, bringing her gaze level with Haelius's.

"Yes," he snapped back at her.

"Why didn't you tell me? Why didn't you explain any of this?" She lifted her hands in exasperation. "Why wouldn't you tell me?"

"I would have!" Haelius rubbed his hand over his eyes. "I would have if you'd given me a chance. Do you think this is how I wanted you to hear it? I just needed some time, to think this through, think of a way I could get us out of this."

"While I have no idea what's happening?" Naila's voice grew louder. "While I let friends put themselves at risk for me, while I have no idea what they're risking?"

"Yes," he said, his voice weary. "If it meant keeping you safe, yes I would have kept this from you."

All of a sudden a thread in Naila snapped, releasing all of the guilt she'd kept tied up behind it. She felt her jaw tremble and her eyes sting. She couldn't keep doing this to him.

"Enough." Malek came to Haelius's side and steered him away from the door, giving Ko'ani a long, lingering look.

Naila felt Ko'ani shrivel under it.

"We've taken you in, Naila, we've promised to look after you. You have the most powerful wizard in Amoria, two of the most powerful women on the Senate – and me. How many other people are so well protected? We'll keep you safe. We're not done yet; we'll figure something out."

"Haelius, is it . . .?" The words blurted out of Naila before she could stop them. "When they searched your apartment, did they take it?"

Haelius knew what she meant without her saying it. He looked away from her, but Naila could still see the conflict in his expression, the war he was having with himself. For a moment, she thought he wouldn't answer her, her heart racing. She couldn't lose it now, not after everything they'd been through.

"Here," Haelius reached into his pocket and produced something which dangled from his fingers, swinging back and forth on a thin silver chain.

Naila's whole awareness bent towards it, reality fading behind it. The obsidian was all she could see, its dark shine like a pool of black ink solidified in mid-air.

"I kept it safe," Haelius said quietly. "But Naila, you have to know . . . when they searched my study, this is what they were looking for."

Naila had been staring at the stone, watching the light slide off the polished black surface, but now her eyes flicked back up to Haelius. "What?"

Haelius, too, was contemplating the twisting pendant, his expression unreadable. "Oriven wants it. Wanted it, from the beginning." He sighed, his shoulders sagging. He looked smaller. Wearier. "When I took it from the archives, it was because I found out Oriven wanted it, *needed* it for some part of his plan. I only meant to keep it long enough to understand it – find out what it is, why Oriven wanted it. And then . . ."

And then Naila had touched it.

It was hard to fully comprehend what Haelius was saying. To relate it all down to this tiny object swaying from a silver thread. How could this be key to Oriven's plans? Why did the High Consul of Amoria want it? And yet Naila couldn't *stop* wanting it. Even now, there was a hunger in her, and she had to struggle against the urge to stretch out her hand and snatch it from Haelius's grasp.

"I don't know if this is the right thing to do," Haelius continued, a twist to his mouth. "He might still come after it – after you. But I don't think he knows yet about the connection between this and your magic. It might be safer here with you than it is with me."

He dropped the shard into her outstretched hand, the silver chain pooling around its irregular edge.

"I made a setting for it – the back is silver, so it should be safe enough for you to wear it. But I couldn't get what you said when you first touched it out of my head: 'how did it break?' So, I made the setting an artefact, capable of changing its conformation in response to, well, in case there's more of it."

For a moment Naila couldn't think past the relief, the giddy sensation that a part of her had slotted back into place. She made herself focus on what Haelius was saying: sure enough, Naila could see phonemes scratched into the silver around its edge and feel the deep throb of Haelius's power locked into the metal; it was no wonder the wizard's magic hadn't yet recovered. She brushed her thumb across the smooth black surface and had to stifle a gasp as her awareness immediately shifted, tilting down to the massive expanse of the Great Lake at her back.

"Thank you," she managed to murmur.

"You must not use it, Naila," Haelius tipped his head, trying to catch her gaze. "You must promise me. Any hope we have relies on you staying hidden – no one else can know of your power. Understand? Promise me you won't use it."

Naila continued to stare at the stone in the palm of her hand, its surface impossibly smooth, unendingly black. This couldn't continue. She couldn't keep putting the people she cared about in harm's way. Every moment she stayed with Malek and Dailem was an incrimination, every time Haelius tried to protect her, he pushed himself deeper and deeper into Amoria's conflicts. She couldn't stay. She couldn't put them in danger because of her.

With her power back in her hands, perhaps there was a way she could get out of Amoria.

"I promise," she lied.

27

HAELIUS

Haelius stood facing the steps of the Majlis, feeling the pressure of people's stares like fingerprints on his skin. He'd traded his robes for an old tunic and trousers, but they did nothing to hide his scars; anyone who worked even adjacent to the Shiura Assembly would know who he was. Another reason he was mad to come here, but what choice did he have?

Haelius didn't approach the wide steps, only waited, knowing it was just a matter of time. Taking deep, even breaths, he tried to slow the rapid thump of his heart. *This is ridiculous*, he told himself. *You're the most powerful mage in Amoria.* That thought did not prevent his stomach dropping when his father eventually appeared at the top of the Majlis steps. Wylian stood for a long moment, as if considering whether or not to descend to his son. Haelius didn't move, well aware that anything he did would have no effect on his father's decision; Wylian was not a man who was easily influenced.

When his father eventually decided to approach, he strode down the steps with a stormy expression.

It was about what Haelius had expected.

"Father," Haelius greeted him with a small bow, and then realised the mage greeting would only annoy him.

Wylian's scowl deepened. "What are you doing here?" He gestured sharply to Haelius's clothes. "Do you think this hides what you are? Everyone in the Adventus knows you're one of them."

And they know I'm your son, thought Haelius, watching the way Wylian glanced uneasily over his shoulder. Out loud, Haelius said, "Well, since you control the flow of information out of the Adventus, I don't imagine it'll be a problem."

It was a mistake. Wylian's eyes narrowed to thin slivers of jade. "Do you think this is funny? Do you have any idea what's happening? People died in those riots, killed by your Surveyors. The Southern Quarter was almost crushed. I know you're safely tucked away in your Academy tower, but out here there is a war brewing."

"I was *in* the Southern Quarter," Haelius snapped. "Who do you think stopped it from being crushed?"

"So that *was* you." Wylian looked at Haelius properly for the first time, his gaze lingering on the raised bruise which still blackened one side of Haelius's forehead. His eyes flicked quickly away; his father had struggled to look him in the face since the accident. "I'm glad to see that your abilities have some use."

There were so many edges to that last comment that if Haelius pushed back, he would only end up cutting himself worse.

"I've come here to help," he said instead, making himself swallow his anger. "There are things I can do. I think I can help. Do you know the Dragon's Rest, in the Southern Quarter?"

"The inn? I wouldn't have thought it was your kind of establishment."

Haelius ignored the tone of his father's voice and continued, "I know the owners. At least, I trust them. I've spoken to them, and they would allow me to create a pattern room in one of their guest rooms. I've begun the work."

Wylian's eyes widened; even he knew the complexity of such a task, though he quickly painted over his surprise with disdain. "You want to create another way mages can invade this part of the city?"

"No – it would only be known to very few people, separate from the existing pattern rooms."

"And someone without magic could use it?"

"I ... no. Even I don't have that kind of power. But we wouldn't use it to move people: there are still stores, the mages aren't starving.

We could use it to smuggle food to the Southern Quarter, buy us a little time."

Haelius held his breath, waiting for Wylian's response.

Despite everything, he was unprepared for the disapproval that twisted across his father's features. "*That's* your answer? Your grand plan? Charity?"

"No. I mean, yes, in a way. Larinne can help us gain access t—"

"Charity that relies on mages? On a senator, no less?" Wylian fixed Haelius with a stare that seemed to burn through thirty years. All that was left was a small boy who'd always given the wrong answer to his father's questions. "We can't trust them. You can't trust *her*. Reveal this plan of yours to a mage and it'll only be a matter of time before they twist it to their own needs."

"No, she— they're people I trust."

"Well, you shouldn't. She's a senator, at the very heart of their council. I'll grant that she's better than most of them, but the situation is changing: we are heading towards war. She's still one of them."

"*I'm* one of them."

Wylian finally looked at Haelius's face, his gaze tracking over the scars. The hardness of that stare sent a chill up the back of Haelius's arms. "You are, and if you had applied yourself to something *useful* then perhaps we wouldn't need the charity of senators."

Haelius felt his magic uncoil in his gut, flickering to life like a re-kindling flame. It was an old argument between them, and Haelius found he had no strength left to guard against it.

"I am one of the heads of the Academy—"

"Yes, and look at the good it is doing us," Wylian replied. "An indulgent pursuit. You could have become a senator, gained influence with the Lieno Council. Instead ..." Wylian gestured with one hand, as if the sight of Haelius himself was enough to convey the uselessness of his choices. "Do you know what I would do with someone too powerful to be rid of, but who I didn't value or trust? I would give them a meaningless ceremonial position. I would put them somewhere I could watch their every move."

For a moment, Haelius couldn't speak. In a few short sentences, his father had taken everything that Haelius had worked for and reduced it to ash in his mouth.

"What would you have me do then?" Haelius knew he was losing control, that every mage within a hundred yards of him would have sensed his magic, but there was no one left here with the gift to feel it.

"Pick a side," said his father. "Whatever you use it for, your power is a force which could tip this conflict one way or the other. Declare for us, and the mages would be forced to acknowledge we are not defenceless."

"You want to use me as a weapon?"

"You *are* a weapon. You all are. Be ours."

"I ..." Haelius stepped backwards, though the movement didn't feel like his own. None of this felt real. "It wouldn't work. It would only lead to war – Oriven has an army. I'd have to kill them before he'd listen to you. Is that what you want? For me to murder mages?"

"Yes, if it proves necessary. War is already upon us. You could use your power to shield us from their magic ..."

"And watch *you* murder mages?" Haelius felt sick. "No. No, I won't do it. Not like you mean."

It was an awful thing to see all the doubt and disappointment Haelius felt at himself appear on someone else's face.

"I didn't think so." Wylian shook his head slowly. "Then you've already picked a side. Go back to your tower, Wizard. And don't return to the Adventus until you really decide to help us."

His father didn't say another word, didn't give him a chance to speak – he turned on his heel and strode away from Haelius, dismissing him as easily as one of his staff.

For a long time, Haelius didn't move. He felt hollowed out, as if his father had scraped away every choice he'd made – every decision he'd used to build his life – and left only an empty vessel. The walls of that vessel were too thin and too fragile, ready to crumple in someone else's grip.

He was so tired.

He felt a powerful urge to be away from the eyes of passing strangers, so he walked, letting his feet carry him away from the Majlis and into the Southern Quarter. The once bustling district was almost unrecognisable, the streets emptier than he'd ever seen them. Haelius found he struggled even to imagine the Southern Quarter as it had once been, his mind instead summoning an image of the night of the riots, the empty streets, the billowing smoke: it felt closer to reality. The traders from Jasser had stopped coming.

Would you come still come here? Haelius asked himself. *If you knew the glass was as fragile as it looked?*

As Haelius walked, he tried to reassemble himself, to swallow the rising shame in the back of his throat. Even now the world felt too distant from him. His power still hadn't recovered from the mending of the dome, and that vital line that connected him to the arcane energies had been stretched away to nothing. He could still sense the magic, but it didn't bend around him as it did before – he walked through the world without touching it.

It was beyond foolish to begin work on something as monumental as creating a new pattern room, but if anything his weakened magic only drove him to it. He needed something he could work towards no matter how slowly. To be without the one thing he could do – that was more than Haelius could stand.

By the time he reached the Dragon's Rest, he felt a little more like himself. Entering the common room, he was struck by an immediate sense of calm. The air smelled of beer and woodsmoke, redolent of life and previous occupants. Even empty as it was, it felt lived in, like a home a family would shortly return to. Haelius found himself imagining Naila sitting here, perched up at the bar or sprawled before the fire. This was where she really belonged, her home, and Haelius wished he knew how to give it back to her.

He turned towards the sound of someone hurrying down the stairs.

"Wizard Akana!" the landlady exclaimed, almost stumbling off the last step.

"Sorry." Haelius felt a sharp pang of guilt for startling her. Of course, this wasn't a home *he* belonged to.

"Thank the Goddess you're here!" She almost jogged across the distance between them, her eyes bright with urgency. "You have to help him."

"What's happened? Is Dillian all right?"

"It's not us," she said, waving away his concern. "Surveyors came here, the day after the riots. They took the priest."

Haelius rocked back with surprise. "The Ellathian? Why?"

"They wouldn't say. They just insisted he come – said they'd restrain him if he didn't."

Haelius rubbed his hand across his eyes and winced when he caught the edge of the bruise.

Brynda watched the gesture with an eagle-eyed sharpness. "He patched that up when Naila brought you here. He helped save you."

"I know—"

"He didn't do anything. He's been a peaceful guest – friendly even. I don't know why he's here, but he's had nothing to do with what happened. I'd swear it—"

"I know, I know." Haelius raised a hand in submission. "Just let me think."

This was an uncomfortable development, though in a way it was unsurprising – Ellathians were the quintessential non-mage, a symbol of everything opposed to magic in Amoria. Yet Ellath was a sleeping dragon no mage should seek to provoke. An Ellathian Seeker could supposedly walk into any country on the continent without fear, so quickly would the fist of the Empire come crashing down on any who did them harm. And mages still fled before that fist. What was Oriven thinking?

"You don't know why the priest is here?" Haelius asked, unable to shake a sliver of doubt.

"He saved you" was all Brynda said to that. "Without hesitation."

"I know." Haelius pushed a hand back through his hair. "All right. I know someone who can help. I'll see what I can find out."

It took him half the day to find Dailem. By the time he reached Justice Tallace, he was one jump away from sending himself back into magical exhaustion. So it was entirely deliberate when he seized control of the prison's magic, making the air hum and the torch flicker with his anger.

Even Dailem's mask slipped a little when he appeared beside her, her dark eyes widening in surprise. "Hae— Wizard Akana," she stammered, failing to keep the shock from her voice. "What are you doing here?"

"I might ask the same thing of you." He was too tired to keep the fury from his voice and too angry with her to try. "I've been searching for you all day, Justice Tallace; I wanted to ask you what possible reason High Consul Oriven could have to risk the wrath of the Ellathian Empire. Imagine my shock when I found that it was not on *his* authority that the priest had been arrested, but on *yours*."

Behind the bars, both the Ellathian and the Dahrani mercenary stirred, edging forward towards the bars. Haelius kept his gaze fixed on Dailem.

"This is hardly Academy business, Wizard." Dailem stood from her chair, her black robes pooling around her feet like shadow. "If you wish to speak to me about this, may I suggest you see me at my office at a more appropriate time."

Haelius felt the two Justice behind him ready themselves as if they thought they might apprehend him, but, compared to him, their magic was little more than the ripple of a pond skater on the surface of the Great Lake. He sent another wave of his power pulsing through the stone and was a little satisfied when the Justice stumbled nervously back.

"I would think starting a war with Ellath was everyone's business."

"I'm not *starting* anything," said Dailem. Her voice remained low and even, but Haelius could hear the fury in every syllable. "I am trying to *prevent* a war."

"By arresting innocent men?"

"Innocent?" Dailem took half a step forward. "An Ellathian priest?"

"He isn't the one behind this, and you know it." Haelius held himself straight-backed, facing down Dailem's anger without flinching. "He helped me – right after the dome broke, he got me into an inn and helped treat my injuries."

"Oh, and I suppose that absolves him from plotting with the Shiura Assembly to overthrow the Lieno Council?"

Haelius faltered. "What?"

The shock felt like someone had just sent ice water through his veins.

"Ah, so your father didn't inform you of that particular plan." Dailem raised one dark eyebrow, a degree of satisfaction in her expression. "The Shiura Assembly has been meeting with this priest, to discuss an alliance with the Ellathian Empire."

"Hang on a minute," the priest finally spoke. He was on his feet now, and he pressed himself right up against the bars, not even twitching in response to the magic-draining phonemes carved into the metal. "I met with the Shiura Assembly, but I agreed to none of their plans. I tried to meet your council and they wouldn't see me! Your fight is with the Shiura Assembly, not *me*."

Haelius stared at him as if he were staring at a ghost. It seemed more likely to Haelius that this was some kind of strange dream than what they both said was true. The Shiura Assembly had sought to ally itself with Ellath? His father, the other Shiura members, had sought out Amoria's oldest enemy to ally against the mages? That just couldn't be possible.

The priest's pale eyes watched Haelius with an intensity that made him want to step away. "You have to believe me," he said. "I didn't agree to anything. I came here to make peace, for gods' sake. Do I look like a war priest to you?"

Haelius shut his eyes for a moment, forcing himself back to his centre. "He's innocent, Dailem. The dome, the silwheat, the artefacts – all of it required some kind of magic. How would an Ellathian priest have done any of that?"

"They might not call it magic—"

"He doesn't have any!" Haelius gestured to where the priest had closed his hands around the bars. Even a foot away from them, Haelius could feel their tug on his power, and the sight of the collar around Entonin's neck was enough to make him feel sick. "The wards aren't affecting him at all. Even the collar has done nothing to him. He doesn't have any power."

Dailem was gritting her teeth so tightly that Haelius could see the twitch of a muscle in her temple. "He could have allies."

"And do you have *any* evidence of that?"

Silence.

Haelius took a step forward, his hands curling into fists, all of him tightening against what he was about to say. "So, you're holding an Ellathian priest, the sacred representative of the Ellathian Empire, with no evidence at all? I'm sure the Senate will want to hear what Oriven and his Justice are doing with their new-found authority."

"You're threatening me with the Senate?" Dailem lifted her chin and huffed out a short breath, almost a laugh. "The Senate doesn't listen to you."

"No, but we both know someone they *do* listen to."

Haelius didn't want Larinne mixed up in this any more than Dailem did, but he had nothing else. Larinne would be as appalled by this as he was, and unlike Haelius she knew exactly how to angle the Senate's attention, levering it like a tool. Yet to stand up and publicly denounce the Justice's actions, angle *herself* against Oriven – that was a risk no one who cared for her would want her to take.

Haelius hated himself for even suggesting it.

That hate was reflected back from Dailem tenfold. For an agonising moment she said nothing, her eyes blazing in the torchlight, her black robes perfectly motionless. Even the Ellathian stepped away from the bars.

"Let me be clear," she said, turning to address the priest and his mercenary. "I am not releasing you. I'm watching you, priest, and my people will never be far away. You will not depart the city: I will know if you try, and the Justice will not allow it. You may return to the Dragon's Rest for now, but you can be sure we'll speak again. Soon." She jerked her chin at the two Justice standing behind Haelius. "Take them back to the inn."

Haelius felt himself sag with relief, and with it the high, keening edge to his magic quietened. All his anger bled away from him, leaving him tired and utterly exposed. He swallowed, waiting for

Dailem to speak, but she said nothing until the prison door had clanged shut behind them.

"What the hell was that?" She dropped each word with a cold fury. "How *dare* you appear in here and interfere with *my* business? You don't even understand what you're blundering into!"

"Don't I?" Haelius answered quietly. He'd braced himself for her anger, but he hadn't anticipated the size of it, like a blade honed so sharp he couldn't see the edge. "It looked a lot to me like you'd imprisoned innocent people."

"Don't be a child. He's an Ellathian *priest*. What reason does he have to be here, if not to spy on us and pave the way for his empire? Every word I said was true. He's been meeting with your father and his cronies, and they've offered an alliance. Do you understand? The Shiura Assembly is trying to ally with Ellath *against* us."

There was that word again: "us". Haelius tried to imagine his father conspiring with Ellathians, plotting to destroy the mages; it was easier to picture than he cared to admit.

"Who cares if he killed the silwheat or broke the dome himself?" Dailem continued, relentless. "I would be willing to bet that he's associated with the people who did. How else did you think I was going to protect Naila, protect *you*?" Haelius flinched. "If I could get some Ellathian priest to take the fall for it, keep non-mages and mages from killing each other, who *cares* if he did it?"

Haelius shook his head. "Dailem, this isn't what I wanted."

"Isn't it?" Dailem took half a step forward, and Haelius felt the angry flicker of her magic. "Oriven is ready to accuse Naila of *everything*, and he'll use her to frame the non-mages for every disaster that's afflicted us. What are you doing? All that power, and what did you use it for? Throwing it around to intimidate me and stop me from actually doing any good? You don't know what it took to keep *you* out of these cells. I'm trying to protect us – if you're not willing to do what it takes to stop this war, then it's at least time to admit that you're *in* it. Pick your side, Haelius."

Haelius opened his mouth but no sound came out; there was nothing he could say that would remotely matter.

"Get out of my sight. Disappear, vanish, go back to your Academy tower." She dismissed him with a sharp wave of her arm and turned away. "Oh, and Haelius, if you *ever* use my sister like that again, so help me I'll—"

Haelius vanished before she could finish her threat.

He appeared on a flat roof of a shophouse, positioned right on the edge of the Mita's District, unsure why exactly his mind had brought him here. The pattern of magic was familiar enough for him to travel, so he'd clearly been here before. He stepped up to the edge of the roof, to a wide street which curved gently away from him. It was lined with pastel-painted shophouses – sky-blue, powder-yellow, pale pink – and mages bustled to the shopfronts as if it were a normal Amorian day. The contrast to the Southern Quarter was sickening.

Ah, of course. Suddenly, Haelius knew where he was. This was the same rooftop from the day his and Naila's lives had finally collided, when Oriven's march had swept through this district and caught an innocent man up in its path. It felt like so long ago, the peaceful scene before him a million miles from that terrible night.

There had to be something he could do. Something that didn't mean "*picking a side*". Which one was he supposed to pick? The side of Oriven was also the side of Malek, Ko'ani – and Larinne. It was the side of his home in the Academy, the young people he taught, the person he'd been for more than two decades. Or should he choose the non-mages, the side who needed a way to protect themselves against magic, who were being starved out of the city. *The side of your father.* Without Haelius, Oriven would destroy them.

Haelius closed his eyes, feeling a breeze drifting from somewhere high in the dome, tugging on the edge of his robes and lifting his hair away from his face.

When he opened his eyes, the pattern of magic lay over the stone and glass of Amoria, one world on top of another. It stretched before him in a web, a rich tapestry of life and energy. The streets of Amoria herself seemed arranged into an array, the lines of a vast spell etched into very her substance. It lay there like an open secret, in a language only he could read.

Perhaps there was another option. Perhaps there was something which could halt the conflict without condemning either side. And perhaps it was a solution only *he* could see.

At last, Haelius had an idea.

28

INTERLUDE

Ra'akea stood at the edge of the Great Lake, as she had done every other day. The beach beneath her feet was less sand, more silt and dirt, but her toes sank into the wet ground and the clear water lapped at her ankles. She could feel each tiny wave as it rolled in towards her, sense every ripple created by her own presence. The lake was deep and vast, stretching away almost beyond the edge of her awareness. To Ra'akea, it was a deep well of strength, a silent ally standing at her back. She was glad of it, after so long moving through this cracked, parched land.

Yet the comfort of the lake was nothing compared to the wrongness she felt from the towering edifice at its heart. The pull was always there, just beneath her thoughts, like a sound just beyond hearing. Ever since that moment in the inn, she'd felt it growing, and now she heard its call even in her sleep. If she listened too directly, it felt like a scraping in her mind, claws extending into a place no one else should be able to reach. There was no doubt now: this was it, this was what had been driving the beasts to madness.

Their quarry had vanished almost as soon as they reached Jasser, disappearing like fish darting away into deep water. The Sha'arin had been coming here, Ra'akea was sure, and now they were waiting just as she was. But for what?

Here, at the heart of this strange human city, something called out to *her* kind, to *her* people. It had created monsters and summoned them halfway across the continent of Omalia. It did not belong to the human world any more than Ra'akea or Tae did. If she wanted to end this, if Ra'akea wanted to protect her people, then she would need to find the source of this power and destroy it.

Yet she'd made no move towards the glass city; she remained in its shadow, never coming closer than the water's edge.

It wasn't fear that held her in Jasser, that kept her rooted to the shore of the lake instead of crossing the long, white bridge. Ahead of her, the sun reflected off the violet glass, a dazzling brightness, the unnatural spires wavering in the heat like a mirage. No, it wasn't fear that stopped her, though she knew she had every reason to be afraid. It was a sense that this was what she should do: wait. Whatever it was, it was coming to her, she was sure of it. The glass walls could no longer contain it. Soon it would leave the city, spreading its poison to the rest of Tokar, and the only way out of Amoria would lead it right into Ra'akea's path.

Whatever it was, Ra'akea was going to kill it.

29

NAILA

The moment Naila stepped out of the apartment she felt like a fugitive. The door clicked shut behind her, making her jump. This was it. She wouldn't be able to open it again – she didn't have the magic to work the lock. Shifting the strap of her bag, Naila made herself turn and look away down the shadowy landing, instead of letting herself look back to everything that she was leaving behind.

This is the only answer, she told herself. *If you want to protect them all, this is what you have to do. No matter what.*

Her footsteps were a muffled whisper against the floor, her bag rattling against her back. It was near noon, but it felt like the quietest hours before dawn. She'd considered slipping away during the night, but it would never have worked: too likely that Ko'ani or her parents would wake as she left, and too risky that she'd be spotted by the Surveyors once she was alone on the streets. Instead, she had waited for days, pretending to read for long, agonising hours, until Malek had finally announced that he was heading out to the Artisan's District and leaving her alone.

Naila had spent so little time outside the apartment or Haelius's studies in the recent months that everything had a faintly unreal quality, as if she'd found a door that opened into a different world.

If walking through the quiet of the Wizard's Tower was strange, stepping out into the Central Dome was stranger still. Around the Wizard's Tower the streets were wide and open, lined either with original glass buildings or newer buildings painted in muted colours.

Naila could hear the twittering of birds and the shrill laughter of children playing nearby; it was Amoria at her most beautiful and her most false, sequestered away from the rest of the world. Naila wondered how long it would be before even the people here would be forced to acknowledge the city's hardships.

Just behind the Wizard's Tower stood the Academy, a building that had loomed so large at the centre of Naila's life for so long. Living with Ko and her family, her lessons with Haelius; all of it had felt entirely separate from the girl who'd lived alone in the shadow of that tower, wondering every day if this would be the day they'd finally cast her out.

In a way that day had come.

I'm not that person any more, thought Naila, looking up to where the Academy tower pierced the curve of the dome high above her head. The obsidian pendant was tucked under her borrowed robes, sitting just beneath the hollow of her throat. Even through the setting Haelius had made for it, Naila could feel its power like a second heartbeat. Not just *its* power; *her* power.

"I'm leaving because I choose to," she whispered.

Somewhere up there, Haelius was working at his desk, pale and tired, surrounded by his empty bookshelves and all the things Naila had already cost him. And in another one of those high classrooms, Ko'ani would be studying for her lieno exams, bent low over her book and chewing the edge of her thumbnail. When Naila tried to imagine never seeing them again, it hurt almost more than she could bear. But this was how it had to be: she was leaving for them.

More than anything, she wished there'd been a way she could say goodbye.

The shortest way to the Southern Quarter was to pass the Academy, into the Mita's District, crossing through Naila's old haunts and then heading directly west. Naila couldn't quite make herself turn in that direction; it felt too much like going backwards. Instead, she took a longer route, along wide, tree-lined avenues and past a still bustling market. She was grateful for Ko'ani's robes – sapphire-blue silk with the Mita's hem glittering on the edge like curling frost. Even hemmed in white, these robes spoke of the wealth of Ko'ani's family, letting Naila slip between the milling mages unnoticed and unchallenged.

Yet she was always aware of the shadows lingering at the edges of these streets, more of them than she'd ever seen before: Surveyors. Oriven's faceless watchers. His influence went beyond the Justice now; any mages who were not allied to Oriven would no longer find themselves called as Surveyors. All they had to do was notice something different, observe the person hiding beneath these robes, and Naila would lose everything. Worse, she'd take Haelius with her.

She kept her head bowed, her hood pulled forward, measuring every step even as her heart hammered for her to go faster. *Don't look at them*, she thought. *Don't give them a reason to look at you.*

Once she was past the market she let her pace quicken to a brisk walk. Here the streets narrowed and emptied. These were the old homes of non-mages, silent and empty now that Oriven had pushed their kind out past the river. Shuttered windows and locked doors lined the street, but there were too many signs that the occupants had left in a hurry.

She didn't register the voices until she was too close to them. The Aurelia was so near that its roar almost swallowed their conversation, only snatches of words reaching her.

The voices were all too familiar.

"... right there. Just carrying on as ... shouldn't be allowed." Tasian.

"Your father should have ... the chance." Marcus.

And beside them both, Celia Oriven.

They had their backs to her, staring across the rushing water and towards the Southern Quarter. There was half a second where Naila could have slipped away unseen, where she might have just turned down a different alley, but the sight of them shook her in a way nothing else could; these were the mages who had held her, who had tormented her and toyed with her like she was nothing. Naila stumbled, her slippered feet slapping hard and loud against the paving stones.

Celia turned first, and then the others. Still Naila didn't run. She lifted her gaze and met Celia's brown eyes with her own, frozen like a mouse in the shadow of a wyvern.

"*You*," said Marcus, the word almost a snarl.

Now that they'd turned towards her, Naila could hear them all too clearly.

"This is what happens when you don't stamp pests out at the source," said Tasian. "They just keep on coming back. Where have you been hiding, rat?"

Naila opened her mouth but her tongue was thick and dry. Their faces were different now. Harder. Crueller. They might have toyed with her before, but this was no longer a game to them; the cracks on both sides ran far deeper than that now. Naila glanced towards the Aurelia, to the high stone bank and the Southern Quarter rising on the other side. If she could only reach it . . .

"Oh no you don't," said Marcus, stepping forward before she'd even tried to run. "You think we'll let you go scurrying back to your hollow friends? Who knows what you've been doing across here, in *our* city?" His voice was trembling with a fury so intense that it pinned Naila with all the force of a holding spell. The arrogant boy with his un-earned pride and jangling bracelets was gone; in his place was a young mage who *hated* her with all the force of a grown man.

"You animals killed his brother." This one was Reilin.

Next to them Celia Oriven stayed strangely silent, her eyes wide and unblinking, the sense of her power growing like the wind gathering before a storm.

Reilin moved first. "*Tenereses persona.*"

Naila's senses came alive with magic, the holding spell shooting towards her like an arrow fired from Reilin's fingers. She felt its path as clearly as if someone had tied a blazing thread to her heart. There was a second. Less than the span of a breath. In it, she stepped and turned the way Haelius did as he cast his spells, sliding out of the path of the Reilin's small magic. It was enough: Naila felt the prickle of the spell on her skin as it flew past her ear.

They stared at her, as if they couldn't quite understand what had happened. Naila's heart was hammering faster and faster, but there was the hot taste of victory in her mouth now. Her hood had fallen back and she stood facing them, eyes blazing, the tingle of power in her own fingertips. If they caught her, she would lose everything.

Marcus recovered first, magic and hatred spitting from his lips. But he was too angry, spinning together phonemes for hurt and pain. His magic felt like a boulder at the top of a hill before it started to roll, terrible but tortuously slow. She was out of the path of his rage before he'd even finished speaking. Behind her, the spell exploded against an empty building, stone cracking and crumbling to the ground. Naila tried not to imagine what would have happened to her had it struck her instead.

But Celia was smarter. Even as Marcus gathered his clumsy magic, she did something smaller, faster. Just a single phoneme: "*Trudo.*"

Naila was struck like someone had slammed their hand into her sternum, knocking the air out of her lungs and launching her backwards. The next thing she felt was her head cracking back against the ground, the metallic taste of blood in her mouth. Her head spun, the violet glass of the dome swinging deliriously above her head. Somewhere ahead of her, she felt the drag of gathering magic.

"No traitor wizard here to save you this time." Marcus's voice sounded distant, like something from a dream.

Get up, get up, get up. She groaned, trying to roll onto her side, but there wasn't any time.

In a moment the next spell would hit her. She didn't have time to move. She didn't have time to get out of their way.

Somehow her fingers found the smooth knot of obsidian at her throat.

Everything stopped.

It was as if she'd been plunged into the waters of the Aurelia, its roar filling her ears. Naila could feel the rush of the current on her skin, the threads of magic which propelled the river on its circular path, even as she still felt the solid certainty of the dry ground against her back. The phoneme *trudo* sounded inside her head like an echo. *Push. Thrust.* The water heard it, too, and it rushed to obey her.

There was the hiss and crash of a wave striking land, followed by shrieks of surprise. Water pattered down around her, splashing against her skin. It filled her with a sense of its strength. She rolled onto her side and pushed herself to her feet, not daring to waste even a fraction of the seconds she'd bought.

It was only a distraction. The mages still stood facing her, their robes pressed wet and heavy against their skin. It had been enough to startle them – to erase the phonemes on their lips – but now they looked at her with a different kind of hate; Naila could see fear burning bright from behind their eyes.

"How did you . . .?" Tasian sputtered, lifting his sodden arms, spitting water.

The ground shone like a mirror. Water crept towards Naila, seeping between the cracks, slowly spreading across the stone. She wouldn't get another chance.

She turned and threw one arm behind her, willing the water to come to her call. In her mind's eye she could see Haelius when he broke the fall of the glass – the way he shifted his whole body and gathered the magic with every turn. The water followed her, joined to her movements as if by invisible threads.

Anima, she thought, *the threads are anima.*

Marcus was already barking his magic at her again, but Naila could feel the water pooling beneath their feet, clinging to their hair and beading on their skin.

Cold, she thought. *Freeze.*

Frost spiralled away from her feet. Marcus was mid-step towards her, bellowing phonemes as if the volume of the words determined the strength of the spell. His foot shot out from beneath him and he fell, his spell lost in a howl. Reilin also slipped, grabbing onto Tasian's arm and almost dragging him down with her. The ice didn't stop at their feet, cracking over their skin, turning their robes milky under a film of frost. Tasian shook his arms like a bird, trying to shrug himself free of Naila's power, and a smile tugged at the edge of Naila's mouth when he fell.

There was a tell-tale prickle of magic, Reilin's mouth moving. These young mages were so much more powerful than Naila and her fledgling power, but Naila was so much faster. Even before she thought the word *freeze*, she was throwing her arms forward, sending a thin whip of water snapping towards Reilin. As she willed it, a chunk of ice broke free and soared forward, slamming against Reilin's forehead. For a moment Reilin wavered, blinked as if she didn't understand what had happened, and then she crumpled to the ground like paper. Watching her fall, Naila felt a distant horror at her own power.

Then there was only Celia.

She stood, a pillar of stillness, her arms held to either side to keep her balance while Marcus and Tasian scrabbled to stand on the slick ice at her feet. She made no move to cast, but her eyes had that distant quality, unfocused, sensing not seeing. Celia stared at Naila with the sight, seeing her in the way only a mage could – her eyes locked on the hot knot of power clenched in Naila's hand.

Naila's heart dropped, her blood as cold as the ice beneath her feet. Every thought of victory fled away from her, leaving her only with the cold certainty that she had done everything that Haelius had begged her not to. This was Oriven's daughter, and she had seen Naila wield anima instead of magic; worse, she'd seen what let her do it.

"What is that? What are *you*?"

Naila heard water splash uselessly to the ground behind her, ice cracking under her feet as her resolve wavered. In a moment, Marcus and Tasian would get back up and everything would be lost, but she couldn't make her mind focus, couldn't make herself move. Her left hand gripped the obsidian at her neck until the silver setting cut into the palm of her hand.

"Hey!"

Behind Celia, a smudge of black entered the edge of Naila's vision. A Surveyor.

No, no, no.

It was over. These had been mita. Children. She could not hope to face down a Surveyor – a *lieno* – on her own. Ahead of her, Celia still waited, her magic ready, her relief as clear as the shadow of the Surveyor growing behind her. To Naila's right was the river, the distant bank, the Southern Quarter and its promise of freedom. She was so close.

The Surveyor was almost on them. When they realised – when they *saw* who she was – that would be the end.

Naila threw her arm towards the river and pulled with all her strength.

The Aurelia herself was much fiercer than the small tributary Naila had used to shield Haelius; the river's power wrested against her, opposing her will with its own. But when it finally answered her call, it came with all its fury behind it. A huge, cresting wave burst up and over its bank, surging between Naila and Celia, the power of a river freed from its banks. Naila willed it to freeze. Creaking and cracking, the water solidified into rippling wall of translucent ice, blue-purple in Amoria's sunlight. Even the water in the river had frozen, solid and shining like glass: a clear path between her and the Southern Quarter. Between her and freedom.

Through the wall, she could just see the blurred shapes of people moving, hear them shouting, the black blot of the Surveyor growing larger with every second.

She turned and ran.

Naila burst into the kitchen of the Dragon's Rest, the back door slamming against the wall. The relief was greater than anything she'd ever felt, and she bent double under the weight of it, sagging forward, her hands pressing hard against her thighs. For a moment she just hung there, her lungs burning, tears swimming before her eyes. When she looked up, it took a moment for the world to come back into focus: the familiar kitchen, the magestone table, the figure sitting with his hands clasped on its surface, his green eyes blazing.

Haelius.

It had only been days since she'd last seen him, but he looked stronger, and Naila could feel the magic of the room shift towards him, trembling with his anger.

She had never been so simultaneously overjoyed and heartbroken to see someone.

"I told you to stay hidden." The words came from between his teeth, as if he'd held onto them as long as he could. "I asked you to *trust* me."

"Haelius ..." Naila tried to find the words to tell him why – why she couldn't let him put himself between her and Oriven. She was exhausted. Now that the adrenaline had bled away from her, a throbbing pain was spreading up the back of her skull. Her back and shoulders ached from where she'd slammed against the ground, and she could feel her tongue stinging and swollen in her mouth. She swayed, just a fraction, but of course Haelius saw.

"Naila?" His eyes changed, tracked over her face, seeing *her* now instead of just the object of his wrath.

Naila closed her eyes against his scrutiny.

She heard him stand, cross towards her, felt the knuckle of one finger tip her face up towards his. When she opened her eyes, the expression on his face almost undid all her resolve to leave.

"Naila," he said again.

"You weren't supposed to come." Her words croaked out as a whisper. "I'm a risk to all of you. It's too much. You can't ask me to hide away while you put yourself in danger – not when I could leave and protect all of you."

"Foolish child," he answered, but all his anger was gone.

He pulled her in towards him, closing his arms gently around her back, letting her lean her face in against his shoulder. He smelled like his study – of old books, candle smoke, metallic magic. Naila couldn't remember the last time someone had held her like this, as if she was a young girl in need of comfort. Her mouth twisted down against her will, her throat thick with emotion.

"I'm not a child." She tried to sound annoyed, but her voice cracked on the last word.

He sighed in a way that was almost a laugh. "I know." Letting go, he stepped back to get a better look at her. "Are you hurt?"

"No." Naila grimaced and reached for the back of her head before she even noticed what she was doing. "I fell and hit my head," she relented in response to Haelius's incredulous expression.

"All right. Come and sit down." He guided her to the table, and for once Naila gave herself up to it, letting herself be led and looked after; after all, it was probably for the last time.

The door to the common room creaked open.

"Goddess, Naila, what are you doing here?" Brynda lifted a trembling hand to her mouth. "It isn't safe – you mustn't stay."

"Ah, Siditi Brynda." Haelius's voice shifted into complete calm; he was Wizard Akana again. "If you don't mind, we're going to stay for a little while, just until Naila has recovered. Could you fetch the priest for me? I understand he has some skill in healing."

Haelius made a small nod to Brynda, and Bryn immediately turned on her heel and marched back out into the empty common room, the door slamming shut behind her. Naila couldn't help but notice that Brynda didn't seem at all surprised to find the wizard in her kitchen.

Haelius himself finally seemed reassured that Naila wasn't about to collapse, and he skirted the edge of the table to sit across from her. As he did, Naila could see a slight tick in his cheek, the set of his jaw – the anger that still sat so clearly behind his calm expression.

Naila braced herself to face it.

"Who did this to you?" he asked, and for a moment Naila didn't know what he meant.

It was as if being in the inn, the sight of Haelius and Brynda, had erased everything that had happened to her since she had left Ko's apartment. Now he was forcing her to remember, to turn and face the reality of what she'd done. She curled forward.

"Oh Goddess."

Haelius twitched, his hand ready to reach for her, but Naila only shook her head.

"Tell me everything."

When she was done, Naila expected his anger – expected him to tell her what an unforgivable fool she'd been. Instead, she found only sadness.

"I'm sorry," she whispered, half wanting him to be angry with her.

"Don't apologise. *I'm sorry.*" He looked down, tugging at the banding which wound round his sleeve. "I should never have let it come to this."

"What? No—"

The door to the common room creaked open again and the priest entered.

"Sorry, sorry," Entonin said by way of greeting, his robes rustling and his bag clinking against his hip. "I was asleep upstairs. Not much else to do when you're imprisoned against your will. Though I guess it could be worse." He eyed Haelius and there was an exchange there that Naila didn't follow.

"Would you mind taking a look at my friend?" Haelius's voice had that calm politeness to it again, retreating behind cool formality. "She took a fall and hit the back of her head."

"Show me." The priest thumped his rattling bag down on the table and looped one leg easily over the stone bench, despite his long robes. He leaned in towards her face, staring at her almost without blinking. This close, Naila found the pale blue of his eyes almost alarming – they were the same colour as the wall of ice she'd thrown between herself and Celia.

"Hard to tell anything when your eyes are so bloody dark." Entonin sighed as if Naila had created her unusual eye colour just to vex him. "You look all right. Turn away from me."

She twisted herself away, her back to both Entonin and Haelius. She felt Entonin's fingers on the back of her head, parting her hair, his touch surprisingly gentle.

The priest sucked in air between his teeth. "You took quite a whack – I'm sure you're feeling that. But it's nothing terrible: a bit of a lump, a nasty bruise. It'll heal on its own, but I'll find something for the pain and the swelling."

Naila didn't turn back but continued to face the wall, her eyes tracing over the orange splashes of old food, the peeling paint by the door. She tried to imagine what it would be like never to see this place again, never to laugh with Brynda and Dillian again. She couldn't make herself picture it.

"Where were you going?" asked Haelius.

Heat rushed to her cheeks. "It didn't matter."

"Didn't it?" The anger was back in his voice, and next to her Naila felt Entonin hesitate for just a heartbeat, his body stiffening. Then he continued his preparations as if he hadn't heard anything; a metal spoon scraping against the side of a jar.

"No, it didn't." Naila looked down at her hands. "What mattered was getting away from here. I just wanted to get somewhere Oriven couldn't find me – where he couldn't use me to hurt *you*."

If anything, that only made Haelius angrier. "And how were you planning to travel, exactly? What's in your bag? Is it packed with money? Enough food for the rest of your life?"

Naila gritted her teeth, feeling the heat of her own anger stirring in response to his. Why didn't he understand? "What should I have done instead? Hidden in Ko'ani's bedroom? Waited for Oriven to take you away again, and me after? Do you have a way out of this?"

Haelius didn't answer, so Naila finally looked back at him. She found him leaning on the table, his head in one of his hands, and her heart broke all over again.

They were saved from speaking by the sound of the door creaking open again, Brynda returning with a lively Dillian in tow.

"Little thief!" he exclaimed, his booming voice propelling Naila right back into her childhood.

She darted up to meet them, exchanging embraces and kisses on the cheek, trying not to wince whenever Dillian patted her on her bruised back.

"Let me feed you!" Dillian clapped his hand on her arm.

"No, I'm not staying, I'm—"

"Nonsense. I'll make you something to send you on your way."

"No, I—"

"Oh, let him," said Brynda with a roll of her eyes. "We've got enough."

Brynda was chewing the inside of her lip, her fingers twisting in the fabric of her apron. She looked smaller than Naila remembered. "So, you're leaving?"

Naila nodded. She wanted to step forward and clasp Brynda's

hands, but something rooted her in place, that impossible distance between them.

"Can you even get out? His companion," Brynda tipped her head towards Entonin. "He says there's Surveyors guarding the entrance to the White Bridge. No one gets in or out of the city without the High Consul's express permission."

"I can help with that," said Haelius.

Both Naila and Entonin turned to look back at Haelius.

"You'll help me get out?" she asked quietly.

"Of course I will. In fact, I think I can help both of you." He glanced towards the priest, who immediately sat up straighter. "Do you know Al Maktaba?"

"The Great Library?" Entonin raised his pale eyebrows. "At Awasef? Of course I do."

"Good. I want you to take Naila there."

Both Entonin and Naila recoiled in shock.

"What do you mean 'take Naila there'?" The priest didn't try to hide his dismay. "That is no small request, Wizard. Awasef is a long way east *and* north of here – weeks of travelling, maybe months with the Queendom the way it is right now. Why in Ardulath's blessed name would I do that?"

Wizard Akana didn't blink as he fixed his gaze on Entonin. Naila could feel the deep thrum of his magic through the stone, and behind her Brynda shifted uncomfortably. "Because that is the price for me getting you and your friend out of Amoria."

That startled the priest into silence.

"I'll fund the travel. I can use my power to get all three of you out on the bridge, past Oriven's guards. All I'm asking is that you make sure she reaches Awasef."

Entonin blew out his cheeks. "No offence meant, Wizard, but what's to stop me from taking your money and leaving Naila here to fend for herself in Jasser?"

"A promise to me, Entonin tyr Ardulath, that you won't." Haelius sat forward, his eyes gleaming. "I am the most powerful mage in a city of mages. Naila has an artefact in her possession that allows me to communicate with her; if you leave her, I *will* know. Consider whether you want me as your enemy."

Naila saw the priest swallow, the tip of his tongue wetting his lips. He turned his pale eyes on Naila, weighing her against his freedom.

"All right," he said eventually. "All right. But I need to speak to Karameth first."

Haelius nodded. "Of course."

Entonin stood, heaving his bag over his shoulder and gesturing to a small bottle he'd left on the table. "Dab a little where you hit your head, and on the bruises on your back, too," he added with a conspiratorial wink. "It will help with the pain."

Naila lifted the small bottle between her thumb and her forefinger. "Thank you."

Haelius glanced towards Brynda. "Could we have a moment?"

"Of course, Wizard." Brynda bobbed in a small bow. "Come on, Dill – let's give them some space."

As soon as the others were gone, Haelius's shoulders dropped, all sense of the great Wizard Akana vanishing with the slamming of the door. Naila sat back down across from him, closing her fingers around the warm metal of the disc. She fished it out of the folds of her pocket and set it down on the table between them.

"This is how you found me," she realised, gazing down at the small artefact he had given her all those months before. It looked exactly as it had when he'd left it on her desk in her old rooms: a small, innocuous circle of metal, green copper etched with shining phonemes.

Haelius nodded. "And Ko'ani. She came to me early this morning – told me she thought you were going to try to leave, or 'try something stupid'."

Naila looked down, her heart aching at the thought of Ko. "She'll never forgive me for leaving."

"She will, given time. I'm not sure she'll forgive *me* for helping you do it, though."

Naila extended one trembling finger, brushing the tip of it

against the artefact. "Is it true?" she asked, dreading the answer. "Can I reach you with this?"

"No." Haelius smiled sadly. "No, you'll be too far from me. Maybe in Jasser ... but no, I don't think so."

Naila had to press her lips together to keep them from quivering. She'd known it really. She would be far, far out of the reach of even the great Wizard Akana; it was dangerous enough for him to try to transport them as far as the bridge.

She'd known all along that this would be goodbye.

"Naila—"

"Haelius—" they said at the same time.

"Why?" Naila continued before he could speak. "Why are you— why did you do all of this? Why me?"

Haelius looked back at her with an infuriatingly blank expression. But then his eyes drifted away from her, his head turning, as if he was searching for the answer outside of himself.

He half sighed, half shook his head before he answered. "I guess, to start with, it was because you're like me."

Naila started to protest, but he spoke over her.

"My mother was a merchant from Jasser, and my father is one of the most influential non-mages in the city. Even before all of—" he lifted a hand and gestured helplessly. "It mattered. Even then it mattered. And it mattered more when I started to show signs that my magic was ... more than what people expected. Different. The Academy was ... well, you know what it was like."

Naila didn't know what to say. Instead, she reached a hand, palm up, across the table. Haelius wordlessly took it in his own, squeezing it between his fingers.

"And how could I not help you?" He smiled sadly. "Naila, none of this is your fault; you deserved better. You deserve better. I'm sorry I couldn't do more.

"Listen, I know people, mages, in Awasef." Haelius released her hand, pressing on before either of them could falter. "I'll give you a letter, let them know it was me who sent you. You might find another teacher, to help you understand your power. You'll be safe there; it will give you time to figure things out. But you need to get out of Jasser as quickly as you can; take the obsidian artefact and get it as far away from Amoria as possible."

Naila nodded, feeling the relentless pressure of words building up behind her lips.

"Come with me." They burst out of her in a single rushed sound.

Haelius raised his eyebrows. "Sorry?"

"Come with me." She looked up at him, locking his gaze with hers. "It's not safe here, especially for you. Come away from Amoria – at least for a while. I know Dahran isn't the safest place for mages—"

"Naila . . ."

"—but I'm sure we'll find a way. You're the most powerful mage on Omalia, and you say there are mages in Awasef, we could go there and—"

"I can't," Haelius said gently. "You know that. My life, my work, my . . ." he hesitated, "my everything is here. I can't abandon Malek, Ko and Dailem." He didn't say Larinne's name, but Naila could see it written on his face. "I can't leave. I belong here."

Naila closed her eyes. A kernel of anger throbbed in the pit of her stomach: anger that she was being forced to leave, anger that Haelius wouldn't see how much danger he was in. She grabbed onto it, desperate to feel something that wasn't loss.

When she opened her eyes, she was surprised to see that Haelius was smiling.

"Good," he said, "that looks more like you."

The jibe cracked apart all her grief and all her anger, and instead Naila found herself trying not to laugh.

"Thank you," she managed to say, her voice wavering. "For everything."

Naila thought she saw a slight tremble at the edge of Haelius's smile. "Thank *you*, Naila." He looked away, his thumb running over the edge of his sleeve. "Come, you should rest as much as you can, and I need to get things prepared. Tonight, you must leave for Jasser."

30

NAILA

Naila didn't think she'd sleep, but she must have, because when Haelius came to wake her she had to wrestle back to waking, her mind groggy and slow.

"It's time," Haelius said, letting her sit up and scrub the sleep from her eyes.

He was perched on the edge of her bed, supplies scattered across the blanket between them. Before she even had time to take it all in, he lifted a packed coin purse and held it out to her, tipping it into her hands with a dull clink. It was so heavy that Naila almost dropped it in surprise.

"I can't—" she tried, but Haelius was already shaking his head.

"You must. There's barely enough here to get you to Awasef. This is the only way I can protect you once you're beyond my reach. Please, I need you to take it."

Naila lowered her arm, cradling the weight of this debt in her lap.

"Be under no illusions – I have bought you passage with these men, but you can't trust them, especially not the Ellathian." Haelius fixed her with a stare it was impossible to evade. "He's helped us before, I know, but I still don't understand his motives, or why he's here. I . . ." He looked down, and for a moment Naila saw the full extent of his weariness. "I wish there were another way." He closed his eyes and allowed himself one deep sigh before he carried on. "There's a life for you out there, Naila, I know there is. Perhaps in Awasef you can find the answers I couldn't give you."

Naila didn't speak. There were no words she could say that could even begin to describe what he'd done for her. Or how sorry she was to leave.

Haelius didn't need her to say anything. He smiled in a way meant to offer comfort, but it only made Naila's heart ache all the more. "Come on. We need to go before it starts to get light."

After that, her time in the Dragon's Rest melted away. She hugged a tearful goodbye to Brynda and Dillian, gave Haelius a letter for Ko'ani and made him promise he'd try to explain, even though they both knew it wouldn't do any good. And then suddenly there wasn't anything left to do, nothing Naila could use to postpone her departure.

Downstairs, the priest and his bodyguard were already waiting, their bags packed and slung over their shoulders. There was a nervous energy about them, as if at any moment this might turn out to be a trap.

"Here, put this on," Haelius said, offering Naila a plain brown cloak with no mage markings. "Try to cover your robes with it. I'm afraid my power hasn't recovered enough yet that I can disguise us and still get us out past Oriven's guards."

Naila took the rough fabric with trembling hands and gathered it about her shoulders. The pristine robes she'd taken from Ko'ani had hidden her so well in the inner city, but here they would do the opposite. Naila looked down at them with a sinking feeling in her stomach; the cloak barely reached her ankles and her robes were still visible from the front, but it might just be enough to slip by someone unnoticed. At a distance.

Haelius himself was dressed in his plain tunic and trousers, and yet without using a spell to hide his scars he was still too recognisable. There were few mages in Amoria who wouldn't know the famous Wizard Akana.

He turned to address the others, his scarred hand opening and closing at his side in barely suppressed agitation. "Listen to me carefully. To get you out of the city, I need to jump all of us far enough that Oriven and his guards won't see us. That kind of distance will be a challenge, and even more so because I'm moving four of us."

The priest's jaw moved as if he were chewing on the wizard's words, the talk of magic stripping away some of his usual bravado. "Can you do it? Is it dangerous?"

"I can do it." When Haelius shifted his gaze to the Ellathian, the priest shrank beneath it. "There will be no danger for you."

For you, thought Naila, screwing her eyes tight against the guilt which slithered in her gut. It was a different story for Haelius. This was everything she'd meant to protect him from.

"Before that, however," Haelius continued, "there will be plenty of danger to all of us. There are few mages in the Southern Quarter, but Surveyors are patrolling these streets, and their numbers will increase once we reach the Adventus. We will need to get within sight of the bridge before I can get us out – and *we must not be seen*. My power is not limitless, and it hasn't fully recovered from repairing the dome. I won't be able to use it to protect us."

The priest and his bodyguard shared a sideways look and then nodded. "We understand."

"Good. Then it's time; we should go."

The others moved away, heaving their bags over their shoulders and murmuring in low, conspiratorial voices. Naila stayed in place, her eyes fixed on where the white hem of her robes slipped out from beneath her cloak. It wasn't enough. None of it had been enough. In trying to protect her friends, she'd put Haelius in more danger than ever.

"Naila?" Haelius's voice was gentle but insistent.

A warm hand closed on her shoulder, making her look up and meet his gaze.

He read her expression perfectly. "I know." He smiled one of his crooked smiles. "This is the only way. Trust me."

"I do," she answered, unable to keep the despair from her voice. "But this isn't what I wanted. I meant to ... I thought leaving would keep you safe."

"A lost cause, I'm afraid." He was trying for humour, but his tone fell too far short. "This is the best we can do – for both of us. Now, come on, there isn't much time."

*

Walking through the Southern Quarter now was somehow worse than it had been on the night of the riots. It felt like moving through a creature long dead, the towering buildings Amoria's exposed bones. Silence thickened the air, every movement straining against it. The only sounds were intrusions – the clatter of a distant scavenger, footsteps of strangers slipping between the ribs of the city with unknown purpose. Naila tried not to look at anyone they passed, sure that people out this night would wish to be observed as little as they did. Instead, she kept her eyes on Haelius's back, stepping into his footsteps as if trying to leave a single set of prints.

Above them, as always, was the curve of Amoria's glass, a bruised indigo against the black of night. Amoria's shell felt thinner than ever, and as Naila walked beneath it she tried not to remember the ugly sound of the glass beginning to break.

Haelius led the way with a certainty that made Naila think he had studied their route before leaving, committing it to memory like the shape of a spell. From behind, he looked almost like any non-mage, his tunic faded to grey in the low light. But Naila could sense the tug of his magic beneath his skin, the constant pull of power no matter how much he suppressed it. It seemed too much to hope that any Surveyors wouldn't feel it, too.

At his shoulder was the Dahrani mercenary, the long sabre strapped conspicuously at his hip. The priest kept pace with Naila, his shoulders bent low, a hood pulled up over his distinctive blonde hair. They all nearly stumbled into Haelius when he stopped.

"Mages ahead," he hissed, even a whisper too loud in the oppressive quiet.

A moment later and Naila could feel them, two bright beacons of power coming down the road ahead of them.

Haelius's fingers dug into Naila's arm, pulling her sideways into an alley, all four of them stumbling into the shadows. They pressed flat against the wall, the stone a wet cold despite Naila's cloak. Haelius angled himself slightly in front of her, his body tight like a held breath. Gradually, Naila became aware of a blankness where Haelius stood, the sense of something being erased. It was his magic, she realised;

he was swallowing his power deep inside himself, burying it behind layers of control.

The mages came closer, echoing footsteps and murmuring voices. Blood rushed in Naila's ears, a distorting pulse which rendered everything distant and unreal. Next to her, the priest pulled a silver brooch to his lips and screwed his eyes shut.

The Surveyors didn't break their stride as they passed, robes swirling about their feet like black water. They were talking like a couple of friends, the conversation so mundane that it felt abhorrent. One of them made a joke, and they both laughed, a strange warbling through the distorting magic. More than ever, Naila felt the jagged edges of Amoria scraping up against each other.

Once they'd passed, the priest made to move away, but Haelius gave a short, sharp shake of his head, his body still rigid with concentration. Only after the Surveyors' magic faded completely did he let go with a gasp, his magic blossoming on Naila's awareness. All that effort just to keep his magic hidden. Naila eyed him worriedly. He wouldn't be able to do that once they got closer to the bridge – once Surveyors were all around them.

Haelius caught her look. "Come on" was all he said. "We need to keep moving."

From then on, Haelius kept them to the smaller streets, running a crooked and parallel path to the main roads. They were circling around the border of the Southern Quarter, and as they drew closer to the edge of Amoria their route disintegrated into a tangle of small streets and abandoned buildings. At least here there were no Surveyors. The outer city was largely ignored, a border of weeds at the edge of a field. Ahead of them, the dome formed a concave horizon, giving Naila the uneasy sensation that she had reached the edge of the sky.

But they were approaching the Adventus fast, the shadow of the Majlis looming above rooftops like grasping fingers. Already, Naila could feel the growing aura of magic, the sense that there were mages gathering ahead.

Haelius beckoned them close. "This is it. We need to move quickly.

Remember – I need to get within sight of the White Bridge to get us far enough."

"Haelius," Naila whispered. "It's surrounded with mages. I can feel them."

The priest stiffened and the mercenary's hand twitched towards his blade.

Haelius only nodded, his eyes fixed on Naila. "I know. At least here the magic of the others will hide mine. Stay close to me. As soon as you see the bridge, grab onto me and I'll get us out." He gave Naila's shoulder one quick squeeze. "Come on. It's now or never."

They walked at a pace quick enough that all Naila could do was focus on her breathing and staying within arm's length of Haelius. The Adventus didn't feel like something dead but something lying in wait. The buildings loomed tall around them, the silent sentinels of Amoria's gateway, and twice Naila thought she caught sight of a shadow on the rooftops; she hoped they were spies for the Shiura Assembly and not for Oriven.

The sharp scent of magic was all around them now. Naila tried to focus on the individual points, picking out where the Surveyors were waiting for them, but her focus blurred like trying to make out too many overlapping lights.

Haelius had no such trouble.

"Right," he whispered, and ducked into a branching street, moments before a Justice and three Surveyors marched past them, their steps in perfect unison.

He moved more freely here, less like he'd memorised their route and more like he knew these streets intimately. They ducked and wove through criss-crossing avenues, pressing into doorways and slipping into alleyways so narrow that Naila could reach out to touch the buildings on either side. Twice Haelius halted abruptly and shoved them back, moments before another patrol marched past. Here they walked in perfect formation, each group made up of three Surveyors and one Justice, and none of *these* Surveyors were chatting or laughing.

The third time they were not so lucky. They were poised at the edge of a main street, backed into a doorway, pressed in so close that Naila could feel someone's breath tickling the back of her neck. The patrol was almost past when one of the Surveyors faltered, their empty face sliding towards them, peering questioningly into the shadows. Naila stiffened, everything in her scrunched tight. They were so close and there was so little to hide them. One step closer and they'd be seen.

Haelius made a quick gesture with one hand, and magic flared briefly on the opposite street, making all four mages whirl round in surprise.

"Did you feel that?" came the distorted voice of one Surveyor. "What was it?"

"No idea," the Justice answered, waving the others forward to check.

There was no time to feel any relief, or to register the squirming doubt at Haelius using his magic; as soon as the Justice had crossed to the other side of the street, Haelius snapped, "*Now!*" and they were moving again.

Naila was half jogging to keep up with Haelius's long stride, a strange pretence at calm while every muscle in her body screamed at her to run. She was desperate to turn around, to look over her shoulder and see if the Surveyors were following. But she kept her eyes forward, her cloak pulled tight, her heartbeat too loud in her ears.

And then, everything they'd been dreading. "Hey! Who goes there? Stop in the—"

"Run!" Haelius shouted.

The world blurred as Naila ran, everything distilled down to the thump of her footsteps and the road tearing away beneath them. She could feel magic building like a storm in their wake, but Haelius was already twisting into a side street and then another, spells smashing into buildings inches behind them, stone and glass scattering into the street. The black pendant at Naila's neck hung heavy with power and promise. All it would take was a touch and Naila would be able to protect them: block their pursuers' paths with slick ice. But she had sworn to Haelius that she wouldn't, that she would trust him to get them out.

The mages were closing in on them on all sides, a seething tide of magic lapping at their heels. Naila saw Haelius hesitate, unsure of which way to turn. His eyes flickered in and out of the sight, as if he was tempted to try the jump even from here. They were still half a mile from the White Bridge, too far even for Haelius to make it. Desperation gnawed at Naila's heart. They needed to get away. *Haelius* needed to get away. If anyone saw him— if Oriven realised what he'd tried to do.

There was no time to think, no turning back. Boots pounded down the road behind them. The priest and the mercenary were already running for the next corner, and Haelius shoved Naila after them. She stumbled into the next street – her heart thumping in her ears.

A Justice was waiting for them.

The priest cursed, Karameth was drawing his sword, and Haelius – Haelius was utterly motionless, pinned as if the Justice already had him in a holding spell. For an awful moment, Naila thought he'd been caught, but then the Justice looked at Naila and she was struck by the same awful force, holding her still without any magic at all.

It was Dailem.

Hope and fear warred in Naila's chest, and she could see the same battle on Dailem's face. Her eyes darted between Naila, Haelius and the Ellathian, her expression torn between horror and an anger so fierce that it struck like the heat of magical flame. Naila realised suddenly that she didn't know what Dailem would do. She didn't know if Dailem would let them go.

It had only been a second, but Naila's life began and ended a thousand times in that moment.

Finally, Dailem lifted one hand and gestured down the street behind her.

"Go," she urged when none of them moved. "*Now*, you idiots."

Naila felt the breath go out of her. She wanted to sag in relief, to fall at Dailem's feet and beg her to take her *home*, to Ko'ani and Malek and their beautiful home in the sky.

But they were running again, Dailem disappearing behind them, Haelius a constant pressure at Naila's back. The mercenary's sword glinted at the edge of her vision.

"Quick! They went this way!" Dailem's voice cut through everything, and Naila didn't know if it was a distraction, or if Dailem had given them the only chance she would.

They'd hardly made it another hundred yards before they heard the thump of footsteps ahead of them, a terrible echo of the thundering footfall in their wake. This time they were on a long, narrow street with high stone buildings on both sides. Naila couldn't see another side street, or even a balcony where they might pull themselves up out of sight. They were trapped.

Her companions knew it, too. They'd stopped, the mercenary raising his sword, the priest reaching for something tucked within his robes.

Haelius turned to look at Naila, and she could see the full whites of his eyes. His breath was short and ragged, and he looked as pale as he had the night of the riots. His expression frightened her more than anything Naila had ever seen. She wanted his guidance, his steady presence, his unending power, but instead she found only fear, raw and exposed. He didn't know what to do.

The pendant was like a buzzing at the edge of Naila's hearing. Her hand moved instinctively, creeping towards the smooth obsidian at her neck.

Time skipped forward, as if it too had been holding its breath. Haelius had her arm in his hand, pulling it away from her neck. "Grab onto me," he called to the others. "We go now."

"No!" Naila tried to pull away. "Haelius you can't – we're still too far, we—"

His magic seized them.

It was the longest Naila had ever been suspended in Haelius's power. She could feel the magic straining in his grasp, a tangle of flickering threads drawing tighter and tighter around them. It picked at Naila's skin, as if the magic meant to drag her into the pattern, reducing her to nothing but anima and magic. Within the void, someone screamed, and Naila couldn't tell if it was real or if the voice had come from inside her head.

But the cry followed them as the spell collapsed and they fell with a thump onto the solid stone of the bridge, the world lurching back into focus. They were enveloped by warm air, a breeze rising off water that lapped and splashed at the stone far below their feet. When Naila opened her eyes, they were further along the bridge than she would have thought possible, well beyond the ability of Oriven's guards to detect them.

As always, the magic had taken its toll. The cry had come from Haelius, his teeth clenched, his body sagging against the carved para-pet. The priest and the mercenary had let themselves sink down to the dusty road, but Haelius clung to the railing, holding himself together through sheer force of will. He was breathing so fast that Naila wasn't sure if it was exhaustion or panic.

She forced herself towards him on trembling legs, her whole body howling in protest. "Haelius?" She reached out for his arm, cursing herself for the thousandth time that she still wasn't a mage, that she still couldn't offer him any power. "Haelius, are you all right?"

His grip tightened and he took a heaving gulp of air, his breaths finally starting to slow. He was doing it for her, Naila realised, to re-assure her, and the thought pressed down hard on an already bruised heart.

"I'm all right," he gasped, sounding anything but. He took another two slow breaths and shook his head. "I'm all right. Are you—?" He turned, too quickly, and winced.

"I'm fine. We're fine. We all made it."

"Just," said the priest, his head tipped back against a marble column, his skin almost the same colour as the stone.

Naila opened her mouth to snap that he had no idea what Haelius had just managed to do, but Haelius interrupted her.

"He's right. Goddess. He's right. I'm sorry, that was too close."

"No, *I'm* sorry." Naila dropped her hand, crossing her arms and folding herself in around her guilt. "This is all my fault. I shouldn't have left. I shouldn't have touched the artefact. I shouldn't have asked for your help."

"Naila—" he tried to talk over her. "Naila. You never asked for my help. I offered it. Remember?"

It was back, that unshakeable calm, the certainty that if she trusted him everything would turn out all right. Now Naila wondered how much of it was real, and how much of it he carefully crafted for her. Goddess, but she'd been hiding behind him for far too long.

Amoria still loomed above them, its purple light leaching into the black sky. It dominated the night, blotting out the stars. On the opposite shore, Jasser was nothing more than a gathering of black shapes, barely visible against the endless dark behind it.

"I can't stay," Haelius said softly. With his back to the city, Amoria's glow formed a halo around his head, hiding his face in shadow. "I need to return home before they look for me."

"Go back?" Naila started at him. "You can't be serious? You can't go back. They *saw* you."

"Only Dailem saw my face."

"And who else could have got us out?"

"Naila—"

"We *disappeared*!"

"Naila!" His voice held the same note of command he'd used to make her run the very first time she'd met him. "We've already talked about this. I have to stay."

"You're going back to be arrested," Naila murmured, her voice pleading and weak next to his resolve.

"Trust me. I'll be fine." Again, that certainty scraped together just for her.

She nodded, not quite able to make herself speak.

"Remember your lessons," he continued, stepping back behind the role of her teacher. "It might not seem like I taught you much about your power, but you've learned more than you know. And remember what I said." His voice dropped almost to a whisper. "Trust in yourself, not them. You have an incredible strength: use it to protect yourself."

Naila nodded, her eyes down, her lips pressed tightly together.

When she didn't answer him, Haelius tugged her towards him, folding her into a last embrace. "Here," he said quietly, as if this would fix everything.

She pressed her head against his shoulder, tears burning behind her eyelids. She had to scrunch herself tight to keep from crumbling. "Will I ever see you again?"

"I'm sure of it," he answered, though his voice cracked a little on the words, and Naila had the feeling the lie wasn't just for her.

When he released her, he turned to her new companions, his back straightening; somehow, he was Wizard Akana again, even without the billowing robes or the scarlet embroidery. "I've kept my side of the bargain."

"You have," the priest answered, hauling himself to his feet with a groan. "Can't say I thought we'd make it. We owe you a debt, Wizard."

The mercenary was already on his feet, having endured their flight far better than any of them. "Thank you," he said in deep, accented Amorian.

"Afwan," Haelius said, *you're welcome*, managing a halting word of Dahrani. "There will be no debt if you get Naila safely to Awasef."

"Well." Entonin turned away from Amoria and towards the dark shore, hefting the bags higher on his shoulder. "We've a long journey ahead of us, but at least it's in the direction of home. We should get going before someone takes too long a look out of all that glass."

Even as Karameth and Entonin both started to move away, Naila lingered, her feet and her heart rooted in place.

"It's time to go," said Haelius. She still couldn't see his face, but she could hear the smile in his voice.

"I don't know how to do this," she whispered, her hands clinging to the straps of her bags to keep them from shaking.

"Yes, you do." He reached for the back of Naila's neck, tipping her head forward so that he could kiss her on the top of her hair. It was an Amorian gesture that meant only one thing: family. "You're losing nothing," he said above her head. "You understand? We'll still be here. I'll still be here. You're leaving Amoria, not us."

Naila's throat was thick with grief. *It meant family.* Had she really just found a family in Amoria only to leave it behind?

She felt him gathering his power to leave her, magic sinking down through the air towards him. "Goodbye, Naila. Be safe. I have every faith that you can do this."

BOOK III
THE STRANGER

31

NAILA

Entering Jasser was like stepping into a wall of noise and chaos. It was loud and fragrant, every part of it in motion, people pouring through the streets like water. There were more animals than Naila had seen in her entire life: a whole herd of dommra plodded past, lifting their crested heads and braying into the still morning air. They were cajoled forward by a single man; he strode alongside them, only occasionally raising his voice and clapping his hands to keep them in line, and yet these enormous creatures inexplicably obeyed.

The children were less obedient, weaving between the legs of people and animals without any fear, their voices ringing out in screams of laughter, their bright faces plastered with dust.

Naila stood on the edge of it, feeling as if she was watching a complex dance of which she knew none of the steps.

She'd have to learn.

"I can do this," she whispered, holding Haelius's last words to her as if they were a spell that would somehow guide her through this.

Jasser roared to life in front of her, the White Bridge of Amoria stretched away at her back. This was it. The beginning of a different life.

It was only just dawn, though Jasser was as lively as the Southern Quarter on market day. The sun rose from behind the city, a swollen, fiery disc rippling in the haze of dust from the desert. It was more brilliant than anything Naila had ever seen, the colours brighter than she could have imagined from behind purple glass.

A hand cuffed Naila on the back of her head.

"No," said Karameth. Naila turned with a start and found she had to blink bright sunspots from her eyes.

"Gods almighty, don't look straight at the sun," snapped Entonin, staring at her in disbelief. "Don't bloody blind yourself before we're even three steps from Amoria. It's like you've never seen the sun before."

Naila bit her lip, her cheeks burning with embarrassment.

They set out down a street that ran parallel to the Great Lake, Karameth leading them. Noise pressed in on Naila's ears, the ripe smell of animal dung and too many humans intermingling in the back of her throat. Dust coated everything. Naila could feel it, gritty on her skin, plastering the soles of her feet inside her shoes. A cart rumbled past them, throwing up a cloud of it, and the man driving it twisted in his seat to watch them, his eyes locked on Naila. She tugged at her cloak, pulling it tight around her shoulders, more aware than ever of the stark white hem that marked her as a mage.

There had always been mages in Jasser, the two cities tied together by more than just proximity, but as Naila looked around now she realised that she couldn't see a single set of Amorian robes in the crowd. Oriven's new order had disrupted the balance of Amoria in so many ways, but now it seemed he had started to wear away its ties with its sister city, too. If there were any mages left here in Jasser, they clearly didn't want to be seen. Naila could feel the press of eyes on her skin from the crowd, and found herself tipping her head forward, letting her hair fall forward in front of her face. It seemed especially cruel to be singled out for *being* a mage.

Somehow, Entonin blended in far better than she did. He had traded his Ellathian robes for something simpler: a loose-fitting shirt and trousers, more suited to travel in the hot climate, all of it in dazzling white; it was shocking to see someone willingly garb themselves in so much of it. The scarf he'd looped round his shoulders was the silver and blue of his order, and there was a large brooch in the shape of a crescent moon fastened in the folds of fabric. Whatever Entonin wore, the shape of the moon was always visible on him somewhere, and Naila wondered if it was a symbol of his god.

"What now?" asked Naila, hurrying her pace to draw alongside the Dahrani.

Karameth almost looked like one of the locals and yet didn't, his bearing too rigid, his red kaftan a different cut from the ones worn by the passing merchants. He turned back to them, his dark brown eyes studying her and Entonin. Naila hoped he couldn't see the exhaustion writ on her face. Crossing the bridge had been *hard*. Her body still ached from her encounter with Marcus and their flight through the Adventus, and her pack dug painfully into her stooping shoulders.

Karameth said something to Entonin in Dahrani and he replied in kind. Naila watched in silence, chewing the edge of her lip, suddenly acutely aware of how isolated she was. She spoke at most a few words of Dahrani, and most of the words Ko'ani had taught her were not exactly useful in polite company.

"We need to find somewhere to stay," said Entonin eventually, his voice as weary as Naila felt. "We only have a few hours until Zuhr – everything will close. We'll find an inn and rest up until the evening market."

"Right," said Naila, as if she had any idea what Zuhr was. Whatever it was, it meant rest, and that filled her with a dizzying relief. She shifted the digging-in straps of her bag and tried to stand a little straighter, unwilling to show her new companions that she was struggling.

Entonin wasn't fooled. His expression looked more like a smirk than a smile. "Don't worry, kid, we'll get you a nice comfy bed at the inn."

"I'm fine," Naila snapped.

"That's a relief." Entonin rolled his eyes as he gathered his own bags back onto his shoulders. "I, for one, am bloody exhausted."

Trying to find somewhere to stay turned out to be a trial. Naila was beyond tired. Every part of her body ached. Blisters had rubbed raw on her heels, making her eyes water with every step. Her weariness made Jasser seem louder, the staring eyes of the locals more invasive, Entonin's smiles crueller. The language just felt like another part of the noise, utterly incomprehensible. She was surrounded and quite alone.

Entonin did most of the talking, leaning casually on the bar and appearing more at home here than even Karameth. Despite his first language being Ellathian, the same language spoken in Amoria, he seemed to speak fluent Dahrani as well. His easy manner quickly relaxed others: within minutes, his laughter would ring out across the room, his bright smile reflected in the face of whoever he was speaking to. But even his charm wasn't enough to get them a room.

"Full again," said Entonin, throwing up his hands in exasperation. "Either that or they don't want to give a room to an Amorian mage." He narrowed his pale eyes at Naila, glaring at her as if she were a particularly nasty stain on his fine robes.

Naila scowled back, blood heating her cheeks. "How do you know it's my fault? Maybe the Ellathian priest's the problem."

Entonin gave a bark of laughter that had nothing to do with humour. "I assure you, me and Karameth had no such issue when *you* weren't with us."

"Well, what do you want me to do about it?" Her exhaustion was coaxing her simmering temper to the boil. She tugged at her silk robes. "These don't mean anything. I'm not a mage; in case you hadn't realised, that's the whole problem."

"How about you try wearing something that doesn't scream 'I'm a bloody mage' then?"

"I don't *have* anything else."

"Enough," growled Karameth, making them both jump.

Entonin let one of his bags drop noisily to the floor, his expression mutinous. Even though she didn't understand the Dahrani words, what he said next sounded an awful lot like "she started it".

Whatever he had said, Karameth ignored him. Instead, he turned and stalked off towards the barman. After a moment of conversation, Karameth turned and gestured to a table.

"Sit, eat. Find room after."

Naila was more than happy to obey.

The seating in the inn was a mixture of tables and benches, much like you'd see in Amoria, or low tables surrounded by cushions, more like the Dahrani style. Karameth picked one of the latter. He stacked the bags at one end of the table, unbuckled his sword from his waist and carefully laid it on the floor next to him, and then sat cross-legged on one of the large cushions, surprisingly graceful for a man of his size. Naila followed his example.

Sitting was such a blessed relief. Every muscle in her tense back softened and relaxed. She even smiled when Entonin collapsed dramatically opposite her, lying across several of the cushions.

Karameth said something in Dahrani, his dark brow furrowed in disapproval.

"Give me a break," Entonin replied in Ellathian. "Will they just let me sleep here? I'll pay good money to sleep on their floor."

Naila rested her fingers on the table. Sandstone, unnaturally smooth. She half closed her eyes and sure enough she could see the residual magic in it: magestone. Everything here was strangely familiar and yet slightly other at the same time, as if Amoria and its influence had seeped into the land around it.

It was no different with the food. The landlord came to their table and started setting a number of small plates in front of them. There were the usual flatbreads and spiced fish, and there was even tchai, though the innkeeper pronounced it "shai" in the Dahrani fashion; but then there was a cold smoked paste which filled Naila's mouth with the taste of woodsmoke and aubergine, and a dish with soft brown cubes soaked in a tomato paste. It was veritable feast after the long months in Amoria since the silwheat died.

She pulled a face at the brown cubes, soft and stringy in her mouth. "Ugh, what *is* that?"

Entonin took a mouthful and sighed with pleasure. "Meat, real meat. Oh gods how I've missed you. It's shahm. Like a dommra, only stupider and better tasting."

"No thank you." Naila swallowed without finishing chewing, feeling it all the way down her throat. "I think I'll stick to fish."

"Your loss," said Entonin, cheerfully reaching for more of it.

"Here," Karameth offered a small dish to Naila, covered in wrinkled brown pellets. *Dates.* A whole plate of them. They were an expensive delicacy in Amoria since every one of them was imported from Jasser, and here they were heaped onto a dish as if it were nothing. She reached for one of the sticky brown fruit and was about to pop it into her mouth when Karameth stopped her.

"This." He took one himself and dipped it into a pale paste and then ate it, careful to show her the stone from inside it, as if he wasn't sure she'd know it was there.

"What is it?" asked Naila, doing as Karameth had shown her.

Karameth frowned in frustration and glanced towards Entonin instead.

"Dates and, uh, gods Karameth, I don't know what you'd call it in Ellathian. Tahina. Sesame paste."

The sweet meat of the date blended perfectly with the savoury of the paste. Naila closed her eyes, savouring the delicious luxury of it. When she opened her eyes, she immediately reached for another one, and a small smile crept to the edges of Karameth's mouth.

"Don't tell me in Ellathian," she said through a mouthful of date. "Tell me the Dahrani words. I need to learn."

Entonin gave her an appraising look. "You want to learn Dahrani?"

"How else am I going to survive out here? Besides, we're going to a Dahrani library, aren't we?"

"Ye-es," said Entonin, drawing the word out into two syllables. "Al Maktaba has the greatest collection of works in all of Omalia: Dahrani, Ellathian, Cerisan, the Brevin cities – it's not all in Dahrani. I could teach you the language, but I don't think your wizard friend included tuition in the bargain."

A little food and a chance to get off her feet allowed Naila to hear the jest in his tone where she hadn't before. "I'll be less annoying if you teach me to speak the language."

"Hmm, I suppose. At the very least, it would mean you could annoy Karameth as much as me."

The rest of lunch and the hottest hours of the day were spent teaching Naila Dahrani. Entonin was her teacher, but Karameth would frequently cut in to correct his pronunciation, much to Entonin's annoyance. She listened carefully and tried to replicate the sounds they both made, but she struggled with the different "h" sounds and with sounds that didn't really seem to exist at all in Amorian. She knew her weary brain wasn't really taking it in, but even this small connection with her companions felt like a precious lifeline.

It turned out Zuhr was the name for the noon hours, where most Jasser businesses closed their doors and the locals sought shade and rest. They waited this out in the inn, Entonin and Karameth eventually lapsing into conversation with each other, speaking entirely in Dahrani.

To start with, Naila tried hard to listen and pick out any words that she might understand, but their exchange passed her by in a blur.

Braving Karameth's wrath, she lay back on the cushions, her aching body sinking into the soft fabric. Her eyelids fluttered against the weight of being awake, all of the exhaustion of the last week pressing down against her. In moments, she was asleep.

"Naila. Naila, wake up," Entonin's voice, raised slightly over the murmur of the common room. "Come on, little mageling, time to get up."

Naila groaned as she heaved herself up, her body, if anything, stiffer than before.

"Where's Karameth?"

"Speaking to the innkeep. He thinks he's found somewhere we can stay."

"What? How did you manage that?" Naila managed to focus her bleary eyes. Sunlight still streamed in through the latticed windows, but the angle had shifted and the patterns had tracked halfway across the floor. How long had she been asleep?

"The innkeeper liked me," Entonin said with a slight shrug and self-congratulatory smile, but Naila caught the way his gaze flitted uneasily across the common room.

"Is something wrong?"

"No." But there was a nervous tension in him, and she could see him toying with a strange silver coin, rubbing it between his thumb and forefinger. "Just the sooner we find somewhere to stay, the better. While you were getting your beauty sleep, *we* were trying to get some information. Things are worse out here than we'd heard."

Naila sat up straighter, fully awake now. She tugged at the hood of her cloak, wanting to pull it up to cover her hair. Was Oriven coming for her? Jasser had seemed so different from the glass city that Naila had begun to feel like she had escaped, but of course they remained within Amoria's shadow.

"What did you hear?"

Entonin gave her a long sideways look, and Naila bit back her irritation rather than voicing it.

"It's a lot of confusion, honestly," he said eventually. "Conflicting reports of floods, fires, entire villages vanishing. No one knows if it's bandits or what. Probably only a matter of time until they start blaming Ellath." He tightened his grip on the coin, his knuckles turning the colour of bone. "Well, it would be more believable than some of the nonsense they're coming up with. Some idiot even claims he saw a dragon."

"A *dragon*." Naila stared at him. Dragons were monstrous elemental creatures from storybooks, bodies bigger than buildings, power enough to burn an entire city to the ground.

"Well, *not really*." Entonin rolled his eyes. "Probably saw a big wyvern and lost their mind. Wyverns are scavengers – carrion feeders – they'd be drawn to any kind of disaster. One man's dog is a frightened man's wolf."

Naila sat back. Her heart was pounding, her head clouded with adrenaline. There was a tiny part of her, lodged deep, that felt – what? Disappointment? Loss? Naila frowned. She didn't recognise this feeling as her own.

Unfortunately, Entonin noticed. "What? Are you disappointed dragons aren't ravaging the land?" He snorted a laugh. "Well, not to worry, you have plenty of real things to be afraid of. If there's one thing everyone is agreed on, it's that *no one* likes what's happening in Amoria. The city is locked down and Jasser can't survive without Amoria. Some of the caravans might think twice about returning; no one wants to deal with mages-turned-zealots." He eyed Naila's robes. "Worse, your terrifying, masked whatevers have been seen in Jasser."

"Surveyors," Naila whispered, a bitter taste in her mouth.

"Right. Well, it looks like we're not out of Amoria's reach just yet."
Entonin glanced up to the back of the room and visibly relaxed.
"There's Karameth. Come on, the sooner we get you out of sight, the
better."

The innkeeper was a different man from the one who'd served them
their food, but he greeted them like old friends.

"Welcome, brother," he said in accented Ellathian, clasping
Entonin's arm. "We are most honoured to have you stay, holy one.
And honoured mage," he bowed to Naila in the mage fashion, making
her feel awkward and embarrassed. "We do not see many of your kind
in our most humble establishment."

Naila tried to wave away his greeting, her cheeks warm; more and
more, she wished she could lose the white hem of her robes.

"You have rooms for us, gracious innkeeper?" Entonin asked,
matching the man's overly polite language. "We thought you had no
space for us."

"Yes, of course, Sidi, though it is only our most luxurious of rooms
that is still available." The innkeeper smiled in a way that was entirely
helpless and apologetic, though Naila suspected he was neither.

Karameth loomed behind them. "Roof," he said by way of explanation, in Ellathian so that Naila could understand.

"Lovely," said Entonin drily, all pretence at politeness gone. "And
how much are you going to charge us for these *most* lovely rooms?"

The innkeeper looked at Naila's robes as if making a calculation,
weighing her against his price, and that was when Naila realised that
the inn had never been full in the first place. "Two silnar, each, for
each night. It includes a meal from our most exquisite cook."

"*Two silnar?*" Entonin barked the words back in his face.

Entonin switched to Dahrani, his words punctuated by angry
gestures. Both he and Karameth rounded on the innkeeper again,
gesturing up the stairs, gesturing to the door, the innkeeper still
hiding behind his polite smile. Everyone sounded angry. Naila felt
her exhaustion roll back over her. When she looked behind her, she
found the eyes of other patrons peering at them from behind their
drinks.

"Well, I hope your wizard made you rich," Entonin addressed Naila so abruptly it made her jump.

Naila barely had time to gather up her things and scramble after Entonin as he stormed towards the stairs. Still, as she closed her hand on the banister, something made her turn and give the common room one last, uneasy glance. Most of the patrons had returned to their conversations, the air filled with the rumble of voices and the clinking of plates, but Naila couldn't shake the sensation of being watched. Just as she was about to turn away, her gaze snagged on a figure in the corner of the room, their hood pulled up even though they were inside. Shadows pooled beneath the hood, hiding their eyes, but Naila was certain they were watching her.

She shuddered and wrenched her gaze away, hurrying to follow Entonin up the stairs.

The rooms stretched the meaning of the word luxurious. There were two adjoining rooms, each with two narrow beds and nothing but a ragged curtain to draw between them. The windows were small and high in the wall, so that the only light was two squares cast on the opposite wall. It was beneath a wind tower at least, so it was cooler than the common room had been, but otherwise the rooms were sparse, with undecorated stone walls and little in the way of furniture.

Entonin flung down his bags. "Luxurious? Horseshit. I've seen dommra with better rooms than these."

Karameth replied in Dahrani and Entonin bickered back. The raised voices, the incomprehensible words, all of it pressed in on Naila's mind. She felt needled by their very presence – these strangers with whom she had no connection, but who had entered her life so suddenly and completely. Exhaustion, loneliness, homesickness: all of it knotted together into anger, and suddenly she couldn't bear to even look at them any more. All she wanted was quiet, to be seated next to Ko'ani with a book on her lap.

She left them to their quarrelling, pushing aside the dusty curtain and retreating to her side of the room. Briefly, she considered lying down on the bed, closing her eyes and letting sleep take her, but even the sight of the bed and its stained blankets felt repulsive, and she could still hear the mumbled words of angry Dahrani from the room next door.

Instead, she crossed the room and pushed open the door to the roof.

The light was almost blinding after the dim interior of the inn. It was late afternoon and the sun still beat down mercilessly on Jasser. Naila took a moment to let her senses adjust, the heat almost dizzying compared to the room behind her. She followed a set of white steps, heat rolling off the stone beneath her feet. Up here, a breeze drifted off the Great Lake, kissing her skin and rippling the silk of her robes against the backs of her legs.

The inn was a square set of buildings around an inner courtyard where animals could be kept, though currently every stable stood empty, only an old, dried-up fountain at the centre of the square. From where Naila stood, she could see the narrow streets which led to the water, square limestone buildings clustering towards the lake's edge. The Great Lake was a dark band of glittering water behind them, stretching out beyond the horizon.

Even without touching the pendant, Naila could feel it. The immense waters called to her, inviting her to sink her mind into their depths. But it was too vast, the enormous expanse of water too much to take in all at once. Instead, she found her mind focusing on small things: the lapping of gentle waves at the nearest edge, the smooth path of a boat cutting across its surface. Threads of magic wove through the water, tied into the very substance of the lake itself.

Naila opened her eyes. Even here, Amoria still dominated the horizon, her violet spires glinting in the sun. Her outline was blurred by heat haze, so the city seemed more like a dream than reality.

Somewhere in there were all the people she loved.

Unbidden, Naila's hands slid into the pocket of her robes, seeking out the small disc Haelius had given her and closing it into the palm of her hand. She could feel the tingle of his magic, a comforting pulse against her skin. She just wanted a moment of familiarity, a last chance to hear his voice in her mind.

Haelius, she thought, *are you there?*
She held her breath, waiting for his answer.
It didn't come.
Naila was alone.

32

HAELIUS

Haelius must have collapsed when he appeared in his study.

He didn't remember it happening, but he awoke on the floor, the sound of the tenth bell ringing in his ears. He pushed himself up on trembling hands and reached clumsily for his desk, pulling himself across to lean against it. He made himself breathe through the cold fingers of panic that were still pressing against his chest. It had been close. *Too* close. He had almost got Naila arrested, or worse, and then the jump to the bridge had come so close to unravelling between his fingers. It had felt too much like the accident – a moment where magic tore through him, a beast he could no longer bring to heel. He'd almost destroyed all of them.

He let his forehead drop onto his knees. *Be safe, Naila. Please be safe.* He'd got her out of the city, whatever it had cost, and he'd let her take the obsidian artefact with her. *Away from Oriven*, he told himself for the hundredth time. *Somewhere he can never find it.*

They would come for Haelius, that much was certain. Naila had been right; they would know it was him whether they saw him or not. He'd come back here to meet whatever fate awaited him, and he didn't know why the Justice weren't already here.

Gripping the edge of the desk, he hauled himself to his feet, pins and needles shooting down his left arm, his neck burning. He fell into rather than sat in his chair.

What to do with his last hours of freedom?

One of the many ancient books he'd pulled from the archives

lay open on his desk, its binding almost crumbled away to nothing. Haelius blinked blearily down at it. He didn't remember picking it up, let alone what had drawn him to it in the first place.

He turned a couple of the frail brown pages, his eyes tracking over the faded handwriting, looking for the reason he'd dug this out from the library archives. It was a book about the founding of Amoria, arrays for the spells which had created the glass, some of the first protection spells woven into the dome. Nothing to explain how the founding mages had managed the magic on such an incredible scale, nothing which might offer him some clue about the power that Amoria seemed to have lost.

On the next page, he found the same answer he kept finding every time he came too close to Amoria's earliest secrets. He ran a finger down the ragged ridge where the pages had been ripped out, the edge so old and worn that it was as soft as cotton. It felt like being mocked, like every time he looked for answers in the right places someone would skip away just a few feet ahead of him, dangling the truth from their fingertips.

On the right-hand page, at least fifty pages deeper into the text than it should have been, was an image so unrelated to anything Haelius was looking for that it felt like a mockery of its own. The painting depicted a vibrant landscape of long grasses and grazing animals, leafy acacia trees – an oasis nestled against a backdrop of jagged peaks, a small town alongside it. Underneath, in a slanted, cursive script was written only *The Site*.

Frowning, Haelius leaned closer, lifting the book so that his eyes were only inches from the page. It couldn't be, and yet it was – five hundred years wasn't enough to change the shape of the earth. Those mountains were the only horizon he had ever known, an early Jasser lying in their shadow. Where this image showed grassland and greenery, Haelius knew glass towers and desert; where animals grazed in the shade of trees, there was now only dry dirt and a land so inhospitable that it had taken magic to coax plants from the soil.

The image of the desiccated silwheat and the crumbling artefacts swam before his eyes. Even the broken dome, with its fine web of stolen magic. What would it look like if mages not only drew on the magic but the *anima*, too, wrenching it from the land itself? Would that be enough to raise impossible glass spires, to create a city like nothing Tokar had ever seen before?

It was Amorian magic. It had always been. All of this was Amorian, in its truest, oldest sense. Somehow, someone had learned their city's secrets, and now they were using it to remake her, to position the pieces exactly how they wanted. Setting Oriven at the very top.

It was him. It had to be him.

The knock came just as Haelius was setting the book on his desk, and he felt a fresh stab of panic. It was what he'd expected, what he'd been waiting for since leaving the bridge the previous night, but he was still unprepared for it. He failed to slow the galloping of his heart or stop the shivering of his magic.

"Come," he called, swallowing to wet his throat.

Three Surveyors entered, faces hidden by their masks, and two Justice followed close behind. One of the Justice lifted her head and Haelius felt a stab of bitter irony. Of course. Of course it was her. Dailem met his gaze with hers, her face carefully neutral. He had no idea if she was here because of their encounter last night, or by pure, dire chance. Regardless, he felt his attention dragged down, drawn to where an awful ring of metal hung from her belt. A magic-draining collar.

For a moment he considered running. It would be too easy. He could feel them gathering their power, and it would be so simple for him to snatch that from them; even weakened, he could draw the magic from the ground beneath their feet, the air surrounding them, leaving them nothing with which to fight.

But then what?

Haelius forced his hands to unclench, releasing his hold on the magic. Only when the Surveyors stepped towards him did he realise that everyone had been utterly still until that moment, their breath held, waiting for his attack. The edges of Dailem's lips were pale, her eyes too bright.

"Wizard Akana," she said, without an inch of familiarity. "Please remain still. We ask that you submit to wearing the collar for the duration of this conversation."

"Is that really necessary, Dailem?" he asked, but, as he spread his hands, everyone in the room jumped, their magic trembling. They were frightened of him.

"These are our orders," said Dailem, nothing in her expression betraying her.

Haelius eyed the circlet of metal at her waist with a tightness in his throat. He could feel it from where he sat, the weight of it, the way it dragged on his magic. If he cooperated, if he let them put that on him, he would lose every advantage he had. Worse, it would muddy his mind: the effect of the collar was greatest on those with the most power. If Dailem put that thing around his neck, he would be helpless.

"If you insist, Dailem." He said her name again, wanting her to feel it, to acknowledge that *she* was the one doing this.

He pushed his chair back so that she could step in next to him, watching her fingers as they clicked open the release that would allow her to fit the collar around his neck. There was an odd intimacy to it. Her braid fell forward in front of his face as she leaned towards him, and her robes carried the scent of her home – of that quiet apartment where he drank tea with Malek and did magic for their daughter.

As soon as the metal touched his skin, he forgot everything else, a wave of nausea rolling through him. It felt like falling, a lurching movement when he should be still, and he gasped despite guarding himself against it. For a moment he lost all sense of where he was, only held on to the edge of his desk with his fingertips, trying to breathe, trying to keep himself from being sick.

When he opened his eyes, all sense of magic was gone, the world dead and grey. Dailem had backed away to the opposite wall, her head bowed; Haelius even imagined that he might see pity there, but that only made him angrier.

As if he'd been waiting for the exact moment Haelius was at his weakest, another figure now stood in the doorway, his robes more gold than black.

Oriven.

"Wizard Akana," he said. "A pleasure to see you again."

"Oriven." Haelius refused to offer him his title, the throbbing headache behind his eyes erasing all possibility of civility. "So, it's to you I owe this humiliation?"

"Please, must we start off like this?" Oriven had a genteel smile on his face, making a show of pausing to admire Haelius's empty study. He crossed the room to Haelius's desk and sat without being invited, his Justice arrayed carefully behind him. "I am High Consul of Amoria – I must take precautions where I can. We both know that you pose a significant risk to my person." He tugged deliberately at the edge of his gloves, and the shame Haelius felt eclipsed everything else.

Haelius was possessed by a desperate urge to reach up and touch the scar on his face, and it took everything in him not to do it. Under those gloves were scars to match his own, on hands that had pulled students away from a terrible fire – a fire *Haelius* had created.

"I was a child."

"You lost control."

"And now I am a wizard of the Academy of Amoria—"

"And you are unpredictable, hostile, and at the centre of every incident in Amoria in the last months."

The anger was easier to feel than the shame. If he weren't wearing the collar, he could have ended this – ended Oriven – and no one would have been able to stop him. The thought was at once terrible and triumphant.

Instead, he'd let them collar him like an animal.

"It is a pity you were gifted such a power and not I." Oriven crossed his legs. "It was always too much for someone like you."

"Someone *like me*?" Haelius almost choked on the words.

This was the crux of it. The reason Oriven had always hated him: the hollow-born who had risen too high.

Haelius wanted to laugh, to rage, to grab onto magic that wasn't there.

"I could have achieved great things with your gift."

"I believe our definition of 'great' differs considerably."

"I quite agree." Oriven waited, still smiling, holding onto his next words like a weapon poised to strike. "I know about your little coup, by the way: the messages you intercepted and passed on to your father."

Haelius's blood turned to ice.

"I've known all along, and really I should thank you for it. It would have been much harder to move against the Shiura Assembly without proof that they were starting to plot against us."

"That isn't—"

"It was more difficult to prove that they plotted with the Ellathian; who would believe they'd seek the aid of our oldest enemy right under our noses? But now it seems that the priest has escaped the city, and he surely could not have done so without help."

The feeling was physical, like someone had struck Haelius in the centre of his chest, knocking the air out of his lungs. The world was dissolving around him, leaving only sensations: the thump of his heart, the buzzing in his skull, the shame, the shame, the shame. Had he *helped* Oriven? Let him use him, just as his father had implied?

"You've dragged quite a number of people into this mess. Imagine my surprise when I found out Lieno Favius hadn't even reported your thefts to my office."

Haelius looked up, the world lurching back into focus. "Reyan didn't know. He had nothing to do with this."

"Oh? That is a comfort. Because, of course, there's his friendship with Lieno Tallace . . ."

"No." The word was out of him too quickly and with too much force.

Across the room, Dailem was motionless, her face a mask of cold stone, but her eyes met Haelius's with an intensity that made him want to back away.

"No," Haelius said again. "She had nothing to do with— she's just a friend. Our classmate, nothing more."

"Good." The genteel smile was still on Oriven's lips, but it was starting to look wrong, fixed and inflexible. "Larinne is a talented senator and an old friend. I would be saddened if she were dragged into this; if she were damaged by her associations."

It was all a trap, one which had been closing on him from long before he let the Surveyors walk through that door. Haelius wanted to thrash his way out of it, but there was nothing to fight against. The collar was strangling him, and he reached up to pull at it, all pretence of calm evaporating. He couldn't think, his thoughts rattling in his head like broken glass.

"What do you want?" Haelius's voice cracked. He knew he'd give Oriven almost anything if it meant keeping Larinne safe.

"The stone," said Oriven. "The artefact you took from the archives. Where is it?"

Haelius had been expecting the question, but he still struggled to find his voice. "I don't know what you're talking about."

Oriven sat straighter, and at last the smile vanished. "I thought we might be past the point where you lied to me. Here, let me refresh your memory. In some of the communications you stole, there was mention of an artefact – a relic from the founding of Amoria. You decided to steal that artefact for yourself."

"What artefact?" Even now, Haelius grasped for answers. "What is it, and why do you want it?"

Oriven lifted a dangerous eyebrow. "You hadn't even worked that out? And they call you a genius." Haelius flinched at the bladed tone in Oriven's voice. "You stole one of the most powerful artefacts of our people and you couldn't even comprehend what you had in your hands."

It was getting harder and harder for Haelius to focus his mind through the fog of the collar. He dug a thumbnail hard into his skin to try to focus. He was so close – so close to understanding. "But it isn't an artefact of our people, is it? It isn't made by us. It isn't meant for us."

"Perhaps not originally," Oriven answered dismissively. "But it is an amplifier of our strength – with it, the mages of Amoria achieved the impossible."

Building the city, by draining the land of its anima, perhaps even creating the desert that surrounded them. The same power which drained the artefacts and killed the silwheat had raised Amoria's glittering towers. Somehow, the obsidian artefact had given that power to the mages. But Naila hadn't drained any anima, she had wielded it – just as Haelius wielded magic – and she could only influence water.

Haelius grimaced through the ache in his head; none of the pieces were quite fitting together.

"Where is it?" Oriven was at the end of his patience.

"I truly don't know."

Watching Oriven's gloved hands bunch into fists, Haelius felt a second of giddy, foolish satisfaction.

And then, just as quickly, it was gone.

"The girl," said Oriven. "The hollow mage. You gave it to her."

"No— I . . ." Haelius's body lurched like he was trying to save himself from falling. "Naila has nothing to do with this."

"Search these rooms." Oriven addressed Dailem, who gave a quick bow and signalled for one of the Surveyors to follow her. Haelius desperately tried to meet her eyes, silently imploring her to intervene; he *knew* she'd cared for Naila. She'd let her go.

Perhaps Oriven knew it, too, because it was only once Dailem was gone that he leaned closer to Haelius and said, "There were four people seen in the Adventus last night, on their way to the bridge. Four people who disappeared right under the noses of my Justice. The Ellathian, his mercenary, *you* and the girl."

"I don't know what you're talking about," Haelius whispered.

"Haelius, please. Enough of this. Nothing you say can protect her. Whatever you do, we *will* find her."

"Why? Allyn, she's just a girl."

"And you continue to lie to me. Twice now she has attacked children of Amoria, this time in front of a Surveyor, and my daughter saw what she can do. Haven't you been insisting all along that this must be magic: the silwheat and then the dome? A type of magic that we don't understand? A hollow mage, able to wield anima as if it were magic – it seems to me that we have our answer."

"And you call *me* a liar." Haelius felt his anger surge through him as violently as magic. "Why do you want the artefact then? Why do you need a power to build cities or create deserts? Everything, the artefacts, the silwheat – all of it has come at the perfect moment for the Consul of Justice. Everything you've ever wanted falling into your hands. You *know* what this power is."

Haelius had expected anger at his outburst, or at least denial. Instead Oriven regarded him with a cool, calculating gaze. "And herein lies your saving grace, Akana. You always did see more than I credited you for." Oriven's top lip lifted in a sneer. "Perhaps there are some baser instincts that can't be taught."

Was this a confession? Before Haelius could speak, Oriven was standing, tugging at the edge of his gloves.

"As usual, you've missed the point spectacularly, but I'm going to give you a chance to figure out the rest." The was a bright, almost feverishness slant to Oriven's gaze. "The dome. The silwheat. I need to know *exactly* how it was done."

But you know. The words were almost on Haelius's lips, but then he looked at Oriven again. His hard mouth, his taut posture, coiled like a serpent ready to strike. Was it fear? It was getting harder and harder to think under the pressure of the collar.

"I will find the hollow girl," Oriven continued. "Crossing the bridge won't save her. Did you really think that it would? Truly, if you cared about the girl's safety you wouldn't have given her the artefact."

I didn't, Haelius wanted to answer, but everything he said only seemed to make the jaws of the trap close tighter.

"This is your final chance, Wizard. I would like nothing better than to see you locked in the cells beneath the city, but I need answers. The silwheat, the dome. I need answers. You have two weeks. Two weeks to find a way to replicate this power, or to defend against it. Otherwise, I will put you where you've always belonged."

But you already know, Haelius thought, uselessly. *You did this.*

But if that were true, why was Oriven frightened?

And then suddenly it was over. Someone was reaching behind his neck to unfasten the collar, Oriven was walking away. Haelius sank forward, his head spinning, bile rising in the back of his throat.

"Naila," he whispered to his empty study. "Naila, I'm sorry."

She had to have made it away from here. She needed to be out of Jasser. If she wasn't, then Oriven was coming for her, and it was all Haelius's fault.

33

ENTONIN

The first thing Entonin did, once they were settled in their abysmal little room, was pray. He eyed the dusty floor with distaste and instead climbed up onto the bed, folding his legs under him and touching his fingertips together in his lap.

Ardulath, father of knowledge, guide me to you.

He emptied his mind, pushing aside the exhaustion, the savage ache in his muscles, the grit between his toes. He tried not to think of Amoria: a whole city of people with the power of gods at their fingertips, poised on the edge of war. He stopped thinking about his new sullen, black-eyed companion. He absolutely did not think about *her* ungodly power, or the threat of the most powerful mage in Omalia should Entonin try to leave her behind.

Not thinking about something was as useful as cutting the shape of it out of a piece of paper: he could block out the thoughts, but the outline of them remained.

Breathe in, breathe out.

He even turned to mentally reciting the tenets of his faith to gain control of his unwieldy thoughts. To meditate on those was to find pillars of strength and stillness in any storm.

The first: all knowledge is only a pale reflection of truth; it is the light of the moon, not the light of the sun.

Knowledge had to pass through and be reflected by frail mortal minds, corrupting it. Only Ardulath could know the full truth, for humans tainted knowledge the moment they had it.

What is that girl's truth? he wondered, failing once again to keep her from his thoughts.

"She's going to be trouble," he said out loud, giving up and opening one eye to look across at Karameth.

Karameth had pulled off his shirt and stretched out along his bed, his dark skin criss-crossed with the paler sheen of scars. Even laid on his back, the man's strength was obvious, his chest lean and muscular. He wasn't unattractive, objectively speaking. Entonin found his eyes following the line of dark hair down Karameth's stomach, and then he blinked and shook himself out of it. That was a stupid idea.

"I'm sleeping," Karameth said, without removing the arm from his eyes.

"Naila," Entonin continued, having to clear his throat to speak. "She's going to bring us trouble."

Karameth lowered his arm and gave Entonin one of his looks. "More than you?"

"Well, you get paid for dealing with *me*."

Karameth sighed and sat up with an air of resignation, pushing the loose waves of his hair back from his eyes with one hand. "Make your point, priest."

"For one thing, she's out on the roof right now. Have you seen her? Everything about her just *announces* that she's from Amoria. Anyone could see her up there."

Karameth didn't say anything, watching him with an infuriatingly inscrutable expression.

"She's never been outside Amoria; it's like travelling with a baby," Entonin kept talking, compelled to fill Karameth's silences. "It's hotter than the war god's temper out there. If she doesn't burn her skin to blisters, then she'll give herself heat stroke."

"Then it will be a lesson well learned." Karameth shrugged, then gave Entonin one of his slow, sideways glances. "You sound almost concerned for her."

"Only because I don't want to have any delay in getting away from this gods forsaken place. If she can't survive an afternoon in Jasser, she's hardly going to survive crossing the desert, is she?"

"You did, and you're the palest person I've ever met, and that includes Ellathians."

"Shows how many Ellathians you know. Have you even crossed the Angustus Sea?"

"I have."

"Really?" Entonin scoffed. "Whatever for ..." his voice trailed off when Karameth looked away, his dark eyebrows furrowed. "Wait, you fought in the Five Year War, didn't you?"

Karameth's scowl still sent a shiver across Entonin's skin, but arguably in a slightly different way than it had done at the start of their relationship. "Leave it."

But Entonin couldn't leave it. This was the most he'd ever learned about the mercenary's past, and it felt like he'd won something precious. The Five Year War was just one in a long history of bloody conflicts between Ellath and Dahran – the last one before their most recent peace, which still felt new enough not to trust but old enough to be wearing thin. It had been a gruelling border conflict where a stalemate between Ellath's numbers and Dahran's mages had left both sides with little more than scrubland and ruined villages. That anyone involved in that grim affair would act as bodyguard to someone from the other side was honestly baffling.

"Were you a soldier in the army or were you still with the Yenisseri's Grand Company?" Entonin pressed, knowing it was unwise but unable to stop himself. He didn't even know Karameth's family name, and a Dahrani without a family was like a wyvern without scales; there were entire wilaya of Dahran where half the population had the same name, and they were fiercely proud of that.

Karameth was just Karameth, and even that was an odd name for a Dahrani.

"I said, leave it."

"You *look* like a soldier. I mean, more than a mercenary. I'm honestly surprised you've survived this long with the Yeni—"

"*Enough.*" Karameth growled the word, and this time the chill ran deeper. Karameth sat forward, his dark eyes blazing, his hands bunched into the sheets at his sides. Entonin tried not to imagine finding those hands around his neck, but instead he couldn't stop imagining it. "Do what you wish about the girl. Renege on your deal with the wizard if you wish, but we will not speak of this again."

"All right, sorry, sorry," Entonin raised his hands in mock submission.

Karameth lay back down and rolled away from him, presenting Entonin with the smooth contours of his back. There were more scars, old ones that had almost faded into the honeyed brown of his skin. As part of learning to heal, Entonin had studied the human form, and his eyes followed the shape of Karameth's muscles, listing off their names in his head, *latissimus dorsi, external obliques.* He found himself wanting to reach out to run his fingers along those firm lines. Press his thumb into the dimple above Karameth's waist.

Instead Entonin made himself heave out a deep breath. He needed to get a grip. His temple didn't care who Entonin took to his bed, but he couldn't think of anything stupider than entertaining these thoughts about a Dahrani man he knew so little about, least of all his *protection.*

Still, he was sorry that he'd driven Karameth to silence. Entonin had begun to enjoy their conversations, exploring the surprising avenues of Karameth's knowledge, prising away small nuggets of information about the mercenary's life. Much as it was fun to bait Karameth, Entonin had never provoked a reaction like this one. In a way, it was a huge success – knowledge hard won – but he found himself sorry all the same.

There was nothing for it but to get some rest, so he followed Karameth's example: he unclipped the silver crescent moon from his scarf, touching it lightly to his lips before tucking it into his bag, and then unwound his blue scarf and spread it out over the bed. It was less than ideal, but it covered the most questionable marks. As he lay down, his eye snagged on the coin he'd set on the bedside table, and another cold shock of fear pulsed through his veins. The coin looked innocuous enough – a silver Ellathian denarius, marked with a crescent moon – but Entonin knew differently. He could see that the crescent was thinner than it should be, waning towards a new moon.

It had caught his eye when he turned to pay the innkeeper at Zuhr, set carefully on the table next to the sleeping Naila, exactly where Entonin would see it. It could have just been forgotten there by the previous customers, but Entonin knew that wasn't true. It had been left for him, and its message was clear to anyone who knew how to read it.

Sleep was impossible with the sound of his own heartbeat hammering in his ears, so Entonin spoke at Karameth's back instead. "We need to leave here soon," he said, prepared for Karameth's sullen silence. "We don't know that the mages won't send someone after us, or after the girl."

"*Go to sleep.*" To Entonin's great surprise, Karameth answered him. "We will find what we need at the night market and then we will buy passage on the first caravan leaving Jasser. Rest: you will need your strength for the journey."

It might have been Entonin's imagination, but he thought he heard the barest hint of apology in Karameth's voice. Or maybe it was resignation. There wasn't much between them.

Entonin must have fallen asleep because he woke to Karameth shaking him. He could tell from the dryness of his mouth that he'd been snoring. He made a disgusted noise and swallowed to lose the prickly feeling on his tongue.

"Wake the girl," Karameth said without any kind of greeting.

"Ugh," Entonin answered, rubbing his face with both his hands. "Why don't you do it?"

The glare from Karameth was about the only answer he could expect to get.

"Fine." Entonin grumbled continuously as he got up. He could feel the mess of his blond hair sticking out at every angle and longed to do something about it. "Naila, get up!" He paused at the ragged curtain separating their beds, reluctant to move it aside. "Naila?"

Fine, well, they were going to have to get used to each other on the road. He pushed the curtain aside and stepped into her side of the room. Blessedly, the girl was fully dressed and asleep on her bed, her hair spread across the pillow like a pool of black ink. There was a sheen to it, like oil, or a raven's wing. For a moment, Entonin didn't say anything. Even in sleep, there was something unsettling about her. He'd told himself it was the strange colour of her eyes, the way she stared, the fact that – whatever she said about being a mage – she wielded an unnatural, gods forbidden power. Looking at her now, eyes closed, defenceless in sleep, Entonin realised it was more than that. She *felt* like bad news.

No wonder Amoria hadn't wanted her.

She stirred, bringing Entonin back to the matter in hand.

"Wakey, wakey, little mage. Time to get up."

She frowned and rolled away from him but didn't wake. There wasn't even a hint of damage to her skin from the sun, Entonin realised with a mixed sense of both disappointment and relief.

"Up," he said again.

When she realised where she was, she started awake and sat up too quickly, staring at him with those disconcerting black eyes. She looked like a suspicious cat, Entonin thought, ready to bolt or lash out with any sudden movement. It made him want to laugh: the idea that *he* was any kind of threat to *her*.

"Did I disturb you?" he asked drily. "It's almost sunset and we need to get to market. There's a water and basin to wash—" he gestured at a chipped porcelain jug in the corner of the room "—but be quick about it. We need to find you something to wear that doesn't immediately announce to everyone that you're a bloody mage."

Her expression immediately darkened, but Entonin turned away before she could say anything, irritated that babysitting this sullen mage had become one of his responsibilities.

Failing in Amoria and now associating with heathens, Entonin thought. How far he had fallen. *Ardulath forgive me.*

Entonin washed himself at the basin in their side of the room. *You could leave her,* Entonin thought again, reaching for his comb. Maybe not in Jasser, that would be too cruel and too close to the wizard, but Awasef was a *long* way. Perhaps the wizard could find out that Entonin had abandoned her, but then what? If he could reach them in Jasser, he would have brought them here himself. Besides, Entonin had recognised the look on the wizard's face before they left; that man was close to the edge, unsure how much longer he had before he fell.

Brushing his hair back into a neat tail, Entonin tied it with a blue ribbon, still fiddling with the knot when he turned around. Karameth immediately glanced away, and Entonin felt a sudden flush to his cheeks; what would Karameth make of his treacherous thoughts? The Dahrani had always seemed too honourable for a mercenary by far.

He *looked* like a mercenary, though. Karameth had dressed in an impressive burgundy kaftan, tied at the waist with a wide black sash. Over the sash, leather belts crossed to his hips, his sword fastened on one side and two daggers on the other. *No, not a mercenary,* Entonin thought. Karameth looked like a soldier, more like one of the Queensguard, if truth be told. Entonin couldn't believe he hadn't seen it before.

He could also see what Karameth was trying to do.

"You're hoping a caravan will take you on as security," Entonin said, looping his blue scarf round his own shoulders.

Karameth nodded. "We need the protection of a group."

Entonin had been thinking the same thing. If the rumours were true, they could be dealing with a large group of bandits raiding the wilaya closest to Amoria.

"You think it'll pay for our crossing?"

Karameth's eyes flicked from Entonin to the curtain separating their room from Naila for just the briefest moment. "No. But if they take me on, they might at least let you come."

"Reassuring." Entonin sighed as he stood up. Apparently gone were the days where being a Seeker meant that people would *ask you* to join them, hoping the gods might bless their journey. Not for the first time, Entonin wondered why he'd listened to Karameth – why he'd set out on this journey with the protection of one man and not twenty.

More like a soldier than a mercenary, Entonin thought again, pursing his lips. *Huh.*

*

The night market was even busier than the morning one, Jasser living for the cooler evenings. A gentle breeze shivered the torches and flapped the fabric of merchant stalls, still carrying with it the scent of the day: lingering warmth, spice, fresh water. Gods but it was good to be outside again.

It was impossible not to notice the changes since they were last here, however. More than a few of the stalls were empty or covered over entirely, and there was no sign of any Amorians – mages or otherwise. The unease was palpable, just as it had been in Amoria, clinging to the streets like an unpleasant odour; it felt like a festival night back home, right at the moment before the night tipped from a spirited celebration into a drunken brawl. Jasser was a town that wouldn't survive without business from Amoria, without the caravans travelling here for magical wares. Entonin thought there would be more than a few of the trading companies who were starting to wonder if they'd bother to make the return trip.

The atmosphere didn't appear to bother Karameth. He led them through the busy streets with ease, his sabre hanging in plain view of anyone who cared to look. Even here, in the shadow of a magical city, people scrambled to get out of his way. Entonin couldn't help the small smile as the crowd parted before them, enjoying the sense of control it gave him after so many months of having no control at all. It was another thing that reminded him of being back home.

Naila was still peering about her with unabashed wonder, but she was more nervous than ever: she'd hunched her shoulders, bowed her head, and Entonin saw her look back over her shoulder three times before they reached the market stalls.

"Keep up, will you?" said Entonin, not entirely unkindly. "What's wrong with you?"

"What?" She started. "No— I just. Nothing."

So, something then. Entonin resolved to keep a closer eye on her.

Their first stop was to find Naila something more suitable to wear. It was easier than Entonin had expected. She listened to Karameth's advice, translated through Entonin, and was more than eager to find something which did not bear the obvious marks of mage society.

She picked dark colours again, but she insisted that the heat hadn't bothered her, and Entonin couldn't deny they suited her. Karameth pulled down a black scarf fringed in gold and moved to show her how to use it, but she recoiled from him.

Karameth threw Entonin a questioning glance.

"What is it?" Entonin translated for him.

"They're—" she stammered, swallowing uneasily. "They're lieno colours. The gold. And with the black, it's Oriven's Justice."

"Oh, please, it's just a scarf." Entonin rolled his eyes. "Gods be good, Naila. Just pick something else then. Though isn't it nice to be able to wear what you want without ascribing some ridiculous meaning to it?"

She considered this, stepping forward with an almost bird-like tilt of her head. She held out her hands and Karameth laid the scarf across them: the fabric was light and soft, its quality apparent even from where Entonin was standing.

"I can?" asked Karameth, and Naila nodded.

He showed her how to wear it over her shoulders in a way which allowed her to lift it over her head as a hood and cover her face if she needed to.

"You have better taste than I thought," Entonin remarked in Dahrani, but Karameth wasn't listening, having already turned to haggle with the stallholder.

When Entonin turned back to Naila, he found her frozen in place. Her face was bloodless and drawn tight, her black eyes staring from between the folds of dark fabric. She was looking over Entonin's shoulder and, compulsively, Entonin turned around to follow her gaze. There was nothing there but the milling crowds of the market, grey shadows and pockets of bright orange light.

"What's wrong?" he asked, a prickle of fear creeping down his spine.

She looked at him with the same expression of horrified surprise, her fingers absently touching at the collar of her robes. Then she deliberately composed herself, closing up her expression like a book.

Entonin scowled and opened his mouth to protest: there was nothing he hated more than secrets that weren't his.

"Come," said Karameth in Ellathian, before Entonin had a chance to speak. "Caravans."

At the south-eastern edge of Jasser they found the travelling merchants and their caravans. There were row upon row of tents, looming black shapes in the dark, and behind them was a greater darkness which swallowed up earth and sky alike: the desert. Here, even Amoria began to release her pale grip on the sky and there were stars, thousands of brilliant pinpoints of light, though no moon had risen yet. Entonin hoped that wasn't some kind of omen.

Of course Naila was staring at the stars as if she'd never seen them before.

The corridors through the tents and wagons were well lit and inviting. Here, merchants sat cross-legged on the ground, their wares spread out on coloured fabric before them. Overhead, the pennants marking the different companies snapped loudly in the breeze, their colours lost to the night. Karameth seemed to know where he was going despite the dark, and Entonin and Naila followed behind him, down the row of tents.

"Let me do the talking," Karameth said, taking Entonin's arm and pulling him close.

"All right, all right." Entonin yanked his arm out of Karameth's grip, his cheeks flushed. "Do you think I'm an idiot? I can see the problems just as well as you can."

Karameth looked at him exactly as if he thought he was an idiot.

Entonin hung back next to Naila while Karameth spoke to a man outside a particularly large tent with a brass fire pit blazing outside it. The man was dressed much like Karameth, with an equally conspicuous sword strapped to his belt. He eyed Naila and Entonin darkly, before beckoning Karameth into the tent.

"Try to look less like a damn mage," Entonin whispered.

"Try to look less Ellathian," Naila snapped back. "Besides, I'd have thought a mage would be useful on the road. The Dahrani aren't as backward about magic as the Ellathians."

Entonin arched one blond eyebrow. *Backward?* Ardulath save him.

"Don't be wilfully stupid. While it might be true that Dahrani *might* be more willing to tolerate your kind under ordinary circumstances, these are *hardly* ordinary circumstances."

She wrapped her arms around herself despite the balmy night air. "Why do we even need a caravan? Can't we make the crossing alone? I thought Nahrayn wasn't a long crossing."

Entonin almost told her not to be stupid again, but he was beginning to feel she couldn't help it. "Were you rich in Amoria?" he asked instead.

"No." Naila frowned, clearly not understanding the question.

"I didn't think so. Were you poor – wait, I mean *really* poor, like there were times where you genuinely didn't think you'd last until your next meal?"

She hesitated, still frowning. "I was a student at the Academy still. I got an allowance – a small . . ."

"So that's a no." Entonin looked at her, *really* looked at her. "I think you never had enough for anyone to bother with you, and I think you had just enough that you didn't have to bother other people. Your wizard has made you rich. Or rich enough to be noticed, at least. And, praise be to Ardulath, I have enough to survive in this wasteland and pay someone to protect that. But do you think Karameth and his sword will be enough if we're set upon by bandits, far from your 'Surveyors' and the Queensguard?"

Naila looked away, her lips pressed together, saying nothing.

And you might be followed. And there are all the reports of trouble on the road. And bloody wyverns to boot, thought Entonin, exasperated. One lesson at a time, though.

An irritatingly bright light dazzled him for just a moment. Scowling, Entonin scrubbed at his eyes with one hand, feeling the frayed edges of his temper begin to ignite. The light came again and Entonin's gaze snapped towards it, ready to give whoever was causing it the full measure of his stare.

In the shadows of the tents, a man leaned casually against a wooden flagpole. He looked much the same as the other caravaners, adorned with a long coat and scarves in the Dahrani style, though he was maybe a little pale. The glint of light had come from a small mirror cupped in his fingers that he'd been using to catch the light of the fire and direct it at Entonin's eyes. Now that he had the priest's attention, he lowered it and held up a small silver badge instead, in the unmistakable shape of a crescent moon.

Entonin felt his throat go dry, the denarius growing heavy in his pocket.

He forced himself to nod, hoping he'd managed to assemble his face into an expression of calm authority. To Naila he said, "Stay here."

"What?" Naila jumped, still every bit the frightened cat. "Why? Where are you going?"

"I have some business to attend to. Don't fuss – Kara will be out in a moment."

She glared at him like she had no reason to do anything he said, and Entonin supposed that she didn't. He wasn't sure that he cared – in a way, it would make his life a lot simpler if she *did* wander off.

The man was waiting around the side of the tent, where the light of torches didn't quite penetrate, everything reduced to monochrome and pooling shadows. He bowed in a manner proper for greeting a Seeker but no more. Entonin didn't bow at all.

"Entonin tyr Ardulath, welcome to Jasser." The man spoke in Ellathian with a very slight Dahrani accent.

"Praise be upon His name," Entonin answered, knowing better than to ask for the man's name in return. "I didn't think to find anyone here."

"You are not the only one drawn to Amoria. There is much to see here." The man's smile was overly bright in the gloom.

Entonin struggled to smother a grimace. He hated all this pretence. "*Drawn to Amoria*", indeed, as if he would have come within a hundred miles of this place if he hadn't been *sent* here.

"Is this yours?" he asked, taking the coin from his pocket and holding it out on the flat of his hand. He hoped it sounded like a polite inquiry and not an accusation, but the rage and humiliation were hard to swallow.

"We had need to speak to you." The man never spoke in the

singular, making it abundantly clear that his words carried the weight of their temple behind them. "We wish to hear about your time in Amoria – the outcome of your mission." They already knew that he had failed. Of course they did, or they would never have summoned Entonin with this particular coin.

Entonin was pleased with himself when he managed to return the coin to his pocket and hold out his other hand without it trembling. "Let me see it."

"How cautious of you." The man raised his eyebrows, but still passed across his crescent-moon brooch, thick and heavy in Entonin's palm. It was cast in some cheaper alloy, not silver like Entonin's. He turned it over and brushed his thumb over the marks on the back, the ridges and indentations placed just as they should be.

"Blessed are those who walk in the light," Entonin said quietly.

"And long are their shadows," answered the man, still smiling that unnerving smile.

Entonin reached back into the pocket of his robes, retrieving the wedge of folded papers, the corners snagging on the fabric as he did so, and handed them over. "Everything you need to know is in there. I made considerable progress in gaining the trust of the Shiura Assembly."

"It was not the Assembly's trust you were supposed to gain."

Really? I had no idea. Aloud he said, "The situation in Amoria has changed. Relations between the mages and outsiders are worse than ever. We won't find any allies in them."

"The priests of Trebaranus will be pleased."

It was a goad, a dig at Entonin's failure. The war priests had been quietly gathering their strength for years, their eyes set once again on Dahran. Very little would stand before Trebaranus's war machine once it started to move, except perhaps an army of Amorian-trained mages.

"Amoria is unstable," Entonin continued, feeling too much like he was defending himself. "On the verge of collapse. Their new leader, High Consul Oriven, is some kind of mage zealot. Maybe we should be more concerned about that."

"That is what the war priests want us to believe."

"*Well maybe they're right.*" The words were out of Entonin's mouth before he could stop himself.

It was a mistake.

The man's eyes narrowed, and Entonin felt a desperation to claw those words back, to beg him not to pass them along. He might as well have wished for rain in the middle of the desert.

"Do you advocate war? Against the mages?"

"No, no of course not." *Ardulath forgive me.* As a Seeker of Ardulath, Entonin should be the last person to seek war.

Ardulath – a god of wisdom, guidance, temperance – only held sway while the Ellathian Empire was at peace. Advocating war was as good as handing the reins of an entire empire to the priests of Trebaranus. It was the last thing any priest of Ardulath would want, and preventing war was one of their temple's fundamental goals.

The mages were meant to be a deterrent: an ally that Trebaranus would never stand beside and a threat they didn't wish to fight. All it would have taken would be turning the tide of one disastrous battle, a moment where Ardulath and their mages could sweep in to save the day. They'd have won the favour of the people of Ellath, the war priest's soldiers, and all would be forgiven; the gods and their children were fickle like that.

Until that moment, it was a dangerous play. Mages, children of Sisephia, were the most hated enemy of the Empire. If the other temples caught wind of it before Entonin's temple had its chance to position them as allies, then the Temple of Ardulath would have no choice but to throw their support behind the war priests or risk the fate of Sisephia themselves. They'd be *leading* the charge into Dahran, while Entonin – well, that didn't bear thinking about. He'd failed, and his failure had left loose threads dangling, hanging there for any priest of Trebaranus – or Itelena, or Baelinne – to find. *He* was a loose end, one that his temple would not hesitate to cut away.

"Well, it is not entirely a loss." The man's expression shifted back into that smile, the smile of a predator who had cornered his prey. "If what you say is true, the Assembly may yet prove useful, as well as the wizard who helped you escape. The company you now keep—"

Something strange happened then. It was just a flicker, a small feeling that coalesced in the pit of his stomach, but Entonin didn't want this man to turn his attention to Naila.

"She's not a mage," he found himself saying, even as part of him still didn't believe it. "She's a part of our deal with the wizard to get out of Amoria. If you wish to make any contact with him, she must be safely delivered to Awasef."

"Yes, the girl." The man's smile was so sharp, Entonin couldn't see the edges of it. "Well, that suits our purpose for now. You may continue towards Awasef. But be wary, Seeker, the rumours you've heard are truer than you realise – the road north is dangerous."

"Really? Are we expecting dragons on the road to Awasef?"

The man said nothing, and Entonin knew sarcasm had been a mistake. The ground had shifted beneath his feet – the coin, the threat, the failure; Entonin was no longer so sure of his position in this exchange. He longed to ask for news of home, his heart burning with it, but he refused to show this bastard anything else that could be used against him.

Instead, he found himself bowing, lower than the man had bowed to him. "I serve at the pleasure of our lord."

"See that you do," answered the man – *not* a traditional response. He didn't bow back at all.

When Entonin returned to Naila he suspected she may truly not have moved an inch. She was pale and jumpy again, twitching like an anxious horse. Karameth was back, though, so that was something.

"And?" asked Entonin, having to work at the casual tone in his voice.

"Where were you?" Karameth rounded on him immediately, as if the priest had been gone for hours rather than a few minutes.

"Just looking around!" Entonin shrugged as casually as he could. "Why, did you miss me?"

A muscle in Karameth's jaw twitched, and for a moment Entonin thought that perhaps the mercenary had genuinely been worried about him. The thought was more pleasing than he cared to admit.

"So, did you get us passage or not?"

"I did," but Karameth grimaced as he said it.

"How much?"

"Ten silnar." Entonin winced. "Each," Karameth finished.

"*Each?*" Entonin let his mouth fall open. "With food and water?"

Karameth shook his head. "And they want us to bring our own animals."

"*What?* This is outright robbery."

"This Amoria business," Karameth couldn't help but glance at Naila as he said it. "They are in high demand. And the crossing is more dangerous. They said a whole caravan went missing last month."

Entonin's blood ran cold. They'd heard that a few people weren't making the crossing. Entonin had assumed it was underprepared residents of Amoria fleeing into the desert, but a whole caravan was a different matter entirely.

Karameth nodded at Entonin's expression. "They think both of you are mages and are not best pleased by that either."

Entonin shuddered at the thought. "You paid them?"

"Yes. Twenty now, the rest on arrival."

"I guess we don't have a choice. Did you get work, at least?"

Karameth made a grunting sound. "I'm not the only one to try, so it took some persuading to make them believe I'm not just an Amorian peasant with a sword."

Entonin stared. Anyone who looked at Karameth and thought he was anything other than an ex-soldier or a mercenary was out of their mind – or smart enough to get him to sell himself cheap.

"How much?"

"Four silnar back when we reach Nahrayn. We leave in two days."

"Two days?" That was more bad news. "We need to leave tomorrow! What are we going to do? Sit here and wait for someone in Amoria to come and murder us in our sleep? At thirty silnar, we ought to be able to dictate to *them* when we leave."

Karameth just shrugged.

"Oriven had better not have sent anyone after you," Entonin

snapped at Naila, switching to Ellathian. "How much do you think he wants you locked up?"

Naila didn't react. She wasn't even listening to him. She was staring off over his shoulder again, every part of her still, one hand clutched at her neck. This time she looked genuinely afraid.

Entonin couldn't help it, his nerves had been poisoned by his interaction with the man behind the tents and now he felt Naila's fear infecting him; he turned to look where she did, straining to see what had caused her so much alarm. There was nothing, but this time Entonin had the distinct feeling someone had just looked away.

"We have to go," Naila said, her voice barely above a whisper.

When Entonin turned back, he found her staring at him, the gold light of the torches caught in the impossible black of her eyes. She was as disturbing as anything he'd seen in the shadows.

Thankfully Karameth was there to make some sense of it. "Magi?" he asked, one hand on the sword at his hip.

Naila shook her head.

"Well, what then?" Entonin snapped, every too-rapid beat of his heart shortening his patience. "Tell us what has had you so bloody spooked all evening?"

"There's someone ..." Naila hesitated, chewing one side of her lip. "I think there's someone following me. Us. They've been following us since the inn."

"Who?"

Naila shook her head again. "I— I don't know. Entonin, do you ... do you get Ellathians with bright blue eyes?"

"Blue ...? Gods, Naila, *I* have blue eyes – is that what has you wound so—"

"No. Not just blue. *Bright* blue. Almost turquoise. And their face ... they didn't look ..." Naila looked down, losing faith in her own words halfway through the sentence.

Karameth and Entonin's gazes met over Naila's head. Clearly Karameth had no idea what this nonsense meant either, but the unease had wormed its way into Entonin, squirming its way right down to his bones.

"Come" was all Karameth said, shepherding them back towards the market. Entonin couldn't help but notice that the mercenary carried himself a little differently, his head raised, his hand resting on the hilt of his sword; it seemed he hadn't entirely dismissed Naila's words, and that wasn't comforting at all.

Entonin found himself falling into step with Naila, watching her out of the corner of his eye. She'd hunched herself smaller, a defensive posture that she'd clearly learned in Amoria, her hand still clutched at her neck. He was annoyed by the pang of pity he felt for her.

"Look. I understand why you're frightened." He cleared his throat, trying his best to sound sympathetic and not annoyed. "The mages probably are looking for us. We're going to have to keep a low profile until the caravan leaves, but two days isn't as ..."

"It's not the mages," she said again, stubbornly. "There's something else."

Gradually, carefully, as if she thought it might catch fire if she released it, Naila uncoiled her fingers from around the thing at her neck. It was a pendant, a shard of what looked like obsidian set in silver. Entonin had caught sight of it before but thought nothing of it, assuming it was some unremarkable piece of jewellery.

Now, though, he could see that he'd been wrong. The pendant was black, true black, so dark that it appeared to drink in the light, but within the black were veins of colour, iridescent blue and emerald-green, like seeing someone's veins through the thin skin at their wrist. Those veins pulsed with life, glowing with a light that was all their own.

"It happens every time the person following us gets close," Naila said.

"Close?" Entonin couldn't help it: he stumbled to a stop and looked back over his shoulder, searching for someone with strange blue eyes.

Naila had stopped, too, cupping the pendant in her fingers. "I've never seen it do this before."

It's just her imagination, he told himself even as he looked behind him. *It's just some malfunctioning mage toy.*

But then he saw her.

She was only a few feet back from them, a hood drawn up around her face, a point of perfect stillness in the moving crowd. Even within the shadow of her hood, Entonin could see her eyes – they were the brightest blue he'd ever seen, clear and shining like aquamarine. No Ellathian had eyes like that.

As soon as she noticed him, she ducked her head and turned away, disappearing back into the seething mass of people. Entonin drew a trembling breath.

"Move," he managed to say to Naila. "We need to get off the street."

34

INTERLUDE

It was a girl. Just a girl.

Ra'akea had waited so long in the shadow of Amoria, ready to bring all of this to an end. But the moment they came properly into view, three weary travellers struggling along the last stretch of the bridge, she'd faltered, her hands dropping to her sides, the water rippling away from her.

She had no idea what she'd been expecting – some human who had stolen too much power, the land shrivelling at their feet – but this girl didn't feel like one of their mages at all. She was a *girl*, barely more than a child. Even in her weariness, the girl looked around her as if everything was a wonder, as if she was surprised and enchanted by everything she saw. How could this be it? How could *she* be the source of the evil that they'd been tracking? She must have been mistaken.

Focus, Tae hissed in her mind, but by then it was too late. The settlement behind them was starting to wake, and the group of travellers had come too close to other humans.

Not yet, Ra'akea answered, trying to convince herself as much as her friend. *The time isn't right.*

But the time wouldn't be right, not now that the group had reached this bustling human town. Ra'akea tried to follow them. She pulled up her cloak and slipped back into the dusty streets, disappearing between the people who emerged, blearily, into the early morning sun, all of them ignorant of the thing that walked among them.

Even following her proved more difficult that she'd anticipated.

Ra'akea was a hunter: she could slip silent and unnoticed in the foot-steps of a deer. But this girl, this *child*, knew she was being followed. It was as if she had a sense for her, some thread that pulled her eyes towards wherever Ra'akea stood in the crowd. The first time their eyes met, Ra'akea knew she'd made a terrible mistake.

The girl's eyes were blacker than the darkest night, and they hooked Ra'akea down in the very core of her being. It felt like being caught within striking distance of a predator you had no way to overcome, knowing you should run but knowing too that running was pointless.

The call of the power was so loud now, it jangled inside her skull, her thoughts unravelling at its touch. For a moment she thought she'd lost everything. This was it. This was the power that had created monsters from her people, had fractured their minds, had left children dead in the frozen ruins of a town. Whatever skin it wore, this was it – this was the thing she had come to destroy.

When the girl looked away, Ra'akea had to fight not to sink down to her knees.

Ra'akea! It was only after three deep, trembling breaths that Ra'akea realised that Tae had been shouting her name.

I'm here, she answered. *I'm still here.*

Tae's emotions were caught up between relief, anger and guilt. *Do you see now? Do you?*

Yes. Ra'akea was reeling, but her mind was sharp. She reached for her strength, for water, feeling the deep power of the lake at the edge of her awareness, a counter-melody to the girl's terrible power. She knew what she had to do.

This was it. The reason she had been searching for. The answer to everything her people feared. There was only one thing left to do.

Not here, she said to Tae, ignoring the sharp lash of Tae's anger. *There are too many people. We'll wait. And when the moment is right, we'll strike.*

35

NAILA

They'd piled back into their tiny room and slammed the door behind them, a good deal more grateful for the dirty stone walls than they had been when they'd left. For a moment none of them said anything, Karameth's hand still flat against the door as if he expected something to break through at any moment. Naila lifted her hand to the pendant at her neck, her fingertips brushing over its glassy surface. She didn't need to see it to know that it had subsided back into blackness.

It was dark, the window offering nothing more than a pale square of light cast high up on the opposite wall, so Entonin fumbled with a battered lamp in the corner of the room.

Wrapping her arms around herself, Naila waited, wanting desperately for someone to break the silence. She knew she ought to say something – reassure them, persuade them not to abandon her to her fate – but she didn't have the first clue what to say. She didn't know what was happening any more than they did.

Who are you? she asked for the hundredth time. *What do you want?*

When Entonin did eventually speak, it wasn't in Amorian. The words were sharp and unfamiliar, and she saw both him and the mercenary glance anxiously towards where the pendant hung below her throat.

Their gaze made her want to recoil, the tone of their voices made her want to run. She didn't know these men, had no reason to believe she was any safer with them than she was out on the street. Listening to their heated words felt like waiting for them to turn on her. It was too much for her to bear.

Naila turned and stalked away from them, shoving her way past the curtain that hung between their rooms.

"Where do you think you're going?" Entonin barked after her in Amorian, but Karameth answered in quiet Dahrani, words that Naila was sure equated to "let her go".

But go where? Naila found herself back on the rooftop, overlooking Jasser and the strange blackness of the Great Lake beyond. There was nowhere *to* go. What could she do, except stay with them until they were clear of the desert? Her other options were to return to Amoria and Oriven's judgement, condemning Haelius and Ko'ani along with her, or brave the desert on her own, and that death was more certain than waiting for the Surveyors to come for her.

Exhausted, Naila sank down to the roof, cradling her arms around her knees. Ahead of her, Amoria glowed relentlessly on the horizon, reminding her that she still hadn't broken free of its grasp. *Haelius*, she thought, leaning forward onto her arms, one hand clasped around the disc he had given her. *Please. I don't know what to do.*

She was still on the roof at dawn. The horizon ignited in a vivid orange, drawing a startling line against the deep navy of the early morning sky. The combination of colours seemed impossible, like they shouldn't exist outside of the realms of magic, yet it was the very magic of Amoria that had kept her from seeing such a sight until now. A sweet-tasting breeze blew off the lake, stirring the cool air and bringing with it the faintest breath of water against her skin. More and more, Naila could sense the water all around her. It lived on the fringe of her awareness: in the air, deep below the ground, in her very breath. It pulled on her attention, dragging her thoughts away from what she could see and further towards what she could feel.

And so it was that she felt them before she saw them.

It was a familiar sensation, like hairs rising on the back of her arms, or the faint metallic taste of Haelius's magic on her tongue. Magic.

Mages.

They weren't casting spells yet, but Naila could feel them readying their power, the sensation passed along to her like vibrations through a web. She stood, even though she knew exactly what she would see. There, by the bridge, only a short walk from the inn, were Oriven's Justice.

Her heart was pounding so loudly it almost drowned out her own thoughts. They were coming for her. The caravan didn't leave for another day, and they were coming *now*. It would take nothing for them to find her – too many people had seen her walking through Jasser in Amorian robes, and none of these people would volunteer to shield a mage in their midst. She should have been more careful. She'd just never imagined that Oriven would care enough about her that he would send Justice out of Amoria to find her.

Stupid, stupid, stupid.

For a moment she only stood there, her heart pounding a steady drumbeat of fear in her chest. Then something compelled her to move, a sensation so powerful that it felt like it came from outside herself. Go, she told herself. *There's no one else here to save you. GO.*

In the span of a heartbeat, she was hurling herself down the steps to their rooms, each jarring footstep sending another jolt of fear through her veins. What would her companions do? Would they come with her? Would they care? Or would they turn her over to the Justice to save their own necks?

"Mages!" she yelled, bursting breathless into the room and throwing aside the ragged curtain. "Mages are coming now!"

Karameth was already up, on his feet as soon as the door banged open. Even Entonin sat straight up in the bed, tense and alert in an instant. He cursed and turned to Karameth, speaking in quick, incomprehensible Dahrani. Naila could feel her fate hanging between them. She strained to hear a word she understood, anything that might offer her the smallest scrap of hope, but she couldn't understand anything.

After only a few seconds, she couldn't bear it any longer.

"I have to go," she interrupted them.

Entonin fixed his pale eyes on her, his expression grim, and Naila held her breath. "We all do. Grab as much as you can. Water first."

For a moment, Naila didn't move, as unable to comprehend the Ellathian words as she had the Dahrani ones. In offering her a lifeline, Entonin had completely untethered her.

"Now!" Entonin snapped, dragging her back. "If you want to stand here and wait for them, be my guest, but *we're* leaving."

Naila stumbled into action, her body trembling with a potent mixture of fear and relief.

They grabbed as many of the packs as they could carry, Karameth loaded with the bulk of them, all of them far emptier than they should have been; they'd begun to prepare for the crossing, but they were far from ready to leave.

"Can you tell where they are?" asked Entonin, his voice strained with the effort of carrying their meagre belongings.

Naila paused with a bag halfway onto her shoulder. Closing her eyes, she let the currents of magic carry her mind away from her, extending her awareness down to the streets below.

"Yes," she answered, her eyes snapping open. "They're coming this way."

"Shit. That gods damned innkeeper." Entonin spat the words. "He'll be bloody rich after robbing us *and* selling us out to the mages."

"Come," said Karameth. He was already at the door, holding it open with his back, bags crowded on his shoulders.

No one needed to be told twice. They stumbled down the stairs, bags colliding and rattling, even their breathing too loud in the early morning quiet. The common room was deserted, crowded with shadows and the grey outline of tables. The only sound was the faint clatter of dishes from the kitchen.

They burst into the courtyard, Naila's heart in her throat. If the stables were empty, then their journey was done before they'd even begun.

Yet no sooner had they crossed the threshold than a dommra made a loud, honking call of dismay, straining at its rope. The stalls were packed with animals, but two dommra and an annaka were tied up at the mounting posts – saddled from a recent arrival or an imminent departure. It was a tiny piece of luck, a sliver of hope that they might just make it out alive. Naila wanted to whoop for joy, but she kept it to a shared smile with Entonin. None of them said a word now, and the only sounds were the rustle of fabric and the crunch of the dirt beneath their feet.

Karameth filled the waterskins while Naila and Entonin loaded as much as they could onto the animals, but it was taking too long. The animals could sense their fear, their eyes rolling. The annaka snapped and hissed at Entonin, refusing to be touched until Naila went and got it herself. She whispered quiet words to the frightened beast and smoothed the soft scales of its neck.

She was fumbling with attaching a heavy waterskin when she felt it – a tingle on the back of her neck. Magic.

"They're here!"

She tried to attach the strap, but her fingers had become clumsy and stiff, fumbling with the buckle. Before she even knew what had happened, Karameth's strong hands had seized her around the waist and heaved her up onto the back of the annaka.

"Go!" he said. He boosted Entonin onto the back of his dommra and then jogged to open the gates out into the street. "Go now!"

"Go, go," called Entonin, striking the dommra across its thick hide. It lurched forwards with a loud cry, lumbering across the courtyard. "Faster, you lazy git, move!"

Naila's annaka ran after it without her doing anything, its loping stride making her sway awkwardly from side to side. She clung to the front of the saddle until her knuckles were white, a waterskin still tucked under her arms. Karameth was right behind them, but so were the mages. The door slammed open again and there were shouts. She felt the white-hot buzz of magic and ducked to one side just as crackling white energy shot past her ear. A grunt and a thump came from behind her and she knew instantly: they had Karameth.

She twisted in her saddle. Karameth was on the ground, hit by a holding spell, his confused dommra stumbling forwards. The mercenary was frozen, his arms and legs still bent as if he were on the back of the animal. Only his eyes still moved, and for a moment they locked with Naila's.

It felt like it happened without her consent, every part of her burning to flee, but Naila pulled hard on the annaka's reins, forcing it to slow, to turn its head back around towards the oncoming Justice. There was no river here for her to draw on, and the Great Lake and all its power was far beyond her reach. But the waterskin still sloshed in her arms. With one hand, she clasped at the pendant at her throat, and with the other she worked the drawstring of the waterskin free.

The world slowed.

She could see the moving lips of the casting mage, his lips forming the words *tenereses persona* over and over. Her own memory swam over the image: Celia uttering the same words, Naila's body no longer her own. But with that memory came the image of Haelius appearing on the bridge beside her, his anger enough to distract Celia and end the spell. That was all Naila had to do: break their focus.

A second mage was already casting, drawing on the power around her. It didn't matter – Naila was faster.

She thrust her hand forward. *Cold, hard, thin, sharp.* Water spilled from the waterskin, hardening beneath Naila's will. A dagger of glittering cold shot forward, straight towards the Justice – and through him. It slid right through his neck with disturbing ease, so quickly that for a moment no one realised what had happened. And then there was blood, so much blood, the mage stumbling forward, gargling and grasping at his neck. His hands were still at his neck when he slumped to the ground.

The annaka screamed.

It swung its head down, and Naila had to cling on, desperate, as it turned and started to run, not even giving her a moment to consider what she'd just done. The world lurched sickeningly around her, the annaka throwing her from side to side. Clinging to the saddle, she tried to look back over her shoulder. They were the sudden flashes of a dream. Karameth was getting up, the second mage had stumbled in her spell, there was the glint of cold, hard steel.

The annaka left all of it behind. It lurched into the streets of Jasser, and Naila could only cling on, a blur of buildings and streets sliding past her in white, grey and dusty brown. There were faces peering up at her from the side of the streets, angry shouts as people stumbled out of her way. No sign of Entonin, no sign of Karameth. She didn't know if Karameth had made it, didn't even know if she was going the right way.

It felt like an eternity before something came into focus beside her, the sound of a dommra's feet pounding against the packed earth, the shouts of a man driving it onwards. Karameth was half on his feet in the saddle, leaning forward, his arm stretched out towards her. He beckoned to her and Naila threw out her reins. Grabbing them in his fist, he immediately rocked back in the saddle, heaving on both the annaka and his own dommra.

At *last* the annaka began to slow, falling into a loping stride with Karameth's mount. All the while, Karameth called to his animal in Dahrani, his voice low and calm, a drop of stillness in an ocean of chaos.

"Hold," he called to Naila, raising the reins in explanation. "More come."

Naila did. She held on with her whole body: her arms tight, her legs clenched against the annaka's back. Her fingers curled into the edge of the saddle, pale and sore from the effort. Karameth led them both through the streets of Jasser, squat buildings and colourful stalls slipping away behind them. She didn't know when they reached Entonin, but suddenly he was there, his dommra running alongside them, every step shaking his narrow body like a leaf.

The spaces between the buildings grew larger and larger, turning into wide dirt tracks and carefully tended fields, fed by the waters of the Great Lake. Then these too gave way to dry ground and the last curling plants, thin-leafed and clinging to the very edge of civilisation. They rushed past a last group of animals, their wide, docile gaze the only thing to mark their passing. Then they were out, past Jasser and out on the wide, flat plain beyond. The desert yawned open before them.

36

LARINNE

Larinne forced herself to stand straight, her chin lifted, even though her every instinct was telling her to shrink down and back away. She'd made sure she was at the front of the room – the first person the Surveyors would see as they entered the office – her subordinates hunkered down at their desks behind her. She heard a cough, an anxious rustle of parchment, but more than that she felt the emptiness of the room: the gaps where her staff members without magic should be.

The procession of uniforms split around her like a black river, surrounding her. A woman broke out of the flow and moved towards Larinne, her boots thumping flatly on the stone floor. She was one of Oriven's new captains, her black robes spiralled with the same golden embroidery as Dailem's. Larinne only distantly recognised her: a lieno counsellor who'd never made Senate, now risen to new heights in Oriven's army.

Larinne tipped her head in greeting all the same but received no such courtesy in return. Even surrounded by Surveyors, Larinne couldn't help her eye twitching with disapproval. "Lieno Junia, is it?"

"*Justice* Junia," the woman snapped, two spots of colour appearing high on her cheeks. Viatrix Junia, Larinne remembered, keeping her own expression carefully neutral.

"Apologies, Justice Junia, of course. How can the Consul of Commerce serve the High Consul?"

"There have been reports that supplies have been going missing. Supplies which are vital to Amoria's survival."

Thanks to Dailem, Larinne was prepared for the accusation, but it didn't stop her heart from dropping a beat. "That is concerning. Do you need my office's assistance in tracking down these supplies? My committia keeps detailed records of market sa—"

"We're actually more concerned that someone in your office had a role in their disappearance." Justice Junia's eyes were as hard as flint, but Larinne noticed the way she failed to entirely meet Larinne's gaze.

Behind her, anxious whispers swept through the room like a breeze.

"*My* office?" Larinne answered, letting some of her true feelings slip between her teeth. "Justice Junia, I think you misunderstand the role of my office. The Committia Agricultura handles the produce of the glass houses, and then their storage is presently the responsibility of the Justice themselves. I'm very sorry to hear that there have been lapses in security."

"There are records which indicate—"

"You're welcome to search our offices, Justice. My staff and I will help you. I'm not sure where you think these supplies could have gone? The markets are heavily regulated, and Amoria's borders are closed. Perhaps you'd like to search our apartments?"

"There will be a search," Viatrix blustered. "And we will be interviewing the members of this committia."

"Is that necessary? I am more than happy to answer the Justice's questions."

"I assure you it *is* necessary. We're aware of your long and loyal service to the Senate, however it has come to our attention that the members of your committia are less than satisfactory."

That was enough. The last of Larinne's restraint snapped. "*Less than satisfactory?* What exactly does that mean? Every member of my staff is chosen by me, so an accusation against them is an accusation against me. Be sure that you wish to make that accusation, Justice Junia."

Viatrix's top lip twitched. "Perhaps you are unaware of the new regulations introduced for the staff of each committia. Members are being reviewed by the High Consul himself, and he found a number of your staff unsuitable."

"Is *this* why my colleagues failed to come to work this morning?" Larinne could feel her assistant's absence, the empty space at her side.

Justice Junia glanced down at a thin book in her hand, scanning the names as if this were a simple administrative issue. "Let me see . . . Ah, yes, the hollows."

Larinne flinched at the word. "The *non-mages*, yes."

"They've been reassigned somewhere more appropriate. This is a committia of the Lieno Council, and as such should be staffed by mages." Viatrix spoke like she was explaining something to a child, and for a moment Larinne's fury was almost blinding.

"I think the staffing of my committia is *my* concern. I—"

"Larinne, please." The honeyed voice came from the open doorway, dripping with unearned familiarity. "I'm only trying to ensure you have the very best people for your work."

It took a tremendous effort to move, like she was struggling against the grip of a holding spell. Larinne made herself turn and tip forward into a stiff bow just as all the Justice around her had already done. "High Consul Oriven."

"Allyn, please. We're old friends, are we not?"

The dark ring of Surveyors parted and then closed again, locking her in with him.

"You are a valued member of the Senate," Oriven continued, oblivious to Larinne's stillness or the fear twisting through her stomach. "And it is vital to Amoria's continued prosperity that this consul function at its highest capacity."

"My staff are excellent—"

"Oh, I'm sure they were, and I'm sure they'll find a new purpose they can apply themselves to with equal vigour. We must not expect people to function beyond their ability, in environments to which they are inherently unsuited – just as you cannot expect a fish to survive out of water." Oriven stepped towards her, himself deliberately moving in too close. The scent of musk and perfume crowded her nostrils, his breath warm on her cheek. Larinne stopped breathing. "People like us, we have a responsibility to our work – to Amoria. We can't let ourselves be blinded by our attachments when we're deciding what's best. It's harmful not only to the city, but to the people we think we're helping."

There was a brightness in his brown eyes, gleaming like the edge of a knife, and Larinne knew he wasn't talking about her committia any more. A gloved finger touched lightly against the bottom of her chin, tipping her face up towards him.

This was it; this was the moment she was supposed to fight for her people – threaten to resign, throw all her strength and experience behind her. But Larinne didn't feel strong. She felt like a butterfly caught in Oriven's grip, more likely to break her wings against his fingers than to persuade him to release her. Here, alone, surrounded by his Justice and his Surveyors, Larinne was afraid.

Oriven only smiled. "I see we understand each other. Now, my associates here are going to speak to your committia and have a look around, but there's no need for our involvement. Perhaps you and I could talk."

He was already speaking to her as if she were the only person in the room, and in a way that was what he believed. None of the frightened people around him even registered in his awareness. He stepped back and gestured to her office.

"Yes, of course," she heard herself answer, already turning as if he'd compelled her to move.

She let Oriven pass and closed the door behind her. The click of the latch had a dreadful finality.

Oriven stepped slowly through her room, claiming the space. He touched everything, shifting papers on her desk, peering carefully at her life, assessing its worth. Larinne had been so sure that there was nothing to find; they'd taken the grain and moved it through Haelius's pattern room to the Dragon's Rest, and then Larinne had carefully erased any record of it. There shouldn't have been enough taken for them to notice it missing, and nothing that let them track it back to her.

There's nothing to find, she told herself, but everything felt different with Oriven's eyes on it. Her body was betraying her, her hands growing cold, her butterfly heart trying to force its way free.

"Don't look at me that way, Larinne. You have nothing to fear from me." Oriven settled himself behind her desk, leaning back into her chair and crossing one leg over the other. It was a perfect mirror of Reyan's invasion of her office, and yet different in every way that mattered.

He gestured to the chair opposite him. "Come. Sit."

Larinne had to swallow before she could speak. "Thank you, High Consul."

He watched her sit, none of the familiarity in his voice reaching his eyes. "The heights of power can be a lonely place, and we've both been disappointed by the people we trust."

"My committia has never been a disappointment to m—"

Oriven waved away her words like an irritating fly. "No more of that. The hollows would have been, given time. And they're not who I'm referring to." He narrowed his eyes, and Larinne felt the last of her hope slip through her fingers.

He knows.

"I can see why you're drawn to him, the promise of his power, but Haelius Akana has finally crossed a line from which he can't return."

"I don't know what you think—"

"I don't *think*, I know. I know everything, Larinne." He was tapping one gloved finger slowly on the edge of her desk. Larinne watched it, unable to tear her eyes away. It felt like he was counting out the last seconds of her freedom. "What I *don't* know is why you ever wasted your time on him. He is, as ever, unworthy of your attention."

Oriven looked at her in a way that felt like fingers dragging over her skin, and every word Larinne had to say lodged in her throat.

"My people are not only looking for the stolen goods. They are looking for an artefact, something Wizard Akana stole from me."

Larinne's heart faltered, her blood cold. She bent every energy she had towards keeping her face still, as if she could project Lieno Tallace like a shield. Behind it, she could feel herself unravelling.

The obsidian artefact. All this was still connected to the stone.

Haelius had finally explained it to her after the dome broke: the way the artefact had remained dead in his hands yet had reacted to

Naila, granting her a power like nothing he'd ever seen, a power which manipulated anima. As soon as he'd said it, Larinne had known they wouldn't escape this confrontation. Everything was too tightly knotted together – the girl, the sabotage, the artefact – and this time she didn't think she could pull Haelius free.

"I won't ask you where it is, because I trust you're not foolish enough to keep this from me." It was a promise and a threat, Oriven reading her silence the way Haelius could read a spell. He tugged on the final thread holding her together. "You can rest assured that Wizard Akana will be punished for his crimes."

"Allyn, what have you done?"

"What have *I* done?" Oriven raised his eyebrows. "I've protected our city, secured a future for mages. Amoria was on the brink of collapse, and I have pulled her back."

"Amoria is on the brink of collapse *now*." It felt like coming untethered from her hope – if he knew everything then she had nothing else to lose. "There's no food, our trade is destroyed, the dome *broke* for Mother's sake. Is this what you want?"

"Just think how bad it could have been if I hadn't intervened." The leather of Oriven's gloves creaked as he balled his hands into fists. "Do you know how the Ellathians were able kill so many of us? How they were able to drive us out when we had magic and they did not?"

He didn't want an answer, so Larinne didn't speak.

"Because there were more of them than us, because we were always kept in the minority. It was the only way they could stand against us. Amoria is *ours*. It is the only place in Omalia where we outnumber them, the only place we are safe. That was changing. I've done what I must to secure our future."

"It didn't have to be this way," Larinne whispered. "We were all Amorians."

"I had no idea you were so hopelessly naive." Oriven uncurled his hands. "I expect that nonsense from Akana, but not from you. I didn't create the divide any more than a hollow-born like him can mend it. He chose his side, whether he'll admit it or not. Have you chosen yours?"

"I serve Amoria. I serve the Senate. I always have."

"I *am* the Senate." Oriven let each word fall with its own oppressive weight. "So, do you intend to serve me?"

Larinne sat with her hands curled in against her stomach, every part of her held utterly still. Even now, she couldn't make herself nod, couldn't make herself say what he wanted to hear.

Oriven's gaze took on a dangerous edge. "The proud Lieno Tallace. Even Akana knows when he's beaten."

"What have you done to him?"

"Nothing, for now. Unfortunately, there remains no one who can do what he can, or see what he sees; his skill is undeniable. It is the only reason he remains at liberty. He has until the end of next week to give me what I need, and then . . ." Oriven shrugged.

Larinne's chest felt so tight she wasn't sure she could speak.

"Now you, you have a different kind of power altogether," Oriven continued. "I could use you, Larinne. You are a keystone of the Senate – a foundation upon which others build their trust. And if you could keep Akana in line, then perhaps there will be a future for him in Amoria. I'm giving you another chance. There is a place for you at my side." Again, Oriven's eyes tracked over her in a way that made her stomach roil: not hungry but possessive. Inescapable. "But only if you do not cross me again."

By the time the Justice left, Larinne was worn away to nothing. She stood at the edge of her offices, watching as the black-clad figures emptied desks and tore open crates. She kept herself steady and calm for her staff, and when the last inch of black fabric disappeared out of her door she still didn't let herself buckle. She turned to a flood of questions and frightened faces, and she tended each one like a wilting flower, giving them comfort and answers, patting an arm, sending them home.

Only when the last of them had gone did Larinne let herself sink down on the nearest desk, a hand over her mouth. The Justice hadn't found anything, of course they hadn't – Larinne had made sure of that – but it had been too close. There shouldn't have been anything which led to her, to any of them.

She couldn't help remembering the words she'd said to Haelius after he'd stolen letters from the Justice: *do you think they need proof?*

She'd betrayed her committia, too. Larinne squeezed her eyes shut. She'd promised this wouldn't happen, but when the time had come to fight for the non-mages on her staff, she'd just stood there, Oriven's hand on her face as if he owned her. Were they gone because of her? Were they fired for their lack of magic, or because Oriven needed to teach Larinne a lesson?

Larinne counted to ten, giving herself those seconds to stay leaning against the desk, to feel her guilt. Then she got back on her feet and forced herself to move.

Haelius. She had to warn Haelius.

The pause before Haelius answered her knock was too long, and Larinne felt the brush of his magic even through the closed door.

"Come."

When she stepped inside, she found him half out of his seat, his eyes narrowed, his hands braced against his desk. The moment he saw her, he rocked back into his chair, his eyes growing round in surprise. The tension in the room dissipated, and Larinne realised he'd been readying his magic, preparing himself to meet a threat.

"Larinne?"

She tried to force her mouth into something resembling a smile but knew she didn't quite manage it.

He was as thin as ever, his hair half on end, but the bruise on his forehead had faded almost to nothing and she could feel that his magic had returned to him. As always, his desk was scattered with fallen stacks of parchment. A few of them had tumbled off the edge of the desk, next to towers of books he'd already managed to rummage up from somewhere.

He tried to push his hair back from his eyes with an ink-stained hand. "What are you doing here?"

"I ..." It struck like an unexpected injury; there was a time she wouldn't have needed a reason. "We need to talk."

It was such a relief to be here, to be back in easy company with the one person she trusted more than anyone else. The air smelled of old leather bindings and musty paper, and it felt more like home to Larinne than her empty apartment ever did.

It made what happened next feel like the very worst kind of betrayal.

Instead of gesturing for her to sit, Haelius scowled and turned his face away from her. "So Dailem told you."

"What? What are you talking about?"

"Oh, I . . . It doesn't—"

"Told me what?"

He looked down, and Larinne took a step towards him, her patience and her resilience long since burned away to nothing.

"Told me *what*, Haelius?"

"*Nothing*," he snapped, and the word lanced straight through her. "It doesn't matter. Just tell me what you want."

Larinne flinched. For a moment, she couldn't trust herself to answer, so she crossed to his desk and bent down to pick up the papers that had fallen onto the floor, gathering them into a pile and tapping the edges together with her fingers. She kept her eyes on them as she set them back on the table, on the sketched lines and winding patterns which looked as much like a map as they did a magical array.

"I came to warn you," she said, her voice flat and inflectionless. "The Justice searched my offices today, looking for the supplies we took and that damn artefact. Dailem warned me just in time, but they're watching my office now. Most of the non-mages on my staff are gone. 'Relocated', or so Oriven said."

"Oriven was there?"

She nodded.

"Larinne, I'm sorry. I—" All his breath left him in a trembling sigh. "He came here as well."

At that she looked up, just in time to catch Haelius rubbing at his neck with one hand. She knew exactly what that meant. "He *collared* you?"

Haelius dropped his hand but didn't answer her.

"Goddess, Haelius, why didn't you tell me?"

"I was going to. I just . . ."

"The High Consul had you arrested and *collared*, and you didn't tell me?"

"I didn't—"

"And Dailem knows? She was there?"

Haelius looked away. "Yes. Look, I was going to tell you. It's just . . . he knew. He knew everything. He knew about the letters I took, even that Reyan knew about them. He knew about Naila, about her magic, about the artefact. I just didn't want to get you involved and . . ."

"*Involved?*" Larinne spat the word in disbelief. "You don't think I'm involved already? You could have warned me! He cornered me, threatened me – and the very first thing I did afterwards was come here to warn *you*. If you had told me *any* of this, I might have been prepared – I might have avoided the Justice descending on my office like I'm a criminal." She covered her eyes with her hand. "Have you even warned Reyan? Told him that *he's* now under Oriven's suspicion?"

Haelius was looking down, his hands buried in his crumpled sleeves. "No."

"Do you think perhaps you should let him know you've brought this to his door?"

When he looked up at her, his eyes were imploring. "I've brought *you* under suspicion. Oriven said you were 'damaged by your associations'. Your associations with *me*. I thought . . . I thought if I could stay away from you, it might be enough. He respects you; more than that, he—" Haelius's mouth twitched with an old bitterness, and it was enough to make Larinne's blood turn cold.

"So, you thought, what? You'd erase years of our friendship, and I would just go and be whatever Oriven wants me to be?" She felt the rough touch of Oriven's gloved hand on her chin and shuddered. "You think that would keep me safe?"

"That isn't what I meant—"

"It's *exactly* what you meant. But it doesn't work like that, I'm afraid. It may surprise you, but I *am* associated with you, and there isn't anything either of us can do about it now." Haelius flinched and she knew he'd misunderstood her, but her anger wouldn't let her correct him; a part of her wanted him to feel every bit as hurt as she did.

"None of this protects me, it only assuages your conscience – lets you run off to play saviour of Amoria."

"I'm trying to find out what broke the dome. I'm trying to protect us." Haelius stood with all the force of his power behind him, and for a moment Larinne knew what it felt like to have the rage of the most powerful mage in Amoria directed at her. "If you want to call that 'playing saviour' then so be it."

"On your own? Will you fix all of Amoria's problems by yourself?"

"Larinne, please."

"No, don't let me stop you."

She looked down at his desk, the blue ink swimming behind angry tears. Which of these scribbled diagrams was the one he meant to use to save them all? There was a familiarity to these arrays that she couldn't place. Her eye caught on one of them, a curved road lined with magic. "These *are* maps," she said aloud. "And arrays. This is ... this is Artisan's Row." She slid out one of the pieces of paper to the middle of the table. "And this is the Southern Quarter, and the Adventus." She stared at the phonemes; runes for holding, for detecting, for breaking. "You've turned Amoria's streets into spells. Haelius, what are you doing?"

"It's not what it looks like."

"Tell me what it *looks like*," Larinne hissed. "Is this for Oriven? Did he get to you ..."

"No! Just listen to me—"

"Why, when you're not telling me anything?" Larinne was taking a step back, her eyes blinking too fast, her head shaking from side to side. "Why have you stopped talking to me?"

"Wait—"

"No. No I want no part in whatever this is."

She turned towards the door, her head spinning, the ache below her throat a noxious and potent thing. Even the thread connecting her and Haelius was beginning to unravel, and she could feel every frayed edge.

She sensed his magic gather before he had a chance to cast it. Without even thinking, she whirled around on the spot and flung out her arm, the words "*induresco repellam*" ringing from her lips. The shield shot across the room with enough force that it sent Haelius's papers spiralling into the air, drifting in front of his startled green eyes. It wouldn't have been enough to hold him, but it surprised him enough that he stopped before jumping in front of her.

"Don't" was all Larinne said, dropping her arm and the shield. "Just don't. I'm going to find Reyan. Someone should warn him that Oriven's watching him now, too."

37

NAILA

Naila's whole body shook as she threw up, her eyes stinging and swimming with tears. Her legs had almost given out when she slid down from the annaka's back, and now she crouched and trembled and tried not to think of the sensation she'd *felt* as the ice dagger slid into the mage's throat.

Karameth and Entonin had stopped but not dismounted, exchanging quiet words while they waited for her. They'd fled for hours, a nightmare ride into the desert, leaving her aching, bruised and shaken. Karameth had led them away from the caravan trail and straight out into the dunes, running the animals hard. But it wouldn't be far enough. Not now that she'd killed one of them. She could still hear the surprised gasp and the wet choking sound which followed. And she saw him fall to the ground in front of her again, and again, and again.

She hadn't heard Entonin jump down and walk over to her. He crouched at her side, ignoring the splatter of vomit at her feet.

"We have to go, kid," he said, his own voice thick with exhaustion.

Naila looked at him but didn't really see him. Only Entonin's eyes were visible between the folds of blue fabric, as much of his pale skin hidden from the sun as possible.

"Come on," he said again, his voice coaxing. "You saved Kara's life. We can't just leave you now."

He was trying to make a joke, but the tone fell flat, and Naila shuddered despite the heat.

Entonin sighed. "I get it, I really do, but we don't have time for this right now. We've left a clear trail for them to follow." He gestured back along their path and the scuffed footprints through the sand of the gully floor. "I don't know how badly they want us but I'm willing to bet they'll follow us for as long as they can. They would have killed Karameth – and both of us if given the chance. You did what you had to do. What are you going to do now? Sit here until they come and kill you for it?"

He was right, Naila knew it, but it didn't make it feel any better.

She forced herself to her feet, her legs and back screaming in protest. She could already feel the bruises from the saddle forming between her legs and she dreaded hauling herself back up onto the annaka.

"Attagirl." Entonin straightened up with the same degree of effort. "Come on. If we cover a bit more ground, Karameth says we can rest tonight. We need to get as far as we can on the supplies we have." He didn't say "pitiful supplies" but the inference was there in his voice: too many of their bags still lay back in their rooms or abandoned on the floor of the courtyard.

Her whole body screamed in protest as she hauled herself into the saddle on the annaka's back. The draconid hissed in anger and shook, trying to wriggle its way free. Its saddle sat halfway up its scaled back, strapped firmly around its chest and arms, and looped around the back of its legs, but it almost managed to fling Naila clear. She hunched forward and clung to the stiff leather with the very last of her strength; it was a long and nasty fall to the hardpack sand beneath their feet.

The first night, Naila didn't sleep. There was still no moon and they couldn't risk any kind of light, so Karameth brought them to an abrupt halt to make camp. If it could be called making camp: they tied the animals to a dried husk of a tree, lay on their backs in the sand and each chewed on a single piece of dried meat, the texture of it making Naila want to throw up. Above them, the sky was awash with stars, the ground darker than the night sky. Both in front and behind, dunes towered above them, the undulating horizon blacker than Naila's eyes.

Every now and again there was a flash of light from somewhere out beyond the dunes, outlining the horizon in unnatural white light. Magic crackled through the air and the sound of voices drifted to them on the wind. Naila held her breath.

"They're not as close as you think," Entonin whispered from beside her. "Go to sleep."

But she was sure the priest didn't sleep either. The next time the strange light swept towards them, Naila saw it reflected in Entonin's eyes.

As soon as the sky softened with the promise of dawn, they were moving again. Their journey snaked between the dunes and along valley floors covered in so much flat limestone that they almost looked paved. They passed a rocky outcrop in the shape of a dragon's skull, wind-carved hollows staring out at them like dark eye sockets, and here Karameth pulled out a ragged map, flattening it against the side of a dommra and marking it with charcoal. They climbed some of the smaller dunes, the sand slipping out from beneath them, and skirted the edges of deadly sand bowls, their sides too steep for even the dommras' wide feet.

It was hot. The sand radiated heat back up against them. Even the wind only served to blow hot air into their faces, stirring up the dust which bit into their skin. They'd smeared black charcoal under their eyes to help protect them from the sun, but the glare still made Naila's eyes and head ache.

Entonin suffered the most. The strip of skin visible from within his scarf and the backs of his hands had already started to burn and, as the day wore on, he kept tripping over the sand, barely catching himself on the reins of his dommra. Three times Karameth called a halt to let the priest drink and wet his face with the precious water, tending to him with a surprising gentleness. He offered no additional water to Naila; she could only look on, trying not to let the envy turn over in her stomach, but it was clear she was faring much better than the priest.

The heat may not have weighed on her the same way it did Entonin, but what she felt keenly was the absence of water. As their own supplies dwindled, it pressed in on her, a low panic in the back of her mind. It was *so* dry. Even the inside of her mouth was cracked and parched. Her sense of connection with the element had been growing since Amoria, and it latched onto the pitiful supply of water they carried with them, aware of the way it sloshed inside the skins with every step. When Karameth shared water with Entonin, Naila felt every drop as it slipped from Entonin's skin and plummeted to the ground, tiny jewels of precious life. Once she tried to catch them, grasping at even that dribble of water, but they were too small and too fast for her new-found power. When the drops hit the sand, the earth swallowed them thirstily, as desperate for water as they were.

Naila was powerless again, in this place with no water.

Even the walking was a trial. Her muscles screamed in protest with each step and blisters formed deep in the hard skin of her feet. It was only when the sun climbed to its zenith, leaving them no shade or shadow to hide in, that Karameth finally let them rest. They used what gear they'd managed to bring to construct something of a shelter, but it offered them little in the way of relief. Sitting in their small scrap of shade, none of them spoke a word, their collective effort bent on surviving.

The quiet must have lulled her to sleep eventually, because the next thing she knew Karameth was shaking her awake.

"Come," he said when he saw her eyes flutter open. "We go."

The heat of the afternoon was just starting to shift, a gentle breeze leading the way into evening. After a day of rest, Karameth let them mount the animals again and they made better progress, though riding only awakened a different set of agonies. Above them, the smallest sliver of a moon hauled itself above the horizon, limning their path with ethereal silver light. Naila saw Entonin lift one hand to the sky and then bring it back to his chest, greeting the moon like an old friend.

By the time they stopped to rest, they were all broken and exhausted, humans and animals both.

"What ungodly magic keeps you so bloody well protected?" asked Entonin, hunched over a small pile of gnarled branches and struggling with a flint; they'd heard neither sight nor sound of their pursuers, so Karameth had finally consented to lighting a fire.

"I don't know," Naila answered, trying to ignore his anger. She touched the hard shape of the pendant beneath her robes, wondering if its power was somehow shielding her from the worst of the heat.

"Well, got any magic spells for this? Feel free to give me a hand."

Naila got up without a word, snatched the flint from his hands and struck the fire herself without a scrap of magic.

"Thank you ever so much. Next time you can—" Entonin was mercifully interrupted by Karameth, the mercenary striding over from where he'd been tending the animals, the map crumpled in his hand.

Naila only half listened to their back and forth, growing more used to being surrounded by a language she couldn't understand.

"Well, shit," Entonin said eventually, though he sounded more relieved than angry. "We might actually just make it out of here."

When Naila looked up, she found Entonin's face changed, his scowl replaced by a look of faint disbelief.

"It isn't far to the next oasis. From there, we should be able to get to Tus'Bala, an oasis town the caravans usually stop at; we might even catch the caravan we meant to travel with."

They were up before dawn, to begin their journey while the air was still cooler, and the whole horrific ritual began all over again. Karameth had baked a single flatbread on the fire the night before, mixed from some kind of powder and a splash of water, so they broke their fast on bread and a few paltry sips of water. Naila held the water in her mouth before she swallowed, relishing the feel of it on her tongue. Three more days to the oasis, and then they could drink as much water as they wanted. It filled Naila's mind as she hauled herself back into the saddle. They would make it. They had to.

They should have realised sooner, when they saw the first of the abal clinging to the dunes, its wispy branches brittle and dead. Not that it would have helped. They'd used everything to get here.

Karameth led them over the ridge, Naila and Entonin close behind, all of them desperately thirsty, their lips cracked, their waterskins empty. Naila's head hurt every time she moved it, as if a cloud of pain were lining the inside of her skull. Entonin sagged on the back of his dommra and even Karameth was starting to stumble over the sand. Their survival, everything they had left, was bent towards this place, and there was nowhere left to go.

They followed the trail of death up the gentle slope of a small dune, past a withered acacia tree, its twisted branches like grasping fingers. At first, the rippling of the heat haze across the basin looked like water, glistening mockingly against the sand. They could see the bed of the oasis, the ground cut by the old paths of water. It was outlined by the desiccated remains of dead plants: thick-trunked adenium, crooked ghaf, date palms – all of them dead.

"No" was all Entonin said, sliding from the back of his dommra.

This is why people have been failing the crossing, thought Naila, her mind too numb to understand what she was seeing.

Death, it turned out, looked much like the rest of the desert.

Karameth only hesitated for a moment. He dropped the reins of his dommra and marched down to the oasis, as if walking forward meant that this couldn't be the end. Without anything else to do, Naila followed him, her annaka padding trustingly behind her.

Getting closer didn't do any good. She could see the hope bleed out of Karameth with every step. Skulls of small animals crunched under their feet, and the remains of the trees loomed all around them, like the ribs of an enormous skeleton.

Once he reached the dry basin, Karameth stopped. He stood in silence, the breeze lifting the trailing ends of his red scarf. There was nothing more to do.

Or was there? Naila pulled the obsidian pendant out from under her robes and pressed it into the palm of her hand. Its smooth surface was cold and hard against her skin, a familiar comfort. She had to be able to do something, didn't she? Her power was water. *Water*. Could she not find some way to use it? Some way for her to bring them what they needed to survive.

Water, thought Naila, longingly, pleadingly. She stretched out her mind, reaching out, extending her awareness like she had in her lessons. In her exhausted state it, it felt like leaving her body behind. The dunes dropped away, and then mountains, out and up to where the air felt wet and sweet again, clouds hanging soft and grey over the tops of the hills. She could feel them like cold mist on her face, the sensation so real she could taste the moisture. *This* was her power. She could feel it, her heart singing to be reconnected with it.

Something else sensed her power, too, something huge and ancient, a shadow just beyond her awareness.

It turned its gaze towards her.

Naila rocked back into her body with a gasp, the obsidian humming and hot beneath her hand. Something had felt her – had sensed her power – had *looked* back at her.

Karameth was watching her now, only his eyes visible from within the folds of his scarf. Naila could see the desperation in them, all his frail hope directed at her.

"Can you?" he asked. "Can you help us?"

She shook her head, her eyes stinging with tears. Only now that she had fallen back to herself had she realised how far she had thrown her mind – nothing would reach them in time.

But Karameth still wasn't ready to give up. He gestured at the ground with one hand. "Here. Underground." He struggled for the words in Ellathian. "Far under. Moya. Water."

Naila didn't give herself time to think. She gripped the pendant and tried again. This time she pushed her mind downwards, sinking deep into the earth. The sensation was dizzying, like falling while standing still. There had been moisture here once, pathways for water, traces of it clinging to stone where before it had reached the surface. She followed these shadows down, deeper into the earth.

It was there waiting for her, just as Karameth said. Water. An underground river.

She lifted one arm and spread her hand parallel to the ground, feeling like she was split between two places, her body on the sand above, her mind in the surging water below. It fought her, more strength in its crashing path than anything she'd ever felt before. Her desperate need flooded through her, more potent than any spell, and in the palm of her right hand the obsidian throbbed like an angry heartbeat.

She lifted it high above her head.

For a moment, nothing. Then there was a rumble beneath their feet, low and threatening, stones rattling against the ground. And then—

It burst up with the force of a geyser, propelling a glittering column high above them. There was the span of a breath before water came tumbling back, pattering onto the dry ground. It splashed against Naila's face and she opened her mouth, letting it slide over skin and onto her tongue. It was warm and sharp, and the most delicious thing she'd ever tasted.

Next to her, Naila heard something she'd never heard before: Karameth was laughing, the sound bright and clear as a bell.

38

HAELIUS

Reyan was dead.

It was Larinne who'd found him, forcing open the door to his apartment when she couldn't reach him at his office, and it was Haelius she'd called on to search Reyan's rooms for signs of magic. Yet when Haelius had arrived, all he'd found was an old man in his bed. Even with the sight, Haelius could detect nothing to suggest that Reyan hadn't just fallen asleep and never woken up.

If only he could believe it.

And who was it who'd really caused Reyan's death? Whose actions had thrown the old man into Oriven's path? While Reyan was in danger, Haelius had been buried in books, tearing through Amoria's libraries for some clue to the great magics that had made her, searching for a power that could drain anima like Amoria had drained the desert.

He'd found nothing. Even now, all he had to show for his efforts were the dusty tomes stacked around his feet. Every time he found a reference to Amoria's founding, he would grab the next book in a fervour, fanning through the pages with a flick of his finger, only to find the answers torn out or sprawling diagrams he didn't understand.

Five days. He had five days left to solve a mystery that had lived for five hundred years.

And while he searched, Amoria fell apart. Even his arrays had revealed nothing. He'd poured so much magic into them, spent so many hours weaving his will into the streets of Amoria, spinning a careful trap for Oriven or anyone who might tried to wield anima like magic. He'd sensed nothing, not a hint of the strange power or anything he could pin to Oriven. All that work, all that magic – none of it had meant anything.

Now Reyan was dead. Oriven was hunting Naila. And Larinne. Larinne wouldn't look at him, had pulled away from him when he'd tried to reach for her arm. He thought he'd been protecting her, and then he'd hurt her in the worst possible way.

With a snarl of frustration, Haelius threw his book across his study. He curled his hands into fists and slammed them against his desk, rattling his ink bottles and sending his pen rolling onto the floor.

What was this for? he asked himself for the thousandth time. *Were you looking for answers to save Amoria, or were you just trying to save yourself?*

There was a tap on the glass behind him, then a patter, and then suddenly it was a roar, the sound rising until it engulfed the whole tower. Rain. Haelius stood with a frown, feeling his body protest after long hours hunched over books. He moved towards the outside wall in a daze, watching the rain pound against the glass, the view of Amoria blurring and running like wet paint. He could feel something, something in the rain that made the hairs on the back of his neck stand on end. Lifting one hand, he pressed his fingers against the glass, shifting his awareness towards magic. Yes, he could feel it – but it was impossible, wasn't it?

"Naila?" he whispered.

It was her power, a trace of it left in the water that now poured down the outside of the glass, as familiar to him as an old friend.

Despite everything, Haelius smiled. Naila was alive, out there somewhere, away from Amoria and free to work her impossible magic.

It could have been something about the rain, or perhaps the memory of Naila, but suddenly Haelius longed for company. He found himself wandering slowly down the Academy corridors, his ears filled with the drumming of the rain. He wasn't even sure what he was looking for until he reached the communal offices and found Malek with his back to him, standing in front of a long curving section of the tower's outer wall. He was silhouetted in grey light, raindrops casting moving shadows across the floor. He didn't turn when Haelius knocked on the doorframe, the sound swallowed by the downpour.

"Malek?" Haelius crossed the threshold tentatively, feeling like he was intruding on a dream.

Malek jumped and turned, and then his face broke into a wide smile. "Haelius! Come here! It's been too long, my friend."

He pulled Haelius into a rough embrace, a sudden shock of contact after so many days alone. It left him feeling disoriented and strange. "I'm sorry. I've been—"

"—working, I know," Malek finished, gripping Haelius's arm, his eyes bright with understanding. "Don't explain yourself – talk to me. What do you think of this, hmm? Somewhat unseasonal."

"You could say that."

"I always forget how dramatic it is here," Malek continued. "It rains heavily in Al Wafra, of course, but the whole of Amoria shakes with it, like she might just collapse beneath it, you know?"

"I do. But remember, this is all I've ever known."

"I suppose it is." Malek turned to look at him, and the corners of his eyes creased with concern. "I was sorry to hear about Reyan."

Haelius swallowed, his throat suddenly tight. "I didn't know him that well, but Larinne . . ."

"I know. Dailem, too. How is Larinne doing?"

Haelius looked down and didn't answer. He couldn't help the feeling that Dailem of all people must know what had happened to Reyan.

"Haelius?"

"I don't know. I don't think she wants to see me."

Malek just raised his eyebrows and waited for an explanation. There was a desk set up against the window, scattered with Malek's notes and tools. Haelius moved them aside with a wave of his hand and pulled himself up onto it, avoiding Malek's scrutinising gaze.

Slowly, word by word, Haelius tried to explain.

When he'd finished, Malek drew a breath between his teeth. "She blamed you for his death?"

"She's right, isn't she? I should have *said* something ..."

"You know Dailem has searched for any sign of the Justice's involvement?" Malek's tone was unusually stern. "She would know if Oriven had moved against him. Really, do you think Dailem would stand back and let that happen? That she wouldn't even tell Larinne?"

Haelius didn't speak; he wasn't so sure he knew the answer.

"Have you even tried talking to Larinne?"

"No," Haelius admitted, averting his gaze.

Without an instant of hesitation, Malek reached up and flicked Haelius between his eyes.

"Don't be a fool. You know, for the smartest man I know, you're often the stupidest." Malek met Haelius's scowl with one of his own. "Your dearest friend is hurting, she needs you, and you're going to hide behind your work and ignore her?"

"It's not quite that simple," Haelius snapped, and he could hear the note of petulance in his own voice.

Malek let out a long sigh, lifting his hands in despair. "Maybe it isn't, but don't pretend you don't know how to fix it. Of course, what do I know? I've only watched you dance around each other for twenty years."

He narrowed his eyes at where Haelius sat on his desk. "You know, I tell Ko'ani off for doing that."

"I always liked your daughter."

"And she you," said Malek, pulling himself up onto the desk next to Haelius. For a moment neither of them said anything, just listened to the rain hammering at their backs. Haelius hadn't told Malek about the deadline Oriven had set for him, hadn't told anyone. He wondered if Dailem knew, if she'd told Malek – did his friend know how little time he had left?

"What if Larinne doesn't want to talk to me?" Haelius asked softly, the words almost lost to the sound of the rain.

"She might not," Malek conceded, and when he caught Haelius's look, he added, "Your friend is the one who tells you the truth, not what you want to hear."

Haelius looked down, staring at his wrists where the gold and red threads had started to fray.

"But if that's true, then you just have to wait, my friend – until she does want to talk to you. But she'll know you're there, and that's what matters."

Haelius closed his eyes and leaned his head back, feeling the hum of Amoria's magic in his bones. "I always seem to be the one who hurts her the most."

"That's because you're the one she loves the most." Malek leaned back too; Haelius heard the thump of his head against the glass. "Dailem ... they're close, but it's complicated. They forget to see each other, they don't have the arguments they need to. *You* are the person she turns to, the person who's always at her side."

How little that had been true in recent months.

Before Haelius could answer, there was an awkward cough from the doorway, and he looked up to find one of the young researchers clutching her books and hovering at the threshold. Haelius could only imagine how ridiculous they looked, climbed up on a desk like students, the wizard with his feet dangling a foot off the ground. He slid off the desk, a hint of warmth in his cheeks.

"Am I interrupting?" Civest stammered.

"No, of course not." Haelius made a pointless attempt to brush his robes straight. "I was just leaving." He turned back to Malek, who'd made no move to get up, apparently unbothered by what the students made of him. "Thank you. Again."

The smile lit up Malek's whole face. "Good. Listen, I'm going to the Artisan's District later ..."

"To the work you actually care about," Haelius said drily.

"You should come. There must be a popina open somewhere. I've missed drinking arak while you sit there and judge me."

Haelius looked away, frowning even as he tried to smile. *Five days,* he thought.

"I'll see," he said aloud.

He moved to leave, standing to one side to let Civest scurry in through the door.

"Haelius," Malek called just before Haelius stepped away. "Talk to her. Today."

Haelius felt a twinge of panic, but outwardly he rolled his eyes and proffered a mock bow. "Yes, Wizard," he said, doing his best to mimic Malek's accent and tone of voice.

"Pah!" was all Malek said to that.

It was mid-afternoon before Haelius resurfaced from his work. The third bell chimed from a clock on his study wall, making him wince. The rain had finally stopped, and the sun was catching in the last of the raindrops, making Amoria sparkle like a precious jewel.

He still hadn't contacted Larinne.

Coward, he thought, rubbing his face with his hands. Even if she didn't answer him, even if she spoke to him only to tell him to go away, Malek was right: he had to do it. He had to tell her that he was sorry.

But perhaps first he owed Malek that drink. Surely he could spare a couple of lousy hours to absorb the gentle wisdom of his friend. He'd speak to Larinne once he'd cleared his head, blown away the dust from these old texts and remembered the sound of his own voice.

Artisan's Row was an easy jump away, and Haelius had met Malek at his workshop so many times. It hardly took any effort to wrap himself in magic and step from his study into the bustling streets of the Central Dome.

It was a shock to find himself so suddenly surrounded by people. Artisan's Row was almost unchanged by the recent months. People ambled slowly between stalls of magical items, bathed in violet sunlight which glittered in the last of Naila's rain. Magic murmured all around him, a soothing hum that resonated in harmony with his own gift. There was the clang of hammering, the rumble of industry, the beating heart of Amoria.

If he closed his eyes, Haelius could let all of that fall away and sense the pattern that lay behind it. Under his feet, his own array followed the shape of the streets like water along a riverbed. This working stretched across the entire northern half of the Market District, a spell fed by both his magic and Amoria herself. It rang with every footfall, every twitch of magic that wasn't his own. It was strangely reassuring to tap into its steady and unaltered path. In a way, it was another reminder of his failure, a sign stamped onto the streets declaring the uselessness of his magic. But still, if it hadn't detected anything here, at least it meant that Artisan's Row remained safe.

His arrival had startled the mages around him, and already Haelius could feel the eyes of people seeking out the scarlet and gold of his robes, tracking tentatively up to find the scars on his face. Haelius ignored them, lifting his chin and striding with purpose down the wide avenue, choosing not to notice the way people scurried out of his path. He could already see Malek at his workshop, his hair pushed back behind by a pair of artisan's goggles, cheerfully greeting anyone who expressed even a passing interest in his wares.

He must have sensed Haelius's arrival because Malek's eyes found him in the crowd almost immediately. The grin crinkling his face was utterly contagious, and Haelius felt an answering smile tug on his lips.

Before he could take another step, magic struck Haelius like a physical blow – a surge of power so great that it made him double forward, his breath leaving his lungs. It tolled like an immense bell, sending his own magic ringing in response. He clutched at his chest, only vaguely aware of the frightened shouts of the crowd. The taste of hot metal coated his tongue, magic filling him up, doubling and doubling, just as it had done with the fire. Some part of him reacted by smothering his own gift, pressing it down deep beneath layers of control, instinct telling him he must have caused this.

But he hadn't. Not this. The magic felt like his, and yet it was entirely beyond his reach. His eyes blurred into and out of the sight, the ground dipping and swaying beneath his feet. He could *see* it, the array – *his* array – burning like a fault line had opened in the earth.

People were starting to run, vendors spreading their arms in front of shelves to protect their wares. Some were looking up at the dome, searching in terror for any sign it was breaking.

In the middle of the turmoil, Malek was a strange point of stillness. He'd remained at his workshop, staring at Haelius, his eyes a question that Haelius couldn't answer.

Is this you?

Then Malek's face changed. His cheeks slackened, his mouth opened and closed as if he was gasping for air. His eyes met Haelius's in an awful, desperate moment.

And then he fell.

They all did. All of the people within the Artisan's District dropped as one, crumpling to the ground like discarded toys.

"Malek!" The cry tore from Haelius's throat, the only sound in a sudden and terrible silence.

He tried to run, but there were too many people fallen in his path. He tripped on an ankle, stumbled over an outstretched hand. Without even thinking, Haelius's magic twisted around him like tangled vines and jumped him the last few feet to Malek's side.

Malek was lying in a pool of rust-coloured robes, one leg folded underneath him, his neck twisted at an unnatural angle. Haelius sank to his knees.

"No, no," he murmured. He grasped blindly at his friend, shaking his shoulders, trying to get him to wake.

Malek's head swung round too quickly. His eyes were still open, but they were flat. Empty. His friend was gone.

"No." Haelius's voice broke, his hand shaking as he reached for Malek's cheek, his chest, searching, searching for some sign of life.

There was no knowing smile, no light in his eyes, no infuriating saying or inescapable wisdom. It had been this morning, only this morning. He'd asked Haelius to come with him, to drink with him, to talk to him. Haelius could have listened, could have come sooner – maybe he could have stopped this, maybe he could have protected him.

"Malek, please." Haelius's whole body was shaking now, a sob lodging itself in his throat. "Please, please don't leave me." Folding forward, he curled his fingers into Malek's robes, pulling on the fabric as if he could drag him back, keep him here. "Please."

When he looked up, the world fractured through the blur of his tears. There were bodies stretching away from him on all sides. People. They were *people*. And they were all dead. He could already feel their magic, their *life*, draining away from them, as if Amoria had taken a deep and terrible breath. He was the only one left alive. But why? *Why?*

He knew, but he didn't want to look.

He had felt it, in that wild surge of power, the taste of it so familiar on his tongue. The roads of the Artisan's District had cracked apart, a broken line slicing the shape of his array into Amoria's skin. There was no magic left within it. His spell had sheared apart, the power coming free. And this had been the result. This. Oh Goddess, this.

His gift answered his grief in the only way it knew how, with more power. Even now, when all he wanted to do was burn it away, it pressed against him, seething beneath his skin. The ground began to vibrate, tiny stones rattling against its surface, and somewhere behind him a glass window shattered. He couldn't stop it, didn't *want* to stop it. Let the ground break apart if it had to, just bring Malek back. *Please.*

Haelius? Haelius didn't know if he initiated the communication or she did, but suddenly Larinne's voice was there, a part of all of this. *Haelius, where are you? What's happened?*

He choked on another sob, this one caught between relief and despair. She was okay, she was alive, and yet now she would witness what he really was. He couldn't pull his thoughts together into words: just grief, images and guilt. *I'm sorry. I'm so sorry.*

I don't . . . Goddess, I . . . He felt her horror as clearly as his own, a terrible moment when he could see all of this through her eyes. Malek. The bodies. The array. It was too much. He couldn't stop it, couldn't shield her from any of it. The connection between them flickered – and then it broke.

Yet Haelius wasn't alone. The Justice were starting to arrive; he could see them, their black robes darkening the edges of his vision. Even Oriven's army wasn't immune to the horror laid at their feet. Someone was screaming, others were on their knees, trying to wake the dead. They would reach him in moments, Haelius waiting for them right at the centre of everything he'd destroyed.

Still, he didn't move, his fingers knotted into Malek's robes.

"Justice! Justice Tallace, there's someone alive over here."

"Who is it? Wait . . . Haelius?" Dailem approached carefully, two

Justice flanking her every movement. Her voice was strained, cling-ing to a thin pretence of control. "Haelius, what is this? Why are you here?"

Haelius didn't know how to look at her, how to show her what was clutched in his hands.

She saw it on her own.

"What—" And then even that veneer of calm was stripped away. "Get away from him."

He couldn't make himself uncurl his fingers. Letting go meant this was over, that Malek was truly lost.

"Get up!" Dailem screamed. "Get away from him."

Finally, Haelius's body moved on its own, stumbling backwards and onto his feet. He made himself look at her, unprepared for the broken shape of her mouth, the raw slash of her grief. She took his place at Malek's side, sinking slowly, as if every movement contained resistance. She didn't grasp at him as Haelius had. She knew her hus-band was gone. Instead, she slipped a hand into the tangle of his hair.

"Senator, please— the Justice are handling this. You don't need to—"

"*Handling?*" Larinne's voice was high and thin. "This is my family. Let me through."

It was clear Larinne had been running. Her hair had come loose from her bun, falling around her face, and the skin around her eyes was streaked and raw from drying tears. She froze when she saw Malek, the sight of him punching through any fragile defences she'd managed to erect. Her eyes tracked slowly to Haelius with a dreadful inevitability.

"Haelius . . ." She'd seen the lines cut through the district, seen the diagrams on his desk. She knew what it meant.

"Please, Larinne, this isn't what it was supposed to do."

"No." She didn't come any closer, keeping Malek and Dailem between them. "No. Tell me this isn't true. Tell me this wasn't you."

"It wasn't. It was . . ." He could feel his magic stir within him, his dreadful power. *Stop it, stop it, stop it.* "It was a source. A . . . a web I could use to detect unusual magic. I made it to hold them – the people who've been doing this, to stop Oriven if I needed to, but it— it was meant as a defence, a way to find them, never to hurt anyone. You have to believe me ..."

Larinne's expression tipped awfully between pity and anger. "You made a *source* for people who drain magic."

"Please," he whispered. "It shouldn't have worked like that— I didn't ... Please, you have to believe me."

He looked down at his hand, at the wrinkled scars written onto his skin. Why had he thought this would be any different? He had only ever meant to find a use for this magic, find some way to justify this vast ocean of power, and yet every time it turned out like this. His magic writhed beneath his skin, control slipping through his fingers. Another window shattered, glass scattering across the ground like rain. None of his restraints, none of his careful layers of control could hold against this grief.

"It was you." Dailem's voice was cold, a dead thing. In all the years he had known her, the many times he had provoked her fury, she had never sounded like this. "You did this. You killed him."

"No, I ... please, it isn't what you think ..."

She stood. "Justice, restrain him."

Larinne flinched but didn't speak, just watched with an expression that broke every last piece of Haelius that remained.

A moment later, Dailem's holding spell hit him like a punch to the gut. His whole body wanted to coil forward, but he was suspended in magic. His lungs heaved in shallow gasps, his heart thrashed in his chest. Even now, he felt the vibration of his power, a will to resist, a fire that refused to go out.

Enough.

The Justice took no more chances. A man in black and gold stepped in front of him, his mouth set in a hard line. He pressed cool fingers to Haelius's temple and uttered a single word.

And then blackness.

It was over.

39

NAILA

On the third day, the impossible happened. It began to rain. Heavy droplets struck against their skin and disintegrated the ground beneath their feet, turning it into a swirling mass of sand and mud. After being starved of water, they were suddenly drowning in it.

Naila had seen rain before from within the protective bubble of Amoria, but it was a different thing to be out in it. With her new senses, it was almost overwhelming. The relentless torrent beat upon the ground and her companions alike, outlining them in a wavering sense of power. If she reached for it, she could trace the path of a single drop of rain as it plummeted to earth, almost slow against the expanse of grey sky. It was too easy to get lost in them: a million raindrops, a million tiny paths of magic.

She kept finding Karameth watching her with steady brown eyes.

"This," he said eventually, jerking his chin up at the sky. "You?"

Naila stumbled, her boots slipping in the sludge and splattering it up the backs of her leg. *Had* it been her? At the barren oasis, she knew she'd reached out for the clouds – stretching her power farther than should have been possible – but could she really have brought the rain? Not even Haelius could accomplish such a feat.

Yet she had felt these clouds, had reached for them, and now they were here.

Ahead of them, Entonin turned to scowl back over his shoulder. His blue scarf was wrapped around his head, sodden and plastered to his skin.

"Then make it stop," he barked over the thunder of the downpour, as unhappy in the rain as he had been in the sun. "This is bloody miserable."

Without the desperation she'd felt at the oasis, Naila hadn't the first notion of how to reach the clouds above them, let alone push them away.

She hadn't even managed to keep herself dry. Every time she touched the obsidian, she was bombarded with the sense of water. Every drop bouncing off the ground, the seething turmoil of the clouds above her head. It was overwhelming, impossible to reach for anything within that chaos. It made her think of Haelius, so sensitive to magic, always living within the noise of Amoria.

Focus. She could almost hear Haelius's voice in her mind. She was thinking about this wrong – trying to take in the entirety of the rain instead of focusing on what she could do.

So much of what Haelius had told her had been lessons, Naila realised now. He hadn't had enough time to train her to use her new power, and yet before they'd even known she could use magic, he'd been teaching her. She had a framework now, thanks to him – a skeleton of knowledge on which to hang her new-found gift. Even the phonemes, useless as they had seemed to her at the time, hadn't so much been for spells but for *ideas*: things she knew she ought to be able to do with magic.

She started with *reject*, pushing the water away from her skin, working it out of her clothes so that it beaded off her like oil on water. She found that she could not only stop the rain from soaking into her robes, but she could extend the barrier outwards, holding it an inch away from her, and then another inch, creeping out until she had a small bubble of dryness that shimmered around her.

People think it's the "spell" that matters – what you say, or how you wave your hands. It isn't. It's your will *that really matters.* Another of Haelius's lessons.

After maintaining it carefully for a time, Naila found that she could make it bigger – extending it to envelop first her annaka, and then further, big enough that Karameth could walk easily beside her and remain dry. It wasn't so hard to increase the size of her influence and, if she was careful, she could maintain it without so much effort: she was beginning to learn stamina and control.

"Entonin," she called out to the priest, "if you come closer, I can keep you dry."

Entonin stumbled in the mud as he turned to glance back at her, his eyes narrow and mutinous, his white travelling robes splattered with brown.

"I'm fine," he said, stubbornly striking out ahead of them. "I don't need whatever *that* is."

"His choice," Karameth said quietly to Naila, a friendly, conspiratorial note to his voice.

He watched Entonin struggle on with a small smile, teasing but not unkind. When Entonin slipped and cursed, Karameth winced in sympathy, but continued to smile in a way Naila hadn't seen before. It felt like Karameth had cracked open a door for her, showing her a little of himself; an offering of vulnerability in return for the trust she'd given him.

The unmistakable warmth of companionship swelled in Naila's chest.

The rain passed away as quickly as it had arrived, continuing west on the new path Naila had made for it. It was not long after that they reached the main caravan route which would take them to Tus'Bala, and from there onwards to Nahrayn and Dahran proper. The trail itself was almost like a road, flat and well worn, and easily traversed by them and their animals alike. It snaked out before and behind them, disappearing into the dunes.

Naila couldn't help but try to feel for the sense of mages on the road, twisting herself in the saddle to look back over her shoulder and reaching out for their power with her mind. There was nothing to see but the flat, dusty grey trail – still dark from the last of the rain – and nothing to feel but the steady, rhythmic sloshing of the water in the skins.

Still, Naila kept finding herself holding her breath, listening, waiting for the sound of someone following in their path; she still couldn't shake the feeling they were being watched.

*

They reached the oasis town, Tus'Bala, with the last of the light, the cliffs looming ahead of them, blue-grey shadows in the twilight. Naila was surprised to find that Tus'Bala wasn't just a camp for travellers but a real town, buildings hugging the edge of the water, fields of what looked like silwheat swaying in the breeze. Voices reached them on the evening air, echoing shouts, braying animals.

At last, some luck.

There was not just one but two caravans waiting for them, one of them the very company they'd meant to travel with, the experienced travellers easily outpacing their own dangerous route through the dunes. The caravans were clustered down by the water, dommra silhouetted against the pale night, firelight reflecting off the surface of the lake.

Karameth went straight to renegotiate their passage and to trade for the supplies they so desperately needed, giving Entonin and Naila strict instructions to *stay away* and let him handle it alone.

"We'll get screwed out here," said Entonin from behind his dommra, lifting a pack down from the animal with a grunt. "It'll be one step above a mugging. Actually, they might just decide to make it an actual mugging and save themselves the trouble."

Naila looked up sharply at Entonin's words. The caravans had their own guards, lean men and women with dark eyes and long, curved blades. She'd been so relieved to see them, their animals heavy with goods and supplies, but now these strangers took on a different, more sinister shape.

Entonin met her gaze over the back of the dommra. "Oh, don't look so bloody grim." He raised his eyebrows, and Naila recognised the thin edge to Entonin's mouth that was almost a smile. "Not everyone is trying to kill you. We don't exactly look worth mugging. And this might be Dahran, but I'm reasonably certain that murdering a priest is still bad luck."

Not that Entonin looked much like a priest any more. His blond hair was matted and untidy, sweaty strands plastered against the side of his face. Black charcoal was smudged halfway down his cheek, disappearing into scruffy, blond stubble. He was a far cry from the impeccably neat stranger she'd met in Amoria.

He still had his brooch pinned visibly at his neck, the silver moon gleaming gold in the torchlight. Maybe that was enough.

"I'm going to get water" was all Naila said, flopping the empty skins over the annaka's saddle. She wet her lips in anticipation. She was going to drain a whole skin before she filled them again.

"Suit yourself. Stick to the path." There was a nagging tone to Entonin's voice. "And come straight back. It's getting dark and the last thing we need is you disappearing off."

Naila rolled her eyes as she walked away, though in truth she had no intention of straying far from their little camp. They'd been alone in the desert for over a week and in a strange way that had kept them safe; more people meant more danger. Her fingers toyed with the pendant at her neck, and she almost thought that she could feel warmth in it beneath her fingers, the same strange power she'd felt back in Jasser. But the heat of the day still hung in the air, and the obsidian was no warmer than her skin; it was just her imagination.

The annaka hissed and lowered its head to Naila's shoulder, its clawed feet scraping on the stony path. She reached up absently to rub along its scaled jaw, drinking in the sight of Tus'Bala in the pale twilight. The dark pool of the oasis was just visible in the last of the light, shadowed by curving palm and acacia trees; cliffs circled one side of the town, as if someone cupped the oasis in great, stone hands.

Torches on long canes surrounded the well, and they blinded Naila to the world beyond the circle of their light. She tied the annaka's reins to one of them and tugged the skins from its back, stooping to lay them on the ground.

And froze.

The sharp point of a dagger, cold and unmistakable, pressed into her back, pain lancing between her ribs. Another hand grabbed her hair, iron fingers digging hard into her scalp, yanking her to her feet with a sickening lurch.

"Do not move, girl," hissed a voice in her ear, a woman's, her face close enough that Naila could feel her icy breath. "Make a sound and I will kill you."

Naila's body seized tight, fear pounding in her skull. She couldn't move, her attacker pulling her tight against the point of her blade. It cut painfully into her skin, burning and cold and – she sensed it, as clearly as the water of the well beneath her feet – made entirely of *ice*.

Naila didn't dare breathe. Slowly, slowly, she raised her hand to touch the pendant at her neck, her finger creeping towards it inch by dangerous inch. She almost gasped with relief when her index finger found the hard shape of the stone.

Melt, she thought.

The blade quivered in response, the shape of it wavering, but then another force snapped it back to solidity. *No.*

"What *are* you?" hissed the woman, the blade biting into Naila's skin.

"You're— you're like me," Naila stuttered, the realisation crashing over her.

The woman's fingers slackened in surprise, the knifepoint easing for just a moment. Then she snarled, shoving Naila away from her, so that she stumbled and fell forward into the dirt.

"I am *nothing* like you."

Scrabbling for purchase, Naila twisted herself round to face her attacker, her boots slipping off the dirt as she tried to back away.

The woman who stood over her looked almost human; almost. She was taller, longer limbed, her movements just a little bit wrong, like something had inhabited the body of a human but didn't know how it should move. Her hood was thrown back to reveal silvery-grey skin and features that looked like they'd been chiselled from ice. She stared down at Naila with impossible aquamarine eyes, the same vivid gaze that had found her in Jasser.

The blade hummed with power. It grew before Naila's eyes: longer, sharper, glistening wet and crystal-blue in her hands. Water, just like Naila – a power that mirrored her own.

The woman levelled it at Naila's neck.

"What are you?" Naila whispered.

"What are *you*?" the woman countered. "And why? Why are you doing this?"

"Doing what? I— I don't understand."

The woman snarled again, her teeth sharp like the jaws of an annaka. She stepped forward with her blade, so close that Naila had to flatten herself backwards to avoid its tip.

"All of it." The woman's voice was tight with anguish. "I have travelled the length of this continent and everything, every disaster, every one of *them*, has been leading me to you. They are drawn to you, but you have been turning them, driving them mad." The woman raised a hand to her head as if something was hurting her. "You're doing it even now, I can hear it. Why? Why would you do this?"

Naila shook her head, her blood as cold as the blade of ice. "I don't know what you're saying. I ... I grew up in Amoria. I've never left the city."

"Yes." Another jab of the blade. "Everything was focused there, on this 'Amoria', until *you* left. Now it follows you, and you leave that place broken behind you."

"Broken? What I don't—" Naila tried to scramble back from her, but the stranger just took a single step forward. "I don't know what you're talking about!"

"Very well." The woman's eyes grew round, almost sad. "I wanted a reason. I wanted to understand. But I will settle for an end."

Everything slowed, distant with a sense of unreality. Naila watched the woman lift her blade high over her head.

No.

As the blade swung down, Naila threw her arms out with all her desperation behind it. Her will collided against the sword, striking against the ice like a hammer and pushing the blade wide, throwing her attacker off balance.

A second. She only had a second. Naila's body scrambled to her feet, but her mind was in the well behind her, grasping desperately.

Come. Come. Faster. Please.

There was a rumble, a roar in Naila's ears, and then a glittering stream of water shot past her and towards her attacker. The woman flicked out her arm and it bent away from her, splattering uselessly against the ground. The gesture had been dismissive, lazy.

"You will not defeat me with water," the stranger said, and the way she said *water* felt different, had a weight to it that Naila understood.

The woman darted forward, the ice flashing bright and deadly. Naila grasped for water, dragging it from the ground, from the air, and threw it in front of her. Her arms trembled as she held it out, a slick shield of glistening ice.

The blade struck forward, ringing against the shield with a high, keening note.

And then the shield shattered.

Naila's hope shattered with it, her will scattering away into glittering pieces.

No.

It couldn't be the end. In that awful moment before the blade hit her, Naila's mind clung to the fragments of ice, let them flow around the woman's blade, threw them forward with every last piece of strength she had.

The blade sank into Naila's shoulder. She heard her voice scream from outside herself, agony swallowing her sense of self.

Somehow, through the pain, she heard another cry.

Ra'akea!

It came both as a distant scream and as if someone had shouted it from inside her own head. Naila saw the woman stagger back, a hand clamped against her side. Black blood seeped from between her fingers, her face frozen in shock.

A wetness was spreading down Naila's arm, sticky and warm, too much for her mind to even comprehend. She wanted to sink to the floor, to curl herself around her pain, to close her eyes. But to fall now would be to die.

"Enough." The woman's voice was a growl. "This ends now."

Before Naila could even react, a torrent of water slammed into her chest, knocking her backwards, forcing the air from her lungs. One moment she was standing, and the next she was flat against the ground, struggling to breathe. Her lungs were paralysed from the impact, her mouth gasping, drowning on air.

The crunch of footsteps and the woman loomed over her, one hand still clutching her side, the other clutching her deadly blade.

Naila was going to die. She was going to die. All she could do was stare up at her end, her eyes wide, her mouth moving uselessly.

No. No I won't. I won't die. There was so much water here after the endless desert. Ancient waterways cut through the earth deep beneath her and she could feel their strength as if it were her own. She wasn't seeing, wasn't thinking. All that existed was the water, her power, her need to survive. She grasped at all of it.

The water heaved, the ground began to shake. Cries of alarm echoed up from the lakeside. Everything rumbled and groaned, cracks forming deep beneath the earth, the land resisting her will. But nothing would escape her.

The woman stumbled backwards, her face changing, all her certainty pouring off her. She looked almost human.

"Stop! In the mothers' name, *stop*! You'll flatten the town – kill all of them!"

Naila gasped, some sliver of reason returning to her. For a moment the earth stilled, and Naila felt all that power slipping between her fingers.

"What *are* you?" The woman said again, her blade quivering in her grip. "Do you even know what you are?"

No, Naila thought, shadows crowding in from the edge of her vision. Her shoulder throbbed, her strength bleeding away along with the last of her power.

There were more shouts now, closer, and the pounding of feet against dirt. Naila wondered numbly if they'd reach her in time. The woman, Ra'akea, seemed frozen in place, but she was still only a step away, her ice blade in her hand.

There was nothing Naila could do. Her strength was gone. Her body cold. The darkness was closing over her, pain stealing her ability to think. Naila's eyelids fluttered, reality swimming away from her.

The last thing Naila saw was the fear on the stranger's face.

*

Naila woke to the smell of woodsmoke and the heat of a crackling fire. Alive. She was alive. *The woman—*

She lurched up and pain shot through her all over again. She cried out and curled forwards, reaching for her left shoulder but too afraid to touch it.

"Don't move, you idiot!" Entonin. It was Entonin's voice. She'd never been so glad to hear the priest snapping at her. "I didn't put you back together just for you to pull it apart."

She didn't trust herself to look up, just leaned forwards, pressing her head against her knees, her body trembling. She was alive.

"Hey, hey." Entonin's voice softened, and a cool shadow passed between her and the fire. "It's all right. You're all right. Here." He dragged a rough blanket up over her shoulders. "At least keep that over you. And try not to move. You've lost a lot of blood – you're going to feel weak for a while. You were ice-cold when we found you, as cold as your wizard friend after the dome broke."

Naila grimaced at the mention of Haelius. Surely Entonin must have realised they were far beyond Wizard Akana's reach now. There was nothing left to protect her, not even that lie.

"That's better," Entonin said, not unkindly, as Naila lifted her head from her knees.

Since she'd last seen him, he'd washed his face and tied back his hair, looking far more like himself. For once, though, there was no condescending smile on his lips – only a look of genuine concern. "How's the pain? Do you want anything for it?"

Her shoulder throbbed angrily. She tried to lift her arm and instantly regretted it, hissing and biting her lip.

"I said *don't* move it. Well, at least that hasn't changed – you still don't do a damn thing I tell you to."

"Hmph." The sound Karameth made was somewhere between relief and amusement. "Good."

"What happened?" Naila rasped, her tongue thick and dry in her mouth. "Where is she?"

"Who? Is 'she' the one who did this to you?"

Next to Entonin, Karameth sat forward, the light of the fire reflected in his eyes. "Did she—" he gestured with his hands, frowning in frustration when he couldn't find the word. "Zilzal?"

"The earthquake," Entonin translated for him. "Was that her?"

"Earthquake?" Naila pressed her uninjured hand against her forehead, her mind reeling. "There was . . ." Naila's voice trailed off, remembering the way the ground trembled with her power, the very earth cracking with the force of her desperation. *She'd* caused the earthquake.

"—a kind of tremor, but the wave off the lake almost drowned half the caravan," Entonin was talking but Naila could only half hear him, a terrible dread sinking through her.

It was the woman who'd stopped her. Ra'akea. *You'll kill them all.* Naila was trembling again, but not because of the pain. *You leave that place broken behind you.* She'd said it as if somehow Naila was the one who'd brought the conflict to Amoria. In her mind, she heard the ground rumble, saw thin cracks snaking up Amoria's glass. Was she right? Was Naila's power some kind of disaster? She'd almost destroyed an entire town, dragged away the water that kept them alive. It wouldn't be the first time she'd killed. Again, she felt the effortless slide of her ice piercing the Justice's throat.

"Naila?" Entonin had moved closer to her again. He touched her arm. "You're all right. It's common to relive something like this, to feel panic. Your body is still telling you to fight or run away. It's all right. Whoever 'she' is, she was gone when we found you."

Entonin's sudden kindness almost undid her. *It's me*, she wanted to say. *I'm the one who almost destroyed everything.*

Instead, she blinked slowly and nodded, trying to swallow the sick feeling rising in the back of her throat. "I . . . I was attacked."

"We realised that," Entonin said drily, sounding more like himself.

"Magi?" asked Karameth.

"Yes. I mean, no." Naila looked down, not knowing how much to tell them. She still needed them to reach Awasef, to get away from here, but she couldn't answer their kindness with lies. "She was like me. She used a power like mine."

Entonin sat back in surprise. "Like yours? Like . . . water or something?"

"Yes. I've never met anyone like that before."

"And she just attacked you? With no warning?"

"She said I ..." Naila's words caught on all the awful things the stranger had said. They couldn't be true, they just couldn't. "I couldn't understand what she was saying. She thinks I'm some kind of threat."

"You and every other person with magic." Entonin's voice sounded a little too sharp, a sudden reminder of what he really was. Yet despite his feelings on magic, he was the one who had saved her.

"It was the person from Jasser," Naila blurted out, her voice trembling. "The one with the pale eyes. She's followed me. Somehow, she's followed us all the way from Amoria. I don't think she's going to stop ..."

Karameth and Entonin exchanged a long glance, and in those agonising moments Naila saw everything come undone. This was more than they'd ever bargained for: they owed her nothing, and without Haelius's threat they had no reason to bring a source of danger with them. They would leave her at Tus'Bala, alone and defenceless, and Naila didn't think she could hold off the stranger a second time.

Karameth shrugged his wide shoulders. "Stay close," he said.

"No more wandering off," Entonin added, as if he were speaking to a small child.

"But—"

"What do you think I pay Karameth for? To look pretty? Besides, we'll be safer with the caravan. He'll not be the only armed guard, for once."

"But I ..." Naila glanced between them, her brow furrowed. "This is more than Haelius ever asked. You ... you must know that he can't reach us here, that he wouldn't know if ..." she hesitated, unable to voice her fears out loud. "If he could have, he would have helped me."

"Well, it's reassuring to know even he has limits." Entonin raised one blond eyebrow. "Naila, we saw how tired he was on the bridge. I haven't the first clue about magic, but I can see when someone's pushed themselves as far as they can go. In Jasser ..." It was Entonin's turn to look down, a hint of colour rising in his cheeks. "Look. You saved us all in the desert, and you saved Karameth before we even got out of Jasser. We'll see you to Awasef. As long as this doesn't get any more out of hand," he added with a disapproving look. "Gods save you if there's anyone *else* who wants to kill you."

Naila let out a startled breath, unsure if she wanted to laugh or cry. "Thank you" was all she managed.

"I'm not a complete bastard," said Entonin, leaning back, his shoulders sinking away from his neck; Naila hadn't seen the tension in him until it left. "Travelling with that arm will be, though, so you'd better do everything I say. Starting with getting that suspicious look off your face."

40

ENTONIN

Entonin stood in the dark, listening to the boats pull at their moorings, the low creak of straining ropes, the rhythmic clink of metal hitting the masts. A breeze was gathering along the river, pushing strands of hair back from Entonin's face and causing his long robes to billow around his ankles. It smelled fresh. Alive. A breathtaking contrast to weeks of suffocating heat in the desert. In front of him, the shadows of boats lined the river like sleeping birds. They'd reached the Jamidi at last, and this branch of the great river would carry them all the way to Awasef.

Entonin ought to have been giddy with relief, but all he could feel was a gathering dread.

The journey from Tus'Bala had been incomparably easier than their flight from Jasser, but it had still been hard. The caravan had set a relentless pace, as keen to be away from Amoria as Entonin was, and he had so many blisters that he would have to entirely regrow the soles of his feet before they healed. When they'd finally reached the top of the mountain pass, able to see down to the high walls of Nahrayn and the glistening bend of the River Jamidi beneath them, Entonin had whooped for pure, uncomplicated joy.

It had represented the moment they finally stepped out of Amoria's shadow and into Dahran proper. Before them was Nahrayn: *two rivers*. The ancient city crouched over the two great arteries of Dahran, controlling everything that came from the west and north. Here was a true city, the domain of Queensguard and thieves alike, gutter rats and noble families. All of these were traps Entonin knew how to navigate, tools he could twist to his own uses. Nothing like the desert.

They were so close now, close to the Angustus Sea, close to *home*. Somewhere down Nahrayn's hot, narrow streets would be a temple to the gods of Ellath – small, forgotten, but a tiny light on the edge of the Empire's growing web. He had been longing for it so much: stepping back into a world where he was protected not only by gods but by the might of an empire as well.

He had forgotten to fear that empire.

Entonin clenched the coin in his fist, feeling the rough edges dig into the palm of his hand. It had been waiting for him at the inn, just like the last one, left in a place he couldn't avoid seeing. And yet everything about this coin was different, at least in all the ways that mattered.

The denarius was cast in a metal so dark it was almost black, and the bloody scent of iron mingled with Entonin's sweat, staining his skin. When he uncurled his fingers, the coin sat like a gaping hole at the centre of his palm. None of the detail was visible in the dark, but it didn't need to be. Entonin wouldn't forget it for all his days. Unlike the coin in Jasser, this coin wasn't stamped with a crescent but a full circle, a smooth continuous edge. But not even a war priest would be fool enough to mistake it for a full moon. This was a new moon, its face hidden in darkness. Ardulath had turned away from him.

He pressed his hand against his forehead, fist and coin together. "Shit," he whispered into the dark. *Father of knowledge, I have walked always in your light. Protect me from . . .* and then he stopped, because why would Ardulath protect him from one of his own?

A voice came from behind Entonin's left shoulder. "Good morning, Brother Seeker."

Whatever he had been expecting, it had not been the cracked and creaking voice of an elderly woman. He couldn't help turning in surprise, only just remembering himself in time to drop into a low bow. Whoever this woman was, she was a member of the Order of the New Moon, his very life clasped in her withered, old fingers.

"Very good, very good." He heard the slight mockery in her voice. "Stand up straight now; my back hurts just looking at you."

Entonin rose slowly, his eyes fixed on this diminutive woman. Even in the dark, he could see she looked as Dahrani as Karameth, but she spoke beautiful, unaccented Ellathian – music to his ears after all the bastardised Amorian he'd heard for so long.

"Good morning," he said, swallowing the words *and what do you want with me?*. Instead, he said, "Blessed are those who walk in the light."

"And long are their shadows," she finished perfunctorily. "Yes, yes. And here I am. One of the shadows." She was clasping a stick in front of her with both hands, and now she used it to hobble to Entonin's side, a slow thump, shuffle, thump, shuffle. Entonin was quite sure the limp was fake – he hadn't heard a sound when she approached. "Young, aren't you?" She squinted up at him. "And you're who they sent to the mage city?"

Because I pissed off the wrong Leader; because I was the best Seeker in Artainus; because I was disposable. Entonin could have said any one of those reasons and it would have been true. "Yes," he said instead.

"And you failed."

Entonin ground his teeth, strangling his reply. "Yes."

"A pity. It will be much harder to keep us from war with Dahran now."

"There was nothing I could do." Entonin's voice sounded thin and petulant to his own ears. "The situation in Amoria has changed. No outsider, no one without magic, could hope to make an alliance there now – least of all an Ellathian, for gods' sake."

"Yes, yes," she interrupted him. "I've seen some version of your reports. A worrying situation. We'll be forced to take action before long." At least this woman spoke plainly, even if nothing else about her was plain.

"Then you'll have seen I wasn't entirely unsuccessful." Entonin grasped at the nothing he had. "I made some connection with the Shiura Assembly, I received help from the most powerful mage in Amoria."

"Ah yes, your wizard friend. I don't think he'll be much use to us."

Something about the way she said "friend" sent a chill running down Entonin's spine. "What do you mean?"

"He's dead. Or he soon will be. The mages intend to execute him."

Oh gods, Naila, Entonin thought helplessly. Even in the short time he'd observed them together, Entonin could see that he'd been like a father to her.

The woman was watching him with her shrewd, unblinking eyes. A full moon had risen, oblivious to Entonin's disgrace, and in its silver light he could see her better – the deep wrinkles carved across her skin like tree bark, the raised veins on the backs of her hands. But her eyes were bright, incongruous with the rest of her face. They didn't look old at all.

"I'm sorry if he meant something to you."

Entonin straightened, deliberately lifted his chin. "No. He helped us. That's all." He had the sense that he was looking over a precipice, and if he didn't turn and push back she would send him plummeting to his death. "Are you going to tell me what I'm doing here or not? I know what the coin means—"

"Oh good." A grin cracked across her face. "I wondered when we were going to get to the point. It seems, young Seeker, that you're wrapped up in a great many interesting things."

Entonin frowned. "I'm just trying to get to Awasef. Look, I did what I could, and getting the girl to Awasef was—"

"*Yes.* The girl. What interesting new friends you have." The woman leaned forward, her weight on the stick she didn't need. "We know something of what happened at Tus'Bala."

Entonin felt suddenly cold.

Gods, how long have you been watching us? The Order of the New Moon was following him. They truly were the shadows to Ardulath's light; the real spies, no matter what Karameth liked to call *him*. If they had taken an interest in Naila, it meant nothing good.

He swallowed, not knowing what to say.

"Why don't you start by telling me about her?" She sounded like a kindly old woman coaxing a child to speak. "Tell me about her power."

"She's not a mage . . ." he started and then stopped. It was knowledge this woman wanted, and knowledge was his currency – his only value. If he didn't speak to this woman, then she'd only use some other way to find out what she wanted to know, and the price of Entonin's silence would be far too high.

Still, it felt like a betrayal.

"What do you want to know?" he asked quietly.

By the time he was done, Entonin felt emptied, as if the old woman had reached inside him and scraped out everything she wanted. He'd told her all of it, every little detail about Naila's life, every word Naila had told them about her encounter at Tus'Bala. Even as he spoke, he kept seeing Naila in front of him, the way she'd changed since Amoria – unfurling slowly as they travelled further from the mage city. She was only beginning to trust them.

This – supplying knowledge to his temple – was Entonin's entire existence, his life, his purpose. He trusted in his god, he trusted in his people. Always. Why, then, was he starting to feel sick?

"Very good," the woman said at last, offering no further reaction to anything he said. "We are satisfied, for now. You may continue on to Awasef as planned, though we'll expect a full report on your arrival."

It was no more than he'd always intended to do, and yet his stomach clenched at the order.

"What is this about?" he snapped, his temper seizing control of his mouth. "This is just a report. Why did you summon me like this? Why the damn coin? I have done nothing but serve. I have crossed deserts, been imprisoned by mages. What reason could the Order of the New Moon *possibly* have to intervene?"

As soon as he'd finished, Entonin felt his anger bleed out of him, leaving him alone to face the consequences of his outburst. He swallowed a gulp of air and tried to ignore the slick feeling on the palms of his hands.

For a moment, neither of them spoke, the woman only watching him with raised eyebrows, dangerous amusement glittering in her eyes.

"You really have no idea who travels with you, do you?" she said at last.

"I don't understand . . ."

"No, you don't. Entonin tyr Ardulath, somehow you have emerged from Amoria with the most dangerous thing that city possessed." She narrowed her eyes and it changed the shape of her smile completely. "You've seen the pieces. Are none of them familiar? Warriors who wield the elemental powers. Strange attacks. A creature with darkness in her eyes."

"That's . . . those are children's stories," Entonin croaked.

"Are they?" The woman didn't appear to blink.

"Just tell me what this is about—"

"Careful, young one. Your questions are pointed in the wrong direction." She waved her hand in an unmistakable dismissal. "You're a Seeker, aren't you? Perhaps it's time to ask your companions who they really are."

Entonin slipped back inside to the same silence in which he'd left. The inn felt deserted. Who knew what time it was? Only the gods kept the hours at this time of night.

He hesitated at the bottom of the stairs, turning the coin over and over in his fingers, the stench of iron and fear still clinging to him. And what else was he bringing back with him? Ardulath may have turned His face from Entonin, but now His gaze was fixed firmly on his companions – on Naila. On Karameth. Was there any scenario in which Entonin could protect them from the Order's attention? And should he want to? He was a priest of Ardulath, for gods' sake, and the Order was the will of his god.

Entonin mounted the stairs slowly, as if the world had grown heavier, his limbs pulled towards the ground. It was only when he turned the corner that he saw the thin sliver of yellow spilling from underneath one of the doors, a rectangle of light cast across the landing. He didn't even have to look to know which door it came from. Karameth was waiting for him.

He thought he'd slipped out without waking the mercenary, but he should have known better. Karameth had noticed when Entonin picked up the coin, and the way he'd looked at him had made Entonin feel uniquely seen, in a way he hadn't felt even among his friends back home. Stripped bare, even within the robes of his faith. Karameth had lingered by Entonin's side without him asking, had stayed silent but present, something Entonin could reach for if only he allowed himself to.

The bedroom door stuck so that Entonin had to shove it to get inside, stirring up a fine cloud of dust and dispelling any notion he might have had of slipping in unnoticed.

Karameth was sitting up anyway, his back against the headboard. His chest was bare, his skin burnished gold by the lamplight, but he was still wearing loose trousers, one leg curled underneath him, the other bent at the knee. His eyes were fixed on the door as if he'd been watching it all night, waiting for Entonin's return.

Entonin shut the door and then sank back against it, for a moment utterly unsure of what he was supposed to say.

"Hi," he said uselessly. "Sorry to wake you."

Karameth glared at him in a way so familiar it made Entonin's mouth twitch in a reluctant smile. It still gave him that uneasy prickle over his skin, a sensation of touch without Karameth moving at all. For once, Entonin was far too tired to make himself look away, to pull his gaze from the straight plane of Karameth's jaw, or the place where his dark hair curled against his shoulders.

Karameth still didn't speak. He knew Entonin wouldn't be able to resist the silence, that it would draw words helplessly out of him.

"I'm fine." Entonin still held the coin, slippery between his fingers. "It was the temple, that was all."

"You could have taken me with you." It was such a relief to hear Karameth's voice that Entonin wanted to laugh.

Instead, he said, "You know I couldn't."

"You hired me to protect you."

"Yeah, but not from them. I don't need ..." Entonin swallowed, unable to finish as Karameth lowered his knee and turned to rise from the bed.

Karameth's trousers were low on his hips, and Entonin had no strength left to keep himself from staring at the line where

Karameth's skin disappeared behind bunched fabric. *The inguinal crease*, he thought stupidly, as if he could hide his desire behind knowledge.

"Did they hurt you?" Karameth asked, and this time Entonin did laugh. It was like an absurd dream, where a play was happening around him but somehow he'd stumbled onto the wrong stage.

"Of course not. You think I'd be here if the Temple of Ardulath had a reason to hurt me? It's fine. I'm fine."

"You are not *fine*." Karameth had come closer, studying Entonin's face as if still looking for some physical injury. Entonin was dressed in the full regalia of an Ellathian priest, but he felt the most naked of the two of them. Karameth was searching him again, *seeing* him in a way no one had for years, and yet somehow the idiot wasn't seeing anything at all.

"I am. Stop it, Kara. I don't need you fussing over me."

Karameth took one more step forward, and there at last was that slow, lingering look. "What *do* you need, then? What can I do for you?"

Oh. Perhaps he wasn't blind, after all. That question obliterated the last fraction of Entonin's restraint. There was nothing Entonin wanted more than to forget, to erase the feelings of doubt and helplessness knotted in his chest. Karameth was so close, it would take nothing to reach out and touch him, and everything not to.

And Entonin didn't have anything left.

It was just a small movement, a tip of a finger on the thin skin of Karameth's clavicle, but it felt like throwing himself off the edge of a cliff. Then his other hand found the smooth expanse of Karameth's back, and he was pulling Karameth with him, tumbling off the face of the world.

Karameth answered him. Entonin had imagined this any number of times – of course he had – but he hadn't anticipated Karameth's gentleness. He tipped Entonin's head towards him, a thumb along his jaw, parting Entonin's lips with his own. He peeled Entonin's robes away from him as if he might bruise the skin underneath, encircling Entonin within the strength of his arms. It was Entonin who bent towards his touch, who pressed his body hard against Karameth's and pulled recklessly, ruinously at the cord at Karameth's waist.

Only when they were both naked did Karameth pause, releasing Entonin and stepping away from him, leaving him cold and yet still drowning under the weight of his desire. Karameth's smile wasn't small now, but daring and wild, his brown eyes glinting in the lamplight.

"So, would you like me to stop fussing over you?"

"Karameth." Entonin's voice came out as a rasp. "Karameth, if you stop now, I swear before all the gods that I will kill you."

Karameth raised a dangerous eyebrow.

"Fine, fire you then. I will ... I will ..."

Karameth pressed a thumb against Entonin's mouth, dragging it across his lips. "Shhh." He grazed his teeth against the side of Entonin's neck, and Entonin thought he might die from need before he had a chance to murder Karameth. "I believe we were talking about what I could do for you."

Then Karameth's lips were at the base of Entonin's neck, and then his chest, then his mouth was trailing slowly over Entonin's abdomen. Entonin's head sank back against the door, his breath coming ragged. When Karameth kissed the inside of Entonin's leg, Entonin made a sound he was not entirely proud of.

Then heat and desire took him, obliterating everything else. He was an outline filled with hot breath, and pleasure, and his fingers knotted in Karameth's hair.

41

ENTONIN

Everything felt different in the hard light of day.

The heat was already starting to build; even in the shade of the canopy, Entonin could feel it in his skin. The boat had slowed slightly the moment Naila had fallen asleep, carried now only by the breeze and not by whatever else it was she'd been doing. She lay sprawled out in the sun on the bow like a sunbathing cat. Try as he might, Entonin couldn't reconcile that sleeping girl with everything the Order of the New Moon had said.

. . . the most dangerous thing that city possessed . . .

Amoria, a city full of heretic mages, capable of reshaping the world as they saw fit, and the young woman who hunched her shoulders and tipped forward her hair to try to avoid the world's notice. How could that be true?

A creature with darkness in her eyes.

Some of the writings in his temple back home were so old that if you so much as breathed on them wrong, they'd crumble away to dust. These stories were older – stories that existed before anything was written down. They were told around firesides, to keep children from misbehaving. No one *believed* them.

Not for the first time, Entonin wondered if this was some kind of test. He had failed them at Amoria, maybe now he would have to prove himself. The Order of the New Moon removed obstacles, tied up loose ends. If the priests of Trebaranus knew his temple had sought a peace with mages and – worse – that they had nothing useful to show for it, then, well, Entonin was a loose end.

Entonin drew his lip between his teeth. All he'd been asked to do was go to the temple to make a report. He just had to sit on a boat for however long it took them to get to Awasef; then he'd deposit Naila at The Great Library and the Order could do whatever they damn well wanted with her. All this talk of war, of strife, of strange attacks: all this was the business of the gods themselves, and lord knows they didn't speak to the likes of him.

Yet here he was.

"Worried?" Karameth asked.

Entonin started. Karameth had been so still that Entonin had assumed he was sleeping. Or had hoped he was. The previous night had been a delicious dream, breathless and intoxicating, and if that was all it had been that would be fine. By the light of day, Entonin ought to be an Ellathian envoy with his Dahrani bodyguard, an appropriate distance between them, an appropriate caution between uneasy allies. Instead, the boat was narrow enough that even though they were opposite each other, they were pressed up together. One of Karameth's legs rested against Entonin's, their knees touching. Once Entonin had noticed it, he couldn't un-notice it, a slow heat creeping through him.

Neither of them made any attempt to move away. In fact, if anything, Karameth had moved closer.

"Just wondering when a particularly vivid dream will cause Naila to sink our boat," Entonin lied.

The complete stillness of Karameth's expression told Entonin exactly how little he'd been believed. He'd become too familiar with those subtle expressions by far. He'd travelled so much, even within the borders of the Empire, that he'd always skirted in and out on the edge of people's lives. It had been an age since he'd spent so long with any one person, and on the road Karameth's face had become more familiar to him than his own. It alarmed him to find that the most constant thing in his life was this Dahrani man he knew nothing about, and it alarmed him more that he didn't know if he wanted that to end.

"What will you do, when we reach Awasef?" Entonin asked.

"Find the most expensive inn in the city and order the best food they have," Karameth answered without a beat of hesitation, and, despite everything, Entonin felt a smile crack across his face.

"Gods, me too. And drink. I mean, I should probably visit the temple at some point."

Karameth gave him a hint of that daring smile, so small it felt like it was meant just for him. At that moment, it was easy to believe they were the only two people in the world; Naila was still asleep, and their helmswoman hadn't said more than two words since they'd come aboard. This was a tiny refuge, the water gurgling and churning around them.

It was an intimacy that was far more dangerous than last night had been.

"Will you rejoin the Grand Company?" The words blurted out of Entonin's mouth before he could stop himself. Sometimes he wondered if this was a compulsion – this picking, this probing for answers. He could have just left it. He could have enjoyed this moment and walked away afterwards. But he couldn't forget that damn woman's words. *Perhaps it's time to ask your companions who they really are.*

Karameth looked away, as Entonin had known he would, and Entonin felt a chill spread up the backs of his arms, the warmth of Karameth's attention sliding away from him.

But to his surprise, Karameth didn't withdraw into silence. "You know the answer to that," he said.

Entonin swallowed. "You were never in the Yenisseri's Grand Company, were you?"

"No."

Entonin sucked in a deep breath. He'd suspected for weeks, months even, but to hear it from Karameth was altogether different. "All that talk at the beginning – that one guard was sufficient, that more would send the wrong message to the Amorians." He dragged a hand over his face. "Gods, I can't believe I let myself go along with this."

Karameth turned back sharply. "It wasn't a lie."

"But you said it so I wouldn't want to hire anyone else, right? Why? So you could spy on me?"

A muscle twitched in Karameth's cheek.

"Gods, Karameth. Who are you? Really? Are you involved in this? Connected to Amoria?"

"*No.*"

"Then tell me! I have to know. You're part of a noble family, aren't you? That's why you won't tell me your name. Some outcast son of a Hakima?"

Karameth closed his eyes, and when he opened them he didn't lift his gaze to meet Entonin's. "In a way."

"Then what is this? Explain it to me."

The pause was unbearable, and then finally Karameth began to speak.

"I was young, in the Five Year War." Karameth clenched his hands into fists and then opened them, as if he was gathering himself to continue. "It was my first command. The conflicts were small, but bloody. We . . . I led my squad into a trap. One set by your war priests." He drew a shaky breath, as undone as Entonin had ever seen him. "It was a massacre. None of them survived. Only I got out of there, and only because someone gave their life for mine."

"Kara, I'm sorry—"

Karameth shook his head and Entonin pressed his lips back together.

"Among them was . . . was a man who was very dear to me. When I returned to Dahran I was a hero. The survivor. They made me a symbol of the war, of Dahrani strength, all because of my failure. I couldn't bear it."

"So you disappeared," Entonin finished.

Karameth looked up, finally meeting Entonin's gaze. There was a bright shine to his eyes, a tightness in the set of his mouth. There were a million other things Entonin should demand to know. Why Entonin? Why an Ellathian after what happened? What was his damn name?

Instead, he placed a hand lightly on Karameth's knee. "I'm sorry."

Neither of them said anything. Entonin could see the flecks of gold through Karameth's brown eyes, the errant strands of hair that had curled onto his forehead. Karameth placed a hand on top of Entonin's, entwining their fingers.

He should let go. He should pull away from this. Having feelings for some runaway Dahrani noble was deeply, *deeply* worse than spending the night with a mercenary.

"Is that *smoke?*" It was their driver from the back of the boat, speaking for the first time in hours.

Entonin fell back into himself with a jolt, snatching his hand away.

The driver had released the tension on their sails, leaving them to flap uselessly above their heads, and now she stood up on the wale to get a better look, the boat only swaying slightly under her movements.

Entonin and Karameth exchanged a glance and then both turned to lean out over the sides.

"Ardulath's light," Entonin breathed. "Is that village on fire?"

There was a sudden cry, a shriek like nothing Entonin had ever heard, so high and so piercing that he thought his head would split open between his hands. For a second, they were plunged into darkness, an enormous shadow passing in front of the sun. And then Entonin saw it. Its shadow tracked across the water and towards the village, wings wider than the river, a sinuous body snaking across the sky. It was terrible. It was impossible. But it couldn't be anything else.

A dragon.

He couldn't help it, his eyes dragged back to Naila, not knowing what he expected to see. Somehow, she was still unconscious, but around her the wooden boat glittered. Frost unfurled across the bow, spiralling away from her. The jagged path of ice from her back looked almost like silver-white wings.

"Children's stories," Entonin whispered.

But they were real. Oh gods, they were all real.

42

LARINNE

Larinne buttoned the black robes up to her neck and lifted the hood over her hair, carefully settling the fabric around her face. Not that it really mattered. Once she activated the device in her pocket, the Surveyor's mask would close over her face, concealing her behind featureless, black shadow. Still, these actions were reassuring, as if taking this care now might somehow protect her.

In her pocket she gripped the artefact in her fingers, the metal growing warm against her skin. It had taken her weeks to secure one: she'd called in favours, swapped duties, waited until she found someone with the right clearances. Weeks of planning for this moment, this uniform, and a plan so paper-thin that Larinne could see right through it, right down to its cracks.

She closed her eyes and released a slow breath. If she hesitated now, if she let herself follow the tangle of possibilities, she would be lost. She'd made her plan, accounted for every outcome she could control, but at the heart of it only one thing mattered: if she did nothing, he would die.

She pressed the artefact into the palm of her hand, closing her fingers tightly around it.

"*Occultos*," she whispered.

A tingling sensation spread from the nape of her neck up the back of her skull, tracking over her skin as the black mask closed over her. When she looked in the mirror, only a shadow looked back.

It was time.

She left her apartment mid-stride, not hesitating, not waiting to hear the door click shut behind her.

The corridor was dark, a long line of flickering lamps bending away into shadow. It was more than she'd hoped for: the landing was deserted. Larinne walked down it with her head high, her black robes streaming out behind her. She was a Surveyor, she was meant to be here, no one would challenge her. With every step, she felt her heart grow steady and her breathing slow. She could do this.

She reached the pattern room without once glancing over her shoulder. It, too, was deserted, the only movement the slow flow of magic spilling endlessly through its intricate pattern. She crossed to the centre of the room, where its attunement to the Central Tower would be greatest, and reached for the artefact in her pocket.

This was another difficult step. Larinne had never seen the pattern of the room she was travelling to: never felt its power or held the shape of it in her mind. She'd found a diagram of it, sketching it out and copying it over and over, but that was a different thing to constructing it with her mind. Now she pictured it, every sweep and stroke, following through the shape as if she were still writing it with her hand. In her pocket, the device grew hot under her fingers – the key that would unlock a path otherwise forbidden to her.

It was working.

There. Right at the back of her mind she felt it, the sensation of a mechanism clicking into place. Magic blazed across her vision, igniting the pattern before her eyes. The power of the room shifted, resonating in pitch with her own gift. Larinne didn't move. She waited, ready, poised, her breath burning in her lungs. The moment the eleventh bell chimed, she let go, and the magic pulled her through, carrying her to a new place.

When she opened her eyes, she was surrounded by stone.

Somehow, the passages below the Central Tower felt darker, even though they were lit with the same line of glowing lamps, light pinned between shadow. The air hung stale and heavy, no stray breeze finding its way through these tunnels.

Despite its differences, she walked down the corridor as if it were just as familiar to her as the landings outside her home. Each footstep rang off cold stone. She could already hear voices from a room somewhere ahead and on her left, and fear crept over her skin like ice.

You're a Surveyor, Larinne repeated to herself. *You belong here.*

It was some sort of common room, with two of Oriven's Justice crowded in over a table. A Surveyor without her mask leaned up against one wall, speaking animatedly, even though exhaustion was writ into the stoop of her shoulders and the shadows under her eyes. Larinne nodded to them as she passed, keeping her feet moving, never even slowing in her stride. One hesitation and she was done.

And then she was past them, back into the shadows and the quiet.

At the end of the corridor was a metal door, banded iron and a tiny, barred window; to go lower she needed the device again.

"*Recludo*," she whispered, one hand on the door handle, one on the artefact in her pocket.

The door whined as it opened and clanged shut behind her, loud enough that Larinne thought it must summon every Justice in Amoria. She gave herself a moment there, standing with her back to the door, letting herself breathe. From here, she should be alone until the twelfth bell, and yet her heart beat harder and faster than ever. Somewhere deep inside herself, she knew it wasn't just the thought of being caught that frightened her; she was frightened of what she would find down there – who she would find, and what they had done to him.

She passed a long row of empty cells before she found his; no other prisoners were kept on the same floor as the fallen wizard, as if his failures might be catching. His cell looked much like any of the others: it was square and dark, the only light coming from a single lamp in the corridor behind her. A thin mattress. A metal bucket. Facing her was a row of iron bars, humming with power, each one etched with phonemes meant to drain magic, more than she'd ever seen in one place. Even with the collar around his neck, they still feared him.

She could feel the wards dragging at her own power as she approached the bars.

"Haelius?" she whispered.

He was there. Just a few steps away from her.

Haelius lay on his back on the mattress, pale as a ghost in the shadows. They'd dressed him in white, the lowest colour, and there was no hem on those robes, nothing to mark him as a mage.

He lay still, so still he barely looked alive. Larinne could only just see the rise and fall of his chest.

"Haelius," she said again, louder this time.

Still, he did not answer her.

Clutching the device in her pocket, Larinne flung back the lock on the cell door and hauled it open. The metal shrieked as loudly as the door above, but this time Larinne didn't hear it. She was already at Haelius's side, sinking to her knees and laying her hands on him as if she had to touch him to know that he was real. She immediately reached behind his neck, through the tangle of his hair, her fingers searching out the latch on the collar. With one hand on the device, she summoned her magic and spoke the words to release him. It clicked apart.

She tugged the cruel metal out from beneath him and then flung it across the room, as far from them both as she could get it.

"Haelius." She closed a hand on his narrow shoulder and shook him lightly. "Haelius, come on, get up."

Still nothing. Panic began to rise like a sickness in her throat. She had always feared what long-term exposure to a collar might do to him.

"Haelius!" she shook him again, hard.

He gasped, drawing a sudden breath as if surfacing from underwater. His hands groped blindly for the edge of the mattress, and then he rolled onto his side and retched, his shoulders heaving. Larinne placed a hand against his back, her thumb smoothing the white fabric. When he was done, he turned to look at her, his eyes confused and unseeing.

"Is it time?" he asked. And then he froze, his hand reaching up to his neck, only just realising it was gone. "Why did you—"

Too late, Larinne realised her mistake. She reached into the pocket of her robes and clicked the device between her fingers, letting the Surveyor mask drop away.

"*Larinne?*" Something in his expression broke. He searched her face with his gaze as if he couldn't believe what he was seeing.

"It's me," she said gently.

His eyes shone in the low light. "Larinne, you can't— what are you doing here?"

Larinne didn't answer, she just threw her arms around him and pulled him close, holding him as tightly as she could. There was a heartbeat of hesitation, and then Haelius closed his arms around her, his fingers digging into her skin as if he couldn't hold her tight enough.

"I'm sorry," she said, easing herself away from him. "There isn't any time. We have to go now. Come on, let me help you up."

She looped a hand around his waist and helped him stand. He was too thin and too light by far, and she could feel him trembling as he found his feet.

"There," she said, forcing herself to smile. She was the one who had to carry them both. "Can you walk? We have until the twelfth bell and there isn't much time."

She waited quietly, giving him a chance to orientate himself. She could almost see him reassembling himself: he glanced slowly around the cell, at his robes, at his hands. He took a deep breath and looked at her, and she could see his expression harden. She was ready for this.

"I know what you're going to say," she said, her voice as stern as she could make it. "We don't have much time, so let's do this quickly."

"I can't come with you."

"I know you think that," she tried to keep her voice steady, "but you can, and you must. Your execution is scheduled. If you don't come with me then you'll die."

"Maybe that's right." She'd known that was coming too, but it still felt like someone had twisted a knife in her heart. "Maybe I should die for what I've done."

There wasn't time to feel it, there wasn't time to feel anything. She had to get him to leave.

She stepped towards him and took both his hands in hers. Again, his fingers pressed into her skin. "Listen to me, I failed you before, and I'm sorry. No, stop, don't say anything, we don't have any time. I can't—" she swallowed, her throat suddenly dry. "I can't stop you once we're out of here. If you want to turn yourself back in, then do it. But I need to get you out of here. Come and talk to me, at least. Let me set this right."

"*I* failed *you*," he whispered, staring at their linked hands.

"Yes, maybe a bit." She squeezed his fingers, tears blurring her vision. "But that doesn't matter right now. You have to come with me."

He pulled his hands out of her grip. "No, it's too dangerous. What if we're caught? What if *you're* caught?"

"It's too late for that. I'm here, aren't I? I promise, I've covered my tracks." She steeled herself, knowing exactly what she was about to do to him. "Come with me, Haelius. I'll be in more danger if you stay, because I won't leave you behind again. I'm not leaving until you come with me."

"What?" He looked horrified. "How can you even say that?"

"Come with me." Larinne set her jaw, her dark eyes cold as stone. "I swear I will let you turn yourself back in, if that's what you want, but for now, just come with me."

His body sagged and he looked down to the ground beneath his feet. "You can't do this."

"I can. And I will. You have to trust me."

It was the word "trust" that undid him. He looked away, his face contorted in frustration. He nodded once, unable to make himself say it out loud.

"Thank you." Larinne felt almost drunk with relief. "We have to go. Now. Can you transport us out of here?"

She saw him turn his gaze inwards, reaching for his power; he flexed the tip of his fingers and then grimaced.

"No, I can't."

It didn't surprise her. "And if I transferred my power to you?"

He shook his head slowly. "I'm sorry, it wouldn't be enough."

Larinne nodded; she'd known it would be this way. She would have to handle their escape.

"Okay, we'll just have to go out the way I came in. I'm going to have to restrain you," she said it as gently as she could. "You'll be able to break the restraints if you need to."

Haelius nodded, his face pinched and pale.

She cast the spell slowly, creating the gold restraints used by Surveyors, taking extra care to make sure they looped only lightly around his wrists. He watched her in silence, the light from her spell reflected in his eyes. This wouldn't be the worst of it, and he knew it. Larinne reached for the cold metal ring she had looped over her belt.

As soon as she brought out the collar, Haelius jerked instinctively away.

"It's not real," she said quickly, holding it out to him so he could touch it. "I removed the coatings; it's only for show. It won't hurt you."

He held his eyes closed for a moment. "I know. I'm sorry, it's just—"

"I know." She held the heavy ring out, seeing the raised red of the skin on his neck and aching for what she asked him to do. "I'm sorry, there isn't any time."

He nodded and turned so she could fasten the false collar around his neck.

"Larinne, I don't think this is going to work. No one will believe I'm being moved."

Larinne didn't look at him, busying herself with checking his restraints and resetting her own disguise. "They don't have to." Her voice was strange and distorted from the Surveyor magic. "Bow your head, don't meet anyone's eye. Not everyone knows you by sight. This level should be empty, and then we just need to take the pattern room to the Dragon's Rest. Can you walk?"

"Yes." He tipped his head into her line of sight, forcing her to look at him. "Promise me you've thought this through: that you'll be safe?"

"Come on," she made herself smile even though he wouldn't be able to see it. "We have to go."

The moment they stepped out of his cell, the watch in her pocket chimed the twelfth bell. Larinne felt her heart skip a beat. They'd tarried too long. Another guard would be coming to check Haelius's cell at any moment. How had they lost so much time?

"Quickly!" She hurried forwards, tugging on Haelius's restraints and pulling him into a stumbling run. She could hear from his ragged breathing that he was struggling, and she wanted nothing more than to turn around and loop her arm through his, let him lean against her shoulder, but she couldn't.

They rushed past the other empty cells, their footsteps slapping against the stone. Larinne counted them. Five, four, three more until they'd reach the stairs. She could see the door up ahead. Just a few more steps.

Before they could reach it, the handle creaked down and the door swung inwards with a teeth-grinding squeal. Another Surveyor stepped into the corridor. Larinne stumbled to a breathless stop, cold sweeping through her. There was only one prisoner on this level – only one person she could possibly have trailing behind her.

The door clanged shut and the Surveyor looked up at her. "Wait. What is this?"

Larinne didn't hesitate. Hot words of power flew to her mouth. Her spell threw the Surveyor backwards, slamming him against the wall. Even as his body smacked against the stone, the next spell was already in her mouth; she stepped forward, reaching for the Surveyor's head as he groggily looked up towards her. The moment her hand touched his skin, Larinne locked her mind with his. He was stunned, weak, his mind standing no chance against her: she struck it with a force which left him slumped against the wall.

Stepping back, Larinne drew a deep breath and balled her hands into fists to keep them from shaking. She glanced back over her shoulder. Haelius could only watch, his eyes creased with worry.

"Come on," she tried to keep her voice even. "Let's go."

By the time they reached the floor with the pattern room, Larinne's heart was beating so fast she thought it would burst. This was it. They just had to make it to the end of the corridor. She could hear the murmur of voices coming from the common room. The Surveyors were there, waiting inside. They just needed to not look up, not look too closely. It would work. It had to.

"Keep your head down," she whispered before they stepped through the metal door. "It's just at the end."

Haelius nodded. He took one of her hands into his and squeezed it wordlessly. Larinne squeezed back, and then pulled her hand away.

She strode out with her head up and Haelius's restraints in her fist, leading him briskly along the corridor. There were other prisoners on this level, and they stared hollowly out from their cells, watching them in silence. She tried not to look at them, just listening to the steady footsteps of Haelius behind her. Would any of them recognise the Wizard Akana? Would any of them say anything if they did?

A bark of laughter from the common room made her heart leap into her throat and she tugged a little too hard on the gold restraints. Haelius stumbled behind her.

Then they were there, past them, walking by the door in full sight of all of them. Two more steps and they'd be clear, Haelius would be clear.

"Hey, isn't that . . .?" Larinne's heart stuttered in her chest. "That's the wizard! Hey! Wait!"

"*Run!*" Larinne yelled.

She whirled on the spot, dropping Haelius's restraints. He ran past her, throwing himself forward, putting his trust in her. She could feel the Justice reaching for their power before they'd even come through the door.

"*Induresco repellam,*" she cried out the words and slammed her hand against the wall, sending an incandescent white shield across the corridor just as they fired two spells towards her. She felt them hit the shield as if someone had struck her in the face, but she gritted her teeth and held it. "*Induresco repellam,*" she repeated over and over, holding the shield in place. She had to stay there, her hand against the wall, her willpower and concentration the shield which protected them. On the other side of it, she could see the Justice preparing to strike her again.

She was trapped.

"Give it up," the Surveyor called to her, while the others prepared their spells. "You can't hold that thing forever."

Go, she willed Haelius, knowing it was futile. *Get out of here.*

Her eyes leapt from one Justice to the next, each of them poised to strike. She couldn't drop the shield to run. One flicker in her power and they would hit her with everything they had.

She tasted it on her tongue, the metallic heat on the air, the prickle of power. It was feeble but it was there. He was next to her, his hand on her shoulder.

"Let the shield go," he said, the hum of magic loud in her ears. "Now!"

As soon as she did, Haelius's holding spell hit all three of them at once, locking them in place.

"Quick," he said through a grimace. "Finish it. I can't hold them for long."

She went to each of them in turn, placing a hand on their foreheads and rendering them unconscious, letting them slump down against the floor.

As the last one fell, Haelius gasped and groped at the wall to steady himself. Larinne ran to help him stand.

"Can you still use the pattern room?" She was breathless as well, barely able to hear over the pounding of her heart.

"I think so." They stumbled together towards it, leaning heavily against each other, her arm around his waist.

"Not far," she breathed, as much to herself as to him. "Just a little further."

The pattern room was right in front of them – their way out, their freedom.

But then the air shimmered, as it always did just before someone's arrival, barring their access until the transportation was complete. Larinne felt Haelius tense in her arms, felt her own heart drop into her stomach.

Someone was coming.

Larinne couldn't move. She couldn't think. Next to her Haelius grasped at his power and failed, sagging heavier against her arm.

A figure materialised at the centre of the pattern room.

Dailem.

She no longer wore the grey of mourning but was back in her Justice uniform, gold embroidery spiralling over the high collar and down the edge of her coat. Her eyes moved from Larinne to Haelius, to the prone forms of the Justice behind them, her face expressionless, no surprise registering in her eyes.

"Dailem?" Larinne choked out, her voice still distorted by the Surveyor's artefact.

"Stop where you are," Dailem answered. "This ends here."

Larinne felt Haelius grasp for magic, but she placed a hand on his chest and he stilled, letting Larinne step forward on her own.

"Let us past," said Larinne.

Dailem pinned Larinne with her gaze, seeming to pierce through the mask and Surveyor's robes, right down to Larinne's core. "No."

"Dailem—"

"I've been waiting for you to do this." A muscle twitched in Dailem's cheek. "I didn't really believe you'd be so stupid, so *selfish*, but I had to be sure. I knew the moment you opened his cell door, the instant both of you crossed over the threshold. How could you *do* this?"

Larinne shivered, the dread trickling down her spine. There'd been so much magic on those bars, so many layers of protection, Larinne had detected nothing unusual about the door itself. She drew three slow breaths, making herself calm down, making herself think.

"No one knows but you," she said, the pleading note in her voice audible even through the distortion magic. "Let us go. This doesn't need to involve you."

"*Involve* me?" Dailem's voice finally cracked. "People are dead, the man I love is dead, because of *him*."

Larinne closed her eyes. Her heart ached – for her sister, for dear Malek, and for Haelius listening behind her. "He didn't kill them. You know he didn't. He made mistakes, I know, but so have I. We all have. You wouldn't expect me to die for them."

There was a beat of hesitation, a moment where Dailem's eyes softened just a fraction, and for a second Larinne thought she might let them go.

"No."

"*What?*"

"I am a Justice, and he is Oriven's prisoner. I won't let you past."

"What are you saying?" Larinne recoiled from her sister. "You joined the Justice to move *against* Oriven, to protect people, to prevent things like this from happening."

The look Dailem gave her was furious, exhausted, impatient. "No, I didn't. I joined the Justice to protect *us*. My family, Ko'ani, *you*. I won't lose anyone else. Time and again, I have watched you put all of us in danger. Enough. Stand aside, and I will take the prisoner back to his cell."

"Wait." Realisation trickled through Larinne slowly. "I didn't understand how Oriven could know about the grain, about what we'd been doing at the Dragon's Rest, but it was you, wasn't it? You told Oriven everything."

"Everything I did, I did to protect you. You needed to be stopped before you went too far, before you went to a place I couldn't bring you back from. And now we're here anyway. Stand aside, before it's too late."

"And Reyan? Dailem, tell me you didn't betray him."

"How *dare* you." Dailem stepped forward, a finger pointed at Haelius. "*He* betrayed Reyan. Enough of this. Stand aside."

"No." Larinne shook her head, caught impossibly between pity and blinding anger. "I know what you've lost, Dailem; don't do the same to me."

"You have no idea what I've lost."

Larinne felt the air change, the lamps flickering as Dailem pulled magic towards her. She was already casting her spell, her lips shaping the phonemes, her hand drawn back. In a second the magic would hit Larinne, ending everything; everything Larinne had worked for, hoped for, longed for.

She didn't move. Didn't make a sound. She waited until the very instant Dailem loosed her spell, magic shivering in her fingertips. She heard Haelius stumble and shout behind her as if he were miles away. "*Wait!*" Saw the bright light of magic arcing towards her. Knew that everything came down to this one second.

Dailem had always been strong, but Larinne had learned magic alongside the most powerful mage in Amoria. In the last instant,

Larinne flicked her fingers, all of her strength and concentration in that simple gesture. A tiny shield flashed into existence. It was a feeble thing, flickering into life and then gone, but it was enough to catch Dailem's spell. The timing was perfect: Dailem's magic dissolved on its surface, sparks scattering away from them.

Casting with her hands left Larinne free to begin her second spell, short, a single phoneme. Before Dailem even registered it, it blasted across the space between them and struck Dailem in the stomach, sending her flying backwards.

Dailem hit the ground, hard, a sprawl of black and gold robes. Larinne couldn't let herself feel it, couldn't hesitate; she was already on top of her, grabbing Dailem's arms and using the gold restraints to lash her wrists together.

Dailem was blinking slowly from hitting her head against the stone, her limbs heavy in Larinne's hands. When she focused her eyes on Larinne, it clearly took effort.

"I could still call for help," Dailem said. "I could still bring them here."

But you won't, Larinne thought, even as she knew she couldn't take that risk.

"I'm sorry" was all she said out loud, wondering if this was all she'd ever say to her – if what she'd done would drive them apart forever. She pressed a hand against her sister's forehead and uttered the words of the spell. Dailem sank against the floor.

When Larinne finally looked up, she found Haelius extending a hand to her, his face taut with worry and grief.

"Larinne . . ."

"I'm all right." She took his hand and let him pull her back to her feet, both of them stumbling and unsteady.

"It isn't too late," he said softly. "Let me go back . . ."

"Come on, we're out of time," she answered, leading him the last few steps, resolutely ignoring his offer. "Can you still use the pattern room?"

"I think so."

"Then go. Go now. I'll follow you."

He hesitated, but only for a moment. She saw him close his eyes, reach a hand towards the pattern room wall, drawing on its magic. Then he was gone, leaving only a faint shimmer in the air where he'd been standing. He was out. He'd made it to the Rest. She'd done it.

The relief almost made Larinne collapse where she stood, but she forced herself to take the last steps, to reach for the unending power of the pattern room. She turned in the last moment, giving the shadowy form of her sister one last, long look.

"Forgive me," she whispered, even though she knew in her heart that Dailem never would.

When she appeared in the pattern room of the Dragon's Rest, Haelius was already on the floor, his back against the wall, his breath coming in ragged gasps. Larinne leaned on the opposite wall and let herself slide slowly to the ground. She closed her eyes, feeling the solidity of the wall behind her back and the stone against her hands. Her lungs burned and her heart still thumped against her ribs, but they were alive. Haelius was free.

They sat in silence, each of them catching their breath. Haelius unclipped the fake collar and hurled it away from him. The room was dark and still, only the tiniest hint of Amorian light creeping in through the open door, painting them both in grey.

She reached into her pocket and clicked off the device, removing the mask of a Surveyor. She started to unbutton the black robes, shrugging them off over her own clothes underneath. She wanted rid of them, wanted them and everything they stood for *away* from her. She tried not to look at the pooling black fabric, tried not to see the dark outline of her sister crumpled on the floor.

When she looked up, she found Haelius watching her.

"What have you done?" he asked, his eyes never leaving hers.

"Nothing you wouldn't have done for me."

"You could have died, Larinne."

"Yes," she said, leaning her head back against the wall. "But I didn't."

"What were you *thinking*?"

"Goddess, Haelius, I was thinking that I didn't want you to die."

A moment of silence, and then, "You shouldn't have come." His voice was barely more than a whisper. "You should have left me there."

Larinne gritted her teeth, hard. "Should I? How could you even ask me to do that? You have no idea what you're asking of me."

She didn't want to have this conversation. She'd been longing for this moment, half believing it would never come. Now, though, she found that she was filled with a desperate kind of anger. She hated the way he kept trying to push her away, couldn't bear the way he spoke so easily of his death, when every mention of it tore her heart to pieces.

She took a deep breath. She'd promised him that they would talk.

"You left me," she said, pulling out the words like splinters. "We face things together, we always have. I wouldn't have survived the council without you and *you*, Goddess, you wouldn't have made it through the Academy without me." She tipped her head back, looking up at the shadowed ceiling. "But when all of this began, you started pulling back from me, pushing me out. You stopped talking to me. It was as if you wanted me to forget you, as if you genuinely believed I might stand by *Oriven*. And then you made these plans, these—" She stopped abruptly. They both knew the consequences of what he'd done.

"You think that you can fix things with some big, grand gesture, but you can't. You think throwing yourself on the fire is the answer, but how can it be, when we would lose *you*?" She frowned, knowing she was hiding behind her own words. "When I would lose you." She tried to press her lips together but they were trembling. "I let you down, I know I did. When I lost Reyan, and then Malek . . . I was angry. Angry with you for acting without me. Angry with myself for not seeing what was happening. But I think I was angriest that I failed you – in those moments where I should have pulled you closer, I pushed you away. You didn't kill them, Haelius. It wasn't you." Larinne knew her voice was cracking now, her cheeks wet with tears. She didn't move to wipe them away. "I should have told you. I should have grabbed you and told you every second until you believed me."

The inn was hung with a heavy silence, not even their breath seemed to disturb the air. Outside, the Southern Quarter was unnaturally still, only the quiet murmur of the Aurelia trickling through the night.

Larinne heard Haelius draw a breath and then stop, the words catching in his throat. He tried several times before he managed to speak.

"I never meant to leave you." He shook his head slowly, the white robes luminous in the low light. "I thought I could protect you, that you'd be safer if you were away from me. Everything I did seemed to make things worse. I had all this power. I didn't know what to do with it. I thought I must be able to do *something* – something that I was *supposed* to do. I never thought— I never meant ..."

"It wasn't your power I needed, Haelius," she said quietly. "I just needed you."

He covered his face with his hands and drew a knife-sharp breath. "I'm so sorry."

His muffled sobs broke her heart. Through all this, she hadn't once heard him cry. She went to his side, gently pulling him towards her, untangling his arms and drawing his head against her shoulder. She felt him shuddering with each breath, swallowing, trying to get himself to stop. Finally, the weight of him sank against her and he let himself cry. She didn't know how long she held him, letting the exhaustion and grief bleed out of him, but gradually his breathing began to slow.

"Mother have mercy," he gasped, tugging away from her and wiping his face with the side of his hand. "Just look at me."

"You're a mess," she said, not unkindly. She reached up and pushed the damp tangle of his hair back from his face. "I brought—" she started and then stopped. She meant to say, "I brought your clothes, some supplies, things you'll need on the road", but she couldn't make herself say it. She couldn't tell him that he had to leave.

He looked at her face like he always did, seeing her in a way no one else ever could. "I know."

"It's in the room next to this one." Larinne made herself look into those familiar green eyes, trying to burn them into her memory. "It's not much, but there's enough to get you to Jasser at least."

"Thank you." His voice was calmer now, steadier, and she knew he was doing it for her.

"Where will you go?"

He made a sound that was trying to be a laugh. "I don't know. Awasef maybe? When Naila left, she asked me to come with her. I should have gone. If I'd left with her, maybe none of this would have happened. Maybe . . ."

He didn't have to finish.

"What about you?" he asked, his fingers tightening on hers. "Dailem saw—"

"Dailem would never turn me in." Larinne said it without a beat of hesitation, but the smallest of doubts crept in behind.

She was too close to him to see his face, but Haelius didn't loosen his grip on her hands. "Even if that's true, there aren't many people who would help me escape. They'll come for you first."

"They won't find anything. If you take the Surveyor robes and the device; destroy them when your power returns. There's nothing else to link me to this."

"Larinne, you know that won't be enough."

"I'm not you," she managed a smile. "I'm well liked on the council. Oriven can't move against me as easily as he did against you."

Haelius heaved a bitter sigh. He didn't believe her, but he had no other answer for her.

"You know I can't leave."

"I know," he whispered. "I just don't want to leave you."

Larinne twined her fingers with his, leaned her head against his shoulder. "I don't want you to go."

For a time neither of them said anything, neither of them moved. Haelius kept brushing his thumb across the top of Larinne's hand, and Larinne wondered if he knew how much that simple gesture undid her.

"You have to go, don't you?" he said at last. He tried to say it lightly, to make it easy for her to leave. "If they go to your apartments and you're not there, then it won't matter that I took the robes."

He was right, she knew he was: every moment she lingered was a greater risk to her. But, Goddess, she didn't want to go.

He squeezed her hand once and pulled away from her. He struggled to his feet, still unsteady, grasping at the wall to pull himself up. Larinne stood slowly, feeling the reluctance weigh heavy in her bones. Standing in the grey light, Haelius straightened the cuffs of his sleeves, trying to smile at her, as if he weren't about to leave his home forever.

She stood in front of him with no idea what to say.

"Thank you," he said, smiling one of his helpless smiles, the corner of his mouth wavering. "For everything."

Larinne reached up to tuck his hair behind his ear, and then she drew her hand back across the curve of his cheekbone, letting it linger against his skin. Haelius leaned into her hand, drawing a deep breath, breathing her in. He placed his hand over hers, his fingertips featherlight on her skin. His eyes burned even in the low light.

"I love you," he whispered.

"I know you do," she said the words with half a laugh, as if it were the most obvious thing in the world. "I've always loved you."

She leaned in and kissed him, his lips soft against hers. She could feel him give way to her, his body bending in towards hers, his hand finding the back of her neck. His lips tasted of the salt from his tears.

It was Haelius who pulled away, stepping back with a gasp.

"Larinne," he said her name like it hurt him. "You have to go. Please, if they find you gone ..."

She nodded, not trusting herself to speak. For a moment, she was possessed with the desire to go with him, to turn her back on Amoria and everything the city had brought upon them: leave behind the mages, the non-mages, even Dailem and Ko'ani.

She knew she couldn't do it.

"I'll see you again," she said, unsure if it was a statement or a plea.

"Yes," he answered, though she could see from his expression that he didn't believe it.

She started to reach for the magic of the pattern room, but her concentration was shattered and the magic kept slipping through her grasp. Haelius tried to smile, and Larinne felt her heart break all over again.

When her magic finally hooked into the pattern room's, she held herself back, making herself look at him one last time, writing him into memory. That narrow, angular face, his tousled hair, the twisting scars on his left cheek, the vivid green of his eyes.

"Don't leave me again," she said, stupidly, as if that weren't exactly what he had to do.

He knew what she meant. "I won't."

Then she let the magic take her, dragging her away from him and back to the Western Spire.

43

RA'AKEA

Ra'akea rolled out of the way just as a wall of flame roared up behind her. She staggered back to her feet, turned, and hurled her spear, ice shivering through the air. The beast raised its great head and screamed, grey wings blotting out the sky. A single breath from its maw and her spear dissolved into mist, the water twisting away into air before she could claw it back to her. This beast was too strong, stronger than any she had faced before. The impossible was happening.

She was losing.

Around her the village burned. Stone blackened and melted into slag. Humans ran screaming, wading out into the river, carrying their young. Somewhere a bell tolled. Ra'akea was at the centre of all of it, exposed, nothing to hide what she was. Her arms ached from fighting, her lungs burned. Smoke and ash clogged her throat. She should never have come. She should never have thrown herself in the path of this beast for the sake of a human town.

But this was *her* fault.

Ra'akea could have put a stop to this. She could have ended everything with the girl. She'd been paralysed by dark, frightened eyes. *"You're— you're like me."* She had been frightened by the girl's power, feared for those small human lives when she shook the ground beneath their feet. She should have killed her then, but instead she had returned to her quarry, searching for the great monster that had led her halfway across a continent. It was an enemy she knew, that she *understood*. But she'd lost her chance to burn away the root cause of this sickness, and now this village had paid a terrible price.

Tae, she thought, desperately.

I am coming. Tae's resolve hardened in Ra'akea's heart, an impossible determination. *Fight. Just a little longer.*

As if the beast could hear them, it beat its wings in a frenzy, hurling ash and rubble up into the sky. Ra'akea held an arm across her eyes, grit and stone grazing her skin. Even now, she could hear the loneliness in the beast's cry. Even now, she felt a sliver of pity.

The beast rocked back onto its vast, coiling body, the whole world trembling beneath it. Its eyes burned the orange of glowing embers, the only colouring of its tribe that remained. It had been a creature of Fire, an enemy to Ra'akea even before the corruption, and yet it had still been one of the Atha. Once this pitiful animal had been a dragon, a living embodiment of its element. If there was anything left to it of its former life, it might still listen to her.

She crossed into the middle of the street, open, exposed, the roar of the flames loud in her ears. Even the air was burning. The beast sensed something had changed and lowered its head, watching her, its clear eyelids blinking slowly across its eyes.

"Child of Fire," Ra'akea called to it. "Tiatha. You do not belong here."

It tipped its head, sliding a little closer, its long body unwinding. There was a rumble that began at its throat and ticked down through its whole body, the sound echoing back on itself within its coils. Ra'akea held its gaze, stared it down as she would a wild animal. For a moment it stilled, considering her, some fragment of its mind making it wait.

Then it screamed.

Orange light appeared at its throat, seeping between the scales of its long underbelly, shading the grey in crimson and touching its feathered back with gold. It was a terrible warning.

Ra'akea grasped frantically at any water within her reach – from the air, from the ground, from the pails the humans carried. It wasn't enough. There wasn't enough. She had let herself get driven back, too far from the river. Even as she drew the water to her, the flames around her roared higher.

With a cry, she threw her own power in the path of the beast's. Just in time – a thin, wall of water shivered between her and all the might of dragonfire. They collided in an explosion of brilliant flames and hissing steam.

She could feel the water dissolving away as if part of herself was being unravelled. Her will wasn't enough. The creature was too strong. It shouldn't *be* this strong.

Heat rolled in waves around her. Her face burned, her eyes stung. Her feet slipped an inch back in the dirt. Then another.

Ra'akea! Tae's cry was desperate.

Ra'akea's arms were trembling, thin trails of sweat trickling down her back.

There was nothing she could do. This was it. This was the end.

I'm sorry.

The torrent of flame vanished. There was a change in the air. A coolness, a moment of respite from the searing heat of the flames. Ra'akea staggered in surprise, her shield of water slipping out of her grip, pattering to the ground. A moment later, a wave of river water washed up the road, rolling over the dusty streets and lapping up against the burning buildings. It swirled around Ra'akea's ankles, filling her with cool relief, with a sense of quiet strength.

The beast coiled away from her, hissing like a flame as it jerked back from the rushing water. Its attention bent down towards the river, its body sliding slowly up around the side of a building, its wings hunched tightly against its feathered back. Ra'akea was entirely forgotten. All it saw was the river.

Not the river. But someone there.

A figure, standing on the very edge of the riverbank. She stood with her arms outstretched, her face lifted to the beast's, her body between the Sha'arin and the humans taking refuge in the water.

It was the girl.

44

NAILA

The dragon turned slowly, first its head and then its body, a ripple of scales, feathers and folded wings. Naila watched it come, watched it consider her with huge, unblinking eyes. For a moment, she saw herself as it would see her, small enough to crush within its coils. Its skull alone was twice as tall she was, and it was crested with a crown of grey feathers that shivered like flames. It bared teeth as long as her arms, and she could smell smoke and sulphur on its breath.

And now it was coming for her.

Every fibre of her being screamed at her to run. Behind her, the Jamidi had burst its banks, brown water surging up the streets at her command, but what did it matter, when faced with a monster like this? Its snake-like body towered over buildings, its wings were wide enough to cover the sky.

The moment the boat had put ashore, Naila had run along the riverbank, her heart pounding so hard she thought she would be sick. She had dreamed of grey wings and whispering voices, and when she'd opened her eyes the obsidian at her neck had been so hot that it burned. She'd *known* what waited for them at the village, and she'd felt the pull of it the same way she'd felt the pull of the pendant, an inescapable weight.

There'd been no hesitation in her when she'd thrown herself between the dragon and the villagers. She hadn't even paused before summoning water to quench the flames, knowing it would draw the creature's attention, pulling it away from the stranger who'd attacked her at the oasis. But now – now she faced the might of this creature, now she stood alone, a girl in front of a dragon: a child in front of a creature older than the human world.

Run, she begged herself.

But she couldn't. Behind her, Karameth was shouting in Dahrani, directing people to the river, and there was the scrape and slide of more people scrambling to safety. Naila was all they had – the only thing standing between this village and utter annihilation. She couldn't step aside.

It didn't give her a chance to strike.

The dragon lifted its head and opened its jaws, brilliant flame spiralling from between its teeth. Naila threw herself sideways, the ground slamming into her shoulder, dragonfire missing her by mere inches. It was so hot. Hotter than anything Naila had felt before, the very air searing the insides of her lungs. Behind her, villagers screamed, flame cresting over their heads. She hadn't even managed to shield them. Naila prayed to whatever god would listen that the river would be enough.

Scrambling to her feet, she forced herself back into the beast's path, legs shaking, her vision blurred from smoke and heat. The dragon hadn't even moved, its long body coiled idly around the building. It regarded her as a cat might regard a dying mouse, deciding whether or not it would toy with her again.

It was a *dragon*. A being so great it had lived only in myth and memory. Naila had dreamed of these creatures, of feathers longer than her arms, the whoosh of wings in her ears. Never had she imagined standing against one. How could she? This creature was ancient, the very embodiment of power and magic. How had she believed she'd make a difference?

She grasped for her power, for the river, arms outstretched, water swirling up and around her as if it trailed from the tips of her fingers. She punched one arm forward then the other, sending stream after stream of water shooting towards it. The jets broke apart harmlessly, dripping off feathers, hissing hot off its scales. Naila's power coiled away into insubstantial steam.

Despair snapped its teeth at her. This wasn't enough – her power wasn't going to be enough. She needed more, so much more than she knew how to give.

Behind her, the river rippled on her awareness, a constant rumble of power at her back. The Jamidi was ancient, too, with a strength that had carved itself into the face of this land, shaping generations of life at the edge of the desert. And fire was its natural enemy.

This time, Naila didn't pick at the river, trying to tug strands of it away; she moved with it instead, twisting her whole body with the flow of the Jamidi, channelling its strength.

"Hold on!" she called to people sheltering behind her, praying she wouldn't wash them all away.

The river came to her call, a towering wave of water with all the strength of the Jamidi behind it. It smashed against the dragon, flattening it against stone, darkening grey feathers to charcoal and old ash.

Cold, thought Naila before the water could coil away, bending her will towards it, seeing crystals of ice before they even began to form.

The dragon screamed, a terrible scraping sound inside her head. It was resisting her, trying to burn her power away, an orange glow bleeding between grey scales. The air was rippling with heat, casting strange fluid shadows across the ground. As soon as any ice would form, it melted again, trickling uselessly away.

Naila clenched both her hands into fists, her arms shaking, her injured shoulder aching with remembered pain. *Cold*, she thought again. *Freeze. Freeze, dammit*. The thought of Haelius came unbidden to her mind, that raised eyebrow, a patient smile. *All that matters is your will*, he'd said, as if it were the simplest thing in the world.

Was her will not enough? Her will was all that stood between this creature and the people hiding at the river's edge, between an ancient beast and companions who had stayed by her side even when they should have turned away. If her will wasn't enough, they would die. *She* would die. And Naila wanted desperately to live.

"Freeze!" she screamed, holding her will between her teeth. It would be enough. It had to be enough. It began at the dragon's throat, milky ice creeping across its scales. The creature recoiled as if she'd burned it, thrashing and shaking its head. The feathers along its back rippled like a guttering candle, frost cutting a stiff and brittle path. It gave an ear-bleeding shriek and stretched out the full length of its body, reaching up towards the sky. Naila thought she'd understood its size, but the sight of it towering over her stole her breath. It stretched as tall as one of Amoria's spires, and when it snapped open its wings it had feathers longer than she was tall. The entire town was in its shadow.

One enormous wingbeat and it launched itself into the sky, trailing water and shimmering ice behind, silver shards falling like frozen rain. Naila had to shield her eyes, her hair blasted back from her face. She watched it go, not letting herself feel the relief that threatened to bubble up from within her chest. This wasn't over.

"Go! Imshi! *Move!*" It was Entonin's voice, calling in a mixture of Dahrani and Ellathian. "Alnahr— the river! GO!"

He was at one side of the ruined street, waving people through, his white robes and pale hair streaked with soot and ash.

"Entonin, hurry!" she shouted, breathless. "It's coming back."

"Go! Go!" he shouted, a high note of desperation to his voice. "Imshi! Imshi!"

The dragon made a single idle wingbeat and banked in the air, cutting through the sky like a knife.

"Entonin!"

It was coming back, bearing down on them at a terrible speed, its wings growing to fill the horizon. Entonin looked up at it, waving people past him. But he was at the centre of the street, terribly exposed, and he wasn't running.

"Entonin, *move!*"

The last person stumbled past, but the dragon was almost on top of them. Entonin didn't move. He stood staring up at the sky, watching it come, hypnotised by the sight of death speeding towards him on grey wings. Naila's heart stopped, time slowing. Fire spilled from the dragon's open jaws, a terrible cyclone of crimson and gold.

There was another shout, and then Karameth was launching himself into the air, his body colliding with Entonin's, bearing them both to the ground. They rolled in the dirt just as the dragon's flames struck, blinding Naila, obliterating any sight of her friends.

No.

Just as at the oasis, Naila was seized by a desperation so potent it almost swallowed her. It rose in a fury behind her eyes.

NO. She screamed it with her mouth, with her mind, and in her echoed a power like nothing she had ever felt before. Strength flooded through her veins, crackled across her skin. Every tiny fraction of water trembled and rang with her voice – in the air, in the ground, in her very breath. All of it was hers.

And she froze it.

The fire from the dragon's mouth flickered and guttered out. The temperature plummeted, ice spiralling away from Naila's feet. All around her, the flames seemed to stagger, to stutter and fail in the face of the blistering cold. The dragon screamed and crashed into the ground, collapsing against an already crumbling building. When it raised its head, Naila could see that every inch of it was covered in clouded ice, muting even the fierce embers of its eyes.

She raised her hands, holding it all in her grasp, tightening her grip. She would force it to feel, force the cold down deep into its bones. Spears of ice smashed against the dragon's side, splintering apart against the hard scales; the stranger was back on her feet, joining her power to Naila's. The dragon cried again, a long, pitiful howl. It slithered back to the nearest building, stone crumbling under the strength of its grip, its feathers flat and creaking under the ice. It was working.

And then there was a second cry.

Naila stumbled backwards, looking up at the sky, unable to comprehend what she'd heard: a cry from a second dragon.

This creature flowed through the sky like water, swooping down to them on wings not of feathers, but of a membrane so thin that Naila could see through them to a muted sky. Where the fire dragon was thick and muscular, crested with feathers like spines, this dragon was delicate and sinuous, its only feathers downy and swaying along its back like reeds. Its body spilled into the flooded streets, sliding beneath the water like it was made to be there. Naila didn't have to see the aqua of its eyes to know this dragon's element.

The fire dragon had used Naila's distraction to curl itself up and out of the flood, clinging to the last husk of a burned-out building, its grey scales hissing steam. The water dragon stayed low in the water, creating barely a ripple as it cut a path towards Naila. There was water everywhere; Naila had flooded the village with the very source of this dragon's power, and behind her every villager crouched in the shallows of the Jamidi, in the grip of this dragon's element. A single wave could wash them all away.

Naila took a step back, her foot sliding on the mud, a chill spreading under her wet clothes. She'd given everything to fight the fire dragon, and now there was another – a creature strengthened by the only weapon she possessed.

The stranger was shouting as the water dragon slid past her, her voice echoing in the strange quiet. "Halt! I am Ra'akea, daughter of Water. You do not belong here, Miatha. I command you to leave."

The dragon ignored her, its body winding through water smooth as glass. Its eyes were fixed on Naila, only Naila, its gaze never moving from her even as its head shifted from side to side. Atop the building, the fire dragon coiled tighter, throwing back the might of its wings to balance itself. It too saw only Naila.

Both of them were coming for her.

"Halt!" Naila shouted in desperation, mirroring Ra'akea's cry. "Stop!"

For a moment she felt hopeless – mad for thinking she might stop a dragon with a shout – and then incredibly, impossibly, they stopped. The water dragon halted mid-stroke, its head low in the water; the fire dragon grew still, its wings folding in against its back. Naila didn't dare move, only her eyes shifting between them. It must be a trap. She was being hunted; at any moment one of the dragons would dart forward and close its jaws around her.

And then the whispering began.

It was quiet at first, a low hiss close to her ears, but it grew, building like a tide, until her skull was seething with it. Naila clapped her hands over her ears, trying to shut them out, but it made no differ-ence – the whispers were coming from inside her head. She could hear the dragons, *feel* them, every thought, every emotion, like a commu-nication spell unspooling in her mind. It was too much, and Naila felt herself double forward, her chest burning as if someone had knocked the air from her lungs.

It was a tangle of hate, of fear, but most of all of *loneliness*. Naila felt it as all the moments she'd failed to find her place in Amoria; all the times she'd walked alone behind a family of mages, or someone had tripped her and called her *hollow*. She relived the look of horrified surprise on Brynda's face when she'd tried to come into the Rest, the moment she'd closed the door on her life with Ko'ani. And she saw Haelius, his face hidden by Amoria's light, telling her that she needed to go, to leave them all behind.

The dragons were grasping at these memories, at her feelings, drag-ging pieces of her away as if they wanted to consume them. It felt like drowning.

"Stop," she gasped. *Stop. Stop. Enough.*

But even as their grip on her lessened, the whispers grew louder, and she began to hear the words laced among them.

We hunger. We need, need, need. Be with us. Be of us. We have come for you. We follow you. We need. Be with us, Mother.

A feeling of revulsion rose in her throat, driving their thoughts away. *No.*

She made herself look up, made herself meet their ancient gaze even though they towered above her.

"Enough!" she called, feeling her power burn through her veins like liquid fire. "Be gone. You are not wanted. I'm not who you think I am."

There was a silent wail, a terrible cry that existed only in Naila's mind. *Mother, Mother, please. We have found you. We must be with you.*

The pendant was hot against her neck, and Naila felt as if her power had possessed her, had seized control of her tongue. "No. Do not call me Mother. I am Naila, mother of nothing and no one, and I do not claim you. Be gone!"

This time they wailed aloud, the sound so terrible that Naila thought her head might split in two. They coiled back from her, unfurling their wide, arching wings.

"Go!" she shouted again. "*Go!*"

They took off as one, the air thundering with their monstrous wingbeats. Naila watched them climb back up into an incongruously calm sky, winding around each other like trailing ribbons.

She'd done it. Somehow, she'd done it.

She'd driven the dragons away.

Sagging with exhaustion, Naila felt her power slipping from her; it was as if someone stronger than her had stepped out of her body, leaving her to deal with the shell that remained. A darkness was creeping in from the edge of her vision and she thought for a moment that she would collapse, until a strong hand seized her arm, fingers digging into her skin. It was the stranger, Ra'akea.

Naila tried to grasp onto the last threads of her strength. She had nothing left – nothing with which to fight if Ra'akea decided that she should die. She made herself look up and meet those impossible aquamarine eyes.

"You saved me?" Ra'akea said the words as a question, as if she didn't believe that any of this was real. "You drove them away."

"Yes," Naila answered, her voice dry and rasping from the smoke.

"Why?"

Naila didn't answer. Her mind was sluggish, her eyelids heavy. Was there a reason she'd thrown herself in the dragon's path? Did there need to be?

"*Why?*" Ra'akea shook her and Naila wobbled in her grip like a rag doll. "I tried to kill you. These people are nothing to you. Why?"

Ra'akea released her suddenly and turned away, hissing with frustration. Naila staggered, only just catching herself before she fell.

"Because it was the right thing to do," Naila offered weakly.

Ra'akea turned back, her blue-black hair whipping around her face, the colour shifting like water. "What *are* you?"

"I don't know." Naila's frustration lodged like a stone in her throat.

All this, and she still didn't know. "I have no idea why any of this is happening. Did the dragons come after me?"

Ra'akea hissed again. "They are not dragons."

"What? But—"

"We call them *Sha'arin*. The lost ones. They were dragons once, but they have become corrupted. They have lost their tribe; their souls."

Naila felt again their desperation, their terrible sadness, and suddenly she understood. "They're alone," she said quietly.

Ra'akea looked back at her, and for the first time her eyes softened, the ice in them melting just a fraction. "Yes."

Naila had so many things she wanted to ask her, but at that moment there was another cry, a piercing call that echoed across the whole valley. It could only belong to one of them: one of the Sha'arin. Both Naila and Ra'akea looked to the sky, and Naila felt her heart tighten like a knot. How could they be coming back?

Another second and they saw it, its long body slicing through the air, its translucent wings folded back as it swooped down towards them. Naila gasped. This creature was nothing like the lost ones. Its scales were the most vivid blue Naila had ever seen, shifting to turquoise and green in the light of the sun. The down on its back flowed like the surface of a stream, dark blue tapering to a white purer than snow. When it landed, the water swirled around it like an extension of its body.

This was a dragon. A real dragon.

It roared again, and the force of the sound sent Naila staggering backwards.

She must die! Naila heard its thoughts inside her head as if they were her own. Its fury was cold, precise, nothing like the chaos of the Sha'arin. It lunged for her, its long body snapped forwards, its teeth bared. Naila watched it come, her blood frozen, her body like lead – there was nothing she could do.

Tae, no! Ra'akea stepped between Naila and the dragon, her arms outstretched. The dragon's jaws snapped closed inches from Ra'akea's face.

It screamed in frustration, swinging its head back. A fan snapped open around its neck, rippling with its anger.

Why do you stop me? She must die. She is the one. She stole their minds, turned them to monsters. You felt it. Can you not hear her song?

Tae— Tae stop. She saved me. She drove them away.

The dragon uncoiled and opened its pale wings, covering everything in an ethereal blue light. The growl swept through its body, making the air tremble with its anger. Droplets of water began to rise around it, like rain falling up into the sky.

It is her. She is corrupting them. Destroying the balance. She must die.

Please, Naila tried to form the thoughts in her mind. *I don't know what you're talking about. I stopped them. I—*

Both Ra'akea and the dragon looked at Naila as if she'd said something horrifying, staring at her with identical blue eyes.

She's in our minds! The dragon howled and shook its head, as if it might fling Naila out. *Stop her. Stop her. Get her OUT.*

Ra'akea turned back to the dragon, her body still between Naila and its jaws. *Listen to me. Please, Tae, listen.*

But the dragon was drawing its head back, its lips pulled into terrible snarl. It darted forward so quickly Naila didn't even have a chance to draw breath. But Ra'akea had already moved, shoving Naila away, her hand slamming into her chest and throwing her out of the dragon's path.

This time, the attack didn't stop short of Ra'akea – it slammed into her, sending her sprawling. She hit blackened rubble and then slumped down into the water.

"Ra'akea!" Naila tried to wade towards her, but the wet ground was slipping away beneath her feet, exhaustion dragging her down. She would never reach her in time.

The dragon swung its head to follow Ra'akea's path, its teeth still bared, its body heaving with each breath. It was half crazed with anger, no longer recognising who stood in its path.

Ra'akea stirred, pushing herself up on trembling arms. She lifted her head, hair plastered against her cheek, her brow crumpled in a strangely human expression.

Tae . . .

Their gazes met and something passed between them that Naila couldn't hear. The dragon's breathing began to slow, its body uncoiling as if it had been released from fury's grip. There was shame there, too, in the rippling of its fan, in the lowering of its head.

Ra'akea stood, though it was clear to Naila that she was hurt. She began a slow walk to Tae's side, her movements too rigid, one arm curled in against her side. When she reached the dragon, she turned and gave Naila one last, long look.

"I must get her away from here."

Away from you, she might have said, but Naila only nodded, her voice dead in her throat.

"Thank you. For saving me." Ra'akea paused, and Naila could feel the weight of what she would say next. "But Tae is right. You are connected to this – to them. I will not hurt you for the debt I owe you, but others will. More of my kind will come for you. You must find out what this means. Find out what you are."

Then she turned and climbed up onto the dragon's lowered neck, grimacing as she pulled herself up onto the down of its back.

Naila watched in silence, her tongue caught between all the things she wanted to say – *What does this mean? Who are you? Why did they call me Mother?* – but she couldn't make herself speak, couldn't risk the dragon turning its fury back towards her.

Instead, she watched them go, along with all their answers. The dragon coiled itself low against the ground and then sprang upwards, stirring up ash and dust, sending waves splashing against Naila's legs. Naila never took her eyes from them, watching them spiral up and up into the pale blue sky. She felt like she was falling, finally dragged beneath the weight of her exhaustion, cold knotting itself around her bones.

Then firm hands closed on her shoulders. "Got you, kid," came Entonin's voice from next to her ear. Karameth's arm looped under hers, taking her weight.

The relief was too much. Naila sagged, letting herself lean into Karameth.

"Thank you," she whispered. She closed her eyes.

EPILOGUE

Entonin wiped a hand across his brow and only managed to smear more ash there. His whole body was covered with it, painting him in mourning colours, and it mixed with the sweat trickling down his face, dripping into his eyes.

He was exhausted, in a heavy, bone-deep kind of way, but he kept himself moving from one thing to the next. He used his knowledge of healing to patch up as many of the wounded as he could, and he helped the people tend to their dead. A village this far from Al Wafra had no priestess of its own, no one to guide its people through their grief. Entonin knew the Goddess's rituals and he'd heard their songs, so he tried to step into the role as best he could. He knew how important faith was at a time like this.

Besides, it was easier to play a role than it was to occupy his own skin. If he kept moving, kept working, he didn't have to think. As the dragon had swept down towards him, something vital in him had crumbled, unable to withstand the impossible sight. The dragon had been ancient, a being beyond reckoning – older even than the gods. It defied so much of what Entonin believed and shook the rest of it.

So, yes, he knew more than anyone how important faith was at a time like this.

Mud squished and slid beneath his feet as walked down towards the river. The floodwaters had receded when Naila had slumped in Karameth's arms, but the damage remained. What wasn't blackened by fire was covered in silt and marked by water. It seemed particularly cruel that this village had been crushed between two such opposing forces. Still, there wasn't much more they could do here; the people needed each other, not strangers or spectators to their grief.

"Those didn't sound like Ellathian songs." Karameth's voice came from Entonin's shoulder.

Entonin glanced back as the mercenary came to stand beside him. Karameth looked as tired and covered in dust as Entonin did, but his dark eyes were watching him as keenly as ever. Entonin could only meet them for a second before his stomach flipped over itself in a way that was entirely ridiculous. He made himself look away.

"Don't tell me – I butchered the pronunciation."

Karameth paused before answering. "No. It sounded … right."

Neither of them said anything for a time, watching the brown water of the Jamidi slide past them, rushing away with a renewed fury.

It was hard to look at the river and not see Naila standing there on the banks, her face raised towards a dragon. Harder still to marry that image with the timid creature they'd taken from Amoria. Entonin didn't think he'd forget that sight for the rest of his life, and it wasn't grey wings and dragonfire that filled his thoughts; it was *her* – the moment she'd stood taller, her voice raised, speaking in a language Entonin had never heard. Her hair had whipped back from her face, revealing a darkness in her eyes unlike anything Entonin had ever seen – the blackness filled them, the whites of her eyes no longer visible. In that moment, Entonin could believe the old stories. He could believe everything the Order feared – this was the Destroyer, an unmaker of worlds.

Fire, water, earth, and air, Entonin thought, his skin prickling. *Bound together by creation … and destruction. By creation and Naila?* The thought was laughable.

Because as soon as the dragons had climbed into the sky, there she'd been again – Naila, swaying with exhaustion. The girl who'd stared at the stars like she'd never seen them before. The one who'd saved Karameth from Amorians, who'd brought them water in the desert. And even here, she'd put herself between people she'd never met and *dragons,* for gods' sake. Without a hesitation. Whatever she was, she had saved them.

The Order would want to know about it.

"Troubled?" Karameth asked.

Entonin had heaved a sigh without even realising he was doing it. "No, I'm just fine, thanks. Nothing much happening with me."

He'd said it more sharply than he'd meant to, but when he glanced over to Karameth he found one of the mercenary's wider smiles.

No, not mercenary, he corrected himself.

"And now?" Karameth pressed.

"Awasef, I guess." It seemed bizarre to say it out loud. They stood in the ruins of a village destroyed by dragons, *real* dragons. Were they really going to continue their journey as if nothing had happened? "Find the Ellathian Temple. Tell them dragons are real and pray they don't want me to do anything about it. What about you? I suppose I ought to call you 'my lord' or something now?"

It was only as he said the words that the thought really struck Entonin: Karameth *wasn't* a mercenary, not really – he probably didn't even need Entonin's coin – but when the dragon had swooped down towards him, that terrible glow in its throat, Karameth had thrown himself into the dragon's path, pushing Entonin out of the way.

"You saved me" was the only thing that actually made its way out of Entonin's mouth.

"So, you noticed."

"No, I mean, yes. But why?" Karameth was frowning at him now, so Entonin just kept talking. "I know you're not just my guard, but that seems a bit beyond the scope of what we agreed. I certainly didn't put 'protection from dragons in the contract' and I know last night was *good*, but... this was a dragon, for Ardulath's sake, and ..."

This time Karameth laughed, the delightful wrinkle of his eyes enough to make Entonin want him all over again. His dark gaze traced over Entonin's face, his expression gentle. Far too gentle.

The only real answer Karameth gave was to tug on the front of Entonin's robes and draw him into a kiss, lips parted, his strong hands pressed into the small of Entonin's back. Entonin let himself be pulled closer, let himself melt against Karameth, his traitorous heart thumping in a way it had no right to.

But he couldn't help the small voice that whispered in the back of his mind, pointing out that he was an Ellathian priest and Karameth was Dahrani nobility. And war was coming.

Well, this is inconvenient, he thought.

Naila felt lost, adrift in a sea of grief that wasn't her own. She might have driven the Sha'arin away, but the village had still been destroyed. People gathered in front of their homes, staring at the rubble, trying to comprehend what had happened to them. Naila saw every blackened stone, heard every sob, and wondered if this was really her fault.

She is the one. She stole their minds, turned them to monsters.

Be with us, Mother.

Naila wrapped her arms around herself. Is this how it would always be? Wherever she went, whatever she did, would she find herself as the problem? The enemy?

She wanted to rip the pendant from her neck and hurl it away from her, throw it as far as it would go and watch it disappear into the Jamidi's depths. But as she reached up her hand to brush one finger against it, she knew it would do no good. Not once during her confrontation with the dragon had she reached for the obsidian – not once had she touched it with her bare skin.

Whatever this power was, it lived in her now.

Her feet were carrying her back down to the river, picking her way through rubble and driftwood. There were a few nods as she passed, the odd murmur of thanks, but more often there were frightened whispers, families huddling together, people making the sign of the Goddess with their hands. Naila didn't blame them. It didn't really matter that she'd saved them, not if she was the one that had brought the beasts here in the first place.

She almost walked straight into Entonin.

"Ah, the hero awakes." He smiled but his eyes were flat and tired, and there were streaks of ash at his hairline, as if he'd pushed a dust-covered hand through his hair.

Naila didn't know how to answer that, so she didn't, standing next to him and drawing her arms in more tightly around herself.

"I see saving an entire village hasn't improved your mood any."

Naila looked back over her shoulder, to the smoking ruins behind her. "Doesn't look very saved to me."

Entonin followed her gaze. "Well, maybe not the buildings." He looked back at her, one blond eyebrow raised. "You saved a lot of lives, though. Mine included."

"I ..." Naila looked down, chewing the edge of her lip. "Could you hear them? Did you hear what they said?"

"Hear them? The dragons?" He half laughed, and then frowned when he realised that's exactly what she meant. "They *spoke* to you?"

Naila flinched, her last bit of hope sputtering out. They hadn't been calling to anyone else. No one had heard them but her.

They called me Mother, she almost said. *They said they'd come for me.* But she found she couldn't make the words leave her mouth.

"You felt it, though," she insisted instead. "Didn't you? When the dragon came towards you, you felt how *wrong* it was. You felt the ... the emptiness inside it."

Entonin was staring at her with his pale eyes. A frown flitted across his face for a brief second, his gaze darting away and then back. When he opened his mouth, Naila expected him to laugh at her, to evade her question with a sarcastic joke.

"Yes," he said softly. "Yes, I guess I did." He looked down. "It was like ... a crack, a tear in the ... Well. In everything."

A place where the world had come undone. Naila's skin went numb, a shiver starting at the backs of her legs and running up through her spine.

"Entonin, what if I ... what if ..." She was breathing too fast. "What if I caused this somehow? What if they came here for me?"

Entonin narrowed his eyes, and for an awful moment Naila remembered what he was. No matter what he'd become to her, she'd just confessed her fears to an Ellathian priest.

"What do you mean?"

"I ... no. Never mind. It's nothing."

A familiar smirk lifted the corner of Entonin's mouth. "All right then, turn around."

"What?"

"Do it! I said turn around."

Naila obeyed, turning away from the river and up towards the ruined village.

"You know these people?" Entonin asked.

Naila scowled at him. "No, of course not."

"Could the dragons have killed you?"

"Yes."

"And yet," Entonin turned to look at her, the smile softer now, "as I recall, you stood between those villagers and . . . I mean, I began to lose count – was it three dragons?"

Naila couldn't help the smile that twisted its way onto her lips.

"I think maybe that's all that matters just now," Entonin continued, though his voice was quieter, less certain. "I'm not really sure things are good or bad. Even the gods aren't *good* – they just are. They do good things, and we serve them and thank them in the hope that they'll do it again."

"How does magic fit into this?" Naila asked, unable to help herself.

"What I'm trying to say, if you'd keep from interrupting me for half a second, is that you did a good thing, Naila."

Naila looked down, her eyes stinging. "Thank you," she whispered.

A breeze swept past them, carrying sweeter air from the river and sending the ash flurrying up into the air, as if the wind itself were trying to clear the damage away. Naila closed her eyes and took a deep breath, holding the cool air in her lungs, feeling it restore her.

She let it out as a sigh. "Where's Karameth?"

Entonin looked up sharply. "He's ... uh ..." He cleared his throat. "He went to ask about passage to Awasef. How far until the next town – see if our boat driver came back or if she cleared off altogether."

"We're leaving?"

Entonin gave her another of his withering looks. "Unless you want to stay?"

"No, I ... I just ..."

"There's nothing more we can do here, Naila. Not unless we stay for weeks." Entonin lifted his shoulders in a small shrug. "It's time we got you to Awasef."

Al Maktaba. The Great Library. It all felt so insignificant now, in the face of everything else.

When they'd set out from Amoria, Naila hadn't given much thought to her destination; she'd wanted only to get away from Amoria, to escape Oriven and his Justice. She'd been too busy looking behind her, thinking of everything she'd lost, to imagine what lay ahead of her. Al Maktaba was the greatest library in all of Omalia. Perhaps the whole world. There would be mages there – mages not tied to the rules and ideas of Amoria – and there'd be knowledge, more than Naila could imagine.

In there, somewhere, had to lie the answers she needed.

You must find out what this means. Find out what you are, Ra'akea had said.

Then that was exactly what Naila would do.

Ko'ani stood alone, wrestling with memory in a place Amoria kept trying to forget.

Artisan's Row curved away from her, disappearing into the no man's land at the edge of the inner city. Unchanged, exactly as it had been on that awful day: empty buildings, abandoned storefronts, workshops with tools laid ready for work or dropped on the floor when their owners fell. A fine layer of white dust covered everything; motes of it hung in the air, ignited by shafts of sunlight tinted purple by the glass dome above her head. Walking down the row of shophouses felt like walking back through time, step by step, hour by hour, back to the day they'd killed her father.

Amoria moved around this place like water around a stone; no one came here any more, as if the deaths had been the result of a curse on the land, and not the arrogant actions of one man. But Ko'ani kept finding herself back here, her footsteps scuffing through the dust, her hands shoved deep into the pockets of her robes, the only life in a dead district.

There was a crack, a sound that ricocheted off the empty streets and the curve of Amoria's glass, and then Ko felt the prickle of distant magic, the hairs raising on the back of her arms.

Ko wasn't frightened. In the long months since the wizard's disappearance, she had stolen back as many of Haelius Akana's spellbooks as she dared. She had studied the magic of the most powerful mage in Amoria, and she knew she was growing to match his strength. Nothing in Amoria was a threat to her.

Still, it wouldn't serve to be seen here.

She ducked into her father's old workshop, sliding into the shadows and dropping behind one of the stone benches towards the front of the shop. Lifting her hand to her lips, she blew the word *spiritus* across her palm. Magic gathered her breath into the smallest breeze, pushing the dust across the path into the shop, covering the worst of her footprints.

She peered carefully around the edge of the bench just as a terribly familiar face stepped into view: High Consul Oriven himself.

He was accompanied by two figures dressed in black and gold, as if they were members of Oriven's Justice, though they looked like no one Ko'ani had ever seen before.

She took a quick breath and plunged her mind in the currents of magic, feeling her fingers hook into power as she drew the phoneme for sound onto the back of the bench. She paused before she whispered the spell, remembering another time and another place, when her best friend had been by her side and her uncle had sensed her spying. She took the nearby magic and twisted it away from her, forming a kind of shield to hide her casting.

The figures stopped abruptly, and for a terrible, paralysing moment, Ko'ani thought they had sensed her, but Oriven only turned to address his strange companions.

"This is far enough, I think." Oriven's voice emerged from Ko'ani's spell as if he had spoken the words right against her ear.

One of the strangers nodded, while the other moved to check the buildings around them, looking in every window and over every broken wall. Ko'ani held her breath.

"This is most unusual, Oriven," said the first stranger, addressing the High Consul without any reference to his title. "I hope you have valuable information for us. It hardly serves any of us to be seen together."

"I agree," Oriven turned around to face his escort, and there was a stiffness to his posture that didn't fit with what Ko knew of the High Consul – the man who had folded Amoria so effortlessly into his grip. "In fact, I believe our association has become unnecessary, as well as unwise."

"Oh?" One of the strangers raised his eyebrows in an expression of benign surprise.

"I have gained control of the council and the inner city; Amoria will be returned to the mages soon."

"Indeed, you have everything you wanted," replied the second man, circling around to stand behind Oriven. "You owe us a great debt."

Oriven straightened, his hands clenched at his sides. With a strange, sinking feeling, Ko'ani realised that he was afraid. "Our agreement has been fulfilled. Amoria is under my control – it will not be an obstacle to your plans."

"Fulfilled, you say?" The expression of the first man remained un-convinced. "I can see that you have what you wanted, but a number of our needs remain unfulfilled. The Wizard Akana, for example—"

"Is no longer a threat. He has been removed from his allies, his resources; he's unstable—"

"And still at liberty," the second figure interjected. "We practically handed him to you on a platter, and you let him and his piece of the obsidian artefact slip through your fingers."

Oriven opened his mouth, but the first of the strangers didn't give him a chance to speak. "That artefact is worth more than you can *possibly* imagine. More than anything else you could offer us, more than this pathetic city, more than your life."

Ko had to bite down on her tongue to keep from making a sound. The stone. The artefact Haelius had given to Naila. There was *more* of it?

"No, you still owe us a debt, Oriven," the man continued, raising a hand and gesturing as if to take in the entirety of Artisan's Row. "And right now, I don't see how you could possibly repay it."

Ko couldn't see the expression on Oriven's face, but she could hear the trembling in his voice. "This? You think I owe you for *this*?" Without his usual confidence, Oriven's voice sounded strange, emptier, as if he was speaking with less air in his lungs. "I never wanted you to do this."

"This is exactly what you wanted."

"Not this. This was too far—"

"Strange," said the one standing behind Oriven, making him turn. "We didn't hear you complaining when we destroyed the city's food supply, leaving many to starve. You had nothing to say when we brought down the dome – that would have killed hundreds, thousands, if we'd succeeded."

"These were mages," Oriven hissed it in a whisper, as if he thought someone might be listening. "You killed my people."

"You wanted this," said the first man, his voice unmoved. "You wanted chaos, fear, mages and non-mages at each other's throats. Did you think there wouldn't be a price? It was *this* that secured your position. It was Artisan's Row that destroyed Akana. We've given you everything you wanted and more, and now we must see to our own goals."

Oriven straightened. Through her spell, Ko could almost feel him gather his magic. "Then our goals no longer align."

It was small, small enough that an ordinary mage might not have felt it: a device being clicked into place, an artefact curled into Oriven's hand. The shift in magic dragged on Ko'ani's senses, and she was sure the strangers would feel it.

The holding spell hit Oriven before he'd even opened his mouth to cast, one of the men catching him with a flick of a finger. They cast as quickly and wordlessly as Haelius, magic wrought into their every gesture.

Ko felt mages arrive in the district like an approaching storm. Justice charged into the street, their hands raised, spells on their lips. Ko leaned forward, almost stumbling from her hiding place. She could barely see their faces – they were too far and moving too fast. She strained to see each one, searching for the familiar features of her mother.

Don't be there, she pleaded.

Fifteen Justice. It should have been a fight, even for someone as powerful as Haelius, but it was nothing. The strangers were too strong. Their power ignited the air, making Ko's lungs burn. It looked like magic cracking away from their feet, but it was the opposite, grey lines cutting through the ground as they drew everything out, carving a web of emptiness around them. One by one the Justice fell, dropping to the ground before they could even mount their attack. All their defences, the magical shields that they'd held up before them, had merely been consumed by the strangers' magic, curling away like paper before fire.

And through it all, Oriven remained motionless, held by their spell, only his eyes moving as he watched his people die.

Ko knew she should run, but she couldn't. She was the same as Oriven, fear gripping her as tightly as any spell.

None of them were Mum, a small voice said in her head. *She wasn't there.*

But she so easily could have been.

One of the strangers stepped towards Oriven, and Ko could hear the man's ragged breathing. Even from here, she could see that something about the stranger had changed, as if a mask had slipped from his face. His skin was paler now, almost transparent, and his hair had turned a strange silver-grey.

"This was foolish," the man said, as if he were reprimanding a child. "What did you think you'd achieve?"

"I . . ." Oriven's voice was strained. "I was protecting my people."

The stranger laughed. "Oh, little man, how you contort yourself around your hate. Now all of these deaths are on your hands, too."

"If you're going to kill me, just do it."

The second figure drew in close enough to whisper in the High Consul's ear. Ko'ani could only just make it out through her spell. "No, of course not. We said you owed a debt, and your life will not repay it. But we can't let this little rebellion go unpunished."

The first man took one of Oriven's hands, lifting it like the limp arm of a doll. Then everything Ko'ani thought she knew about magic dissolved in front of her eyes. Power surged towards them; she could feel her own magic lurch in her chest as if it might rip out of her.

It *was* ripping out of Oriven, magic and anima pouring out of him like blood. His skin blurred at the edges, leaching into the air as if his body couldn't quite contain him any more. His face turned grey, laced with tiny fissures which cracked out across his skin. The scream of agony was the worst thing Ko'ani had ever heard.

Oriven's hand disintegrated, crumbling into dust.

It all happened too quickly. Panic gripped Ko'ani's heart. Her concentration evaporated and her listening spell collapsed, releasing its magic back into the air. It was so little, barely a shiver of power, but these were no ordinary mages.

They turned as one towards her hiding place.

No, no, no. Ko'ani scrambled backwards, her arms shaking. She couldn't hear them any more, but she could *feel* them coming towards her with all their dreadful power. Her mind was fogged with panic. She couldn't grasp the magic, she couldn't form spells, she didn't know what she could possibly do. They were coming to kill her.

No.

She'd studied how Haelius had transported himself with magic, had suspected that all her training had given her enough power to do it. She'd even memorised the shape of the magic in her room, watching the way it flowed through the Amorian glass, knowing one day she'd use it to try and bring herself back there. Only fear had kept her from trying it – the fear that trying and failing could kill her.

Now it would kill her not to try.

They were close, the air buzzing with their strange power. Ko'ani shut it out. She took a deep breath, closed her eyes and reached for magic. Her power spiralled out around her, and Artisan's Row vanished.

GLOSSARY

The Academy: The prestigious magical school at the heart of Amorian society. All mages must learn control of their magic there before they can join Amorian society.

Adventus: A wealthy non-mage area in the outer city, where the Majlis is situated.

Allyn Oriven: A prominent mage politician in Amoria, leader of the Committia Justice, in charge of the city's security. Attended the Academy alongside Haelius and Larinne.

Anima: The "prime element": the energy that defines all things. Mages cannot influence anima directly.

Amoria: A glass city founded at the edge of Dahran by mages fleeing the Ellathian Empire.

Ardulath: The Ellathian god of knowledge and wisdom.

Artainus: Capital city of the Ellathian Empire.

Artefacts: Magical devices created by mages. They can be made so non-mages can use them.

Array: A complex interweaving of written phonemes to create a physical manifestation of a spell.

Aurelia: The canal which circles and criss-crosses Amoria.

Awasef: A mountain city in Dahran, home of the Great Library. Awasef means *storms* in Dahrani.

Baelinne: Ellathian goddess of fertility, harvest and fresh water.

Brynda: Landlady of the Dragon's Rest. She took Naila in as a baby.

Celia Oriven: Daughter of Allyn Oriven and classmate of Naila.

Committia: Sections of the Lieno Council responsible for running different parts of the city.

Consul: The leader of a committia and a senior senator in the Lieno Council.

Dahran: The Queendom of Dahran is the country neighbouring Amoria. Dahran means *two ages* in Dahrani, signifying its long history and the different peoples who have lived on this land.

Dailem Tallace: Senior senator in the Lieno Council. Larinne's sister, Malek's wife and mother of Ko'ani.

Dillian: Husband of Brynda and cook at the Dragon's Rest.

The Dragon's Rest: An inn in the Southern Quarter of Amoria and the place Naila lived before the Academy.

Ellath/The Ellathian Empire: A vast and powerful holy empire to the north of Dahran. Ruled by priests of the Ruling Six temples.

Entonin tyr Ardulath: An Ellathian priest and Seeker of the Temple of Ardulath.

The Goddess: The Goddess is the deity and creator in Dahran's monotheistic religion. Amorians also worship the Goddess, though religion has a lesser presence in the mage city.

The Great Lake: A vast enchanted lake that surrounds Amoria, preserved by the magic of Amoria's creators. It provides a water supply and food source for Amoria.

Haelius Akana: A wizard of Amoria's Academy and the most powerful mage of his generation, despite his non-magical heritage. Tutor to Naila and dearest friend of Larinne Tallace.

Hakima: The typically female ruler of a region (wilaya) of Dahran.

Hollow: An Amorian derogatory term for a person without magic.

Itelena: Ellathian goddess of cities, commerce, governance and civilisation.

Karameth: A mercenary and bodyguard of Entonin. Very little is known of him, not even his full name.

Ko'ani Tallace: A young and talented mage. Best friend of Naila and daughter of Dailem and Malek.

Jamidi: The largest river in Dahran, running much of the country's length from west to east.

Jasser: The sister city to Amoria; a settlement that skirts the edge of the Great Lake on the Dahrani side. Jasser means *bridge* in Dahrani.

The Justice: An army of trained mages created to keep the peace in Amoria. Under the control of the Consul of Justice, Allyn Oriven. Their uniform is black edged in gold.

Larinne Tallace: Consul of commerce and a senior senator in the Lieno Council. She is Haelius's dearest friend and sister of Dailem Tallace.

Lieno: The highest rank of mage. Robes of Lieno are edged in gold.

The Lieno Council: The ruling council of the mages. All Lieno are invited to sit on the council.

Mage: A person with the ability to wield magic.

Magic: A mysterious power linked to anima. Mages can use and alter magic to affect the world around them.

Al Maktaba: The Great Library of Awasef. Al Maktaba simply means *the library* in Dahrani.

Malek Thidan: A Dahrani mage and Haelius's assistant and close friend. Father to Ko'ani and husband of Dailem.

Majlis: The seat of the non-mage council, the Shiura Assembly.

Mita: The lowest rank of mage and the rank of all mages until they sit their ranking exams. Mita robes are edged in white.

Mita's District: A district close to the Academy which once housed trainee mages in dormitories.

Mudammir: A figure in Dahrani religion known as *the Destroyer,* opposed to the goddess.

Mustashaar: A member of the Shiura Assembly. Mustashaar means *counsellor*.

Nahrayn: A fort town straddling the confluence of the two main branches of the Jamidi River. Nahrayn means *two rivers* in Dahrani.

Naila: A mita at the Academy who cannot control magic. Referred to by her peers as "the Hollow Mage".

Omalia: The continent containing Amoria, Dahran and the Ellathian Empire.

Pattern Room: A room which allows mages to safely transport around Amoria with magic.

Phoneme: The sounds combined in a spell to control magic.

Popina: A type of wine bar frequented primarily by mages, found in the inner city.

Ra'akea: A mysterious stranger tracking attacks across Omalia.

Reyan Favius: A senator, Consol of Communication and old friend of the Tallace family.

Ruling Six: The six temples which rule the holy Ellathian Empire.

Rudimenta: The elements which make all things: air, fire, water, earth and anima. Also the name of a strategy game played in Amoria and Dahran.

The Sallow Lady: The Ellathian goddess of death.

Seeker: A high-ranking member of the Temple of Ardulath. A diplomat, ambassador and curator of knowledge. Many outside Ellath see them as spies for the Empire.

Sidi/Siditi: A respectful address for a man/woman, originating in Dahran.

Sil/Silnar: The currency of Dahran and Amoria.

Silwheat: The main grain crop grown in Amoria's glasshouses. So called for its value.

Sisephia: The former Ellathian goddess of magic. She was cast out the Ellathian pantheon, her temples burned and mages hunted to extinction within the Empire.

The Senate: Senior members of the Lieno Council and the true rulers of Amoria.

Shiura Assembly: The council of the non-mages in Amoria. The Shiura have more influence in the outer city and connections in Dahran which make them influential in Amoria's trade.

Solis: Also known as *the sunset district*. A leisure district with many tea houses and wine bars.

The Southern Quarter: The largest part of the outer city, adjacent to the Adventus. It is less affluent than the inner city, but it is a bustling centre of trade.

Surveyor: An anonymous law enforcer of Amoria. Lieno are selected at random to serve, their identities concealed by magic and large black robes.

Tae: The mysterious companion of Ra'akea, connected to her by a deep mental bond.

Trebaranus: The Ellathian god of war.

Trianne: The second highest rank of mage. Their robes are edged in silver.

Tokar: The name of the world in which The Outcast Mage is set.

Tus'Bala: A small oasis town situated in the desert between Amoria and Dahran proper.

Vetra: The second lowest rank of mage. Their robes are edged in bronze.

Al Wafra: The capital of Dahran. The name means *place of prosperity* in Dahrani.

The White Bridge: The bridge between Amoria and Jasser, crossing the Great Lake and connecting the glass city to mainland Dahran.

Wilaya: A region of Dahran typically ruled by a Hakima and her family.

Wizard: A leader of the Academy. Strictly, this is the highest rank of mage, denoting the most powerful magic users in Amoria. The robes of wizards are edged in red and also in gold to denote their dual status of Lieno. There are currently only eight wizards in Amoria.

Wylian Akana: A prominent member of the Shiura Assembly and father of Haelius Akana.

Yenisseri's Grand Company: A famous mercenary company in Dahran, to which Karameth belongs.

ACKNOWLEDGEMENTS

I can't believe I'm writing these – it's such a pinch-yourself moment as a new author. Firstly, I'd like to thank you, the reader, for joining Naila and her disaster family on this mad journey. It is a dream to be able to share these characters with you, so you've truly made this writer's dreams come true.

Thank you so much to Robbie Guillory for taking a chance on this book and his brilliant editorial suggestions, which I'm still mad I didn't think of, and to Bethany Ferguson for her early edits. Thank you to James Long, Nazia Khatun, Joanna Kramer and everyone at the Orbit UK team, as well as Bradley Englert, Nick Burnham and all the Orbit US team. A huge thank you to Ellen Rockell for the incredible cover and Rebecka Champion for the stunning map. Thank you also to Mohamed Ghalaieny for his advice and expertise on the cultural sensitivity read – any remaining mistakes in the text are mine. I'm still learning how many people it takes to make and champion a book, so if I have missed any of you then I'm truly sorry and thank you!

Thank you to the BookCamp Mentees: Laura Sweeney, Sam Pennington, Imogen Martin, Katie McDermott, Kathryn Whitfield, Joanne Clague, Nicola Jones, Jon Barton, Ina Christova and Adam Cook. You have been an amazing support through all things and I'm so proud of how far we've all come! Thank you especially to Georgia Summers, my publishing guru and partner-in-five-hour brunch – thank you for helping me through some of the hardest decisions on this journey.

To the Scream Team, Lyndsey Croal, Cat Hellisen, Raine Wilson, Katalina Watt, Dave Goodman, Erin Hardee and Morag Hannah, thank you for being the most wonderful crew to navigate the perils of publishing with; you held my hand through some of the hardest times and I treasure both your friendship and advice. Thank you to Catriona Silvey for the writing and cheese time, even if cheese and therapy might be a more accurate description (still much needed). Eve Power, another writer, friend and sometimes therapist – thank you for *all* our Zoom calls, your wisdom and your friendship. Thank you to the Glasgow Science Fiction Writers Circle and the Edinburgh Science Fiction and Fantasy community for being the most welcoming and talented bunch of writers I've ever met.

A huge thank you to the British Fantasy Society and to every author who ever took the time to chat to a newbie writer. The SFF writing community in the UK is a wonderful space where so many people I admire have stopped to offer me wisdom or advice (even as I garbled incoherently at them). The con crew and members of the 3 a.m. red wine club – you know who you are – thank you for being outstanding people (and for making sure I would eventually go to bed).

To my dear friends, thank you for putting up with me. All the excitement, angst, random monologues about writing and publishing – you have listened to it all with such patience. Especially thank you to Chris and Jen Hall (and Emily and Logan too). Thank you for all the support. I'm lucky to know such wonderful people.

To my family, Mum, Dad and Lucinda, thank you so much for supporting my writing and all my notions. Mum, thanks for suggesting I pick up that copy of *The Fellowship of the Ring*, and Dad for making me watch *Legend* at an impressionable age (look what you both started), and Lucy for reading early work that no one should have to read (sorry). Speaking of early work, thank you to Jennie Dring and Helen White, who were there at the beginning. Helen – you have read everything I've ever written, helped with edits, squeed when I needed you to and kicked my ass when it was deserved. The dedication is true – without you none of this would exist!

Lastly, to my wonderful husband, Omar Kooheji. I don't know

where to even begin. You have supported me in a way no one else ever could. So much of this book is yours too – thank you for sharing your culture with me, making me a part of your wonderful family and holding my hand in literally every conceivable way. You are my favourite dork. Honourable mentions to Leon hugs, Ada's constant sabotage of my desk and the late but great Tiffin-Black-Toe.

ABOUT THE AUTHOR

Annabel Campbell writes fantasy with fierce female characters, disaster wizards and all the fun tropes.

She lives near Lanark, Scotland, in a village where most of her neighbours are sheep. She has a PhD in cardiovascular science, and when not making things up for a living, she works from home as a Medical Writer.

Her other joys are red wine, playing games, or showing you too many pictures of her dog. Her evil cat overlord occasionally lets her leave the house.

Find out more about Annabel Campbell and other Orbit authors by registering for the free monthly newsletter at orbit-books.co.uk.